I0775667

Praise for Detective Emilia Cruz

CLIFF DIVER

"From the moment I started the first one, I couldn't put it down. . . Her work touches on important issues affecting Mexico in a real, human way and is exciting, fast paced and utterly gripping." – *Mexico Retold*

HAT DANCE

[Emilia] is a force to be reckoned with." – *Mystery Sequels*

DIABLO NIGHTS

"Amato brings her characters to life with her vivid writing style and sets them on the streets of a Mexico steeped in Catholicism and corruption." – *OnlineBookClub.org*

KING PESO

"Danger and betrayal never more than a few pages away." – *Kirkus Reviews*

PACIFIC REAPER

"Carmen Amato . . . out does many of the best crime authors out there." – *Artisan Book Reviews*

43 MISSING

"A fast-paced procedural . . . a real page-turner . . . a very original plot." – *The BookLife Prize*

Also by Carmen Amato

DETECTIVE EMILIA CRUZ SERIES
CLIFF DIVER: Detective Emilia Cruz Book 1
HAT DANCE: Detective Emilia Cruz Book 2
DIABLO NIGHTS: Detective Emilia Cruz Book 3
KING PESO: Detective Emilia Cruz Book 4
PACIFIC REAPER: Detective Emilia Cruz Book 5
43 MISSING: Detective Emilia Cruz Book 6
RUSSIAN MOJITO: Detective Emilia Cruz Book 7
NARCO NOIR: Detective Emilia Cruz Book 8
MADE IN ACAPULCO: The Emilia Cruz Stories
THE ARTIST/EL ARTISTA: A Bilingual Short Story
FELIZ NAVIDAD FROM ACAPULCO: A Detective Emilia Cruz
Novella
THE LISTMAKER OF ACAPULCO: A Detective Emilia Cruz Novella

GALLIANO CLUB SERIES
ROAD TO THE GALLIANO CLUB: Prequel
MURDER AT THE GALLIANO CLUB: Book 1
BLACKMAIL AT THE GALLIANO CLUB: Book 2
REVENGE AT THE GALLIANO CLUB: Book 3

THRILLERS
AWAKENING MACBETH
THE HIDDEN LIGHT OF MEXICO CITY

KING PESO

A Detective Emilia Cruz Novel

Carmen Amato

KING PESO copyright © 2016, 2023 by Carmen Amato All rights reserved.

No parts of Carmen Amato's novels and stories may be reproduced in whole or in part without written permission from the author, with the exception of reviewers who may quote brief excerpts in connection with a review in a newspaper, magazine, or electronic publication; nor may any part of the books be reproduced, stored in a retrieval system, or transmitted in any form or by any means electronic, mechanical, photocopying, audio recording, or other means without the written approval of the author.

KING PESO and the Detective Emilia Cruz novels are works of fiction. Names, characters, places, and incidents are the products of the author's imagination or are used fictitiously. Any resemblance to actual events, locales, or persons, living or dead, is entirely coincidental or used with permission.

Certain long-standing institutions, agencies, and public offices are mentioned, but the characters and situations involved are wholly imaginary.

Published 2023 by Laurel & Croton (second edition)
Trade Paperback Edition

Identifiers: ISBN: 979-8-9885363-4-5 (print)
ISBN 978-0-9853256-6-4 (ebook)

Regarding names and monetary conversion

Regarding Mexican names: It is the custom in Mexico to use two surnames. The first is from the father's family and is always used. The second surname is the name of the mother's father. The second is sometimes dropped in conversation and/or to shorten the name in keeping with American and European naming conventions.

Conversion rate: For the purposes of this novel, $US1.00 = 10 Mexican pesos.

Spanish words: A glossary of Spanish words and terms commonly used in the Detective Emilia Cruz series is included.

Money is a good servant but an evil master.

Mexican proverb

CHAPTER 1

Under the midnight sky, the ocean glowed like mercury. Waves charged at the shore, retreated, and surged again. Emilia Cruz Encinos made her way across the balcony to lean over the stone wall and watch the Pacific fight against gravity.

If only all these people would leave. Emilia needed to be alone in this spot high above the rest of Acapulco. Close her eyes and feel her heart beat in rhythm with the ocean. Draw in big breaths of salty darkness. Settle her mind.

Prepare herself for what she would face tomorrow.

"Day after day I listen to Tony talk about his real estate investment club, eh." The shrill voice made Emilia wince as she pulled her attention back to the party. Guests were everywhere, mingling between the spacious living room and the balcony, which was nearly as large. The speaker next to Emilia was Jane Wilcox. She and her husband Tony were the Canadian owners of the Santa Rosa hotel.

"His real estate investment club, eh," Jane repeated in her accented Spanish. The breeze ruffled her short gray hair as she waved a wineglass to punctuate her words, red liquid sloshing up to the rim. "Buildings and occupancy. Rate of return." She paused to suck down more wine, then fixed Emilia with a glassy stare. "Is Kurt a member?"

Emilia forced a smile. "Kurt and I don't talk about money."

Her stolen moment was over. Emilia led Jane back through the sliding glass doors into the living room in hopes of foisting the tipsy Canadian off on someone else. From across the crowded space, as if he'd heard his name, Kurt Rucker cocked his head and caught Emilia's eye. He gave her a discreet wink, his wavy blonde hair haloed by the chandelier. Lean and muscled from his disciplined regime of triathlon training, he wore perfectly pressed khaki pants topped by a white polo shirt with the logo of the Palacio Réal hotel; his usual understated look of wealthy gringo hotel manager.

When Emilia returned the wink, he turned back to the two men with whom he'd been chatting. Both were fellow board members of the Acapulco Hotel Association. Twenty board members and their spouses were in the penthouse apartment Emilia shared with Kurt at the Palacio Réal, invited to watch the Sunday evening Copa America kick-off match between Uruguay and Mexico and dine on the buffet supper catered by the hotel's 5-star restaurant. The Copa America soccer tournament was the biggest sporting event in the Western Hemisphere, with more than a dozen national teams competing for the region's most prized trophy.

Mexico had prevailed over Uruguay an hour ago. Dessert and coffee were served and eaten. Emilia wanted all these strangers to get out so she could prepare for tomorrow. She needed to find Jacques Anatole, the Palacio Réal's head chef and Kurt's best friend. If

Jacques and the kitchen staff made a production about cleaning up, perhaps the guests would get the point.

She realized Jane Wilcox was looking at her expectantly.

"I'm sorry?" Emilia asked, trying to keep the irritation out of her voice.

"I said, you might be young and in love, eh, but make sure to talk about money." Jane swayed a little. She had to be on her fifth or sixth glass of wine. "Every girl needs to know where she stands, eh. With your looks, you could catch as much money as you wanted."

Emilia pretended to laugh and took a sip from her own wineglass to avoid a reply. Maybe it was because she was tired, or worried about tomorrow, but Jane Wilcox's words struck a raw nerve. Talking about whether or not she loved Kurt, or if he loved her, wasn't a place Emilia was willing to go.

Te amo. I love you.

Such small words. Such a big commitment.

"Emilia, I want to tell you what a beautiful outfit you have on." Magda Porchenko joined them. Like Jane, Magda was in her fifties. She had blonde hair scraped into a tight bun and wore a white caftan that looked casual yet hideously expensive at the same time. The Porchenkos were Russian and owned the Pacific Lotus on the western side of Acapulco Bay.

"Thank you," Emilia said.

"You're so fit," Magda marveled.

Emilia smiled. "I try."

She'd borrowed the teal silk pants and halter from her friend Mercedes and paired them with her own chunky turquoise necklace, the one bought after making detective. With her straight dark hair out of the way in its usual ponytail, the halter top showed off Emilia's abs and biceps. Carefully applied makeup hid the scar on her upper right arm; a legacy from being shot not so long ago.

"Darling Emilia." Magda put a claw-like hand on Emilia's wrist. "You never told us how you and Kurt met."

"We're dying to know," Jane slurred in agreement. She edged closer. "Kurt's the most eligible man in Acapulco and all the ladies at the tennis club . . ." She stopped to guzzle more wine.

"Are terribly jealous," Magda finished her friend's sentence.

All the norteamericano women are terribly jealous that a Mexican woman snagged him instead of one of their own, Emilia thought.

"Here, of course," she said brightly. "We met here. In Acapulco."

"But details, darling," Magda cooed. "We need all the dirty details."

"We can live vicariously," Jane giggled. "I'll bet he's a powerhouse in bed, eh?"

Emilia glanced at the adjacent dining room, where the buffet table still bore the remains of dessert as well as a silver coffee service with the hotel monogram. "I think this is our last chance for dessert."

"Don't change the subject, darling." Magda tightened her grip on Emilia's wrist. "Was it a blind date? Or were you out clubbing?"

Magda's husband Sergei Porchenko was probably Russian mafia. Emilia wasn't about to admit to his wife that she was a cop or that she and Kurt had met because of a major drug smuggling investigation.

"Well, if you must know—." She closed in on Magda, bumping into Jane in the process. The Canadian woman stumbled and the contents of her wineglass rained down on Magda's bosom.

Magda gave a squeal of dismay as a dark stain bloomed over the sheer white fabric of her caftan.

"Oh, Magda," Jane exclaimed loudly. "I'm so sorry."

"My God," Magda shrilled. "This is ruined."

Tony Wilcox barreled up. "Christ, Jane," he barked to his wife in English. "Are you drunk again?"

"Entirely my fault," Emilia apologized.

"Oh, Magda," Jane exclaimed again and burst into tears.

"Let me get you a cloth," Emilia said to Magda.

Two minutes later, Magda was in the guest bathroom with a helper from the kitchen staff, having the stain dabbed with club soda. The Wilcoxes called for the valet to bring their car around. Kurt gave Emilia a rueful grin as he left to walk them down to the lobby.

To hell with all of them, Emilia thought as the door to the penthouse closed behind Kurt. She left the other guests talking in the living room, went to the kitchen, and slumped into a chair at the table.

Jacques and two of his helpers were there. The chef glanced at Emilia, poured a glass of water from a fancy bottle, and set it in front of her.

Emilia sat without moving as the helpers cleared the buffet, shuttling back and forth with trays between the kitchen and the dining room. Jacques supervised, meticulously packaging up leftovers. She knew he didn't normally cater events himself but had done so tonight as a favor to Kurt.

A few months ago, when Kurt had asked her to move into his new penthouse apartment at the Palacio Réal, Emilia had come on weekends. Not only was there the issue of what her family would say about being unmarried and living with a gringo, but there were practical considerations. The Palacio Réal was on the southeastern edge of Acapulco Bay, a long commute across the city to the police station which housed the detectives squadroom. And her mother Sophia, who'd hovered between reality and fantasy for years, still needed Emilia.

But the commute was manageable and when Sophia remarried, Emilia began to stay at the hotel more frequently. Little by little, her things migrated to the penthouse. Clothes, mementos from her childhood, awards and certificates from her police career.

But sometimes, like tonight, it was hard to convince herself that she belonged there.

Jacques gave the helpers a platter of food and let them take it into the unused maid's quarters behind the kitchen. Emilia and the chef were left alone.

"Jacques," Emilia said, her head propped by a hand. "Do something. Make these people leave."

The white chef's jacket and loose checkered pants disguised the man's slim frame as he leaned against the stainless steel counter and crossed his arms. Like Kurt, Jacques was a competitive runner and swimmer. He had jet-black hair, a large nose, and a sharp, almost pointed chin that gave his face mobility and character.

"Aren't you supposed to be in the other room playing hostess?" he asked.

"I'm done." Emilia flapped her free hand at the door to the dining room. "I'm horrible at this sort of social thing."

Jacques chuckled. "Especially when you hide in the kitchen."

"Don't joke," Emilia reproved him. "This is important to Kurt's career and I'm a disaster."

"Let Kurt worry about his career."

"That's easy for you to say," Emilia said.

The chef's face grew serious and his eyebrows went up. "Emilia, it is foolish to worry," he said. "No matter how difficult things get, you will always be much better for Kurt than Suzanne."

Emilia blinked. "Suzanne?"

Jacques nodded. "How could you think otherwise?"

Emilia had no idea who or what he was talking about.

"Em." Kurt appeared in the doorway and held out his hand to her. "Come and say good night. People are leaving."

An hour later, wearing a soft cotton nightshirt, Emilia propped her elbows on top of the waist-high wall edging the balcony. The tile floor was cool under her bare feet as she stared down at the moonlit ocean, letting the rhythm of the waves soothe her. The outside lights were off and the darkness was peaceful.

The balcony was one of her favorite things about living in the penthouse at the Palacio Réal hotel. Wrapping around two sides of the apartment, it was accessible from every room. Teak chaise lounges, a dining table that could seat 12, cobalt cushions, glazed pots full of geraniums and trailing greenery combined to make it the perfect escape.

The sliding glass doors leading to the master bedroom were open. Thanks to the hotel's professional decorators, that room was straight out of a magazine, with tasteful touches of blue warming the otherwise all-white color scheme. The rest of the apartment was just as streamlined and elegant. Kurt kept telling Emilia that they could redo the penthouse any way she wanted, but it was already nicer than any home she'd ever seen, let alone lived in.

This side of the balcony overlooked the marina,

private beach, and the famous two-level Pasodoble Bar that formed the heart of the hotel. A dozen ceramic lanterns, each as big as a barrel, created a dramatic barrier of flames and color between the water and the edge of the Pasodoble's lower terrace. Pinpoints of lights bobbed in the inky sky beyond the shore. Emilia knew they were reflectors on the floating dock anchored in the middle of Puerto Marques, the bay-within-a-bay that was part of the secluded charm of the Palacio Réal. The hotel was an architectural marvel; seven stories of luxurious hospitality clinging to the cliffs along Acapulco's southeastern edge. Diplomats, rock stars, and global business tycoons stayed at the Palacio Réal for the world's finest food, accommodations, and relaxation.

The Pasodoble was open to the ocean on two sides and bounded by the hotel's immense lobby on the others. The ocean's rhythm, along with guitar music and gentle laughter, floated up to Emilia. Even at this late hour people drank and danced, unaware of the woman looking down upon them.

"Just how drunk was Jane Wilcox?" Kurt asked.

He knew. Emilia turned around as Kurt joined her on the balcony.

His bedtime attire of tee shirt, cotton boxers, and bare feet did nothing to lessen the combination of natural confidence and personal power that Kurt Rucker wore like a second skin. Maybe it came with his job as manager of Acapulco's most exclusive hotel or was forged during his years as a Marine in his country's military. Either way, his confidence had been a magnet for her since the day they met. That was the first time she saw a man with eyes the color of the water beyond the cliffs at La Quebrada and felt a handshake she didn't want to release.

Emilia felt her face get hot; she could never keep anything from him. "I just bumped her a little," she confessed. "Are you mad?"

"No," Kurt said. "I was ready to punch Tony in the mouth, so your timing was impeccable."

Emilia accepted one of the two small glasses he carried. Brandy. She was learning about the finer things in life from him. "Punch him? Why?"

Kurt touched his glass to hers. "Let's just say that Tony found you very attractive and wasn't shy about letting me know how lucky I am. As if I needed that oaf to tell me."

He leaned in and gave Emilia a kiss that nearly made her knees buckle. When they came up for air Kurt put his arm around her and they watched the ocean's relentless chase.

"Is that why you've been out here?" Kurt asked. "You thought I was mad?"

"A little," Emilia admitted. "I'm thinking about tomorrow, too."

Kurt played with the ends of Emilia's hair as the breeze lifted it away from her shoulder. "What's going on tomorrow?"

Emilia leaned against him as she sipped some brandy. "I've been ordered to attend a meeting tomorrow morning at the mayor's office."

"Monday morning with Carlota," Kurt said with sympathy. "What's on the agenda?"

Emilia had dealt before with Carlota Montoya Perez, Acapulco's charismatic mayor. Every interaction had left Emilia both awed by the woman's commanding presence and repulsed by her political machinations.

"I'm not sure," Emilia said. "Chief Salazar's office called me with a royal summons on Friday afternoon. Everyone in the squadroom thinks it's a task force to look into the El Trio murders."

"An El Trio task force?" Kurt's arm tightened. "What's Carlota got to do with that?"

"Maybe she'll give us a pep talk." Emilia heard the false humor in her voice.

In the last few months the Acapulco police department had been thrown into disarray and Emilia knew she was partly to blame. She'd been the one to unknowingly take on the powerful head of Internal Affairs, who together with a lieutenant from Organized Crime and a vigilante group from a small town outside Acapulco, was shipping drugs to *El Norte* aboard a cruise ship. By a wholly unforeseen set of circumstances, Emilia had broken the ring. Both of the dirty cops were killed, but not before one of them shot her.

Maybe it was just coincidence, but since then violent crime in Acapulco had spiraled while arrest rates declined. The execution-style murders of three law enforcement officers in as many weeks had thrown the situation into sharp relief. Dubbed the El Trio murders by the press, the fatal shootings had become a rallying cry for improved security. Tensions were high in the police department as every cop wondered if they were next. Emilia was no exception, but she had a better reason than most.

"The El Trio victims were all senior, weren't they?" Kurt asked.

"Well, you know about Captain Espinosa," Emilia said. "Killed last week. He was the *federale* in charge of the investigation into the killing field at Gallo Pinto."

Kurt nodded.

"Captain Vega was the second," Emilia went on. "He was on Chief Salazar's executive staff. He took over that big arson case."

Kurt finished his brandy and set the glass on the smooth stone topping the wall. "And the first?"

"Javier Salinas Arroliza was my contact at the state attorney general's office on the El Pharaoh casino money laundering mess." Emilia thought back to that case, tossed out when key evidence mysteriously went missing. But Salinas had salvaged something from the wreckage before the casino reopened. "He was one of the good guys. So was Espinosa."

"What about Vega?"

"Hard to know."

Kurt waited.

The Copa America party had kept her busy all weekend; now the fears she'd tamped down since the phone call on Friday bubbled up again.

"There's one more thing I need to tell you." Emilia set her empty glass on the wall next to his. "I think I'm on the task force because I worked with all three victims."

She'd crossed paths professionally with all three of the murder victims, although none had been a close colleague. She hadn't even met Salinas, just talked to him a couple of times on the phone. But he'd been honest with her and done what he said he would do. A rare and rapidly disappearing commodity these days.

"Who else worked with all of them?" Kurt asked. "Silvio? What does he think?"

"Franco worked with Vega on the arson case, too." Franco Silvio was Acapulco's senior police detective and Emilia's perpetually surly partner. "But he never met Salinas or Espinosa. He wasn't invited to the meeting, either. None of the other detectives were."

"Even Loyola?" Kurt asked.

Emilia shook her head. Loyola, who was junior to Silvio, had been made acting lieutenant of detectives several months ago. He now rarely worked cases. "Not invited. He only knew Vega from the arson case."

"What are you telling me, Em?" Kurt paused. "That you're a target, too?"

"I don't know. Maybe." Emilia stared at the lights twinkling in the dark ocean as the unseen swimming dock bobbed. "The El Trio killer could be another cop. Someone on the inside who is being specific about their victims."

"I can't believe you waited to tell me, Em," Kurt said, exasperation and sudden anger in his voice. "You live here. If you're in danger, that means everybody in this hotel is in danger. I have to know things like this."

Emilia bristled. "I'm telling you now, aren't I?"

Kurt turned to look at the ocean again, elbows propped on top of the wall. "I guess what I'm trying to say is that I wish you were invested enough in us . . . in this relationship . . . to tell me things when they happen. Not a week later. Because you're thinking how things impact us. Not just you."

Emilia concentrated on the pinpoints of light out in the bay. Why did they keep having the same conversation and why was it always so hard?

Kurt raised his eyebrows at her, clearly waiting for a response.

"I just . . . I don't know," Emilia floundered. "You're talking about . . . commitment. But I'm in one world and you're in another."

"That's not true, Em."

"Take the people who were here tonight," Emilia said. "They're your colleagues. But we can't even tell them I'm a cop or how we met because we don't know who they'd tell."

"Right now, I'm talking about you and me," Kurt said. "Forget those other people."

"They ask questions I can't answer," Emilia said.

"So we'll figure it out," Kurt said.

"Okay," Emilia said. She didn't have the energy to fight tonight. "I'm sorry."

"Okay," Kurt echoed, his anger spent.

He put his arms around her and Emilia pressed her cheek against his shoulder. "I won't live scared," she whispered.

"I won't let you," Kurt said into her hair.

They stayed quiet for a long moment on the darkened balcony, as the distant sounds of surf and strings sighed through the night breeze. Her strength came from being with him, in this oasis that he'd created. Some days it felt as if Acapulco was crumbling under the assault of the cartel and gang violence that saw multiple murders on the city's streets every day. The tourist zone around the lip of the bay was so far immune to the chaos, but in Acapulco's hilly inland neighborhoods, life was cheap and lost value every day. But up here, in his arms, it still mattered.

"Jacques said a funny thing tonight," Emilia said.

"What was that?" Kurt asked. He drew back to look at her but didn't release Emilia from the circle of his embrace.

"That I was better for you than Suzanne."

"Suzanne Kellogg?" Kurt blinked. "Jacques said that?"

"Yes." Emilia gave a tiny smile. "Who's Suzanne?"

Kurt's face was unreadable. "An old girlfriend," he said. "I met her when I worked in Las Vegas. Before I moved to Mexico."

"Was she special?" Emilia felt suddenly awkward asking the question. They'd skimmed over each other's past relationships; the past wasn't important amid the urgency of life in Acapulco.

"For awhile." Kurt kissed Emilia's forehead then picked up the empty brandy glasses. "Come on, Em. Let's go to bed."

Emilia woke abruptly, seized with an unfamiliar feeling of dread. The bedroom was bathed in moonlight. She squinted to see the display on her cell phone, plugged into its charger and glowing faintly on the bedside table. It was 2:15 am.

Kurt's side of the bed was empty. Emilia touched his pillow; it was no longer warm. The bedroom door was partially open.

The hall light clicked on. Emilia heard a muffled grind as the sliding door to the hall closet was pulled aside, followed by the scrape of hangers along the metal rod. Rattling noises ensued. Emilia pictured what was in the closet; two surfboards, tennis racquets, scuba and snorkeling gear, his bike helmets, boxes of winter clothes Kurt never wore.

After a few minutes, the closet door slid closed and the hall light went out.

Kurt came into the dark bedroom. He stopped at the end of the bed and looked around the room, as if it was unfamiliar. Emilia was on the verge of sitting up and saying something when he went to his dresser, a tall piece of furniture full of clothing folded to his precise specifications by the hotel laundry. A moment later he turned on the lamp and methodically combed through the top drawer where Emilia knew he kept odds and ends; cufflinks, a box of loose change, several different watches, the letters and photos his parents and siblings in the *El Norte* state of New York occasionally sent.

"Damn," she heard him mutter. Kurt closed the drawer, switched off the lamp, and left the room.

Emilia got out of bed and found the old flannel shirt of his that she used for a robe. Getting it on over her nightshirt took concentration. Despite weeks of physical therapy her right arm was still stiff from the gunshot wound.

She went down the hall. The living room, furnished with leather sofas and scrubbed pine occasional tables, looked even larger now that the guests had gone. Pale stucco walls were illuminated by the night sky shining through the glass doors and framed by open white draperies.

Kurt was slumped on one of the sofas, elbows on knees, head in his hands.

Emilia snapped on a table lamp, suddenly afraid.

Kurt's head popped up. There was an expression of desolation on his face Emilia had never seen before.

"What's going on?" Emilia asked.

He ran a hand through his hair and that indefinable confidence came rushing back, reanimating his handsome features like water filling a glass. "Did I wake you up?" he asked.

Emilia sat next to him on the sofa, unsure of what she'd just seen. "Trouble sleeping?"

"Thought I'd get a snack," Kurt said, with the feigned artlessness that Emilia had seen too many times across an interrogation table. "I didn't eat much with all those people here."

Emilia hesitated. If you're hungry, why were you sitting here in the dark?

A phone shrilled from the bedroom.

"Yours or mine?" Kurt frowned.

Emilia stood up. "Mine."

She jogged to the bedroom, skirted the bed, and reached for the phone. It stopped ringing. Emilia checked the call log.

Silvio.

Best partner and worst enemy.

"Problem?" Kurt appeared in the open doorway.

"Silvio." Emilia gave a grimace as she held up the phone. "No doubt he's drunk and wants to gloat, the *pendejo*."

"Tell me you bet with him," Kurt said.

"He was offering really great odds." Emilia hadn't planned on telling Kurt about her little flutter on the Copa America match. "I put down 200 pesos. It was the smallest bet he would take."

Before Emilia fought her way into the detectives squadroom, Silvio and his then-partner Manuel Garcia Diaz had been involved in a shootout during a drug bust.

Garcia was killed. Initially accused of setting up his partner, Silvio was suspended without pay during the investigation. To make ends meet, he became a bookie, running bets on boxing and *fútbol*, and kept the sideline going even when reinstated.

"Your partner is an illegal bookie," Kurt said. "And you are aiding and abetting."

"The entire police department is aiding and abetting," Emilia said dryly. She tossed the phone back on the bedside table. "Do you still want that snack?"

"Snack?"

"You said you were hungry."

"Right. Sure." Kurt smiled a little too widely. "I'll make us something." He disappeared down the hall.

Emilia went into the bathroom. Her stomach knotted as she washed her face. Kurt was the one whose life was an open book, the one who shared from the heart and pushed for commitment. She was the one who kept secrets and stalled when things got too serious.

But now, it seemed as if that dependable dynamic was gone. Something was wrong and Emilia didn't know what it was.

She only knew that Kurt had lied to her for the first time.

Not sure why she was doing it, Emilia turned on all the lights as she returned to the living room. The dining room chandelier came to life and illuminated the doorway to the kitchen. The lights were already on in there, bouncing off the stainless steel appliances and glossy Italian cabinetry.

Two glasses of wine stood on the table. Kurt was busy topping *chupata* rolls with thin slices *of jamón Serrano,* tomato, and avocado. "One sandwich or two?" he asked as Emilia sat down.

"Just one."

Kurt put the sandwiches on a *talavera* pottery platter and slid one of the glasses next to her hand. "Here you go."

Emilia took a sandwich despite the tension in her stomach. "Second party of the day."

"Just the kind of people we are." Kurt touched his glass to hers.

"Is everything okay?" Emilia asked after a minute or two.

"As long as you're okay, I'm okay." Kurt poured them both more wine.

"I just—." She was cut off by the distant ring of her phone.

"Yours again, Em."

Emilia stood up. "If this is Silvio drunk and butt dialing me, I'm going to slay him."

She stalked down the hall to the bedroom, torn between fury at Silvio and worry that her relationship with Kurt was washing away like sand in a storm. The phone's ring was insistent. As Emilia hit the button she saw that the caller wasn't Silvio, but the central police dispatch desk.

"Detective Cruz," Emilia answered.

"This is the desk sergeant from Dispatch reporting a home invasion." The male voice on the other end of the line sounded tired.

"Why call me?" Emilia said, not bothering to mask her annoyance. "Get it out to the night duty unit for that neighborhood."

"The caller asked specifically for you. Detective Emilia Cruz."

Emilia lowered herself to the edge of the bed. The knot in her stomach tightened into a fist. "Okay," she said. "Give me everything you've got."

"Male caller. Couple minutes ago. Reported a home invasion. One victim. Female, 42 years old. Multiple gunshots to the upper chest. Claims she's been dead less than four hours."

"How would he know?"

"Didn't say."

And you didn't ask. This sounded like the shooter calling to taunt the police. And he'd named her. Emilia felt sweat bead up on her forehead. "Location?"

The sergeant named a neighborhood known for poverty and violence. It was a combat zone full of street kids where gangs ruled at night and only one cop dared to walk.

She'd been there before.

Emilia found herself nearly doubled over, the phone still pressed to her ear. "Did the caller identify himself?"

"No. Just kept repeating a number. Said it was a badge." The sergeant on the other end was getting testy with all her questions. "Said to call you and have you come. That neighborhood, we figured it was some sort of hoax. The captain here thought you should be aware. You got any enemies in that area?"

"Did you run the badge number?" Emilia demanded.

"No," the sergeant said sulkily. "We can get somebody to do it in the morning, if you think it's important."

"Run it," Emilia nearly shouted. "I'll hold."

She forced herself upright and held her breath as the clack of computer keys traveled through the line. Blood pounded in her ears and every nerve stretched to the breaking point.

Less than a minute later, the sergeant cleared his throat. "We got a hit," he said. "The badge belongs to Detective Franco Silvio."

CHAPTER 2

The mayor's conference room was as big as a parking lot. Small groups of men in twos and threes ranged on the periphery of the room, where brocade chairs and occasional tables encouraged intimacy. Or secrecy. Conversations were low and hushed.

The white jacketed waiter led Emilia to the vast table in the center of the room. He pulled out a chair and Emilia sat down. Next to a cup and saucer, a folded place card boasted her name. The waiter came back with a silver coffee pot. She thanked him, wondering if he knew that he'd just saved her life.

A couple of big swallows and much-needed caffeine began to make itself felt. Cookies were set out on the huge mahogany table. Between coffee and sugar, she just might stop feeling like a zombie.

She'd been up more than 24 hours and hardly remembered driving from the crime scene back to the Palacio Réal. There had been barely enough time to wash up, put on her one dressy suit, and make it to the mayor's office in time for the task force meeting. Her eyes were swollen from the good cry she'd had in the shower, but Emilia was sure that with Carlota in the room, few would be looking at her.

Emilia took a handful of cookies and looked around. The table was ready for 20, with little place cards by each setting.

Emilia wondered how many of those around the table would be members of the actual task force.

Although she'd been in the mayor's chambers before, she'd never been in this particular conference room. A giant seal of the city of Acapulco, with a hand grasping stalks of wheat, filled the center of the far wall. The opposite wall was a gallery of dramatic photographs. Emilia recognized the cliffs at La Quebrada, the Fuerte San Diego, a cruise ship lit against a midnight sky, a view of Isla Roqueta at the southwestern lip of the bay.

The waiter refilled her cup. Several men took seats on the other side of the table. Coffee cups were filled as the men looked around as if they, too, had never seen the conference room. Emilia marked them as possible task force members.

Two men stayed in a corner by a carved sideboard. One wore a police uniform and was easily recognized by his trademark bald head, beaked nose, and the amount of gold braid on his shirt. Acapulco's chief of police Rodrigo Salazar was in his late fifties. He was slim, fit, and testy.

The other man was Victor Obregon Sosa, the head of the police union for the state of Guerrero.

From their body language it was clear the conversation was terse. Obregon ended it with a jerk of his head, then wheeled around towards the conference table. Chief Salazar stalked out of the room.

The waiter came around again and Emilia gratefully

accepted a third cup of coffee. A fresh plate of cookies appeared and she took two more, knowing that in another ten minutes she'd be hysterical from caffeine, sugar, and grief, but also still awake.

More people came into the room. A young woman in a fashionable black skirt suit took the seat next to Emilia. "Hello, I'm Claudia," she said.

The woman's place card read Claudia Sanchez Rangel. Emilia shook the proffered hand. "Detective Emilia Cruz."

The woman's eyes widened and she leaned closer. "Oh, I know," she exclaimed breathlessly. Wavy hair streaked auburn by a skilled stylist fell over one shoulder. "I've been simply dying to meet you."

Emilia was caught off guard by the reaction. Had she missed some sort of introductory message with biographies of the task force members?

"Was there an email?" she asked.

"Oh, no." Everything Claudia said was delivered with childish excitement. "I just went to Carlota's office and she told me."

"Oh." Emilia decided that Claudia was some sort of administrative assistant. She didn't have the maturity or reserve usually found in a skilled investigator. Maybe she was a secretary and had information about the task force members. "Who else did she tell you about?" Emilia asked.

"I'm so excited to be working with you. May I call you Emilia?" Claudia took a sip of her coffee, making a guppy face to avoid smearing her dark red lipstick. Her nails matched her mouth. "Isn't this the best coffee? We'll have to have this kind in the office."

Emilia smiled weakly but didn't reply. Claudia reminded her of a rich teenager in her mother's Sunday clothes. She might be pretty and expensively dressed, but she didn't belong there.

The waiter filled Emilia's cup again.

More people sat at the table. Emilia didn't know any of them, but she would soon. They were the members of the El Trio task force. Despite sleep deprivation and images from last night that wouldn't leave her head, Emilia felt her spirits rise. Or maybe it was just the coffee.

Obregon dropped into a seat across the expanse of polished mahogany tabletop and snapped his fingers to get the waiter's attention. He looked at Emilia. "Long night, Detective Cruz?"

The head of the police union was dressed in his customary black, as if always building the mystique that powered his empire. Obregon had a network that reached throughout the state of Guerrero, much of it due to "businessmen" whose business was using law enforcement to best advantage.

Emilia knew that Obregon's hands were dirty, but at the same time she'd seen him use his influence to save lives and attain justice. He was the mayor's frequent escort, yet often made it clear to Emilia that sex was on offer. It was always best to walk carefully around him.

"Have you heard about Silvio?" she asked in reply.

"If you're talking about your partner, everyone has heard," Obregon said laconically as he accepted a cup of coffee from the waiter. "Silvio outdid himself this time. Of course, it was just a matter of time."

Emilia didn't understand what he meant, but before she could reply there was a small commotion by the door. Chief Salazar came in and held the door for Acapulco mayor Carlota Montoya Perez. The mayor walked through flanked by two bodyguards and followed by a staff of three men and two women, all dressed in dark suits. In contrast, Carlota strode across the room wearing a dark pink lace jacket with bracelet-length sleeves and a matching pencil skirt that skimmed the top of her calves. Jet black hair brushed her shoulders and framed the well-known face. Carlota's makeup was so perfect as to be nearly invisible but Emilia knew no woman was that gorgeous without some help. Her age was a well-kept secret; Carlota was 25 or 50 or any age in between.

Everyone, including Emilia, got to their feet. Carlota went around the room, shaking hands warmly and exchanging air kisses. When she came to Emilia, the mayor greeted her like an old friend. Carlota took the place next to Obregon, leaving the seat at the head of the table empty. Chief Salazar sat opposite Carlota. Her retinue sat at the other end of the table.

Carlota waved a hand at the waiter, making a diamond tennis bracelet sparkle in the sunlight coming through the tall windows.

Once everyone's cup was full and the servers withdrew,

Carlota thanked those around the table for coming. Emilia mentally flipped through a catalogue of every cop she knew. She didn't recognize anyone besides the chief and Obregon.

No one besides Chief Salazar was in uniform, either. That meant that the members were from plainclothes assignments, like Special Operations, rather than from uniformed units. Or maybe some were from the state attorney general's office, there to work the Salinas angle. Hopefully Acapulco's task force was also drawing on federal law enforcement units that operated in street clothes.

Carlota stood up and addressed those around the table. "As you know," she began. "Security issues are uppermost in my mind as we prepare for Acapulco's Olympic bid. After a 90 day study period, my staff has come up with a proposal that Chief Salazar joins me in supporting."

Carlota continued to talk in general terms about Acapulco's valiant efforts to contain street violence and convince tourists, businesses, and the Olympic selection committee that the city was safe, happy, and ready. As Carlota went on and on, Emilia drank the last of the coffee in her cup and wished the waiter had left the pot. Sitting still in this comfortable chair, she could feel the exhaustion and heartbreak in her bones.

Everyone around the table appeared to listen intently as the mayor spoke. There were smiles and nods but no interruptions. Carlota was an engaging speaker; plus she looked just like all the famous billboards dotted across the city. They featured her perfect smile and exhorted citizens to recycle, throw trash in new decorative bins, and support the city's Olympic bid. Nobody recycled, the decorative bins were constantly vandalized, and Acapulco didn't have the infrastructure to host the Olympic games, but the mayor's vision translated into great popularity poll numbers.

Carlota beamed at the group around the table. "Now I'd like to introduce our esteemed chief of police, Rodrigo Salazar. We have partnered on this new proposal and he can explain it so much better than I." Carlota sat down to a hearty round of applause.

Now that the preliminaries had been taken care of, Emilia was eager to listen. Chief Salazar would talk about the task force, introduce the members around the table. Let them dive into the El Trio case files and catch a killer.

"First, my thanks to the mayor for this meeting," Chief Salazar said, remaining seated. "Since coming to office, she has been a strong supporter of law enforcement. She has a progressive view of how the police can help Acapulco welcome visitors."

Mostly by shaking them down for bribes. Emilia swallowed the thought and tried to look attentive, helped by the rush of caffeine and sugar. She'd heard that Chief Salazar had taken the murder of Captain Vega pretty hard. Vega had been on the chief's executive staff.

Chief Salazar droned on about aligning police resources

with Carlota's vision for Acapulco and finished to applause without ever mentioning the El Trio murders. Carlota said something to an aide and the lights in the conference room dimmed. A screen unwound from the ceiling and the city seal appeared as music played.

They watched a documentary about an all-female police unit in India that had cut crime in half in a major city. The women wore matching saris and headscarves. Several spoke on camera, lauding their unit's effectiveness and the impact on the city. The camera panned out after that, showing patrol units of two women walking their beat, talking to beggars and calling in a burglary with little radios clipped to the fabric swathed across their chests.

"Aren't they clever?" Claudia whispered to Emilia. The younger woman squeezed Emilia's hand where it rested on the table, as if they were best friends catching a movie.

Emilia made a fist and subtly shook off the other woman.

She looked around the room. Everyone was watching the screen except Obregon. He was making notes on a pad with a silver pen, a half-smile on his face.

The film wrapped up with comments by the mayor of the city in India. His popularity had risen remarkably since the all-female police unit began patrolling the streets. People trust them, the mayor said. *That means the people trust me, too. Crime is down, and more visitors were coming to the city now. Women feel safe going out. Life here is good, thanks to the new police unit.*

Emilia stifled a yawn and hitched herself into a different position to keep from falling asleep. Women in saris had nothing to do with the El Trio murders.

The lights brightened and the screen reeled back up into the ceiling. Carlota went to a podium angled to face the table. "Acapulco is a modern and vibrant city that welcomes the world," she declared. The diamond bracelet again caught the light as Carlota tossed back her hair. "To our beaches. Our skyscrapers. Our shops and markets. Our conference venues and our businesses. Our challenge is to keep our visitors safe. With style."

A ripple of obligatory laughter ran around the conference room.

Carlota smiled. "That is why, after much discussion with Chief Salazar and head of the police union Victor Obregon Sosa, I have decided to form an all-female auxiliary unit. This unit will be Acapulco's doves of peace." She paused dramatically. "Las Palomas. The Doves of Acapulco."

She waited for applause, which came in an enthusiastic wave. Stunned, Emilia found herself clapping along. Surely this new unit was just the first of a number of issues the meeting would address. The El Trio task force had to be next on the agenda.

Carlota accepted the accolade with a smile of ownership. She raised her hands for quiet and continued. "Chief Salazar has promised me that the unit will be operational within 30 days. I have no reason to doubt his word, especially given our selection to head it up."

Emilia glanced at Obregon. He licked his lips at her and she focused on Carlota again.

The mayor extended a manicured hand toward the woman next to Emilia. "Please join me in congratulating Claudia Sanchez Rangel from my own staff. Claudia, please stand up."

Claudia got to her feet and beamed at Carlota. There was a smattering of polite applause.

Emilia didn't know whether to laugh or cry. How could Las Palomas be a police unit if it was headed by one of Carlota's office minions? Claudia Sanchez Rangel probably didn't have the first idea how to run a police unit.

This was another one of Carlota's ideas that was all about image and nothing about reality.

Claudia continued to stand as Carlota swept her gaze around the table. "Claudia will be ably assisted by her chief of operations, an officer hand picked by Chief Salazar. Please join me in congratulating Detective Emilia Cruz Encinos."

Emilia gave a start, knocking over her empty coffee cup.

Claudia reached down and grabbed Emilia's hand, pressuring her to rise. As Emilia got to her feet, feeling like she'd been struck with a bag full of wet sand, Claudia pumped their joined hands into the air. The room erupted into another round of applause.

Across the expanse of polished wood, Obregon licked his lips again.

"I'm so excited," Claudia mouthed to Emilia.

"Stop it," Emilia hissed. She snatched her hand back and sat down.

Claudia resumed her seat, lower lip trembling.

Carlota began talking again, but the mayor's words were lost on Emilia. Surely this was all a mistake. They were here to talk about the El Trio murders.

Her breath came in little caffeine-fueled gulps as various people around the table were revealed to be from Carlota's public relations machine or Obregon's union organizers. The group discussed the aggressive timeline, office space that the union was willing to provide, and Carlota's press appearances to announce the formation of the Las Palomas unit.

Claudia agreed with everything, as if she had a choice.

Finally, Carlota declared Las Palomas a reality that would bring peace to the streets of Acapulco. The meeting was adjourned to another round of applause.

When the mayor stood to leave, so did Chief Salazar. Emilia bolted to her feet. She had to talk to him, make sure he understood last night's horrible tragedy. Surely, he would not reassign her to this ridiculous unit if he knew.

Meaningless chatter swirled around Emilia as she worked her way around the room to where Chief Salazar stood talking with some of Carlota's staff. People she didn't know shook her hand and wished her well. Small talk was obviously expected; Emilia smiled weakly and murmured her thanks.

Chief Salazar moved towards the door, still in discussions with several men. Emilia broke out of the pack of well-wishers.

But Claudia Sanchez stuck to her elbow. "Detective Cruz, I'd like to schedule our first team meeting for this afternoon."

"Not now," Emilia said.

She pushed past Claudia, shouldered a suit out of the way, and edged close to Chief Salazar.

"May I have a word with you, *mi jefe*?" she asked, trying to keep the urgency out of her voice.

"Cruz," he said. The single word was laden with irritation at her interruption.

"Two minutes, *mi jefe*. Thank you." It was dangerous to be so presumptuous, Emilia knew, but she couldn't help it.

Several of the suits with the police chief smiled indulgently as Emilia kept up with the knot of people with Chief Salazar. They passed into the hallway outside the mayor's reception area. The chief's security detail stayed with the group.

"What is it, Cruz?" Salazar's words were clipped.

"I greatly appreciate your confidence in me, *mi jefe*." Emilia started on her hastily composed speech, despite the multiple pairs of eyes staring at her. "But I'm a detective. Not a chief of operations. This assignment should go to someone with more compatible skills."

"Cruz, you will select candidates, train them, and get those women patrolling the streets of Acapulco within 30 days. And it was the mayor who has confidence in you, not me." Salazar looked at his watch. It was heavy and gold.

"*Mi jefe*," Emilia said, refusing to be dismissed so quickly. "I'm on a critical case right now. My partner's wife was murdered last night."

"Your partner's wife?" One of the suits positioned himself at Chief Salazar's elbow and pointed at Emilia.

"Yes," Emilia started. "A home invasion."

Salazar shook his head. "What happened last night was unfortunate, Cruz, but the investigation will go forward without you. The mayor's new unit is just as important." He walked away, the entire group moving with him.

Just as important?

Emilia felt the blood pound in her head as she glued herself to Salazar's side. "*Mi jefe*, with all due respect, I request that my assignment to Las Palomas be given to someone else. Or at least delayed while the investigation is ongoing."

Chief Salazar stopped and stared at her as if astounded.

"We can give her some time," one of suits said.

Chief Salazar gave the man a thin-lipped smile. "We have many excellent detectives," he said. "Detective Cruz often has trouble remembering that she is not the only one."

"Please, *mi jefe*," Emilia pleaded. "This could be related

to the El Trio murders."

The suits excitedly exchanged glances. "The El Trio murders?" one of them exclaimed. "Are you saying there's been another one?"

"There should be an El Trio task force," a second suit opined. "Good for Carlota's image."

Another man chimed in, concern all over his fleshy face. "That's Acapulco's biggest public relations mess right now. We all liked Detective Cruz's file, but if she's on the El Trio thing, we can get someone else for Las Palomas."

Emilia didn't know who the suits were, but today they were her guardian angels.

Chief Salazar's smile was so tight his face looked like a mask. "Unfortunately, there is no El Trio task force," he said stiffly to the cluster of suits. "The Acapulco police have the jurisdiction to investigate Captain Vega's death and my office is doing so. The attorney general's office investigates their own, as do the *federales*. There is no task force combining all three. But of course, we are all cooperating and sharing information and each of the crimes will be solved with all possible speed." His glance narrowed and focused on Emilia. "As for you, Detective Cruz, you'd do well not to question the capabilities of your fellow detectives."

"No, no, of course not, *mi jefe*," Emilia said hastily. "If this crime had happened to anyone else, I wouldn't be asking. But this is my partner."

"We can give Detective Cruz some time to sort things out, can't we, Chief Salazar?"

It was that distinctive female voice, always pitched between command and cajole. All heads swiveled to see Carlota standing in the hallway a few feet away.

Obregon was at her elbow. "Carlota, I think we should let Chief Salazar make that decision."

Carlota gave a frosty smile. "The El Trio situation is a public relations black eye. We can give Detective Cruz a week, shall we say? I'm sure she'll show some impressive results."

The hallway was crowded with competing agendas Emilia didn't understand. The tension between Carlota, Obregon, and Salazar was practically visible, arcing between them like electricity. It included her, too, and Carlota's remark about "impressive results" felt like a warning.

"Of course." Chief Salazar's face betrayed nothing. "A week for Detective Cruz to get her affairs in order, wrap up current investigations, and clean out her desk."

"Excellent." Carlota gave a regal nod and swept by. Minions followed in her wake like a school of fish. Obregon stayed with the suits, clearly enjoying the sight of Salazar being put in his place by the mayor.

"Gentlemen, will you excuse us?" Salazar said pointedly.

Obregon and the suits moved down the hallway. The security detail backed away a step, leaving Salazar and Emilia alone by a gilded console table.

"How dare you attempt to negotiate with me." Salazar's

face flushed with suppressed anger as he spat out the words. "You will take the jobs that are assigned to you and behave like a police officer who understands the concept of chain of command, instead of a little girl who doesn't like the games played in the schoolyard. Carlota may have helped you out today, but she won't be there the next time. Do you understand me, Detective?"

"Yes, *mi jefe*," Emilia murmured.

Chief Salazar strode away, back to the suits and Obregon, his security detail maintaining their respectful distance. He spoke to the group of suits, they all shook hands, and the suits disappeared into the mayoral offices.

Salazar and Obregon were left alone near the exit. Obregon glanced down the hall at Emilia. Salazar spoke to one of his security detail. The man came back down the long hallway and pointed at Emilia. "You waiting for something, Detective?"

Over his shoulder, it was clear that Salazar and Obregon were arguing.

"No," Emilia said. She went back into the waiting room.

Emilia leaned against the wall and closed her eyes. The caffeine and sugar that had propped her up for the past two hours were gone.

"Detective Cruz, I'm so glad I found you." It was Claudia Sanchez again, but no longer Emilia's new best friend. She thrust out a cell phone, the gesture full of shaky bravado. "I need your contact information."

Emilia blinked at the woman.

"We need to schedule our first planning meeting," Claudia continued. "I'd like to make it the same time every week. We'll meet in my office in this building until we move to the Las Palomas headquarters."

She paused and looked at Emilia expectantly.

Emilia didn't move.

After a moment of confusion, Claudia went on doggedly. "We have a lot of decisions to make. Carlota has given me a file full of her ideas. We really need to focus on the uniforms. Carlota wants something with that signature Las Brisas pink."

"Do you have any idea what it means to be a cop in this city?" Emilia asked abruptly.

"I . . . I majored in public administration and security in college," Claudia stammered. "I've been working for the mayor for almost two years."

Emilia was nearly speechless with sudden fury. "Have you ever listened to your partner describe how he came home to find his wife a bloody dead mess?" She launched herself off the wall. "Paid a snitch on the street for information to keep your friends from being killed? Scraped bodies off a sidewalk after a gang fight?"

Claudia took a shaky step away from Emilia. "You're not being very nice, Detective Cruz."

Emilia's anger fled as quickly as it came. Claudia's face was puckered with the effort not to cry.

The situation was hopeless.

"I have to go," Emilia said.

CHAPTER 3

Emilia walked into the squadroom to see a dozen uniformed cops clustered around Loyola, the bespectacled former teacher who was now acting lieutenant of detectives, as he handed out flyers and rattled off instructions.

Detectives Macias and Sandor were over by the long wall used to display information about active cases. It had already been turned into the murder board for the shooting death of Isabel de Silvio. Her picture, obviously copied from her national identity card, or *cédula*, topped the board. Below it, photographs of the crime featured the woman's body crumpled on a stairway. A dark puddle of blood spread beneath her.

On the other side of the big room, two desks were shoved into the corner which previously had hosted the coffee maker. Technicians armed with coils of wire and blinking equipment were obviously installing a hot line call center. Three uniforms were squeezed into the space; two spoke into headsets while the other typed assiduously on a computer keyboard. From its new perch on top of the filing cabinet, the coffee maker gurgled as the carafe filled with the promise of more caffeine.

Emilia got a wave of acknowledgement from Macias as she skirted Loyola's impromptu briefing and went to her desk. It was pushed nose-to-nose with Silvio's so that the backs of their computer monitors touched. Her partner's coffee mug, with a puddle of brown sludge at the bottom, sat forlornly by his keyboard, a painful reminder of their discussion of the El Trio murders on Friday.

Like she did every morning, Emilia unlocked her desk, opened the deep file drawer, and dumped her shoulder bag on top of the binder containing Emilia's personal files on women who'd gone missing in Acapulco. She shoved the drawer closed just as a uniformed courier came into the squadroom, stopped for a moment to take in the noise and the chaos, then made a beeline for her.

"Detective Cruz?" he asked.

"Sure," Emilia said. "What have you got?"

He handed her a large gray envelope and left.

"That was fast," Emilia muttered. The crime scene report from Silvio's house, no doubt.

She unfastened the clasp and pulled out a log of calls related to a cell phone number. Emilia stared at the printout for a full minute before it clicked. This was the record of calls made to and from the cell phone of Yolanda Lata, a dead hooker whose daughter Lila was one of the missing in Emilia's binder. Emilia had found Yolanda's phone by accident weeks ago and had requested the phone records in hopes of picking up Lila's trail again.

"You got something, Cruz?" Sandor called across the room.

Emilia shook her head. "Another case," she said. "But it'll wait."

"God help us if anything else comes in today," Sandor grumbled.

She dropped the cell phone record into the desk drawer with her bag and the binder and joined Macias and Sandor at the murder board. Macias had sketched in a brief timeline but like the start of every investigation, there was precious little information. Sandor tacked up two more photographs of the dead woman. Emilia swallowed hard as she looked at the photographs of the crime scene. It had been hard to look at the real thing last night; today's gory images were no easier.

Loyola wound up his instructions to the uniforms and asked if anyone had questions. Emilia counted a dozen young men wearing bulletproof vests with POLICIA stenciled front and back. Bulky task force radios weighted belts already laden with guns, nightsticks, handcuffs, and pepper spray. Primary radios were clipped to shirt collars. Emilia knew the old radios were an emergency measure in case the primary radios got jammed. More and more frequently, the drug cartels were learning police radio frequencies and blocking them in neighborhoods like El Roble where business was brisk and violence was high.

These were the cops who'd be going door-to-door to ask questions but also to display a show of force. The message was clear: the killing of an Acapulco cop's wife in a home invasion scenario was a high profile case being taken very seriously. A few of the uniforms asked questions about what to expect in El Roble, would they be out of there before sundown, how many suspects could they gather up. Emilia noticed their uniforms sported a small white diamond on the shoulder, the symbol of the Special Assignments unit. Like the Special Weapons and Tactics unit, Special Assignments officers had specialized skills.

Macias saw her looking at the group. "Silvio's old unit, you know. Before he made detective."

"*Madre de Dios*," Emilia said. "El Roble is going to get a surprise."

Considered one of Acapulco's elite units, Special Assignments was called out when there was a need for breaking doors, heads, and rules. Recruited for size, strength, and toughness, the members were the thugs of the police department. The unit was informally known as the Ball Busters.

Calling out Special Assignments meant that Loyola was going big with the investigation and Emilia felt her spirits lift. He'd been acting lieutenant for a couple of months now and the stress of the job was taking its toll. The former teacher had been a solid investigator, and a fairly honest one, but as the head of the detective squadroom he was crippled by indecision. Every move had to be vetted with Chief Salazar's staff. As a result, many cases went untouched and even the least competent detectives were frustrated to the breaking point.

The Ball Busters thundered out amid barking orders, the stomp of heavy boots, and the slap of nightsticks against palms as the men revved themselves up. Most of them probably didn't know Silvio, but his reputation as both detective and bookie stretched far and wide. Bad things had happened to a fellow cop—and a famous one at that—and they were out to get payback.

Air rushed back into the squadroom. There was a moment of quiet then a blast of urgency as phones rang, the hotline techs gathered up their equipment, and the uniforms in the corner debated procedure.

"Cruz. Macias. Sandor." Loyola gestured tiredly at his office door. "In here."

Emilia dropped into one of the cheap plastic and chrome chairs in front of the scarred metal desk. The sickly green walls, fluorescent lighting, and mountain of files gave her an instant headache. Macias and Sandor seated themselves as well.

Loyola took off his spectacles and pinched the bridge of his nose. "We're throwing everything at the Isabel de Silvio case. Hotline in place, teams in El Roble, forensics working the scene. Dr. Prade is doing the autopsy later today, but from what we know I doubt there's going to be much more for us there." He resettled his glasses in place and looked at Emilia. "First piece of business. Tell us about the El Trio task force. Can they help? What can they give us?"

Emilia shook her head. "There is no El Trio task force."

Both Macias and Sandor exclaimed, "What?"

Loyola half rose from his chair behind the desk. "Explain."

Emilia felt sick having to tell them. "It was a meeting

about a new unit Carlota is sponsoring. A female patrol unit called Las Palomas. I'm supposed to be the chief of operations."

Loyola's eyes bulged behind wire rims as he slowly sank back into his chair. "Nobody told me."

"Not a good time to dance off to some sweetheart job, Cruz," Sandor said angrily.

"I don't get a choice," Emilia said. "Chief Salazar was there and made it crystal clear. I go over on Monday."

"Nobody told me," Loyola repeated.

Emilia clenched her fists on her thighs. "I get to stay here for the rest of the week because, as she put it, Carlota expects us to produce impressive results. Apparently for her, El Trio is a public relations nightmare."

"Cops are getting killed," Macias exclaimed. "And this is about public relations?"

"Exact words."

Macias let loose with a string of invective. Sandor looked angry.

Loyola took off his glasses again and polished them with the end of his tie, an article of clothing he'd never worn as a detective. "Go back to the business about there not being an El Trio task force," he said. "Why not?"

"Chief Salazar claimed competing jurisdictions," Emilia said. "I don't think he's convinced that the murders are related."

"That's crazy." Macias leaned forward in his chair. "The shooter was going for Silvio and got Isabel by mistake. A fourth victim for whoever this *pendejo* is."

Loyola held up his hands in a *not-so-fast* gesture. "What about Silvio's bookie business?" he asked. "It happened the night of a Copa America match. Maybe somebody didn't like his gambling odds. Got mad at Silvio and killed his wife to teach him a lesson."

"Maybe the wife was the intended target," Sandor suggested. "She had an enemy in the neighborhood. She cheated at cards. Had a lover who wanted to get even after she kicked him to the curb."

"Please, Isabel did not cheat on Silvio or at cards." Emilia knew that like she knew her own name. "Isabel was not the intended victim. Nobody had a personal reason to kill her in the middle of the night. She was a nice lady who made meals for homeless kids."

"She was a cook?" Macias asked.

"Isabel cooked for the homeless kids in El Roble," Emilia said. "Dinners a couple of times a week. Probably fed 40, 50 kids each time in the courtyard of their house."

"Like a welfare program?" Loyola asked, squinting at her across his desk.

Emilia nodded. "Something like that."

"Why?" Loyola asked.

"It doesn't matter." Emilia looked at each of the surprised men in turn. They'd worked with Silvio for far longer than she had. "I can't believe you don't know. It's why Franco kept on with the bookie thing. He made enough to buy the food so Isabel could keep feeding the kids."

"*Rayos*," Loyola swore. "This is going to be on the news tonight and the mayor is going to be screaming about another public relations nightmare. 'The saint of El Roble gunned down in her own home.'"

"And the El Trio killer still out there, picking off cops," Macias added.

"The press will make the connection to El Trio," Emilia said. "Even if Chief Salazar's office doesn't."

"All right, all right." Loyola closed his eyes and pinched the bridge of his nose again. "We work this on the theory that either Silvio was the intended victim, a fourth El Trio, or he's got an enemy who wanted to send him a message by hurting the wife."

"You know I worked with all of them," Emilia said. "Salinas, Vega, Espinosa. Silvio."

Quiet settled over the room. Loyola dropped his hand and opened his eyes.

"Any one of us could be next," Macias said. He and Sandor shared a look.

"Do you know something, Cruz?" Loyola asked.

Emilia shook her head. "I don't have anything more than you do."

Loyola put his glasses back on and began writing on a pad. "All right. We'll hit this as hard as we can, as fast as we can. With any luck, the Ball Busters will shake things up in El Roble, scare somebody into giving up a lead. Somebody will have seen something."

Emilia was glad that for once, Loyola was leading

instead of waiting for orders. He and Silvio had been colleagues and rivals for years. Loyola's appointment as acting lieutenant created tensions between the two men exacerbated by Loyola's crippling deference to his superiors.

Everyone knew that Silvio was senior and the better administrator and investigator. But a combination of scandal and bad attitude had stalled Silvio's career long ago.

"Cruz." Loyola pointed his pen at Emilia. "For the time being, stay off the streets until we know more about what's out there. I want you on old case files. Get a uniform to help you go through everything. Silvio's old files from when he worked with Fuentes and Garcia. If this is another El Trio, there will be some hidden link to the other victims."

"All right," Emilia said.

"Macias and Sandor, you get with Silvio again. We left him at his cousin's last night, probably still there. Take him through anything and everything that could be relevant. He can fall apart later."

"What about the autopsy?" Macias asked.

"I'll go," Emilia said. "She was my friend."

To her surprise, Loyola nodded. "As soon as Prade tells you anything, call it in."

"We got Ibarra directing things in El Roble," he went on, naming his former partner who now worked solo. "They'll keep up the pressure as long as it takes. Castro and Gomez can follow up on anybody bothering Isabel, following her, anything like that." The acting lieutenant's pen swung to Macias and Sandor, both of whom were scribbling in their notebooks. "We need the preliminary crime scene report. The techs were all over that place last night. They should have at least the prints by now. I'll put in the request for the house phone records, see if they've been getting calls from unknown numbers. Maybe they had a stalker."

They talked through the next steps before Macias and Sandor walked out of the office. They were an effective team who'd arrived at Silvio's house last night shortly after Emilia called for backup. It had been a relief to see them instead of Castro and Gomez.

In addition to being the least effective and most dishonest team, Castro and Gomez had both accosted Emilia in the restroom reserved for detectives, as if being female meant she was fair game. Emilia fought her way out each time, leaving her colleague bruised and bloody. Bad feelings remained on all sides.

Loyola picked up his phone but set it down when he realized Emilia was still in the office. "What?"

"This new police unit I'm assigned to," Emilia said. "It's a joke. Run by a 5-year-old *chica* admin type. You have to get me out of it."

"I would assume that I'd be informed before one of my detectives is reassigned," Loyola said cautiously.

Emilia rattled the phone on Loyola's desk. "You talk to Chief Salazar's office a dozen times a day. You have to know someone who can reason with him."

Loyola sighed. "This is not the time to be your usual pain in the ass, Cruz. Let's work Silvio's case first. I'll make some calls later."

Emilia nodded, realizing that she was exhausted from too little sleep, emotional strain, and the bombshell that had fallen on her that morning. "Thank you."

An hour later she had a young uniformed cop seated at Silvio's desk, accessing old case files from the online archive. She wrote out a list of names on a pad next to him. If he found anything he was to print out the entire file.

She found herself compulsively checking her rearview mirror all the way to the morgue.

"What happened?" Emilia asked the morgue technician as she followed him down a hallway. She'd never seen the morgue so crowded. Two metal rolling carts were stacked with body bags. As Emilia walked by, another attendant shoved one of the carts into motion. Wheels groaned in protest. It had been designed to carry four bodies, not eight.

"Riot at the bull pen," the technician said over his shoulder. "Looks like a big knife fight. Guards broke it up."

Emilia didn't need to hear more to know that the bodies would reveal both stabbings and gunshots. The bull pen was the nickname for a temporary holding prison for men on the north side of Acapulco. The squat cinderblock facility was perpetually full to bursting with gang members, thieves, and other criminals. Most were awaiting charges, which under Mexican law didn't always come quickly. Others were nominally out on bail but couldn't raise the cash so the men stayed put.

Inmates were fed once a day and dependent on family for additional food, plus clothing, soap, and other sundries. There were few cells; the majority lived in concrete rectangles holding 40-60 men. The pens were a nightmare environment where the strong ruled and the weak were raped. A few bodies were hauled out every month.

The morgue technician pushed open a thick metal door and handed Emilia a surgical mask to tie over her mouth. Dr. Prade, Acapulco's medical examiner, was already in the room, bending over a flaccid female body.

He looked up and nodded at Emilia. The doctor wore a plaid shirt and surgical scrub pants, making for an incongruous outfit. It didn't matter; Emilia respected him, not only for his obvious medical skill and dedication to a difficult job, but because he treated her as respectfully as he treated the male detectives. Moreover, Prade knew about the list of missing women Emilia kept and always let her know if an unidentified female passed through the morgue.

"I've already placed time of death at between midnight and 2:00 am this morning," Prade said through his mask.

"Okay." Emilia had been in the room plenty of times, but this was the first time that it was personal. The body on the table had been a good, kind woman. Emilia had sat in her home, eaten her food.

Emilia fastened her mask in place, found one of the tall stools by the metal worktable where Prade wrote his reports, and got out her notebook.

Prade began his commentary, speaking into the recording microphone dangling from the ceiling.

"Three shots to the upper body. Large caliber handgun."

She heard the clink of metal on metal and glanced up as Prade dropped a blunted metal bullet into a bowl from a pair of long thin tongs. "All three bullets removed." He described the location of each in medical terms.

Prade's assistant took photographs with a small digital camera.

"From the trajectory," Prade said. "It would appear that the victim was shot at fairly close range while facing her assailant. The assailant was standing below her."

Emilia closed her eyes for a moment, reliving the moment she'd stepped into Silvio's house. It had been organized chaos, with the ambulance, two carloads of uniforms, and a van with an army of sleepy crime scene techs. As everyone fanned out, Emilia saw Isabel on her back, tumbled across the middle of the flight of stairs, arms and legs splayed awkwardly like a rag doll forgotten in the rain. Her head rested on the edge of a step; chin pushed into the neckline of the nightgown bunched around her thighs.

"The shooter was at the base of the stairs," Emilia said. "Judging from the blood above the body, I'd guess Isabel was shot as she was coming down the stairs. She slid down several steps as she fell."

"Thank you, Detective," Prade said crisply. "Please keep editorial comments to yourself until we are done."

The autopsy seemed to go on forever. Prade's voice was detached and clinical. "No sign of struggle. Nothing under the victim's fingernails. No bruising anywhere on the body."

Emilia scribbled his words into her notebook. "Rape?" she asked faintly.

It took some time before Prade answered. "She was not the victim of rape."

Emilia let out her breath.

When Prade was done, he came over to Emilia as she sat clutching her notebook. His assistant took over the job of sewing up the body before placing it in a temperature-controlled drawer. Isabel was luckier than the bodies from the bull pen prison. Those would remain stacked in their body bags for who knew how long. The morgue's army of char women mopped constantly.

"Let me buy you a cup of coffee, Detective," Prade said, taking off his mask.

Emilia took off her own mask, too. It was damp with tears.

"Did Silvio ever talk about his wife's illness?" Prade asked. He stirred sugar into his cup.

"Illness?" Emilia echoed. "What illness?"

"So I take it the answer is no." Prade sipped coffee. "She had advanced endometriosis with severe uterine fibroids and scarring. She'd probably had multiple miscarriages with at least one dilation and curettage procedure that left her with excessive scar tissue."

"No." Emilia found herself cringing inwardly. "He never mentioned anything about that, only that she'd had miscarriages."

"She likely experienced excessive bleeding on a regular basis," Prade said. "Lived with a great deal of pain. She was also extremely anemic, which is a side effect of the bleeding. The bloodwork from the autopsy will take a day or two, but I don't need tests to see that."

"Is that why they never had children?"

"Without a doubt." Prade shook his head sadly. "She should have had a hysterectomy long ago."

The coffee shop was a few blocks from the morgue and the short walk had helped to clear Emilia's head. She hadn't expected the autopsy to be so traumatic. Thankfully, she had been there alone, without Macias or Sandor. Or Silvio himself.

The coffee was dark and strong and for the second time that day, Emilia was downing it as fast as her cup was refilled. "Did you autopsy any of the El Trio victims?" she asked.

Prade stopped with his cup halfway to his lips. "You think there is a connection between the El Trio killer and Silvio's wife?"

"It's possible the killer came for Silvio and got Isabel by mistake," Emilia said.

"A fourth El Trio killing?"

"Yes."

"A great leap of logic," Prade warned. "Given the number of fatal shootings in this city every week and the El Roble neighborhood in particular."

"I worked with all of them. Salinas, Vega, Espinosa. And Silvio."

Prade put the cup back in the saucer. "They were all senior officers. No doubt they worked with many other law enforcement officers over the course of their careers. You shouldn't read too much into it, Emilia."

"Still," Emilia said as she pulled out her notebook. "We are going to look at everything and anything."

"All right." Prade nodded. "I did the autopsy for Captain Vega. None of the others were autopsied in Acapulco."

"Why not? They all died here, didn't they?"

"Salinas's family refused to allow an autopsy. Espinosa's murder was handled by the *federales*. They have their own medical examiners."

"That's right," Emilia said. "Espinosa introduced me to two of them when we worked that case in Gallo Pinto. They said they knew you." She flipped to a new page in her notebook. "Okay. About the Vega autopsy. Did anything stand out?"

"Captain Vega was killed by two shots from a large

caliber handgun," Prade said. "Either were fatal. One pierced his left ventricle and the other was an execution-style shot to the head. There was nothing more than that. No sign of a struggle, no bruising, nothing. He was an extremely fit man, probably a runner."

"No struggle. The same as Isabel."

"That isn't much of a connection."

"Shots from a large caliber handgun at close range," Emilia went on. "Another similarity."

Prade leaned back. "Most shootings in Acapulco are with a large caliber handgun. Domestic killings aren't rare in this town, either."

Emilia put down her pen. "What's that supposed to mean?"

Prade raised his hands. "I'm a great admirer of Franco Silvio's professional skills. But are you so sure he didn't kill his wife? Their physical relationship couldn't have been very satisfying for him and he's a bad tempered man at the best of times."

"No." Emilia laughed, no doubt from rising hysteria rather than humor. "Silvio can be a jerk, but he didn't kill her."

Prade swirled the coffee around in his cup. "Are you forgetting his past?"

"The unending scandal," Emilia said. "The death of Manuel Garcia Diaz."

Of course, it was inevitable that someone would connect the death of Silvio's past partner with Isabel, but Emilia hoped it stayed out of the news. After all, Garcia died long ago, when Emilia was a uniformed cop pounding the pavement in a bulletproof vest, herding drunks off Acapulco's scenic Costera Miguel Alemán and chasing kids who jumped the turnstiles at the CiCi Water Park.

"Silvio was cleared," Prade admitted. "But many people still think he killed Garcia."

"Why?" Emilia asked.

"The rumors," Prade said simply. "If there was no basis in fact, they would have died down by now. Whoever is keeping them alive probably knows the truth."

Emilia felt a little sick. "Do you really think he killed his own partner?"

"Garcia was also killed with a large caliber weapon at close range," Prade said.

Emilia closed her notebook. The pleasant taste of coffee was now sour in her mouth. "That's the way everybody dies in Acapulco."

CHAPTER 4

The squadroom was quiet when she got back. The Ball Busters, along with Castro, Gomez, and Ibarra, still combed El Roble. The hotline phones were silent. The uniforms in the corner drank coffee and chatted in low voices.

Emilia felt a ridiculous spurt of resentment at the young uniformed officer occupying Silvio's desk chair. He was still clicking through old case files and hadn't found anything significant while she was gone.

Macias handed Emilia a printout.

It was the preliminary crime scene report. The techs did a thorough job at Silvio's house but found nothing. All the gates, doors, and windows were locked and there was no sign of forced entry. No finger prints other than those of Silvio and his wife on door knobs or window latches. The house was surrounded by a 10-foot wall topped with razor wire. The wire was in good shape with no signs of sagging or breaks.

The living room had been disturbed. The other rooms appeared tidy and normal. The television and DVD player were there, as was a radio in the kitchen. The house contained no other major electronics or personal electronic devices. Some pieces of gold and silver jewelry were still in the victim's bedroom, along with a cell phone and a handbag containing wallet, keys, and some cosmetics.

Emilia put down the report and went over to the murder

board. Sandor had already written out the obvious questions.

She read the first aloud. "How did the shooter get in?"

"Either the shooter had a key or was already in the house before Silvio left," Sandor said. "not a break-in."

"Or she let them in," Emilia said.

"Dressed like that?" Sandor tapped the picture of Isabel's body in its blood-soaked white nightgown.

Emilia nodded. "Maybe it was someone who pretended to need help. Isabel might have let in someone if she thought it was an emergency."

"Good point." Sandor scribbled on the board.

"Did Silvio give you anything?" Emilia asked.

"Nothing new." Macias joined them in front of the wall of gory pictures and unanswered questions. "You wouldn't believe the crowds at his cousin's house. A parade of people with food and holy cards."

"I told you, everybody in El Roble knew her," Emilia said. "She fed all the homeless kids."

"This is garbage." Loyola was suddenly at Emilia's shoulder, waving a copy of the same crime scene report she'd just read. "What are we paying these *pendejos* to do? Sit on their asses?" He glared at Emilia. "You got anything else from the autopsy?"

"No, just what I called in. Isabel was shot from below. The shooter was likely at the foot of the stairs as she came down. Prade will have his full report for us in the morning."

"Fuck, fuck, we got nothing." Loyola's face was red with either anger or frustration. "The story is already online. The saint of El Roble gunned down in her own home. Just like we predicted."

"Tied in to El Trio?" Macias asked.

"Not yet." Loyola stomped back into his office and slammed the door.

"And no calls asking to join efforts with any of the other El Trio investigations," Macias said softly.

Emilia went back to her desk, powered up her computer, and time flew by. She and the young uniform at Silvio's desk reviewed the cases that connected her to the three El Trio victims. Emilia knew them by heart but reread each, hoping against hope that there was a detail related to Silvio that she'd overlooked.

Salinas, the first El Trio victim, had been her contact at the state's attorney general's office on the El Pharaoh casino money laundering case. Silvio had led the raid that closed the casino but she'd done the liaison work. As far as Emilia knew, Salinas and Silvio had never met.

An arson case brought Silvio into contact with Vega, the arrogant captain from Chief Salazar's office. Vega had taken over the case and Silvio briefed him. There was no collaboration or coordination afterwards.

There was no link at all between Silvio and the case involving Espinosa, the *federale* and third El Trio victim. Silvio didn't work that case and never met Espinosa. Emilia knew little about the *federale* officer and his law enforcement career other than his role investigating a killing field she'd stumbled upon.

Out of all the cases, Silvio was most involved in the El Pharaoh money laundering mess. Indeed, Silvio had led the raid on the casino, Emilia by his side. They seized evidence and closed the casino, sure that it was doing a roaring trade in money laundering for drug cartels.

Key documents went missing, however, before being properly logged into police custody. She and Silvio suspected fellow detectives Castro and Gomez for the loss of evidence, but like so many other things, were never held accountable. The El Pharaoh reopened. The casino was more popular now than ever before.

Emilia got up and made a fresh pot of coffee. Macias and Sandor got access to the traffic camera database. A fresh team came to manage the hotline and had nothing to do.

The text on her computer screen blurred. Emilia sat back and closed her eyes and tried to make sense of the last 24 hours. This time yesterday she was worried about making a good impression on the members of the Acapulco Hotel Association. Those concerns seemed so irrelevant now.

The chatter of the uniforms staffing the silent hotline grated on her nerves. Emilia pulled out the envelope with Yolanda Lata's cell phone record and gave it to the loudest. "Please run traces on all the numbers in this log," she instructed him. "Incoming and outgoing. I need everything you can find."

Ibarra arrived an hour later. Emilia jumped to her feet, as did Macias and Sandor, a silent question on all faces. Ibarra was a stocky chain-smoking bachelor who smelled like a chimney and lately sported a cotton duster from an Australian clothing store, making him look like a Latino gnome who got lost in the outback. He rarely spoke to Emilia. Unlit cigarette dangling from the corner of his mouth, he spread his hands to indicate they were empty after hours knocking on doors in El Roble. He disappeared inside Loyola's office.

One of the Ball Buster sergeants came in. Again, all the detectives rose to their feet. He shook his head. "Nothing so far." He stayed in Loyola's office for five minutes and left. Ibarra stayed inside with the acting lieutenant.

Macias and Sandor took a break from watching camera footage and fetched pizza. Emilia brewed another pot of coffee. There were no city security cameras close to Silvio's house. They all agreed that it was pointless to keep reviewing the feeds.

She'd lost track of time when the hotline uniform brought back the printout of Yolanda Lata's cell phone records, plus a neatly typed note summarizing his findings.

Emilia's heart sank. "That's all?"

"Yes, señora."

"Detective," Emilia corrected him.

"What?"

"Never mind." Emilia was too tired to give him a lesson

in how to deal with superior officers who were female. Not that he was likely to encounter many.

Two of the four numbers the late Yolanda Lata had called or texted were no longer in service and there was no information on either. A third number belonged to the beauty school that Emilia knew was run by Yolanda's husband. The fourth number was a cell phone that was in service but registered to the president of Mexico.

"We checked and rechecked," the uniform said. "That's the name associated with the number."

Emilia nodded. Cell phone registration was mandatory but easily gamed. She'd heard that at last count over 100 cell phone numbers were registered to the president. "Let me try the number."

The outgoing hotline connection was untraceable so Emilia dialed the number from that workstation. A warbling male voice answered. "*Digame.*"

Emilia hung up without speaking. The distinctive voice on the other end was that of Chavito, a pimp for whom Yolanda had worked off and on for years. Chavito had already told her all he knew about the late hooker and her missing daughter, Lila. Once again, Lila's trail had evaporated.

Macias and Sandor left. Eventually Loyola and Ibarra left, too.

At midnight, the uniform at Silvio's desk asked if he could go home. Emilia let him leave. She gathered up her shoulder bag and stumbled out after him.

Fatigue heightened the fear that had shadowed her for too long. Four people murdered. The El Trio killer was picking off law enforcement officers who were all connected by some invisible thread that she should be able to see. Except that she was too stupid.

Driving back to the Palacio Réal so late at night was nerve-wracking. Everything was a potential death trap; a light in her rearview, a deserted intersection. She ran three red lights and drove the Carretera Escénica like a Formula One racer, spinning the heavy Suburban without warning off the highway and into the turnoff for the Palacio Réal. She almost rammed the *privada* gate leading to the cliffside development.

Her hands shook as she gave the vehicle keys to the hotel valet and punched the button for the elevator. Kurt woke up when she came into the bedroom. He might have said something but Emilia was asleep before her head hit the pillow.

CHAPTER 5

The sense of urgency in the squadroom was just as intense on Tuesday. Teams were back on the streets in El Roble, running down leads about unfamiliar cars and bar talk between drinkers who'd bet on the Copa America match. Loyola's phone rang constantly. In between calls he barked out orders that he was the only one to speak about the Isabel de Silvio case to either the press or Chief Salazar's office.

Current cases were put on hold, at least for the next two days. Dispatch sent over details of overnight shootings and Ibarra was tasked with getting the cases transferred to another unit. Emilia overheard the holding cell desk sergeant say that the Acapulco police could be called upon to investigate the deaths at the bull pen prison. With any luck, that sordid mess would be handled by Chief Salazar's office.

Emilia and the same young uniform started on the cases Silvio had handled with his late partner, Garcia.

It didn't take long before Emilia realized that they couldn't access older files stored in an archive system. It took her two hours and three cups of coffee to get access, only to have the ancient database freeze when she entered a search term.

The door to the lieutenant's office crashed open. Loyola tore through the squadroom, struggling into a suit jacket as he went, and disappeared without speaking to anyone.

Emilia caught Sandor's eye over the top of her computer monitor. He shrugged.

At noon the system administrator told Emilia that some files were corrupted and the system was basically unusable, despite the millions of pesos spent on transferring files into its new state-of-the art database.

The alternative was to go over to the central administration building and request the paper files from the Records department.

The young uniform went off to get some lunch. Emilia sat at her desk and took out the food she'd brought from the hotel. Jacques would probably be appalled if he knew she was eating his balsamic roasted vegetable ravioli cold. With a plastic fork.

Loyola walked into the squadroom, walking appreciably slower than when he'd left. He had a file folder in one hand and a crumpled handkerchief in the other. He looked at Macias and Sandor. "You two." The file folder fluttered in Emilia's direction. "Cruz. My office. Now."

Once they were all assembled, he took off his jacket, sat behind his desk, and plied the handkerchief across his forehead. Loyola appeared to have aged 10 years in two hours.

"What's going on?" Emilia asked.

"We got Silvio's phone records," Loyola said. He rested his free hand on the file folder. "Home and cell for both him and the wife."

"They had a stalker," Macias said immediately.

"No," Loyola said. "Where were you Sunday night, Cruz?"

"At Silvio's," Emilia said. "The crime scene, remember? Same as all of you. Until sunrise."

"Before that."

"At home," Emilia said.

"Alone?"

"No."

"Got anybody can swear to that?"

"Yes. We had a Copa America party." She leaned forward. "What are you getting at?"

Loyola refused to meet her eye. "Silvio called you. Right around the time of death for the wife."

Emilia blinked. "That's right."

"What?" Macias and Sandor said it at the same time.

"Why didn't you say anything, Cruz?" Loyola opened the file folder, extracted a phone log, and handed it to Macias.

"I never picked up." Emilia shrugged. "It didn't make any difference."

"Unless it was supposed to be some sort of signal," Loyola said.

"What are you talking about?" Emilia asked. "It was the middle of the night. I thought Silvio was drunk and butt-dialing me. By the time I got to my phone, it had stopped ringing. Dispatch called a few minutes later."

"It's here," Sandor said, peering over his partner's shoulder. "Two outgoing calls from Silvio's phone during the autopsy's time of death window."

"Were Silvio and his wife having problems?" Loyola asked. "They argue on the phone a lot?"

"No," Emilia said. "He didn't talk to her on the phone while he was working."

"So they didn't get along."

"That's not what I said."

"Girl on the side?" Loyola snapped.

"No, and I'm not liking this line of inquiry," Emilia said. It was too reminiscent of Prade's words after the autopsy. "Are you implying that Franco killed his wife?"

"The gate was locked, Cruz," Loyola said. "Nobody tampered with any of the doors, locks, or windows."

"We've been over all of this," Emilia countered. "Somebody had a key. Or Isabel knew them and let them in."

She looked at Macias and Sandor. Both detectives shrugged.

Loyola shook his head. "Middle of the night? In her nightgown? Not likely."

"You don't have a motive." Emilia folded her arms. "Franco and Isabel had been married over 20 years. Why kill her now?"

Loyola coughed. "Silvio never had a partner like you before."

"I'm not following," Emilia heard herself say.

"Everybody took bets on how long the two of you would

stay partners," Loyola mopped his face again. "Longest bet was two months. But something clicked, you know. You two made quite a team."

A rushing sound filled Emilia's head.

Loyola leaned over the desk and snatched the phone logs out of Macias's hand. "I saw the autopsy report," he said. "His wife was sick. Used-up. Silvio probably spent more time with you in the past six months than he did with her in the past six years."

"We've been working like dogs." Emilia couldn't believe what he was saying. "With the results to prove it."

"You took it to the bedroom," Loyola said with a snort. "Eventually Silvio decides the wife is in the way. You're a lot hotter and you're always right there. Why does he need the old bag? Maybe she knew. Complained. Didn't like being replaced by a pretty girl cop. Silvio saw him and you in a new life on the beach in Ixtapa, I don't know."

"This is nuts," Emilia exploded.

"You helped him plan it," Loyola said. "Figured out the right night, made sure you both had a good alibi. He kills the old bag. Calls you to give you the 'mission accomplished' signal. But he forgets to make it look like robbery before calling Dispatch. Wasn't thinking clear. Kind of impatient to celebrate, you know what I mean?"

If Emilia could breathe, she could move. If she could move, she'd shoot Loyola in the head.

"After all, this isn't the first time something bad has

happened to someone close to Silvio." Loyola scrabbled to find the folder's open edge. "Got away with the whole Garcia thing a couple of years ago. So why not do it again, right?"

He nervously snatched at the folder. A snowfall of white paper fluttered to the floor.

No one else in the room moved.

"I've got it," Loyola said hastily. He slammed the folder closed and scooted back his chair to pick up the mess at his feet.

With Loyola bent over, Emilia half-rose in her chair. "Cruz" and "Confidential" were written in small block letters on the cover of the folder.

Loyola straightened up and Emilia hastily settled back in her chair. Loyola rifled through the retrieved papers, plucked out a handwritten memo, and jammed the rest back in the folder. He held out the memo to Sandor and jerked his chin at the door. "You two take Cruz's statement."

Macias and Sandor reluctantly got to their feet.

"Wait a minute," Emilia said. The fight or flight instinct was kicking in and she was ready to brawl. "Yesterday, we were all about the El Trio murders. How can you sit here now and say Franco killed Isabel when yesterday he was the intended victim?"

"Yesterday you were hiding a phone call," Loyola said. "All wound up over the coincidence that you worked with the El Trio victims. Throwing us off the scent."

Emilia jumped up. "Just to be clear, this doesn't have

anything to do with Silvio being a better detective or my knee in your crotch a couple of months ago?"

Macias made a sound like a snort disguised as a cough.

"Back off, Cruz," Loyola warned. "For all we know you're the El Trio killer. Maybe you and Silvio together. After all, you knew all the victims. Maybe the two of you killed the others just so when you got to the old lady, it would look like a serial killer knocking off law enforcement. Make us think he was supposed to be the next victim. That would be Silvio's style."

"This is such a load of shit," Emilia said furiously. "Silvio's been a burr under your saddle ever since they made you acting lieutenant. I can't believe you'd stoop low enough to pin the murder of his wife—."

Loyola bolted to his feet. "Shut up, Cruz!"

"That's a two for one, isn't it?" Emilia shouted, so angry she couldn't see straight. "Get rid of your biggest problem in the squadroom and boost your solve rate. Chief Salazar will fucking love you."

"Cruz, I could arrest you right now," Loyola roared. "Charge you when hell freezes. You want to remember that."

"I'll remember—."

Suddenly both Macias and Sandor were at Emilia's elbow, opening the door and shoving her through. "Shut the fuck up, Cruz," Macias said under his breath.

"Wait a minute," Loyola snapped as the little parade was halfway out the door.

"What?" Emilia tried to turn but Sandor had a grip like iron around her right bicep. The old wound throbbed.

"Clean out her desk," Loyola said, speaking to Macias and Sandor. "If she's got any keys, collect them up. One of them probably unlocks Silvio's house."

Each of the new interrogation rooms had an audio feed, one-way mirrors, a single table, and three chairs, plus cameras in the ceiling and a hidden squawk button in case a cop needed emergency help. There was a narrow anteroom outside where watchers could hear the audio and observe the interrogations, although at the press of a button the interrogators inside could block both window and sound. The space age techniques didn't mask the traditional interrogation room aroma of stale coffee, old sweat, and fresh fear.

Out of habit, Emilia walked to the side of the table reserved for the police interrogator. Macias held up a hand. "Cruz."

He indicated the opposite side of the table. The side with steel loops in the table to restrain a prisoner's handcuffs.

The gesture jolted Emilia down to her shoe soles. She reluctantly took the proffered chair and crossed her arms.

Her anger was still racing at full throttle. She'd watched as Sandor took everything out of her desk, in full view of all the uniforms. Castro and Gomez, like two village idiots, smirked and catcalled the entire time. Emilia had stared fixedly at the photograph of Isabel's dead body on the murder board, until Macias shoved her out of the squadroom and made her follow Sandor down the hall to the interrogation rooms.

Macias switched the one-way mirror to a solid opaque sheet and turned on the recorder. He stated that they were there to take the statement of Detective Emilia Cruz Encinos regarding the death of Isabel de Silvio.

He asked Emilia to state her full name, rank, and badge number.

And address.

"The Palacio Réal hotel." There was grim satisfaction in the look of surprise that flitted over both detectives' faces. They all knew that one night at the Palacio Réal cost more than an Acapulco detective made in a month.

"The Palacio Réal?" Macias asked. "How are you affording that, Detective Cruz?"

"My boyfriend is Kurt Rucker. The general manager of the hotel. I live in his apartment with him. Which makes it highly unlikely I had a motive for a relationship with anyone else."

"Rucker." Sandor said. "Is that the same guy who pulled the mayor out of the El Tigre restaurant?"

She'd been with Kurt when he'd plunged into a burning restaurant to save trapped patrons. Carlota had been one of them. "Yes."

"Let the record show that Detective Cruz voluntarily

gave updated personnel information," Sandor said for the benefit of the recording.

"Detective Cruz, please give your whereabouts during the date and time in question."

Emilia steadied her breath against the waves of anger coursing through her body. "I was at the Palacio Réal hotel. We hosted a party for the board of the Acapulco Hotel Association. About 40 people attended. All the guests saw me there."

Macias and Sandor exchanged a sideways look.

"I never left," Emilia continued. "I was at the Palacio Réal until Dispatch called about 3:00 am with information about a shooting in El Roble."

"Can you name any witnesses who saw you at the hotel?"

"Yes," Emilia said. "The head chef. The kitchen staff who set up the buffet. The valet who can verify my car was parked in the underground garage all day. The hotel is loaded with closed circuit television cameras, too. I'll give you the name of the head of security. We know each other. I'm sure he'll be willing to have you look at hours and hours of footage while whoever killed Isabel de Silvio picks out his next target."

Macias gave a tight smile. "All these people work for Rucker, don't they?"

"Call everybody who came to the party." Emilia folded her arms. "Start with Tony and Jane Wilcox. They own the Santa Rosa hotel. You know, the pink hacienda downtown. Magda and Sergei Porchenko. They own the Pacific Lotus. I spilled wine on her. They'll remember me."

She'd end this utterly stupid line of inquiry into Isabel's death by sabotaging Kurt's career. There would be a scandal when the rarified world of the Acapulco Hotel Association was tainted by one of their board members living with a cop. Kurt would be blackballed, lose his position on the board. Maybe even get fired by the Palacio Réal chain of hotels.

"Anyone else?"

"*Madre de Dios*," Emilia swore. "Call the Association office. Get a list of the board members. Call them all."

"Cruz," Macias said warningly. "You know the kinds of questions we have to ask."

Emilia took a deep breath and exhaled very slowly.

Sandor held up the handwritten memo Loyola had given him. It was covered in hastily scribbled lines. "Are you in a personal relationship with your partner, Detective Franco Silvio?" he read tonelessly.

"No."

Sandor wrote down Emilia's reply before reading the next question. "Did you know his late wife, Isabel de Silvio?"

"Yes."

"Describe the nature of your relationship with her."

"We were friends. Not close, but friends. Talked a few times at Silvio's house."

"Did you know if there was trouble in the marriage?"

"No," Emilia said. "No trouble."

"Did she want him to quit the bookie business?"

"No. I think it was important to both of them so they could keep feeding the neighborhood kids."

Sandor's pen scratched against the paper. Macias watched his partner. Emilia plotted ways to destroy Loyola.

Eventually Sandor put down his pen and upended the box containing the contents of Emilia's desk. Her shoulder bag thumped onto the table, followed by the heavy binder containing the *Las Perdidas* files. A shower of loose papers, snacks, and an old cosmetics bag followed.

Emilia kept her temper in check as Sandor opened her shoulder bag and picked out a set of keys. "What are these?" he asked.

"Keys to my mother's house." Emilia rattled off the address.

He rifled through her wallet, finding the keycard to the penthouse at the Palacio Réal. He spoke to the ceiling. "For the record, Detective Cruz is in possession of a keycard for the Palacio Réal hotel."

It was a half-hearted job, both detectives sheepish as they poked through Emilia's things. Finally Macias put everything except the keys back into the box. "We'll have to take these," he said.

"Sure," Emilia said, loading as much sarcasm as she could into the single word. "You do that."

Sandor noted for the record what time the interview ended. Detective Cruz had cooperated fully. He turned off the recorder, picked up the handwritten memo that now included his answers, and left.

Emilia drummed her fingers on the table. "So are we done with this nonsense?" she asked Macias.

"I don't know, Cruz." Macias got up and paced. He was the best looking detective in the squadroom, with wavy hair and deep set eyes. She didn't know if he had a personal life; he and Sandor were always together and a little apart from the rest of the squadroom.

"The El Trio killer is out there," Emilia warned. "The more time we waste, the harder it will be to find him."

"I know."

The door to the interrogation room opened. Sandor motioned for Macias to step outside. The door closed behind him.

Her anger had ebbed. Emilia concentrated on taming her breathing and thinking logically. This interview was a formality. Loyola had done a good job marshalling resources to find Isabel's killer; he wasn't going to derail the investigation because of one unanswered phone call. She should have said something, but between the Las Palomas job surprise and the murder investigation, she'd simply forgotten about Silvio's call.

No, this was a tiny distraction. They would find Isabel's killer. There would be a connection to the El Trio murders they hadn't yet found. It was hiding in plain sight.

Sandor and Macias came back into the interrogation room.

"We'll need you to leave your badge and gun, Cruz," Sandor said.

Emilia stared at the two men. "You took my statement," she said. "We're done."

Macias gave his head a tiny shake.

"Leave your badge and gun," Sandor repeated. "Loyola says you're to report to your new assignment on Monday."

"You're kidding," Emilia looked from Sandor to Macias and back again. "I'm suspended?"

"You're on a break," Sandor said. "Take your stuff. Leave your gun. And badge."

Emilia slowly drew the handgun out of her shoulder holster and laid it on the table. Neither Sandor nor Macias made any move to pick it up.

She slipped her badge lanyard over her head. The shiny detective badge clanked against the worn table top when she set it down. The lanyard coiled on top of it.

"What's going to happen to Silvio?" Emilia asked.

"Loyola's assigned a team of uniforms to pick him up," Sandor said. "Taking him over to the bull pen."

"But he's a cop," Emilia gasped. "He could get killed in there."

Sandor shot a glance at the recording button. Emilia followed his glance. It was off.

"Listen, Cruz," he said in a low voice. "This isn't time to be the loyal partner. If I was you, I'd keep my mouth shut and my head down. Loyola's wound real tight. Let things with Silvio take their course."

"Am I free to go?" This time Emilia couldn't keep her voice from shaking.

Sandor nodded.

She slung her bag over her shoulder, picked up the file box and wheeled for the door. Macias opened it for her.

The walls on either side blurred as she rapidly made her way to the rear exit.

"Hey, Cruz." The duty sergeant at the desk by the holding cells put out a hand to stop her. "Tough news about Silvio's old lady. Tell him I'm real sorry."

Emilia managed a smile and a nod. She juggled the box with one hand to shoot him with her thumb and forefinger, the same as always.

She shoved open the door and stepped into the hot afternoon sun. In a minute she was inside the Suburban with the air conditioning going full blast and the vehicle emitting its usual symphony of metallic rattles. She rested her forehead on the steering wheel and tried to collect herself. This was wrong. This was so wrong.

CHAPTER 6

"Since when are you my sister?" Silvio asked.

"Since yesterday," Emilia said, her voice barely above a whisper. "I had to turn in my badge and gun. Loyola thinks I was your accomplice."

Silvio didn't look as bad as Emilia had expected. His face was drawn with fatigue but otherwise he was holding up well. The former heavyweight boxer hadn't been in the ring in years but retained the solid muscle mass and crew cut of his youth. Silvio was dressed in his usual attire of jeans and white tee shirt, both now streaked with grime. The bull pen didn't issue uniforms, ensuring that prisoners fought over status symbols like rock band tee shirts. The exception was shoes; all prisoners wore cheap prison flip flops. In the plastic sandals, Silvio's feet were dark with dust.

"What's supposed to be the motive?" he asked.

Emilia swallowed hard. "We're having an affair and wanted Isabel out of the way."

To her surprise Silvio laughed. "One thing I've always admired about Loyola," he said. "The way he knows his people so well.

Emilia managed a smile. "It's a skill, all right."

Silvio's amusement faded into grim stoicism. "Did he claim this is just like how I set up Garcia all those years ago?"

"Something along those lines." Emilia didn't mention

that the medical examiner had said the same thing but pushed a plastic grocery bag across the tabletop. "I brought you some stuff."

As Silvio sorted through the clothes, soap, and foil-wrapped food, Emilia dared to look around. The reception area for prisoners was a series of chicken-wire cages, each enclosing a table and two chairs. Prisoners entered from one side and family members from the other. There were guards on both the prison and freedom sides but none seemed concerned with what went on inside the mesh cubicles.

She counted six cages, all occupied by a male prisoner. Most of the visitors were female; the exception was a priest.

"Cigarettes," Silvio said approvingly. "How did you get them in?"

Emilia knew he'd need the cigarettes as barter goods. "I brought four packs," she said. "The guard was nice enough to take two."

Emilia, her shoulder bag, and the parcel for Silvio had all been thoroughly searched by a male guard before she was allowed to enter the prison. Without the free passage her badge would have guaranteed, she'd anticipated the ordeal but that didn't make it any easier. The "gift" of two packs of cigarettes, however, kept it to a minimum and convinced the guard not to take the food.

"You brought a book?" Silvio held up a paperback.

Emilia shrugged. "Thought it might help to pass the

time."

Silvio tossed it across the table to her. "No distractions. Not in this place."

It was then she noticed that his hands were cut and bruised.

"How bad is it?" she asked.

"It's a good place to be right now." Silvio flexed his hands. A trickle of blood ran between two knuckles. "Can beat the shit out of anyone I want."

She'd been Silvio's partner for nine months and had come to know him as well as anyone in the squadroom. The big man was street smart, menacing, and often callous. He was also a clever and tireless investigator. His initial contempt for her as a female in the otherwise all-male squadroom had gradually eased when Emilia had proven herself to be a match for his intelligence and fit enough to take on any challenge.

Emilia stuffed the unwelcome paperback into her bag and pulled out her notebook. "Do they know who you are?"

"Not yet." Silvio unwrapped one of the burritos she'd bought from a downtown street vendor. "Any leads yet?"

"Nothing solid," Emilia wrinkled her nose against the stink of urine and body odor wafting from the man and woman in the cage next to them. "When I left they were running down some cars."

"I needed this fucking food, Cruz," Silvio said, as he swallowed down half the burrito. "But coming here wasn't your best idea if Loyola thinks you were my accomplice."

"Loyola can go to hell," Emilia said. "I'll get a new badge on Monday."

"El Trio task force?"

Emilia shook her head. She'd forgotten that he didn't know the outcome of Monday's meeting. "There's no El Trio task force," she said. "I'm assigned to a new unit. Carlota is backing it."

She briefly recounted the meeting in Carlota's office, including meeting Claudia Sanchez and the encounter with Chief Salazar.

"So Macias and Sandor are running after nothing and you're reassigned," Silvio said. He put down the burrito and looked around as if seeing the prison for the first time. "Guess I'd better get used to this."

"This is crazy," Emilia said. "Loyola can't make this stick and he knows it. I'll prove your alibi, and you'll be out."

"You're already suspended, Cruz," Silvio said. "Don't kill your career over me."

"I'll do what I want, Franco." Emilia poised her pen over her notebook. "What time did you leave the house?"

It was the first time she'd ever won a staring contest with him. Silvio finished the burrito and reached for the next one.

"We were supposed to go over to my cousin Antonio's at 7:00 pm," he started. "He got a new widescreen television. "I spent the afternoon doing the point spread, taking in a few more bets."

Emilia began a timeline in her notebook with *7:00 pm.* "You and Isabel both planned to go?"

"Yes." Silvio swallowed a bite. "Walk over. It isn't far." He gave her the address.

Emilia had never met Antonio but Silvio had mentioned him occasionally and she knew they were drinking buddies as well as close family members. "Who knew about your plans to go to Antonio's?"

Silvio shrugged. "Wasn't a secret. Family. Neighborhood friends who were coming. You. Whoever was in the squadroom listening to us talk on Friday."

Emilia took down a dozen names of men with whom Silvio had shared his Copa America viewing plans before Sunday's match. Macias and Sandor had the same names, but given what had happened, she couldn't trust that they would follow up.

"So why didn't Isabel go over to Antonio's with you?" she asked.

"Said she didn't feel good. Female problems."

"Did you tell anyone she was staying home?"

"She called, talked to Antonio's wife."

"What time?"

"Couple minutes before I left the house. She said she was going to go to bed early. I left. Walked over there around 7:00 pm, just the same as we'd planned."

Silvio displayed no emotion. He didn't say if he'd kissed his wife for the last time. Told her that he loved her.

Emilia drew in a breath, forcing herself to stay in

investigation mode. "So Isabel was home by herself after 7:00 pm."

"Everybody at Antonio's knew she was home alone."

"I need the names of everyone who was there," Emilia said. The guard was looking at her suspiciously and she wondered if he was going to try and confiscate her notebook.

Silvio reeled off half a dozen names of friends and family members, many of whom were the same people who'd known of his plans ahead of time. As Emilia wrote she thought that the party at Antonio's had probably been more fun than the event in the penthouse.

"Were you there all night? You never left?" Emilia scribbled questions for those at the party. Would any of them be involved? It was unlikely, but she'd check. She found herself writing as if in a rush; the stink and noise of the prison was magnifying the emotional drama of the questions she had to ask.

Silvio nodded. "We ate, drank beer, yelled at the screen. I stayed at Antonio's until around 2:00 am. Walked home."

"How drunk were you?"

"I could still walk a straight line."

"Anybody go with you? Or you walked home alone?"

Silvio finished the last burrito. "Must have passed a dozen or so *halcones* doing sentry duty for their rock and rollers. Not exactly witnesses who would attest to having seen me."

He was right; even if they could find them, kids who acted as lookouts for drug gangs didn't make reliable witnesses.

"Okay, so you walked home alone." Emilia gave him a *keep going* hand roll.

Like all the houses in the neighborhood, his was surrounded by a tall concrete wall, bisected by two corrugated metal gates. The pedestrian gate was the size of an ordinary house door. The other gate was for vehicles and controlled by an automatic opener. At night, the entire front of the property was illuminated by a large mercury light. He'd turned it on before he left; a routine security precaution.

The big exterior mercury light was still on as Silvio unlocked the pedestrian gate. As he crossed the courtyard to the house, the motion-detection light by the front door flickered on.

Everything worked normally. There was nothing about the house to indicate what he'd find inside. Silvio's dry, factual manner, exactly the way he dissected every other murder case, was unnerving.

"You're sure that both the gate and the door were locked?" Emilia said.

"Both the door and the gate lock automatically when closed," Silvio said. "The same key opens both. If they're closed, they're locked. And they were both closed when I left at 7:00 pm."

The living room lights were on. The room was messy and he wondered if Isabel had been rearranging the furniture. He remembered thinking it was odd that she would do that when she'd said she wasn't feeling well.

He'd headed for the stairs and their bedroom on the second floor.

That's when he found Isabel, in her nightgown, sprawled on her back mid-way down the stairs to the second floor and congealed blood over the steps.

"Prade's done the autopsy," Emilia informed him. "The shooter was below her, probably at the base of the stairs."

"You know the rest." Silvio crushed the burrito wrappers into a ball, as if to close the discussion about Isabel's death. "We talked through it all at the station."

He'd drawn his weapon and gone room-by-room to see if the assailant was still there. Once he'd cleared the house, he went back to Isabel's body on the stairs and stayed there until the first patrol car showed up. He hadn't checked if anything was missing.

He didn't mention calling her and Emilia didn't prompt him. She wondered if he even remembered that he'd given his badge number and not his name when he called Dispatch.

"Nobody broke in," Emilia said. "The doors and windows were locked. The techs didn't find any prints."

"Ballistics?"

"Not yet," Emilia said. "Look, would she have opened the door for someone?"

"No," Silvio said immediately. "She would have

called me if someone had come to the house at that hour." He held up a hand. "And don't bother asking if she had a lover. I went over all that nonsense already with Macias and Sandor."

"Did they ask if you had a lover? A jealous one?"

"Of course," Silvio said. "You know I didn't step out on Isabel. But the easiest answer is always the husband, right?"

"It's Loyola's answer until we figure out how the killer got in," Emilia said.

"I had my key," Silvio said. "Isabel's key was still in our bedroom. The only other person with a key to the house is my cousin Antonio. He and his wife have a spare to ours and we have one to theirs."

"Have you been officially charged?" Emilia asked.

"No," Silvio said. "Do you think this is Loyola's idea? Or is he somebody's puppet?"

Before Emilia could reply, the couple in the next cage started shouting at each other. He was a *pendejo* who'd never made a peso he didn't drink and she was a *bruja* who was going to burst into flames the next time she went into church.

The guards on either side of the cage perked up, snickering at each other through the wire mesh and angry hand waving.

Emilia leaned forward so Silvio could hear her. "Until yesterday afternoon, the number one theory was that someone had come for you and got Isabel instead. The fourth El Trio murder."

"All the people you've worked with are getting nervous,"

Silvio said. "You're just a fucking good luck charm."

Emilia nodded. "I've been through all the case files I could get my hands on. Ours. Cases you worked before. Nothing stood out."

"Could be someone who is just targeting random law enforcement." Silvio flexed his hands again.

"What about your bookie business," Emilia said. "Anybody mad at you? Felt they were cheated?"

"Not that I know of," Silvio said.

"Owed you and couldn't pay?"

"Like brainless *chicas* who lost a big bet?" Silvio almost smiled.

"Don't joke," Emilia said.

Silvio rubbed his forehead. "Probably had a couple of big losers. I don't remember exactly who. It'll be in the books."

"What books?"

"My account books," Silvio said. "You didn't think I memorized all those bets, did you?"

"No, of course not," Emilia said. "Where are the books? Did you have them with you at Antonio's?"

"No, they should still be in my office at the house." Silvio mimed the size of a rectangle. "Two basic accounting ledgers. From the *papelería* down the street."

"Green?" Emilia asked. Most office supply stores sold one style of fabric-bound ledger. Virtually every small business in Mexico used them. "Linen-covered?"

"Yes."

Emilia thought back to the crime scene reports she'd seen. "I don't remember any books in the evidence reports. They're probably still in the house."

"So you could get them," Silvio said. "Antonio can help you identify the big losers."

"He's in this with you?"

"He helps out. The bets on Sunday's match are still outstanding. Antonio can look up the bets if he gets the ledgers."

Emilia pressed a hand to her forehead. "I hate your *maldita* bookie business," she swore. "The house is locked down. It's a crime scene."

"I had to surrender my key," Silvio said. "Antonio might still have his."

"What about Macias and Sandor?" Emilia asked. "When you talked to them, did they say they were going to get the books?"

"No, it didn't come up."

"Okay." Something told her that Silvio's bookie business wasn't the reason Isabel had been killed but it was a loose thread that couldn't be left hanging. Emilia nodded. "I'll figure it out."

"You know, as long as we were together, there was hope we'd have kids someday," Silvio surprised Emilia by saying.

His words caught her unawares and Emilia felt a sudden lump in her throat.

"Isabel never could hang onto a pregnancy," he went on, without anger or grief in his voice. "Went to good doctors, too. Lost six or seven over the years."

"She had advanced endometriosis," Emilia said.

Silvio raised his eyebrows.

"From the autopsy," Emilia said.

"So she fed every kid in the neighborhood." Silvio spoke as if he hadn't heard Emilia's last word. "Gave her some peace to take care of all the lost kids. But it never replaced wanting our own."

"I guess not," Emilia said lamely. She felt stunningly helpless.

"She would have been a good mother." Silvio's gaze went to the couple in the next cage. The woman reached across the table and slapped the prisoner. The guards chuckled; obviously they'd seen this show before.

"Yes, she would have." Emilia closed her notebook and breathed hard to keep herself from breaking down.

Silvio stared at the back of his hand for a long moment then rubbed absently at the dried blood. "Fatherhood. I would have fucked it up anyway." He gave an odd laugh.

"Do you want me to call a priest?" Emilia asked.

Silvio looked up and the moment was over. "I don't need a priest, Cruz," he said with a touch of his usual gruffness. "I need those account books."

The cage door on Silvio's side swung open. "Time's up," the guard announced.

Silvio stood. "How's Hollywood?"

It was his infuriating nickname for Kurt. "He's okay," Emilia said.

"Make the time count, Cruz," Silvio said. "You know what I mean?"

Emilia couldn't reply; the lump in her throat made words impossible.

Silvio collected the plastic bag of clothes and food and walked out of the cage. Emilia watched as the guard shoved him toward a scratched metal door. Her partner passed out of sight and the door clanged shut behind him.

Emilia blundered past the guard on her side of the cage. He made a clumsy attempt to grope her as she passed.

The key to Silvio's house burned a hole in the pocket of Emilia's jeans as she drove into the El Roble neighborhood that afternoon. Compared to the bull pen, the place didn't look so bad.

Same smell. Fewer guards.

El Roble was a small *barrio* in Acapulco's hilly northern suburbs, far from the moneyed circle of white hi-rises that ringed Acapulco Bay and graced the city's best-selling postcards. Tourists who came for Acapulco's famous sun and fun never made it as far inland as El Roble, where every night street gangs aligned with rival cartels fought proxy wars for territory.

Every structure in the neighborhood was surrounded by cement block walls topped with broken glass and razor wire. From the street, the high walls presented a continuous barricade with flat roofs and satellite dishes poking above wire and glass. The cement was painted with faded advertising for beer and tequila and streaked with years of rust from roof-mounted water tanks and air conditioning compressors. Most of the walls were pocked with bullet holes.

Emilia slowly cruised down Silvio's street. His house was fronted by a faded blue two-story wall, one of the few swaths of cement in El Roble without graffiti. The wall was topped with the usual razor wire above shards of broken glass cemented into the top, a low-tech but effective deterrent to anyone trying to climb over.

As she rolled past the wall, Emilia saw that the corrugated metal gate was open like the gaping mouth of a flat blue face. A police crime scene van in the courtyard occupied the space where Silvio parked his vehicles. Figures in crime scene gear crossed between the house and the van.

Emilia circled the block, torn between coming back later or brazening it out with the crime scene techs. There weren't that many and she probably knew those at the house. Maybe they didn't know she'd been suspended.

She pulled to the curb in front of a small grocery store with pineapples and mangoes in wooden bins by the door. She cut the engine but kept the keys in the ignition, took out her phone, and pretended to be texting, all the while watching the street ahead of her. Silvio's house was half a block away and she could see the open gate. Maybe there would be enough activity to give her an idea of what was going on.

A couple of small boys in rags and flip flops squatted on their haunches by the curb, playing a game with stones. Housewives with plastic shopping bags came out of the store and joined a small cluster of neighbors across from Silvio's. They watched the techs through the open gates.

A male figure in tech gear walked out of the open pedestrian gate, cell phone clapped to his ear. Emilia recognized Julio Rodriguez, a senior tech she'd worked with before and who had never seemed to resent her presence as the only female detective, as did many of his colleagues.

Loyola had either sent the techs back in because they'd found nothing on their first pass. Or he was planting evidence to convict Silvio. Maybe her, too, with whatever had been in the file folder with her name on it.

As Emilia watched, Rodriguez punched a gloved finger at his phone's display. He pocketed the phone and looked down the street in her direction. Emilia automatically checked her rearview mirror.

Too late, she recognized Ibarra's ancient unmarked black sedan with the dinged front fender. He always said it was so old it was theft-proof; no one knew how to stick a key in a door lock any more.

Emilia dove for the floorboards, banging her right arm on the center console. The mended bone in her upper arm sang out.

The sedan passed but she knew Ibarra would recognize

the Suburban. As if to prove it, her cell phone rang, causing her to flinch and bang her arm a second time. Her fingers went numb and she dropped the phone.

She groped around the floor with her left hand. The display showed the call had come from Loyola's cell phone. No doubt he was riding shotgun.

"*Madre de Dios*," Emilia muttered. She was a grown woman and a police detective and she was cowering on the floor of a car.

She slid back into the front seat. The sedan parked across from Silvio's house, blocking the worried gaggle of neighbors.

Her phone rang again. This time Emilia took a deep breath and hit the button to talk.

"Cruz," Loyola's voice barked through the connection. "Get your ass out of there."

"Hi, Loyola." Emilia kept her tone neutral. "How's it going? Been shining my badge for me?"

"Don't give me any of your crap, Cruz," he snarled. "Get out or so help me, I'll get a couple of uniforms to arrest you."

Emilia hit the disconnect button and tossed her phone onto the passenger seat.

She headed south through central Acapulco, hit the Costera Miguel Alemán, and turned east toward home. She was furious with herself for blundering along, for not thinking things through, for forgetting who held the power.

She should never have gone to Silvio's house so soon. Now Loyola could twist things around. Point to her lurking near the house as proof of guilt. Maybe even claim she had come to cover her tracks.

Emilia slammed her palms against the steering wheel in frustration.

She stared up at the bedroom ceiling, where a soft angle of moonlight sliced across the stucco. It wasn't just that she was afraid for Silvio, she was afraid for herself. Telling Kurt that she wouldn't live scared was one thing, grappling with all of the fears in her mind was another.

Fear of being the next El Trio victim and never knowing why.

Fear that Silvio wouldn't make it out of the bull pen alive.

Fear of who she was without a badge.

Kurt was still up. He was in the office down the hall and Emilia could see a halo of light through the open bedroom door. The furniture in the office was dark, sleek, and modern, and she imagined him rifling through the drawers of the chrome and mahogany desk to find something he didn't want her to see.

Whatever it was, and wherever it led, her imagination was probably worse than the truth. Emilia pushed aside the coverlet and followed the light down the hall.

Kurt sat at the desk, going through a file box. More were

stacked on the floor. Emilia recognized them as several stored on the top shelf of the room's spacious closet.

"Hey," Emilia said from the doorway.

He was absorbed in what he was doing and her voice caught him by surprise. Emilia watched his expression shift from anxious intensity to false casualness.

"Did I wake you?" he asked.

"I couldn't sleep," Emilia replied. "What's in the box?"

Kurt closed the box. "Paperwork."

"Kind of late for that, isn't it?"

He held out his hand and Emilia came to his side. He put his arm around her waist. "I'm sorry I woke you up," he said. "Things are so busy with the Acapulco Hotel Association I thought I'd get some work done when it was quiet."

"Okay," Emilia said slowly. *Madre de Dios* but he was a terrible liar.

"You should go back to sleep." Kurt jostled her a little. "I'll be there in a minute."

Emilia pulled away from him. "Sure."

Kurt came to bed five minutes later. He kissed her and was asleep almost immediately.

Emilia slipped out from under the covers, went to the balcony and stared at the ocean. She'd never felt so alone.

CHAPTER 7

Under the clear morning sky, the sign for Mercedes Sandoval's dance studio advertised tap, jazz, and ballroom lessons. The studio was in a small strip mall on the edge of the central Acapulco neighborhood Emilia thought of as her own. It was where she knew everyone and she paid the rent for the house where her mother and stepfather lived.

A heavy security grille fronted the dance studio's metal brown front door. It matched the grilles over the windows. Curtains kept anyone from seeing in but showed that the lights were on. Emilia rang the intercom buzzer gouged into the green concrete wall while juggling the outfit she'd worn Sunday night, a cardboard tray of lattes, and a paper bag of pastries. She was rewarded with a metallic voice asking who was there.

"I have breakfast," Emilia announced into the small speaker panel next to the door. The buzzer sounded and Emilia opened the security grille. A key turned in a lock on the other side and the brown door swung open.

"Why aren't you at work?" Mercedes didn't wait for an answer but hustled Emilia into the studio, locking the door behind her.

"I brought back your outfit," Emilia said.

Mercedes took the cardboard tray. "I love friends bearing gifts," the dancer said and sniffed appreciatively at the aroma of fresh coffee. "But you're usually at work this time of day."

She led Emilia across the big open space containing nothing more than a portable stereo sitting on a chair in the corner surrounded by stacks of CDs. One wall was mirrored. The wood plank floor was worn almost to smooth whiteness. Emilia followed the dancer to the single room that served as office, bedroom, and kitchen.

When Emilia was young, Mercedes was a successful ballroom dancer. Emilia and her mother Sophia lived with her father's brother and family and it was always an event in the crowded apartment when they stayed up late to watch ballroom dancing competitions on television. Sophia's eyes had sparkled at the swirling fabric of Mercedes's dresses and her handsome husband's powerful moves. The husband had died at the height of their fame, leaving Mercedes to return home and scrape together a living as a dance teacher.

The former dance champion was a decade older than Emilia, but moved with a grace and strength that made her appear years younger. The two women were about the same size, but Emilia carried more muscle in her calves and upper body. In comparison to Emilia's black tee, skinny jeans, and sandals, Mercedes wore a loose pink sleeveless tunic, capri-length leggings, and ballet slippers. A loose braid of dark hair hung down her back while unruly wisps curled around her forehead, framing thick-lashed eyes.

Mercedes set the cardboard tray on a table draped with gauzy print fabric and eased out the two coffee cups.

"What did Kurt say when he saw you in that halter top?"

"He approved," Emilia said. She looked around the room, jumpy and tense. She'd driven into central Acapulco from the Palacio Réal checking the rearview mirror every other second. Standing in line at the coffee shop had been nerve-wracking. She saw the faceless El Trio killer everywhere.

"What's the matter?" Mercedes asked as she handed Emilia one of the coffee cups.

"Silvio's wife was murdered. He's in jail and I'm suspended."

Mercedes caught her breath. A hand flew to her throat. Even that gesture was balletic and graceful.

In a few short sentences, Emilia told Mercedes about the events of the past few days. The dancer had never met Silvio but knew him well from Emilia's stories.

"*Por Dios*, Emilia," Mercedes said sadly. "What's going to happen now?"

Emilia pried the lid off her cup and took a big swallow. "I have to find out who killed Isabel. And the others. Somehow."

"But you just said . . ." Mercedes fetched the bag of pastries from the table.

"I have some leads." Emilia selected a *concha*. Once again, sugar and caffeine would get her through the day. "People who knew Silvio was out and that Isabel was alone at home."

"You'll talk to them?" Mercedes sipped her own coffee. "Alone?"

"It's a place to start." Emilia drank more coffee and felt marginally better. She wasn't going to hide. Badge or not, she was still a detective. "I need to figure out how the killer got into the house. Right now, the fact that there wasn't any break-in supports Loyola's theory that Silvio killed Isabel."

"Silvio's a pretty grumpy guy from what you've told me," Mercedes said. "Does he have enemies?"

"Only at work," Emilia said with a rueful laugh. "But he's got this side business as a bookie. An unhappy gambler could have killed her."

Mercedes gave a shiver. "Do you think that's what happened?"

"Maybe." As the caffeine began to do its work, Emilia realized she was saying too much. The less Mercedes knew, the better. She forced herself to brighten. "I could use your advice on another topic."

"Something else?" Mercedes probed. "Besides being suspended and the murder of your partner's wife?"

"I think so."

"You're not sure?"

Emilia put her empty latte cup on the table and came back to sit on the bed with her legs curled under her. "When you were married, did your husband ever lie to you?"

Mercedes frowned. "That's an odd question. I guess he told a few white lies. Nothing that ever mattered."

"Kurt has started lying to me," Emilia said.

"Are you sure?"

"The night Isabel was murdered, he got out of bed to look for something. All over the apartment. When I asked, he said he was hungry, but I know he just made that up on the spur of the moment."

"What was he looking for?"

"I don't know." Emilia dug out the last pastry. "It happened again last night. He was up in the middle of the night. Said he was getting work done while it was quiet."

"You don't believe him, I take it?"

"The problem is that all this started after I asked about Suzanne." Emilia broke the pastry in two.

Mercedes took the proffered half. "Suzanne?"

"The chef at the hotel said something about her," Emilia said. "When I asked Kurt, he said that she was an old girlfriend from when he lived in Las Vegas."

"So?"

Emilia swallowed before replying. "What if she's here? To get Kurt back."

Mercedes stopped in the act of dunking her last bite of pastry into her coffee. "You think he hid her in a box and forgot where he put her?"

"This is serious, Mercedes," Emilia said. "Suzanne gave him something. He can't remember where he put it. But he needs to find it before I do."

"Emilia," Mercedes said sadly.

"Maybe she wasn't just a girlfriend. Maybe he's trying to find their marriage license—."

"*Por Dios*," Mercedes broke in. "Do you have any proof he's looking for something related to this woman?"

Emilia narrowed her eyes. "Kurt lied to me."

"Listen to me," Mercedes said sternly. "Not so long ago you thought he was carrying on with the hotel concierge. That dull, skinny—."

"Christine," Emilia supplied.

"And it was all your imagination. Wasn't it?"

"Yes," Emilia admitted reluctantly.

"Silvio's situation is making you crazy," Mercedes said. She finished her breakfast and brushed crumbs off her tunic. "It seems to me that you have two choices. Talk to Kurt and find out what's going on. Or search the apartment until you either find something incriminating or realize you are being an *idiota*."

The brash sound of Emilia's ringtone stopped her retort. Emilia didn't recognize the number on the phone's display. "*Bueno?*"

"Emilia, it's Claudia."

The name meant nothing to Emilia. "Claudia? I'm sorry, I don't know anyone named Claudia."

"I am the head of Las Palomas." Frostiness blew through the connection. "You are the chief of operations."

Emilia closed her eyes. One phone call was all it took to go from despair to ridiculous. "Claudia, of course. How did you get this number?"

"I had to call people."

Emilia didn't reply.

Claudia nervously cleared her throat. "There's a planning committee meeting this afternoon that I'd like you to attend. We're discussing our branding strategy. And uniforms." She rattled on, giving Emilia the details of the Las Palomas meeting.

Emilia made no move to write down anything. She waited until Claudia took a breath and cut in. "I'm not available until Monday. I thought you knew that."

"Lieutenant Loyola in your old office said—."

"I'm in the middle of something right now," Emilia interrupted. "Text me the address of where I'm to report on Monday."

"But Lieutenant Loyola said you were available now," Claudia protested.

"Lieutenant Loyola is a *pendejo*," Emilia said and disconnected.

She left the dance studio feeling marginally better. A cup of coffee and a hour of friendship was enough to get her refocused.

The priority was getting Silvio out of the bull pen and finding Isabel's killer. Emilia might not have her badge, but she was still a detective who could do her job, even if it meant looking over her shoulder every two minutes.

At the same time, she decided that Kurt wasn't the sneaky type. He was just working too hard.

Emilia marched all over Acapulco to find the friends with whom Silvio had watched the Copa America match at his cousin Antonio's house last Sunday. One by one, they corroborated Silvio's alibi. They'd expected to see both Silvio and Isabel at Antonio's. All the wives were friends and they were surprised not to see her. Everyone was visibly upset about Isabel's death and Silvio being in jail. All of them wanted to know when Isabel's funeral would be.

To Emilia's surprise, none had spoken to the police. Nor did they want to make a statement at a police station. Everybody wanted to help Silvio, of course, but felt that the less contact with the police the better. Cops were all crooks.

Even Silvio, but he was a bookie, too, so it didn't count. The two occupations cancelled each other out.

El Roble logic, Emilia surmised.

After the third such interview, Emilia called Macias as she plodded back to the Suburban in the blistering heat. Sweat darkened her tee shirt as his cell phone went to voicemail. Emilia kept her message brief. "This is Cruz. I have witnesses who can corroborate Silvio's alibi. Call me back."

Felipe Garcia was the fifth and final name on Silvio's list. Garcia worked in a scuba supply and sporting goods store on Paseo de Pescador near the dive action at Playa Manzanillo. It was a prime location for both tourists and locals and the store had the happy vibe of athletic youth and outdoor life. Huge posters of surfers, divers, and beach volleyball games were everywhere. Racks of brand name apparel marched along a center aisle, while signs in English and Spanish hung from the ceiling, directing shoppers to departments by sport. Surfboards marched along a wall like an army going into battle against the waves. Colorful wetsuits and scuba gear, along with the latest high tech dive equipment, enticed divers. A long counter dominated the rear of the store, where patrons could sign up for dive trips and get their air tanks refilled.

I should bring Kurt here. The thought barely registered before a good looking man approached her.

"Can I help you?" The man had long straight hair parted in the middle that accentuated his hawkish nose, dark-lashed eyes, and high cheekbones. There was a lot of *indio* in his bloodline, Emilia decided.

"I'm looking for Felipe Garcia."

"That's me."

"I'd like to ask you a few questions about Franco Silvio," Emilia said. "I understand he's a friend of yours."

The young man grinned. "You must be Franco's partner, Emilia Cruz." He shook her hand with a firm grip. "Come on to the back. We can talk without being interrupted."

He led her through the store, nodding to employees, who like Felipe, seemed to be in their mid-20's. They all wore cargo shorts and a red polo shirt with an embroidered store logo. The customers were beach crowd types in shorts, tees, sundresses, and flip flops. If the number of people in the store was any indication, the place was doing well.

Felipe ushered Emilia into a small office with two desks, a semicircle of cheap folding chairs, and stacks of cardboard boxes. He held out a folding chair as if he was Emilia's date in a restaurant, then took the seat next to her.

"This is my office but we also have staff meetings in here," he said with a wave of explanation. "Sorry it isn't cleaner but we've been really busy lately. The Copa America is good for business."

Emilia smiled as she looked around at the jumble of boxes and packages of sports equipment shoved up against the walls. "Are you the manager here?"

"And owner." Felipe's proud grin faded quickly. "Have you caught whoever killed Isabel? Is that what this is about?"

"No," Emilia said. "Not yet. The investigation is ongoing."

Felipe nodded and tucked his hair behind his ears with a practiced gesture. "Is Franco still in jail? Antonio called right after they took him. I've been up there twice to bring him food. Are you going to get him out?"

"I'm trying." Emilia liked Felipe immediately, including his rapid-fire manner of shooting out questions.

Felipe leaned forward in the folding chair, knees on elbows. "How can I help? What do you need?"

Emilia got out her notebook and flipped to the timeline page. "Can I ask you a few questions about Sunday night?"

"Of course."

Emilia went through the questions and got familiar answers. Felipe and his wife got to Antonio's at about 7:30 pm. Silvio was already there. They left about the same time he did.

Felipe referred to Silvio as Franco, in a way that implied a real friendship. Emilia wondered what Silvio would have in common with a hip young owner of a sporting goods store.

"Have you known Franco long?" she asked.

Felipe raised his eyebrows as he thought. "Eleven, twelve years," he said. "Something like that."

"That's a long time," Emilia said, slightly surprised. "How did you meet?"

"He and my brother Manuel worked together," Felipe said.

Garcia, of course. The name was so common, Emilia hadn't made the connection. "Manuel Garcia Diaz?" she verified. "Silvio's late partner?"

"Manuel was my older brother," Felipe said. "I was 19 when he died."

"I'm so sorry for your loss," Emilia said sincerely.

"Thank you," Felipe said. "Manuel and Franco were partners for seven years. They did everything together. It was like I had two older brothers."

Emilia nodded, glad to learn about this side of Silvio.

"He's been there for us all these years." Felipe looked around. "Helped me buy this place. Taught David how to box."

"David?"

"My younger brother. David was just a kid when Manuel died and it set him adrift. Wanted to be an actor. Got involved with heroin. Franco helped him get himself together. Now David even has an acting job of sorts. But I don't think any of us ever really recovered from losing Manuel, you know what I mean?"

Emilia gave a half smile. "Everyone I know lives with the dead tugging at their souls."

"Franco and Isabel are like family," Felipe said, his voice breaking. "Losing Manuel drew us even closer. We might have lost Manuel, but we weren't going to lose Franco and Isabel, too."

Emilia closed her notebook, trying to fit the pieces together. Even respected colleagues like Prade weren't above repeating the old rumors, long since officially dismissed, about the death of Manuel Garcia Diaz. But from this conversation, it was clear that the Garcia family harbored no such concerns.

"I'm sorry," Emilia said. "I know this is hard. I just have a few more questions."

Felipe tucked his hair behind his ears again. The practiced gesture seemed to help him center himself. "Go ahead," he said.

Emilia opened her notebook again. "Do you have a key to Franco's house?"

"No."

"Do you know anyone who had a key to his house?"

"No."

Emilia nodded as she wrote. All of Silvio's friends had the same answers. "Franco's bookie business," she went on. "Did he ever talk to you about people who placed bets with him? Anyone angry?"

Felipe smiled. "My mother doesn't approve of gambling so he never talked about it with us."

"Did Franco ever talk about another woman?" Emilia asked.

"Besides you?"

"Me?" Emilia put down her pen.

"He said you were smart. Not as smart as Manuel but you were honest like Manuel and he knew where he stood with you."

"No," Emilia said. "I meant if Franco ever . . . said or did anything that gave you an idea he was seeing someone else."

Felipe straightened up in the chair. "No, never."

"What about Isabel?"

"You mean carrying on behind Franco's back?"

Emilia gave a tiny nod.

"No," Felipe said firmly. "Neither of them. Never."

"Thanks." Emilia stowed her notebook in her bag and stood up, feeling tired and wrung out. She'd sweated through her tee shirt so many times it was crisp with salt. "I really appreciate your time."

Felipe stood, too. "Can I get you some water? Coffee?"

Emilia slung the strap of her bag over her shoulder. "No,

I have to get going."

"Wait." Felipe darted over to a pile of cardboard boxes stacked by the far desk and came back with a package of socks and a handful of protein bars. "Look, it's not much, but we have these great socks. They're for runners. Nice cushion to keep your feet from getting sore. And you look like you could do with something to eat, too."

"Thank you," Emilia said, touched. "You just made my whole day."

He led her through the store, where customers chattered in the aisles and the registers kept up an electronic chant. "I'm glad we finally met," he said. "Stay in touch. Anything we can do for Franco, you let us know. Or if you need more socks. Or a surfboard. Or whatever. Give a call. Come by."

Emilia grinned. "I will. Take care."

She walked back to the Suburban and dialed Macias yet again. The connection went directly to voice mail. *Again.* "Why haven't you called me back?" she demanded of the faint hum at the other end. "I've talked to five witnesses who can all place Silvio at—."

An electronic tone cut off Emilia in mid-rant. A metallic voice informed her that the inbox was full.

Emilia swore and broke the connection. Sandor's phone also went to voice mail.

She shoved her phone back in her bag and checked her watch. It was nearly 5:00 pm.

As she shifted the Suburban into gear, she was glad

she'd met Felipe Garcia. She'd always imagined Silvio as a loner, respected yet feared at work. It was nice to know that Silvio had other people in his life.

But only one stupid enough to break into a crime scene and find his *maldita* bookie ledgers.

CHAPTER 8

On Thursday afternoon Emilia drove into El Roble. Silvio's neighborhood looked the same; battered buildings, anxious people. Nothing survived long in the blighted *barrio*, she decided.

Good women only lasted 42 years.

She learned her lesson and parked further away from Silvio's house this time. With her shoulder bag slung across her body, she strolled towards Silvio's house. There was a pair of latex gloves in her jeans pocket from the emergency stash in the Suburban.

The street was bereft of cars or people save for half a dozen boys by the curb in front of the small grocery store. A street sign was cemented into the sidewalk and apparently served as rallying point. Some of the boys listlessly tossed stones into the gutter. As Emilia neared, they scuttled closer to the store, like crabs seeking shelter.

"Hey," Emilia said by way of greeting. She wondered if any of them were the *halcones* who'd watched Silvio return to his house after the Copa America match.

"*Puta*," one of them replied. "Give me money." His voice was breathy and strained. He was nine or ten years old, dressed in flip flops, dirty jeans, and a tee shirt that had once been orange but was now striped with dirt. A clear plastic soda bottle dangled just below his chin, suspended by a bit of string like a necklace.

His friends laughed, but their laughter was aimless and their eyes were unfocused. Two of them held plastic soda bottles close to their faces while the others wore the same bottle necklace as their leader.

The cop called them "glue boys." The kids put glue in the bottom of empty plastic bottles and sniffed the fumes that wafted up all day long. The high from the glue cut hunger pangs and diluted the misery and loneliness of being homeless in a combat zone. Street gangs sometimes paid a glue boy a couple of pesos to play lookout, but after a year or two on glue, the kids' brains were fried and they weren't reliable.

"You all going to school this morning?" Emilia asked.

The boys scattered, laughing inanely.

Emilia slowed as she crossed the street and approached the faded blue wall marking Silvio's house. The block was nearly deserted. No tech vans, no identifiable cop cars. No people hanging around.

The exception was a glue boy. The straggler was very young, six or seven at the most, wearing the standard uniform of glue bottle necklace, tee shirt, ragged jeans, and flip flops. Someone had been taking care of him, however, as his hair was neatly barbered, his shirt was relatively clean, and he looked as if he'd had a few regular meals of late.

When Emilia reached the edge of the wall he ran off with an awkward, shuffling gait.

Silence hung over the worn cement like a storm cloud. A crisscross of crime scene tape barred the pedestrian gate with its flimsy warning of PROHIBIDO EL PASO. Emilia worked one end loose, unlocked the gate, and slipped inside.

The courtyard was empty. Both Silvio's police sedan and the truck he owned were gone. Plastic tables and chairs were stacked against the side wall, ready for Isabel's next meal for El Roble's lost children.

The house was the same faded blue as the front wall, but enlivened by a yellow door and a terra cotta pot of geraniums. Emilia used the same key to let herself into the house.

All the lights were off and the entranceway was dim. The air in the house was sour and stung her eyes. Emilia followed a suspicious stink and an angry hum to the foot of the staircase.

Halfway up, a writhing dark mass covered three steps.

Flies. Thousands of flies.

"*Madre de Dios*," she blurted.

No one had bothered to clean up the blood after removing Isabel's body. The flies were gorging on it. The smell was overwhelming.

Gagging, Emilia hauled the hem of her tee shirt over her mouth and nose. She stumbled backwards. Once in the living room, where weak sunlight shone through the curtains, she coughed and caught her breath again.

The living room was messy, just as Silvio had said. The sofa and chairs were pushed at odd angles. Two pictures were propped against the wall and she could see the faded squares where they had once hung. The television and DVD player were still there, however, as was a stack of DVDs. A few popular action movies seemed right up Silvio's alley while Isabel probably enjoyed the cooking show boxed set. Two children's movies, one with cartoon cars on the front and another showing a bulbous purple animal, were hidden at the bottom of the stack.

She passed through the tidy kitchen on the way to Silvio's office located at the back of the house. Just to satisfy herself, Emilia checked the back door and the windows before moving on. No sign of a break-in, just like the crime scene report said.

Silvio's office enjoyed the clutter of a man who spent a lot of time engrossed in the sports pages. Emilia thought back to the last time she'd been there. She and Silvio had downed beers at the table and set up a sting, unaware that they would net the crooked cop who led Internal Affairs. Dark humor and raw tension had sat with them at that planning session, as did the confidence that Emilia could rely on Silvio in the midst of crisis. Now she had to play that role for him.

She snapped on the latex gloves and began rifling through the newspapers, magazines, and Copa America brackets strewn over the table and chair seats. It didn't take long to realize that the ledgers weren't on the table or on the bookshelves, which were full of scrapbooks, boxes of old trophies, and rolled-up posters. A basket held battered boxing gloves.

Emilia looked around; sure she had missed something. But the room was small. There was no closet or storage cabinet. She searched the room a second time.

Thirty minutes later she'd found out everything she ever wanted to know about Silvio's former boxing career, all the sports news from the last two months, and his best guess for the final Copa America matchup. She didn't know anything about two green linen-covered accounting ledgers, the kind everybody in Mexico used.

With her shirt once again pulled over her nose and mouth, Emilia stepped over the angry swarm of feasting flies and went upstairs. She hadn't planned to search the house but maybe the ledgers had ended up somewhere else. Isabel could have moved them after Silvio left to go to Antonio's. The crime scene techs could have picked them up and misplaced them.

There were two bedrooms and two bathrooms on the second floor. The master bedroom was tidy but plain, the bed dressed in white sheets and a dark green blanket. The bedclothes were flung back on one side as if someone had just gotten up.

On the dresser, two silver frames showcased photos of Isabel and Silvio. In the most recent one, Silvio wore his trademark white tee and squinted at the camera while Isabel smiled and shaded her eyes with one hand. He had his arm around her and she wore a floral apron over a brown dress. In the background, children sat at plastic tables like the ones Emilia had seen stacked in the courtyard.

The other photo showed a young couple, excited about the future and grinning into the camera. Isabel was trim, with long wavy hair. Silvio looked every inch a heavyweight champ.

Emilia tried to reconcile the happy youth with the scowling, often surly man she rode with every day. Bad things had happened between the two pictures and they had changed him. Emilia felt as if she was intruding into a part of his life that Silvio would not want shared, looking at things she did not have permission to see.

The feeling stayed with her as Emilia explored the room.

The ledgers were not there.

The second bedroom evidently was Isabel's storage space. Boxes containing dried goods like beans, rice, oil, and pasta were stacked along one wall. All were neatly labelled.

Again Emilia searched patiently and methodically. She even shoved boxes away from the walls in case the ledgers had fallen or been hidden.

The ledgers were not there.

The ledgers weren't in the bathrooms, either.

Emilia stood on the stair landing, unsure what to do. She drifted into the master bedroom, worked the recent picture of Silvio and Isabel out of its silver frame, and stuck it in her shoulder bag. It might come in useful and she knew she wasn't coming back to the house any time soon.

The smell of the blood and the thick swarm of flies made her gag again as Emilia returned to the first floor. She combed each room again, working fast. Her hands were damp with sweat inside the latex gloves.

The ledgers were not there.

She found herself back in the kitchen after a third pass through Silvio's office. Emilia opened the back door, stepped out, and sucked in El Roble's version of clean air.

The back patio was a small tile affair, with a set of white plastic chairs surrounding a café sized white plastic table. A pretty flower garden grew against the back of the house, with fat roses nodding on glossy green stems and chili-colored hibiscus spreading above low flowering plants, the names of which Emilia could only guess. On the other side of the back door, a vegetable garden was heavy with a crop of tomatoes, peppers, and eggplant. Between the garden and her storeroom, Isabel had been well stocked to feed the army of children forever knocking at her door.

A small shed, painted to match the house, leaned against the faded blue wall enclosing the property. The shed had likely been the chauffeur's quarters before El Roble's drug-fueled decline.

The shed's corrugated metal roof extended like a canopy over an outdoor work area with a sink and stone counter. A single red cloth was pinned to the clothesline above the sink and flapped gently in the late afternoon breeze.

Emilia tried the door to the shed. It was unlocked and swung inward.

A louvered window let in enough light to reveal a garden shovel and narrow rake propped in one corner by a neatly coiled hose. A long narrow table held a bag of dirt, an old basket, a neat stack of small terra cotta pots, and hand tools corralled in an old coffee can.

The floor was swept clean, except for a blanket folded into a lumpy rectangle. Glad she still wore her gloves, Emilia picked up the wad of cloth. Something fell out and clattered against the concrete floor, making her jump.

She dropped the blanket, shoved at the door to let in more light, and saw a small plastic child's toy with sliding numbered tiles. Emilia bent to pick it up and saw something shiny under the table.

It looked like a curled tube of toothpaste after every bit was squeezed out. But this tube was metal. Emilia unrolled it. Cracked red lettering proclaimed multi-purpose glue. The best adhesive for metal, wood, and plastics.

"And small boys," Emilia muttered.

She stuffed the tube in her bag, next to the photo of Silvio and Isabel. Emilia retraced her steps through the house, let herself out the front door, crossed the courtyard, and finally slipped through the gate. She smoothed the crime scene tape back into place before stripping off the gloves and wadding them into a pocket.

The glue boy who'd been in front of the house was back, hunched by the edge of the cement wall as if trying to make himself invisible. Despite the bottle around his neck, Emilia recognized the posture of hunger. She hoped that she had never looked like that when she was his age.

"Hey." Emilia strolled towards him, deliberately casual and unhurried.

The kid watched her approach. His chin came up.

"Is this your corner?" Emilia asked. He looked ready to take flight if she said the wrong thing.

His eyes focused. Emilia took it as a good sign that the glue hadn't yet rotted his brain.

Emilia came a step closer. "You hiding from the other boys?"

"They don't scare me," the kid said. His words were slurred but both audible and intelligible. He folded his arms, careful not to jostle the plastic bottle near his throat. The tee shirt heralded the Barcelona soccer team. The plastic flip flops were a size too big. His feet were dirty.

"What's your name?" Emilia asked.

"Rio."

"Hey, Rio. I'm Emilia. Can you do a job for me?" Emilia held out 50 pesos. "Go over to the *abarrotes* store over there and get me some chips. Get some for yourself, too, if you bring them back right away."

"The kind in a can?"

"If that's the kind you like."

The kid darted forward, took the money, and flapped his way down the block. Emilia leaned against Silvio's wall. She watched the boy and checked her text messages at the same time. Claudia Sanchez had sent three. Emilia deleted them without reading.

Rio was back with two cans of chips, faster than she would have expected. Emilia popped the top on one and let him keep the other. He didn't open it.

"You're not supposed to go into the house," he said.

"Are you going to tell on me?" Emilia offered the open can.

Rio hesitated before taking a chip. "Señora Isabel isn't home any more. Nobody made any food yesterday."

Emilia watched the chip explode into pieces as he stuffed the entire thing into his mouth at once. Rio was so young, yet death was commonplace in his world. "Did you eat here?" she asked.

The neatly barbered head nodded. He swallowed the chip and raised his hand hesitantly for another. "Are you going to cook now?" he asked.

Emilia offered the can again and he took two chips this time. "Did you know Señora Isabel?" she asked.

Rio coughed. A few crumbs sprayed out of his mouth and into the plastic bottle dangling below his chin.

"Señora Isabel was nice, wasn't she?" Emilia pressed.

Rio stuffed another handful of chips into his mouth but couldn't control the sudden tears that cascaded down his cheeks.

"You liked her," Emilia said. "I liked her, too."

Rio nodded, chest heaving. "I liked being inside. It was safe."

Emilia was suddenly face-to-face with the childhood misery that Isabel de Silvio had fought. "You mean inside the gate? To eat?"

"And work."

"You worked for her?" Emilia imagine Isabel taking in the child, cutting his hair, doing her best to be a counterweight to a rudderless and often brief life on the streets.

Rio nodded again. His tears continued to flow even as he took the rest of the chips in Emilia's can.

Emilia knelt to be on his level. "What did you do for Señora Isabel?" she asked.

He looked toward the house and the crime scene tape barring the entrance. "Watered the garden. Picked tomatoes."

"I can see that you'd be a real good helper." Emilia gently took the second can of chips from the boy, every instinct telling her to keep probing. "Did anyone else help, too?"

Rio watched her hands as Emilia pried the foil off the top of the can. "Who's going to make rice and beans now?"

"I don't know." Emilia held out the can to him. Emilia wondered if he was making up things to get the chips. "Who else came to work for Señora Isabel?"

"Only me," Rio said with a spark of pride.

Emilia smiled encouragingly. She could see Isabel's heart going out to this child. "You must be special."

"Señora Isabel let me watch television," he said. His tears had left two lines down his grubby cheeks.

"Inside the house?" she asked.

"A movie with talking cars," Rio said. "There was one with a purple dinosaur, too."

Emilia froze with a smile on her face and the chip can held out to the boy. Without prompting he'd described the children's DVDs she'd seen in the living room. Had Isabel taken care of him in Silvio's absence and the child somehow killed her? Or had he seen who had?

Her mind raced, trying to figure out the best angle. "Did you watch television Sunday night? Four nights ago?"

Rio put a hand to his mouth as if to bite another chip. "It was a secret."

"I love secrets," Emilia said.

Rio blinked at Emilia, then broke into a snuffling laugh. "I watched television. When Señor Franco wasn't there."

"That was your secret?" Emilia pressed. "Señora Isabel let you come in the house on Sunday when Señor Franco was gone?"

Rio put his finger across his mouth as if to quiet Emilia. The glue was taking effect. First, he'd be giddy, then stoned and sullen. "At night, too."

"Sunday night?" Emilia didn't know if Rio understood the passage of time or not.

"Lots of nights."

"But at night Señor Franco was home," she pointed out.

"I took care of the garden at night." More snuffles of

mirth.

Emilia smiled as if she understood the joke. "Did Señor Franco let you in at night?"

Rio ran a forearm across his nose, careful not to disturb the soda bottle below his chin. "No, I used the key."

Emilia's mouth went dry. "You have a key?"

"Señora Isabel gave me a key," Rio reached for another chip.

"Can I see it?" Emilia asked.

Rio shook his head with a slow, dopey move. The glue was softening his cognitive abilities. "I don't have it any more," he said.

Emilia resisted the urge to grab him by the shoulders and rattle him until the fog lifted and the child's brain speeded up. "What happened to the key?"

Rio looked down the street again, toward the grocery store. The sidewalk was still empty.

Emilia tapped the can of chips to get his attention again. When his head wobbled back in her direction, she asked, "Did you lose the key, Rio?"

"No," he whispered.

"Did you give it to somebody?"

"No."

"What happened to the key, Rio?" Emilia said. "It's important that you tell me."

"Do you need it to cook the rice and beans?" He blinked at her.

Emilia offered up a mental prayer for forgiveness.

"Yes. That's why I need to know where the key is."

Rio rubbed his eyes with fingers dusted with salt. "I sold it."

"You sold the key that Señora Isabel gave you? Why?"

"The big boys wanted glue."

"Who did you sell it to?"

"The man."

"The man." Emilia smiled at him. Assurance. Trust. Encouragement. "Does he have a name?"

Rio found the last chip and stuffed it into his mouth.

"Tell me about the man, Rio," Emilia urged. "Why did he want to buy your key?"

Rio shrugged.

Emilia shifted her position. Her leg muscles were beginning to protest the prolonged squat. "How did he know you had the key?" she asked.

"He was here."

"Four nights ago? When Señora Isabel was home?"

Rio drew a circle on his forehead near his hairline. "The circle man was here."

"The circle man?" Emilia wasn't sure she'd heard him correctly. "On Sunday or another day?"

Rio's thumb again inscribed an imaginary circle on his forehead. "The circle man," he repeated.

"Did he have a hat with a circle on it?" Emilia's mind flashed through logo possibilities: sports teams, businesses, political campaigns.

Rio blinked at her very slowly. "When are you making

the rice and beans?"

"Soon," Emilia said. "Tell me what day the circle man came."

"What day," Rio parroted.

Emilia decided on a different tack. "Did the circle man ever ask you about books? Green books that Señor Franco had?"

Rio half turned away from her, ignoring all the positive vibes she was sending. "He, he . . . I didn't talk to him."

"But you sold him the key," Emilia said hastily. "You said he was here. You must have talked to him. Do you remember his name?"

Rio stiffened. Emilia followed his gaze. The glue boys were clustered on the sidewalk in front of the grocery store again. All stared at Emilia as she crouched next to Rio. She felt fear emanate from Rio's thin body.

"Are you afraid of the other boys, Rio?" she asked softly. "Do you want to come with me and find a safe place to sleep?"

"Go away," Rio mumbled. He turned and started to shuffle away.

Emilia reached for the boy's arm. "Rio, wait—."

The boy slammed a fist into her face with a shocking display of strength. Emilia jerked backwards and came up hard against the faded blue cement wall. As her vision narrowed and fireworks went off inside her skull, her cell phone chimed with the notification of a text message.

Rio took off, half running, half shuffling, his flip flops

slapping against the sidewalk.

CHAPTER 9

Emilia retreated to the balcony with a mug of coffee and watched the hotel come to life below her. Colorful umbrellas bloomed along the beach, the breakfast buffet went up on the lower terrace of the Pasodoble Bar, and staff readied the marina for boat trips to the private island the hotel owned a mile offshore.

Kurt joined her, already dressed in a starched and monogrammed button-down shirt, khaki pants with knife-edge creases, and polished loafers.

"Didn't I tell you it would all work out?" he asked. He touched his coffee mug to hers in a toast. "Solid alibis, both of you."

Yesterday in front of Silvio's house, with her vision still hazy from Rio's punch, Emilia had read the text from Macias that said she and Silvio were cleared. She'd called him and was almost drunk with relief to hear that Silvio would be released Friday morning. Emilia was to report to the squadroom to pick up her badge and Silvio's release papers before collecting him at the bull pen.

"You did," Emilia said. "But things in Mexico so rarely go the way *gringos* think they should."

"I can't argue with that," Kurt said.

"I'm sorry for last night," Emilia said.

Kurt put down his mug and lifted Emilia's hair to examine the bruise on the back of her head. "It doesn't look so bad this morning," he said. "The eye is worse."

"Can we say I had a car accident?" Emilia asked. "Your staff is bound to ask questions."

Last night, she'd been a wreck with a bloated left eye and blood-soaked tee from the nasty cut on the back of her head. Christine, the hotel concierge, had spotted Emilia as she wobbled across the lobby of the Palacio Réal, hoping to escape into the elevator without being seen. Instead, the skinny blonde *puta* had over-reacted with a screech of alarm, alerting everyone in the lobby. Emilia loathed the woman at the best of times but never so much as last night.

"We'll have to say someone else was driving," Kurt said. "Unless the kid punched your car, too."

The guard at the police station gate recognized the Suburban and waved her through without asking for a badge. Macias and Sandor met her in the entrance and snuck her past the guard desk.

It seemed to Emilia that she no longer belonged in the squadroom. Her desk was bare and empty, a reminder that her presence was temporary. Silvio's coffee cup was still by his keyboard, as if he'd just got up for a moment and would be right back. The sludge of coffee in the bottom was beginning to mold. Emilia reminded herself to wash it before she brought him back to the squadroom.

In comparison, the desks of both Macias and Sandor were heaped with files. Another paper mountain covered the desks of Castro and Gomez. Neither were there and Emilia assumed they were out on the streets, fucking up another case.

"We're so far behind, it's a joke," Sandor said.

"Loyola needs to find some fresh meat," Emilia observed and removed her sunglasses. Isabel's death scene photos were gone from the murder board wall, replaced by Acapulco's latest violent crime. Two men and a woman shot on a sidewalk, no doubt with a large caliber handgun. They all looked relatively young.

Before either of her colleagues could answer, Loyola stalked out of his office. "Well, Cruz," he said and gestured to her black eye. "Looks like you got yourself into a bit of trouble while you've been away."

"Car accident," Emilia said.

"With somebody's fist," Loyola snorted. The acting lieutenant looked as if he hadn't slept in weeks. Behind wire spectacles, his eyes were red-rimmed and sunk into dark circles of fatigue. His skin was ashy and his clothes were rumpled.

"Not your problem," Emilia flashed back. "Let's get Silvio out of the bull pen."

Loyola's mouth twisted into a begrudging smile as he put her gun and badge on her desk. "There you go, Cruz," he said. "You get to be a detective again until Monday."

"I'll be sure to check the calendar," Emilia replied. She scooped up her badge, slipped the lanyard over her neck, and checked her gun before securing it in the holster under her left arm. It felt good.

Loyola nodded at Macias and Sandor. "You two can brief her on the latest developments and make sure she gets the paperwork." He shifted his attention back to Emilia. "Pick up Silvio and bring him back here. I want him to know we've been working his wife's case."

"You've had an arrest?" Emilia asked, looking from Loyola to the other two detectives.

"No, but we will," Loyola said. "The important thing is that Franco's been cleared. We need him back on the job. This place is going in the shitter. With you out he'll team with Ibarra."

Over Loyola's shoulder, Macias raised his eyebrows in a subtle *let-it-go* signal.

"Okay," Emilia said to Loyola. "Thanks."

The phone in Loyola's office rang. He gave a grunt of exasperation, went into the office, and slammed the door.

"What's going on with him?" Emilia asked.

"Three more homicides last night," Macias said. "We're so short-handed nobody's even got time to file reports let alone investigate."

Sandor shook his head sadly as he led them back to his desk; it was pushed against that of his partner like Emilia's and Silvio's desks. "This is getting crazy."

"What about Isabel's murder?" Emilia asked. "It's been

five days."

"Nothing," Macias admitted as he dropped into his desk chair. "Some scared neighbors blaming the neighborhood kids. A guy who wanted to place bets with Silvio. No prints, no match for the rounds. Nothing that is going to take us anywhere."

"Do you have the evidence reports?" Emilia asked. "I want to check something."

"Sure." Macias shuffled through the papers on his desk, found a printout, and passed it over.

Just as Emilia thought, no green linen-covered accounting ledgers were on the list of items taken out of Silvio's house.

"What's going on, Cruz?" Sandor asked.

Emilia lowered herself into a chair by the side of Sandor's desk. "Don't ask me how I know," she said. "But Silvio's bookie ledgers are missing from his house."

Sandor held out his hand and she gave him the evidence roster. Macias came around to stand behind his partner's chair. The two men were silent as they reviewed the list.

"You're sure?" Sandor said at length. "Should we send the crime scene techs back in?"

"Don't waste their time," Emilia said. "The books are gone. I'm sure."

"It's a gambling thing? Not part of the El Trio mess?" Macias asked. He leaned against his partner's desk.

"Maybe," Emilia said. "I talked to this kid yesterday

who hangs out around Silvio's house. One of the strays who ate there when Isabel fed the neighborhood kids."

She told them briefly about Rio and the boy's story of selling the key. They tossed around a couple of theories as to the identity of the "circle man" and agreed that a ball cap with a sports emblem was the best explanation.

"We can print out a couple of logos, find the kid again, and get him to identify which one this circle man was wearing," Macias finally decided.

"Maybe if Silvio sees the logos, he'll have an idea of who it could be," Emilia offered. This was the part of the job she loved; sorting out seemingly abstract and unrelated details, brainstorming next steps with other quick minds. "Might have seen someone hanging around the neighborhood with a ball cap with a certain logo on it."

"Fuck, we're wasting time talking." Macias swung around to his own desk chair, tapped his keyboard and the printer across the room by the copier coughed into life. It spit out a sheaf of papers. "You go pick up Silvio, bring him back here."

Sandor collected the papers and gave them to Emilia. "Loyola needs to sign them," he said.

"I know the drill," Emilia replied. She looked at the two detectives. "Thanks for helping."

Macias nodded. "Silvio didn't deserve this."

Emilia crossed the room and tapped on Loyola's office door, the papers in her hand. When she heard him respond, she cracked open the door. "I need you to sign the release papers."

"Give them to me," Loyola said.

Emilia came in and slid the papers on the desk. Loyola looked even worse than he had before, as if stress was mounting by the minute.

He pulled the papers close and began to read, his head bobbing nervously and his lips pinched in concentration.

Emilia stepped closer to the desk, looking for the file with her name written on the upper edge. It wasn't there but the two-drawer safe in the corner of the room was unlocked. The top drawer was open a few inches and she could see file folders inside.

"I thought you should be the one to pick him up," Loyola said. "Partners and all."

"Thanks," Emilia said. "I wouldn't have wanted anybody else to get him."

Loyola signed the documents with a shaky hand. His signature came out loopy and erratic. He caught her looking at his handwriting, impatiently gathered up the sheaf of papers and rattled them at her. "Bring him straight back here," he snapped. "I don't suppose Silvio will be in a good mood but we need to talk."

"Sure." Emilia stuck the papers in her bag.

"And like I said," Loyola went on. "You can keep your badge until Monday when you go to your next assignment. They want you for this new unit, Cruz. Christ the King couldn't get you out of it."

As Emilia walked down the familiar corridor leading

to the parking lot at the back of the building, she shot the sergeant at the holding cells with her thumb and forefinger, the same as always.

But nothing felt the same.

With a police badge dangling from its lanyard around her neck, the bull pen was an entirely different place. Emilia went in the Officials Only entrance, showed her badge to the wizened man in a bulletproof glass booth and received a nod of acknowledgement that made his oversized prison guard uniform flap around him. A solenoid buzzed, a heavy metal door opened, and Emilia went into the inner processing area where the release papers were collected. A receptionist pointed to a coffee urn and told her Silvio would be brought out in 15 minutes.

The room was stuffy and hectic. Guards passed through and harassed the receptionist. Two different families tried to plead for the release of men who didn't have enough money to pay their bail. Both families were practically shoved out of the processing area, the women in tears. Emilia's thoughts hopscotched from Kurt's nocturnal searches to Rio's circle man to Loyola's folder with her name on it. The back of her head itched. Her eye hurt like hell.

It took three hours before Silvio appeared, clad in the same tee and jeans but with his own cross trainers. He carried a small plastic bag containing his phone and wallet.

Silvio jutted his chin in an *I'm-all-right* motion that made her forget everything else. Neither said anything as they both signed more paperwork. Finally, Emilia led him out to the Suburban.

"Did they make an arrest?" he asked as soon as they were both inside the vehicle.

"No," Emilia said. "But we've got some leads."

The administrative side of the bull pen complex was enclosed by a wall topped with electrified wire and accessed by a single gate barred by a long horizontal pole. Emilia expected to be asked for the prisoner release receipt she'd been given but the guard merely left his cinderblock hut and leaned on the barrier's counterweight to raise the pole blocking the exit. He didn't put much effort into it and the aluminum pole banged against the roof of the Suburban. Emilia didn't stop; one more dent hardly mattered.

"Got your badge back, I see." Silvio leaned back against the passenger seat.

"Until Monday. I'm still reassigned."

Silvio squinted in the rush of sunlight as the prison grounds fell behind. "Find someplace that sells food."

"Sure," Emilia replied. She pointed over her shoulder to the back seat. "There's some clean stuff in that bag for you."

Silvio pulled out a blue Palacio Réal tee shirt that she'd scooped up in the gift shop on her way out of the hotel.

"I didn't have time to pick up anything else," Emilia

said apologetically.

Silvio reached over and slid down her sunglasses until they rested on the tip of her nose and she had to look over them to keep her eyes on the road. "That shiner got anything to do with Hollywood's fist?"

"No," Emilia said and resettled the sunglasses in their proper place. "Nothing to do with Kurt."

Silvio unfastened his seat belt and peeled off his grimy tee shirt. Emilia chanced a quick glance. His knuckles were cut and raw and his muscled torso was spotted with bruises, but his body was solid as stone. Biceps and abdominals flexed as he pulled the clean shirt over his head.

"Do you need to see a doctor or anything?" Emilia asked.

"I've been in jail, Cruz," Silvio said. "Not the plague ward. I'm fine."

"Okay."

The Palacio Réal tee fit him well. Silvio flipped his old tee into the back seat, and rifled in the glove compartment for Emilia's phone charger. He plugged in his phone and dug out his wallet.

"What do you know." There was sarcasm in every syllable. "Not a peso in it."

Emilia glanced at the open wallet. The prison system was notorious for corruption; the theft of a few pesos was hardly a surprise. "How much did they take?"

"Couple hundred pesos," Silvio said. "At least my *cédula* is still here. And my keys."

"I'm to bring you back to the squadroom," Emilia

informed him. "Loyola wants to brief you, give you back your badge."

"Does he now," Silvio said, his voice again laced with sarcasm. "First, you can tell me what you know. With food."

Emilia muscled the Suburban to the curb in front of an outdoor restaurant on Calle Escudero. White plastic tables, roofed by green cloth umbrellas, formed a semicircle around what was little more than a food stand. The place was one of Silvio's favorites and a frequent stop for the duo when work took them to the old part of Acapulco. Patrons were locals, not tourists, and the food was plentiful and cheap.

The specialty was *tostadas* topped with seafood ceviche. Emilia paid for two melamine platters encased in disposable plastic bags and heaped with crisp tortillas and seafood marinated in lime, tomatoes, and onions. Silvio asked for two *Cocas*; Emilia bought three bottles of cola for him and a glass of sweetened *aqua de jamaica* hibiscus tea for herself.

They commandeered one of the small tables and Emilia watched as Silvio wolfed his food. She gingerly chewed one of her *tostadas*, the black eye twinging with every bite. Halfway through, she gave up and put the remains of her meal on his plate.

Silvio shoveled it down and wiped his mouth with a paper napkin. "Leads but no arrest. What the fuck has been going on?"

Emilia clasped her glass of cold *agua de jamaica* with both hands. "Do you remember a little boy in your neighborhood named Rio?"

Silvio stared at Emilia. "Yeah. Maybe seven, eight years old. He runs with the glue boys. So?"

Having her sunglasses on helped; somehow they were a welcome barrier between what Emilia had to say and Silvio's intensity. "Did Isabel ever talk about him?"

"Once or twice. She knew all the kids. What are you getting at, Cruz?"

"She gave him a key to the house."

"No, she didn't," Silvio said. It was an automatic response.

The child she never had. Emilia plowed on. "Isabel gave him a key so he could sleep in the garden shed."

"No," Silvio said again. "Isabel would never have given a key to the house to some drugged-up kid without telling me."

Emilia dug out the used tube of glue from her bag and set it on the table. "I found this in your shed yesterday, along with a blanket and a kid's toy."

Silvio stared at the tube without speaking. A couple walked by their table and took the next one over, setting laden plates under the green umbrella and laughing over some shared joke.

The neighborhood was nice, with shops lining the streets and a small park behind them. Tinny music from the food stand's ancient boom box competed with the sounds of traffic and the chatter of passersby.

"You're telling me," Silvio said finally. His voice was dangerously low. Intensity had been replaced by incomprehension, a rare look for the big detective. "That this kid had a key so he could sneak in. Isabel arranged it and didn't tell me."

"He talked about watching movies in the house after he did jobs for her," Emilia said. "There are some kid DVDs in the living room. Rio knew which ones."

"I don't fucking believe this." Silvio shoved the spent glue tube across the table.

A light breeze fluttered the plastic covering Emilia's platter and somewhere a bird called to its mate. Emilia looked in the direction of the birdsong but all she saw was blue sky, slow-moving cars, and a line of palm trees shading the street.

"He was special to her, Franco," Emilia said softly. "His hair's cut. He's cleaner than the rest of the kids."

"Okay." Silvio swiveled to face Emilia. He was back in control. "Let's go on the theory that she gave him a key. Did the kid kill her? Is he in custody? Did you at least get the key back?"

Emilia held up a hand for him to stop. "No, he didn't kill her. And no, I didn't get the key back. Rio sold the key."

Silvio stared at her. "Who'd he sell it to?"

"I don't have a name," Emilia said. "But I think he sold it to someone who had been watching your house enough to know the kid had access."

"Watching the house?" Silvio repeated. "I've got my own *halcones* in El Roble. Someone would have told me."

Of course Silvio had his own watchers; they probably reported things to him for a few pesos and his promise of protection. It was an asset she and Macias and Sandor hadn't taken into account.

"Rio said one thing that might lead somewhere." Emilia lowered the sunglasses to trace a circle on her forehead. "He said he sold the key to the circle man. That's how Rio described him." She repeated the gesture. "Does that mean anything to you?"

Silvio shook his head. "The circle man? No."

"A ball cap maybe," Emilia suggested. "Something with a circle logo on it. Macias and Sandor are researching logos. Maybe when you see them, it will ring a bell."

"Is that all the kid had to say?" Silvio asked.

"When I tried to get more out of him, he tagged me in the eye and I bashed my head into the wall by the gate."

"The kid gave you the eye?"

"I told you Kurt had nothing to do with it."

"Was the kid doing glue when he talked to you?" Silvio gestured to his neck.

"Yes," Emilia admitted. "But he was still able to reason and remember. I think he was telling me the truth."

"What about the crime scene reports?" Silvio asked. "Prints. Ballistics? Anything?"

"No," Emilia said. "But at least now we know how the

killer got in."

Silvio passed a hand over his face. "I still find it hard to believe that Isabel would have given out a key and not told me. She was a cop's wife for 20 years. She knew the danger."

"There is something else," Emilia said. "Your accounting ledgers are gone."

"What do you mean, gone?"

"Not in the house," Emilia said. "Not picked up by the techs for evidence. Your cousin doesn't have them."

Silvio leaned back in the cheap white plastic chair and drank deeply from his last bottle of cola. His face got the look of deep concentration Emilia knew well; she could almost see the gears meshing as her partner tried out various connections that would break open the investigation.

"Anyone who wears a ball cap with a logo on it ever bet with you?" Emilia asked. "And lose big?"

"That's the lead?" Silvio asked. "Our best lead?"

"I think so," Emilia said.

"Not El Trio?" Silvio asked. "There's no connection?"

"Doesn't look like it," Emilia replied and finished her *agua de jamaica.*

Silvio stood up. "I've got business at the morgue."

It was late afternoon before they got to the squadroom.

Emilia's head hurt and she was emotionally exhausted.

The trip to the morgue had been unbelievably hard. Silvio insisted on seeing Isabel's body. Prade pulled out a drawer to reveal a naked gray body rendered clinical by the slices and stitches of a full autopsy. Silvio didn't react, just stared as if to convince himself Isabel was truly dead. When he nodded, Prade rolled the body back into the freezer. Emilia went to the restroom where she splashed cold water on her face and took an aspirin. Silvio said something about a funeral as they got back into the Suburban. Emilia replied but had no idea what came out of her mouth.

As they'd done with her that morning, Macias and Sandor met them in the entrance.

"Good to see you, Silvio." Both detectives embraced their colleague.

"Got your car in the back lot," Sandor said as they made their way to the squadroom. Several uniforms left their desks to shake Silvio's hand and say they were glad to see him. The holding cell guards left their post to clap him on the back and express condolences.

Everyone stepped carefully around the topic of Silvio's recent sojourn in the bull pen.

Loyola came out of his office as Silvio and Emilia came into the squadroom with Macias and Sandor.

"Franco," he said, falsely hearty. He held Silvio's badge. "Good to see you again."

In retrospect, Emilia should have expected what happened next. Silvio grabbed Loyola's outstretched hand, swung him around, and suddenly the acting lieutenant was caught in a wrenching headlock. His mouth opened in a soundless gasp and his wire-framed spectacles flew off his face. Silvio's badge skittered over the worn linoleum.

"My wife is murdered and you lock me up?" Silvio's voice was low. "I don't know who you're taking orders from, but it ends right now." He drew Loyola's head backwards, making the other man emit a hoarse rasp of air.

"Franco, stop!" Emilia shouted.

"*Oye*," Macias exclaimed. Sandor raised his voice, too.

"Do you understand me?" Silvio thundered. The muscles in his arms bulged as Loyola flailed against his captor.

"Yes," Loyola gurgled. "Yes, yes."

Silvio abruptly shoved Loyola away from him. Loyola cannoned into Emilia's desk and saved himself from a bad fall by clutching the edge.

Emilia picked up Loyola's glasses and held them out. The air in the squadroom crackled with anger and electricity.

Loyola replaced his glasses on his nose with a trembling hand. He coughed a couple of times and cleared his throat. "Okay, Franco," he said. "I know you're pissed and maybe you have a right to be. But people are still killing each other in Acapulco and we have work to do.

We need you."

"Like you needed me at the beginning of the week?" Silvio was still close to Loyola, his menace real and immediate.

Loyola was so shaky that Emilia almost felt sorry for him. "Macias and Sandor are handling Isabel's murder investigation," the acting lieutenant said. "They'll brief you on the latest developments."

Emilia held out Silvio's badge, trying to think of something to diffuse the tension in the room. "Franco. Look—."

"Take the weekend to get your feet under yourself again," Loyola said to Silvio, not paying any attention to Emilia. He adjusted his glasses again and sidled around Silvio towards his office. "We'll see you on Monday and forget today's unpleasantness."

"You're a fucking *pendejo*, Loyola," Silvio said in disgust. "Who told you to get me out of the way, eh? I know you didn't think it up on your own."

Loyola spread his hands. "Look, Franco. We had to play by the book on this one."

"The book?" Silvio roared. "Whose fucking book are you talking about?"

"I'm sorry about Isabel," Loyola flung back. "But no forced entry, no robbery. You know as well as I do that the husband is the prime suspect every time."

It was the wrong thing to have said. Silvio's fist connected with Loyola's face, lifting the slimmer man off the ground and disintegrating his glasses before Loyola crashed to the floor, tumbling against Emilia's desk on his way down. The impact rocked the furniture enough to knock the coffee mug off Silvio's adjacent desk. It shattered on the floor, spraying coffee scum and sharp shards against everyone's feet.

"Look, Silvio," Loyola croaked as he struggled to his feet, blood streaming from his nose. "Don't think—."

Then Silvio was at him, hands buried in Loyola's shirt collar. Loyola's feet bicycled ineffectually as Silvio's momentum carried them across the room to culminate in a heavyweight's body blow. Loyola doubled up, snot and saliva dripping down his chin. Silvio landed another punch to the ribs, next an uppercut to the jaw that sounded like a crack of thunder. Loyola's eyes bugged as he smashed against the murder board. The pictures of the three homicide victims fluttered off the wall.

It took the combined efforts of Emilia, Macias, and Sandor to peel Silvio off Loyola. Silvio shrugged off the detectives and jabbed a finger in front of Loyola's nose. "Don't wet yourself, Loyola," Silvio snarled. "You're not worth killing. This was just a little farewell present from me to you."

Still leaning against the wall, Loyola's chin and shirt front were red from the blood steaming from his nose. "You know how the system works," he wheezed.

"Fuck the system." Silvio looked around the room, his gaze sweeping over the scarred floor, dented metal desks, the half-destroyed murder board, his fellow detectives. "Consider this my resignation."

"No," Emilia heard herself protest.

Silvio turned to Macias and Sandor standing in shock next to Emilia. "Do what you think you need to do," he growled. "Just don't get in my way."

He walked out, leaving them all stunned, as if the room had been struck by a swift and violent tornado.

Loyola raised a hand to his lip and it came away bloody. He slid down the wall until he was sitting on the floor. "Well," he said faintly. His eyes rolled back in his head.

"*Jesu Cristo*," Macias said.

With Silvio's badge still clutched in her hand, Emilia ran out of the squadroom.

She headed to the rear of the building near the holding cells, knowing that Silvio would look for his truck. The sergeant who'd been on duty Tuesday afternoon was there and nodded his head at the hallway leading to the exit.

Silvio was almost to the door. Emilia skidded to a halt and blocked his way. "Franco, take it," Emilia began, holding out his badge to him. "You need it. This isn't the time to make hasty—."

"Move it, Cruz." He made no move to take the shield. "I know what I'm doing. I had a week to do nothing but think."

"Thinking in a place like that doesn't count," Emilia said. "We should—."

"Get out of my way, Cruz," Silvio ordered.

"No," Emilia said. "You didn't tell me—."

Silvio reached around her and shoved open the door. Emilia was propelled backwards into the parking lot still clutching his badge as he strode between the rows of cars toward the impound section. "Franco, please," Emilia said. "This isn't fair. You can't just walk out on me like this."

Silvio stopped and looked up at the sky. He drew a deep breath. "Tell Hollywood thanks for the shirt," he said.

Emilia thrust the badge at him again. "Take it, Franco."

"Let me do this my way, Emilia," he said.

"Your badge means access," Emilia said. "Whatever turns up—."

Silvio grabbed Emilia by the neck of her shirt. For an awful second she thought he was going to punch her, too, but he just moved her to the side and kept going.

"Franco, please," Emilia called.

A moment later he had found his truck and climbed inside. The vehicle started with a jolt, swung out of the parking space, and headed for the gate. As soon as the barrier rolled aside, Silvio gunned the engine and the truck shot into the street.

Emilia stamped the tarmac in frustration. She stuck his badge in her back pocket and strode back to the squadroom. It was empty. Shards of Silvio's broken mug were everywhere. The homicide photos from the trashed murder board were scattered by the copier. Some were spattered with blood. Emilia wondered if Loyola's nose was broken. Maybe Macias and Sandor had taken him to the police clinic.

His office door was ajar. Emilia rapped. When she didn't get an answer, she peeped inside. The room was empty. She went inside and closed the door.

Afternoon haze showed between the slats of the horizontal blinds covering the single window. Emilia went to the desk, looking for the file folder with her name on it. She rifled methodically through the clutter on top. The file wasn't there. She moved on to the desk drawers and the trash.

Footsteps and a garble of voices made her stop. Emilia realized that Castro and Gomez were back in the squadroom. *Madre de Dios*, but she didn't want them to catch her in Loyola's office. She was stuck there until they left.

She moved noiselessly over to the safe, praying that the department's usual inefficiencies meant that no one had changed the safe combination since she'd briefly occupied the office a year ago.

The clicking of the dial seemed ridiculously loud as she spun it to the first number. The murmur of male voices continued through the closed door. She spun the dial to the left and settled on the second number; another spin to the right for the third. The handle didn't pop the way she expected and she stood up before remembering that the dial had to be set to zero before the drawer would open. She squatted down again, carefully aligned the dial to zero and the handle popped with a clang.

Castro and Gomez stopped talking.

Emilia froze, her heart pounding in her ears. Castro laughed and their chatter resumed. She took in a lungful of air and slowly slid open the top drawer of the safe.

The front was full of upright personnel files. There was a jumble of papers and folders at the back. She pulled out a handful and pawed through. The folder with her name was on the bottom. She put it on the floor and shoved the other folders back into the safe.

There was a single rap on the door before it swung open. "Hey, *jefe*."

It was Gomez. The detective was tall and wiry, in fashionably torn jeans and a tee shirt advertising a local band called Muerte Guapo. In his mid-30's, he wore his hair pulled back in a lank ponytail and had a thatch of chin hair struggling to grow into a beard.

"Cruz," he said. He leaned around the doorway to see if anyone else was in the office. Satisfied that they were alone, his lips curved into a half-smile. "Didn't expect to find you here. Waiting for me?"

"I was waiting for Loyola," she lied.

"You're going to be a long time." Gomez glanced at his watch. "Macias and Sandor took him to the hospital. We heard Silvio broke his face."

"I'll head out," Emilia said.

Gomez took a step back but continued to block the doorway. "*Oye*," he called over his shoulder. "Cruz has graced us with her presence."

Castro appeared behind Gomez. He was a shorter and swarthier version of his partner, also clad in jeans, tee, and ponytail. "How you doing, Cruz?" he asked.

"Just leaving," Emilia said.

"I don't think so," Gomez said. The lazy half-smile spread into a sneer. "Seems to me that this is the perfect time for you to give us both a little sugar."

Castro snickered. Gomez came into the office, the other man on his heels. The latter shut the door. The office was suddenly much, much smaller.

"Open the door, Castro," Emilia said.

He shook his head. "Scores to settle, Cruz," he said.

Gomez lifted his chin at Emilia. "Remember that day in the bathroom, Cruz?" he asked. "Just having a little fun and you spoiled it."

She remembered it all too well. He'd come into the detectives bathroom behind her and locked the door, saying that he'd waited long enough. It had been a raw fistfight between commodes and sinks that left the white tiled floor slick with blood. Emilia finally laid him out with a broken metal partition from the toilet stalls. She'd been stupid enough to think she was buying some goodwill with the department by not reporting the assault to the police union. Nor had she lodged a protest when Castro cornered her in the same bathroom in front of an audience and she'd rammed his head against a urinal so hard the porcelain cracked.

"We're past that," Emilia said. Her gun was a reassuring

pressure against her left side.

Both men came toward Emilia as she stood near the safe. "Nah, it's going to be different this time, Cruz," Gomez said. "The best you ever had."

Castro snickered again.

Emilia sidestepped, putting the plastic and metal chairs that fronted Loyola's desk between herself and the two men. "Not going to happen."

Castro grabbed one of the chairs to pull it away. Emilia snatched at the top and they were suddenly locked in a ridiculous tug of war. Emilia let go and Castro overbalanced, the chair scything through the air and carrying him crashing into the opposite wall.

She heard a click and the barrel of Gomez's handgun swam into view, his face red and angry on the other side of the weapon.

Emilia's fingers closed around the neck of Loyola's desk lamp and swung hard. The metal edge of the shade sliced into Gomez's cheek. He gave a shrill yell, stumbled backwards, and his gun went off. Plaster rained from the ceiling.

The office door opened, letting in light from the squadroom. "What the fuck is going on in here?"

It was Ibarra. The scent of cigarettes preceded him. He stood in the doorway, taking in Castro on the floor, Gomez holding his gun in one hand and his bloody cheek in the other, and Emilia breathing hard as if she'd just finished a marathon. All were sprinkled with plaster dust.

Castro picked himself up. "Hey, just letting off a little steam," he said.

"Get out, both of you." Ibarra grabbed Gomez's gun and spun him out of the room. Castro followed, grinning like it had all been a joke and slapping white dust off his tee shirt.

Emilia brushed the plaster out of her hair and replaced the lamp on Loyola's desk with a shaky hand.

"What the fuck are you doing here, Cruz?" Ibarra asked.

"I was waiting," Emilia said.

"What for?"

"Waiting for Loyola."

"Why?" Ibarra righted the chairs.

"To see if he's okay."

"Why shouldn't he be okay?" He caught sight of her badge on its lanyard around her neck. "What's the deal with your badge?"

"Loyola gave it back so I could go up to the bull pen and get Silvio."

"Shit, I told him not to do that." Ibarra took a pack of cigarettes out of his shirt pocket. "Where's everybody? The squadroom looks like a fucking war zone."

"When Silvio got here Loyola tried to give him his badge back," Emilia informed him. "They had words. Silvio resigned and punched him. I think Macias and Sandor took Loyola to the hospital."

"Ah, fuck." Ibarra paced a few steps in extreme agitation, rapping the pack of smokes against his thumb. "Okay, Cruz, here's what we're going to do. You're going get out of here and stay out. I'm not your biggest fan, but I don't like this kind of shit and neither does Loyola."

"Hey," Emilia said hotly. "I didn't ask for this—."

"Nobody said you did," Ibarra said. "Go to your new job and be happy you made it out alive, okay?"

Emilia looked around the room, wondering why she had been there in the first place, until her eye fell on the file lying on the floor by the safe. She picked it up.

"What's that?" Ibarra asked suspiciously.

"It's mine," Emilia said. She showed him her name on the cover.

He saw and nodded. "You okay to drive?"

"I'm fine," Emilia said.

She grabbed her shoulder bag as they walked through the empty squadroom. Ibarra lit a cigarette as soon as they were outside.

"Thanks," she said when they got to the Suburban. "I probably would have shot Gomez if you hadn't come in."

"The *pendejo* would have deserved it." Ibarra greedily inhaled smoke. "Like I said, be glad you got a new job and don't have to deal with this shit any more."

Emilia got into the Suburban. Ibarra slapped the door closed. She locked the vehicle and Ibarra nodded his approval. The sun had sunk below the roofline, darkening the parking lot. Emilia watched his dim figure and the glowing end of his cigarette recede as he returned to the building.

It was the most interaction she'd had with him in three

years. He was Loyola's partner and one of the detectives who'd opposed a female becoming a detective. For most of the time they'd been in the squadroom together his attitude had been one of disdainful indifference, as if her presence was tolerated because it was also unacknowledged.

She left the lot and turned the Suburban east towards the Palacio Réal. After a minute she realized that Silvio's badge was still in the back pocket of her jeans. She pulled it out and dropped it into the console between the two front seats.

Reality sank in as she drove. Somewhere in the back of her mind, she had always believed that when Silvio got out of the bull pen they would solve Isabel's murder. Claudia and Las Palomas would be forgotten. Emilia and Silvio would go back to being the detective team with the highest solve rate in the squadroom, arguing through every investigation with that unique mix of mutual respect and outright exasperation she'd come to relish.

Emilia never thought it would end like this.

She'd spent nearly three years in that squadroom, fighting to be accepted, refusing to be intimidated, learning as much as she could, and proving that she had the skills and guts to do the job as well as any of her male colleagues.

Yet they were still ready to rape her in the lieutenant's office.

The road ahead blurred. Emilia started to shake and had to pull over.

CHAPTER 10

"Kiss me for luck, Em."

"What?" Emilia asked groggily. She pried her eyes open. The bedroom was dark, although the haze behind the drawn white drapes told her dawn was coming. "What's going on?"

"It's the half marathon at Zihuatanejo, remember?" Kurt stood by the bed dressed in running shorts and a singlet with a number pinned to the front. "Jacques is waiting for me."

"Oh no." Emilia struggled to a sitting position. "I said I'd go with you."

"You're not going anywhere today," Kurt said firmly. "You need a day off. I already ordered you breakfast for nine o'clock. Go back to sleep for another four hours."

He bent to kiss her and Emilia put a hand on his cheek. "I hope you win."

"No, hope that I beat my old time and don't throw up at the finish line."

Emilia's lips curved into a grin under his.

She woke up again when room service rang the penthouse doorbell. Fortified with an omelet and clad in shorts and a tank top, Emilia took a cup of manzanilla tea and the folder from Loyola's safe into the dining room.

She opened the folder to find Silvio's phone records, then the handwritten list of questions Loyola had given

Macias and Sandor last Tuesday. The questions were not in Loyola's nervous scribble or any other hand she recognized, in contrast to the terse answers in Sandor's familiar block print. She lifted the memo aside to find copies of her last two annual evaluations, the personnel action promoting her to detective, and a letter of commendation from her old patrol unit.

A copy of a posed group photo was stuck to the letter. About 20 men stood facing the camera.

A few wore uniforms but the majority were in suit and tie. Emilia couldn't think what relation the photo had to her; it certainly wasn't her graduation from the police academy more than a dozen years ago, or a photo of the ceremony in which she'd been promoted to detective.

There was nothing on the reverse. With the picture face up again, Emilia studied the faces. They were a diverse bunch; Latino, white *gringo*, Asian and black. The few uniforms were just as diverse. They could be police or military.

One uniformed figure was slightly familiar. Emilia walked over to the sliding glass doors to hold the photo up to the light. The face was long, with a faint sneer. She couldn't be sure, but it looked like Vega, the police captain from Chief Salazar's staff who'd been the second El Trio victim.

She went back to the table, laid the photo to the side and the next page stared up at her. It was the crime scene report of the murder of Captain Helios Vega Corona.

"What's going on, Loyola?" Emilia murmured.

A parking garage security guard found Vega dead in his car shortly before dawn. Vega was killed by two rounds from a heavy caliber handgun, one of which had lodged in the driver's side door. From the angle, the killer almost certainly had been sitting in the passenger seat when Vega was shot. No prints, fibers, or other evidence of the killer was found. The captain was last seen leaving Planet Hollywood the previous evening around 11:00 pm.

She flipped to the next page and found Prade's autopsy report. Time of death was between midnight and 1:00 am.

Other pages appeared to be from Vega's personnel file. A certificate of promotion to captain, with the date circled. He'd been a captain for almost three years. Certificate of achievement for a training program in *El Norte*. A letter of commendation from Chief Salazar for heading up a financial crimes task force last year. Again, the date was circled.

The next thing in the file folder was a ballistics report.

Three 9mm rounds had been extracted from the body of Isabel de Silvio, female, age 42. All rounds had been examined and tested to determine the profile of the firing weapon. This was obtained by the unique striations on the projectiles created by the imperfections on the interior surface of the weapon. The resulting profile was compared to the national database of all weapons profiles used in crimes in Mexico. A match was established.

The weapon used in the murder of Isabel de Silvio

matched weapons profile ACA-10258. The signature at the bottom was that of Orlando Hernandez Soto, head of the ballistics lab.

Emilia caught her breath. Macias and Sandor claimed the ballistics report was negative. No match against anything in the database.

She kept reading, not realizing that she was holding her breath. Weapons profile ACA-10258 was established three weeks ago. Known matches: 1.

A second ballistics report showed that one 9mm round had been extracted from the body of Helios Vega Corona. Another had been extracted from the vehicle in which the victim had been found, which was registered to the victim. Both rounds had been examined and tested to determine the profile of the firing weapon. The resulting profile did not match any other weapons profile currently on record and so was assigned new number ACA-10258.

The third page was a list of all crimes catalogued to weapons serial number ACA-10258. Murder victim: Vega Corona, Helio. Murder victim: de Silvio, Isabel. This report was also signed by the head of the ballistics lab.

There was nothing else in the folder.

Emilia stood up, too agitated to stay seated. She went out to the balcony.

Isabel and Vega had been killed by the same handgun. Loyola knew it. But if he knew, why didn't Macias and Sandor know? Why have them chasing nothing when clearly they should be back to the El Trio murders, back to the theory that Silvio had been the intended target?

Macias and Sandor would want to follow up. They were good cops who were clearly frustrated with the little they had to go on.

She paced across the tile floor, hair ruffled by the breeze. If Isabel's death was connected to the El Trio murders, did that mean Silvio's missing bookie ledgers were irrelevant? Yet, it was hard to believe that it was mere coincidence that the ledgers went missing the same day his wife was killed.

She didn't know if she should call Silvio with the information or not.

Emilia needed something stronger than tea or coffee. She headed back to the dining room and Kurt's selection of expensive liquor displayed on the buffet. As she poured herself a drink, her thoughts circled back to the question of why Loyola would not have shared the ballistics report with Macias and Sandor.

More than that, why did he hide information relevant to the El Trio murders by disguising it as her personnel file? Emilia thought back to her last conversation with the acting lieutenant. He'd been stressed to the breaking point.

Was Loyola the El Trio killer?

She spent the rest of Saturday in front of Kurt's

computer, hunting online for reports of the El Trio murders. She'd read a few at the time of each shooting but now her purpose was different.

After a few clicks, she realized how little real information was in the news. But she wasn't surprised. Journalism was nearly as dangerous a profession in Mexico as being a cop. Every year journalists were murdered or made to disappear for reporting on cartel crime and government corruption. True investigative journalism was a death sentence. As a result, it was safer to publish speculation or sensationalism rather than real news.

Most of the articles she found focused on politicians' calls for action to end the drug gang violence in Acapulco and the state of Guerrero. Of course, as Acapulco's popular standard-bearer, Carlota was quoted numerous times. Chief Salazar was quoted as well.

Emilia even found an interview with Obregon as head of the police union for Guerrero. He was the master of saying nothing, but the interviewer had gushed over his crime fighting rhetoric and stretched the interview to a dozen paragraphs. The interviewer had probably been some clueless *chica,* tremendously impressed with his enigmatic smile and the mysterious persona he cultivated, like the way he always wore black. Obregon probably slept with her afterwards.

Evening shadows stretched across the room as Emilia made a timeline of El Trio events. Javier Salinas Arroliza from the state's attorney general's office had been the first victim. The lawyer had been found in his car, dead from two shots to the head, execution style. The car was parked on a quiet side street about a block from a favorite restaurant near Playa Hornitos. He'd reportedly eaten there alone that night. One website displayed a photo of Salinas's car. The driver's side window was so splattered with blood it was completely red.

The news reports she found about Vega's murder corroborated the report in the folder. Police captain Helio Vega Corona had been killed in his car after dining out. There was no picture of Vega's car. Vega left behind a wife and two children.

The third victim was *federale* Juan Carlos Espinosa, who died six days after Vega. The officer had been killed in a parking lot near Playa Bonfil, a rustic beach that catered to surfers. It was 45 minutes south of Acapulco. Espinosa had been found in his car by a pair of early morning joggers staying at the nearby Bonfil condo complex. Espinosa was survived by his ex-wife and four children.

Emilia stared for a long time at pictures of Espinosa; an official portrait in uniform in front of the Mexican flag, and a grainier photo of a body held upright by a seat belt with the back of its head blown off. He'd been one of the few *federales* with integrity and didn't deserve to have this be his memorial.

Each of the victims had been in their cars and behind the wheel when they'd been killed. The cars were parked and the ignition was off. No doors found open, no windows smashed, no bullet holes suggesting a drive-by shooting. Each had been armed, yet their weapon had not been drawn or taken by the killer.

The obvious answer was that the killer was in the car with each one. Not a random carjacker, but someone they'd all known and been friendly enough to sit with for a chat. There had been an element of trust between victim and killer.

Three law enforcement officials. Three men executed in their cars. Emilia circled the dates in her timeline; she'd find out what Loyola had been doing each night in question.

If Silvio was to be the fourth victim, there had to be a reason why the same method wasn't used. Why had the killer gone to Silvio's house instead of killing him in a car like the others? A home invasion in El Roble had to be much riskier. The killer had to surveille the house, looking for a weak spot. Which he found in the form of a glue boy named Rio.

The logical answer was that the killer simply didn't know Silvio as well as the others. That ruled out Loyola; he certainly knew Silvio well enough to be in a car with him.

Maybe Loyola wasn't the killer. But another law enforcement official was the likeliest type to know all of the El Trio victims. Loyola had even said it could be her.

Did the circle man wear a cap with a police emblem? If so, the only cops bold—or dumb—enough to wear a police emblem when out of uniform were the Ball Busters.

Emilia got up and stretched, surprised to see the night sky beyond the sliding glass doors to the balcony. The room was dark, except for the square of light projected by the computer screen. Kurt was late. The thought made her uneasy.

She drifted onto the balcony. Below her, the Pasodoble Bar was busy. The happy sounds of a steel drum band floated up. Couples danced on the beach while waiters in the hotel's trademark blue floral shirts served specialty cocktails.

As Emilia went back to the desk to shut down the computer, she realized there was another possible answer. Each of the El Trio victims was killed near a restaurant or a beach. Places the men might have taken a date.

Maybe a woman was killing her lovers. Or men who had rejected her.

On the one hand, it meant that Emilia herself wouldn't be a target.

On the other hand, however, it meant that Silvio knew the killer. She was suddenly glad she hadn't called to tell him of the connection between the murders of Isabel and Vega.

Emilia slumped into the desk chair in front of the computer. She'd believed Silvio when he said he hadn't cheated but maybe the whole drama at the police station was a front because he knew something and didn't want to answer any more questions.

As she examined the theory, Emilia imagined a scenario in which Silvio and the woman were no longer on speaking terms. Execution in the car like the others was impossible. So the woman hired someone to find a way into Silvio's house. Perhaps Silvio's ledgers had been stolen simply to make the home invasion look like a burglary. But why those ledgers when so many more valuable and obvious things could be taken?

It was a workable theory, except for the fact that Emilia believed Silvio when he said he never cheated on his wife.

The phone rang, scaring a small scream out of her. Emilia took a deep breath before answering.

"Bueno?"

"Em, we're downstairs in the bar," Kurt said. "Come celebrate."

"Celebrate?" Emilia echoed. "Did you win?"

"Yes," Kurt said. "Jacques is opening the champagne now."

"Give me five minutes," Emilia said.

She threw on a dress and sandals and met him in the Pasodoble. They toasted Jacques, who'd finished six minutes after Kurt. The two men were tired but went over the race in detail, until Emilia imagined herself on the beach at the finish line, shouting herself hoarse.

Make the time count, Silvio had said.

CHAPTER 11

"Emilia," her mother reproved her. "Did you get in a fight at school?"

"I work now, Mama, remember?" Emilia said impatiently. The black eye had faded since Rio's punch three days ago, but there was still an impressive purple half-moon above her cheekbone that no amount of makeup could hide.

"Of course," Sophia said. "I don't like to see you bruised like that. You play too rough."

"It was an accident," Emilia said, knowing it was hopeless to argue. "But it's fine."

"How are you, señora?" Kurt stepped out of the church pew and kissed Sophia on the cheek. "It's good to see you and Ernesto again."

"Mama, you remember Kurt—er, Carlos," Emilia said.

"Carlos." Sophia's face broke into one of her vaguely happy smiles as if she had received a gift but didn't know what it was. "You're Emilia's friend from school."

Kurt shook hands with Ernesto, who trailed his wife as they all walked toward the open door at the back of the church. Ernesto and Sophia had been married nearly three months, yet the itinerant knife grinder remained a broken soul. Sophia had found him wandering the neighborhood market and brought him home. His name, Ernesto Cruz, was the same as the husband Sophia lost when Emilia was a toddler. The loss had prompted the nervous breakdown which left Sophia in her own version of reality. Emilia still didn't know if her mother understood that this Ernesto was not the man she'd married as a teen.

Sophia prattled on to Kurt about people he didn't know and Emilia took a last look at the altar. Sunday Mass at San Juan de los Pinos and the social hour afterwards was one of the sacrifices of her move to the Palacio Réal. The church was no longer convenient. Besides, Kurt wasn't Catholic and Emilia found herself forgoing Sunday Mass to be with him on the one day of the week neither of them worked. He came with her from time to time, however, treating the experience as a social experiment. But for Emilia, visiting the little church now was a sweet sharp pain.

Padre Ricardo, by the steps in his threadbare vestments, greeted parishioners as they left the church and made for the garden. He beamed as Emilia and Kurt followed Sophia and Ernesto, the last to leave.

"So nice to see you again, Señor Rucker," Padre Ricardo said.

"And you, Padre." Kurt smiled and shook hands with the priest. "A rousing sermon."

They talked for a few minutes before Emilia drew the priest aside. "Padre, do you have a moment?"

"Of course," he said. "Here or shall we go inside?"

"I need to talk to Berta," Emilia said. "And I'd rather not do it alone."

"You found her granddaughter?" Padre Ricardo asked. "Is it bad news?"

"No." Emilia raised her hands in resignation then let them drop. "I don't think I'm going to find her."

"Is she dead?" Padre Ricardo had brought the missing teen to Emilia's attention and she knew he wanted a happy ending as much as she did.

"Not that I know," Emilia said. "I simply don't have anywhere else to look. It's only fair to tell Berta." She heard desperation in her voice.

Padre Ricardo frowned. "That's not like you, Emilia. You always seem to find a way. I often think of you as indefatigable." He cocked his head to one side. "Were you in an accident?"

Emilia pulled her sunglasses off the top of her head and settled them on her nose to hide the fading black eye. "In a way," she grimaced. "I was questioning a little boy and he hit me."

"Just how little was he?"

"Too little," Emilia said sadly. "And scared."

Padre Ricardo shook his head. "Things seem to get worse every day. My prayers are with you."

Emilia tilted her head in the direction of the refreshments table on the far side of the church garden, where a stern-faced woman in a dark brown dress filled paper cups with coffee for thirsty churchgoers. "Best to get it over with sooner than later."

Padre Ricardo nodded. "I'll come with you."

Parishioners stood in happy groups around the garden, adults drinking coffee while children played noisily, fueled by a Sunday treat of *limonada* and store-bought cookies. Padre Ricardo and Emilia threaded their way through to the table and the woman attending to the refreshments.

"Berta," Padre Ricardo said. "Thank you for volunteering again this week."

"I haven't anything else to do, Padre," Berta sniffed. "But you know that."

"Emilia has come to talk to us about Lila," Padre Ricardo said gently. "Perhaps we could go sit inside the church. Anyone who wants more coffee can help themselves."

Berta's eyes narrowed at Emilia but she moved around the side of the table and grabbed a scarred leather handbag off a nearby folding chair. Padre Ricardo took her elbow to guide her across the lawn. Their progress was slowed by people seeking to chat with the priest. Each time, he begged their pardon and said he'd be back shortly.

Emilia stopped to tell Kurt she was going inside for a few minutes.

"Sure," he said, with a sideways glance at Sophia. "Take your time."

"Just a few minutes," Emilia said and squeezed his arm. He was the only *gringo* there, tall and blonde, standing out in a linen *guayabera* shirt and starched khaki pants. "I promise."

Emilia followed Berta and Padre Ricardo to the church and turned to look before she went in. She felt vaguely guilty for abandoning Kurt to the challenge of making small talk by himself with her mother and Ernesto but he didn't seem to mind; Kurt was in command of any situation; be it the fanciest restaurant or the lowliest *barrio* crowd. He caught her eye as he said something that made Sophia laugh and winked the same way he'd done that night in the penthouse. Her heart clenched and Emilia winked back.

She went into the church just as Berta and Padre Ricardo sat down in the last pew. Padre Ricardo took Berta's hand. "Nothing bad has happened," the priest said. "Emilia just wants to talk."

"I want to tell you that I've been looking, but I don't have any new information about Lila, Berta," Emilia began. "The best thing I can say is that there isn't any evidence that Lila is dead. But there isn't any evidence that she is alive, either. The fact is I don't have anything at all."

"But you were looking," Berta looked from Emilia to Padre Ricardo.

"I was but I've hit a dead end," Emilia said. "There's nothing new to tell you, no more leads to follow. I thought her mother Yolanda's phone would be helpful but it wasn't."

"Yolanda," Berta scoffed. "You see? I always said no good would come of that skank. And I was right."

Emilia swallowed hard. "Lila's been gone nearly eight months now, Berta. The odds are not good we'll ever find her. I'm sorry."

"All you gave me was fancy talk about that no good Yolanda," Berta sniffed. "But I don't need you no more. Lila wrote me a letter. She's fine. She got herself a job. Sent me 200 pesos, too. Not like that worthless mother of hers."

"You got a letter from Lila," Emilia gasped. "That's wonderful."

Berta opened her big purse and took out a scrap of paper. It was half of a photograph, with a torn and ragged edge. In a pink tank top and skinny jeans, Lila Jimenez Lata smiled into the camera, her china doll features and short black hair immediately recognizable. A male hand was at her waist but the rest of him was undoubtedly in the missing half of the photo.

Lila stood in front of a wrought iron fence. There was a yellow stucco building in the background, with a grassy area bordered by tall red canna lilies. A corner of the building was visible and shone with something smooth and gold, like part of a sign affixed to the stucco.

"Where is she?" Emilia asked. "Did the letter say where she is?"

Berta bristled. "She didn't say, just that she has friends and a job."

"How did you get the letter, Berta?" Emilia pressed. "Did you have to go to the post office to get it? Was it delivered to the house by a messenger?"

"She sent me 200 pesos, more than her mother ever made," Berta snapped. "And you ask me about the envelope?

Her father would be proud, God rest his soul."

Emilia swallowed back a retort. "Berta, would you mind if I made a copy of the picture?"

"Use the printer in the sacristy, Emilia," Padre Ricardo said.

Berta looked reluctant to surrender the photo but Emilia plucked it out of her fingers and ran into the church.

"So just the picture," Kurt said.

"Berta seemed much more impressed with the fact that the girl sent her money than with trying to find her." Emilia handed it to him. "Where do you think it was taken?"

Kurt took off his sunglasses to study the image. Next to him on the doublewide chaise lounge, Emilia sipped her mojito and watched him. His ocean-colored eyes filled with concentration and he absently rubbed his cheek with his knuckles.

The breeze off the waves rustled the palm fronds roofing their *palapa*. After church they'd driven to La Luna, the new five star resort on the far side of Playa Revolcadero. They both needed to relax, Kurt had declared, and he wanted to check out the competition. To Emilia's surprise, he'd reserved one of the secluded and thatched cabanas for the entire afternoon, so far out on the beach they were chauffeured in a dune buggy. The cost was probably more than she made in six months but would hardly put a dent in Kurt's wallet. She knew he made a preposterous amount of money and had minimal expenses. The penthouse came with the job, as did meals.

"I'm not going to be very helpful." Kurt handed back the photo. "I don't recognize the building. It might not even be in Acapulco. For all you know, she could be in the Bahamas."

"No, I think she's alive and well and still in Acapulco." Emilia stuck the photo in her bag. "If I didn't have to start this stupid job tomorrow, I could look for the building. How many buildings in Acapulco have a shiny gold sign?"

"I don't know." Kurt grinned. "On another topic, your new boss is going to be mighty impressed with your eye."

"I've been directed into this job." Emilia gingerly touched her eye. "They can hardly complain if I'm not what they expected. At least that stupid Claudia stopped texting me."

"That's the spirit," Kurt said.

Emilia laughed. For the first time in a week, she relaxed. Silvio was out of the bull pen, and Loyola got what he deserved. She wouldn't have to see Castro and Gomez any time soon. Lila wasn't dead.

It was a better day than most.

The red and white fabric walls of the cabana were pulled back and tied to the stanchions supporting the thatched roof. Their chaise faced the shore. The sky was royal blue lacquer above a restless ocean. They'd already had a swim, gently wrestling each other through the waves.

Kurt rolled onto his side and pressed up against her. "I'm thinking of an appetizer before dinner."

"Here?" Emilia felt her cheeks get warm.

"Here," Kurt murmured.

There was no dishonesty in his eyes. Emilia could lose herself in those eyes, in his arms, in the way he made her feel. The suspicions she'd poured out to Mercedes now seemed ludicrous.

Kurt tied the canvas walls of the cabana in place and they made love on the chaise as the breeze sighed through the fabric. Kurt was an intense and powerful lover and like so many other times, he left her gasping for air but stronger than before. Healed, renewed, and exhausted.

Emilia felt the sweat dry on her bare skin as they lay together afterwards. Shadows crept up on the cabana walls as they listened to the unseen surf and the rustle of the thatch.

Kurt hoisted Emilia to her feet for another dip in the ocean. As tendrils of extravagant color portended another gorgeous sunset, a fleet of waiters catered dinner to the cabana, making Emilia feel like slightly sandy royalty.

Late in the evening, they headed home to the Palacio Réal, driving west on the Carretera Escénica. The road was a ribbon of tarmac carved from the face of the cliff, two dark lanes without guardrails or a safety net amid a dramatic scene of mountain curves and glittering ocean.

The Palacio Réal was part of an exclusive gated

community built into the cliff face below the highway. From the huge *privada* gate, a steep cobblestone road led down to the water, the only means of access for a few dozen private villas, a luxury condominium building, and the hotel at the bottom.

Emilia yawned as they reached the turnoff.

"Almost home," Kurt said. The guard swung open the *privada* gate and the SUV bounced onto the cobblestones.

Just beyond the first curve, Kurt's headlights picked out a red reflection on the opposite side of the road. He slowed and Emilia saw a car half hidden in the foliage. The car was parked at an angle, although well off the road. They passed and Emilia realized the rear driver's side door was ajar.

"This does not look right," Emilia said.

"Hold on," Kurt said.

He spun the vehicle and started back the other way, coming to a halt behind the parked car. Emilia snatched her gun out of her shoulder bag while Kurt found a flashlight in the glove compartment.

The night air was still as Emilia approached the rear of the vehicle, guided by Kurt's steady beam. She used the muzzle of her gun to fully open the door. There was nothing in the back seat. There was no sound or movement, only the coppery smell of blood.

"Hold the light higher," Emilia said.

Kurt lifted the beam and she heard him swear in English. Emilia rose up on her toes to see over the front seat.

A man in an Acapulco police uniform was behind the

wheel but slumped over, his bloody head resting on the passenger side.

"Don't touch anything," Emilia said, more to herself than Kurt.

It took 25 minutes for a patrol car to arrive, followed shortly by the crime scene techs and a body wagon from the morgue. Ibarra pulled in behind the tech van, his clunker belching exhaust.

Ignoring Kurt, Ibarra nodded at Emilia as he pulled out his phone, a cigarette dangling from the corner of his mouth. "Did you call in the *placas*?" he asked her.

"Yes." Emilia held up her own phone to signal that she'd called Dispatch with the license plate numbers. "Still waiting for them to call back."

The crime scene techs set up a noisy diesel generator. Mounted on tripods, two big searchlights emitted an electronic whine as they stabbed the darkness. The army arrived and took charge of the *privada* gate. Ibarra introduced himself to the commander as the police officer in charge and snapped out orders to keep the press away from the crime scene. Emilia didn't say anything else, just waited with Kurt beyond the reach of the searchlights.

Finally the team from the morgue eased the body out of the car and laid it on a gurney.

"Another cop," Ibarra said to no one in particular.

Emilia wished she had a sweater; she was shivering despite the warm night air. The private road leading to the Palacio Réal was not like the public parking areas where Salinas, Vega, and Espinosa had been found. It was no coincidence that the body was there. The El Trio killer had left his latest victim as a message for her.

The senior crime scene tech walked over to Ibarra. "Male victim. Probably mid-40s. Been dead awhile. Shot three times but not in the car."

"They wanted it to look like the El Trio killings," Emilia suggested.

The tech shrugged. "Looks that way. You want to try for a visual?"

Led by the tech, Emilia and Ibarra stepped inside the funnel of light. Kurt hung back, arms folded, hip resting on the fender of his SUV.

Emilia found herself looking down on the body of a middle-aged man with a receding hairline and a thick waist. He'd been shot in the head, execution style, like the El Trio victims. A dark stain across the front of his uniform blouse revealed two more wounds near the center of his chest. The body smelled of old blood and feces. Emilia was strongly reminded of the disgusting mass of flies infesting Silvio's house.

Ibarra took a last drag on what was left of his filterless cigarette, then flicked it away. A red glow arced through the air before disappearing into the night. "Look familiar to you, Cruz?"

Emilia realized she was hugging herself so hard her elbows hurt from the fingers digging into them. "He's familiar, but I can't place him," she said.

"It's Hernandez," Ibarra said. "Chief of Ballistics."

CHAPTER 12

El Cuarto, the headlines screamed the next morning. The fourth victim of a killer targeting law enforcement! Another execution! How can Acapulco's law enforcement officers defend us if they can't defend themselves?

The gory details of Hernandez's death followed, along with an official photo of the late ballistics expert. There was no shot from the crime scene. To fill space and entice readers, the murders of Salinas, Vega, and Espinosa were rehashed with lurid delight.

Thankfully, the media had already forgotten Isabel and her death was not mentioned. It was old news. After all, someone was killed in El Roble at least once a week.

Emilia compulsively bought every paper she could find before starting off for the Las Palomas office building. Someone had murdered Hernandez to ensure that a whitewashed ballistics report ended up in the official case file on Isabel's murder.

Who else knew about the original report besides Loyola? Who knew she'd taken the file folder?

Those questions had Emilia up at dawn. She reread the ballistics reports on the deaths of Vega and Isabel before hiding them inside waxed paper in the freezer of the penthouse, under a container of something Jacques had left. Wearing a look of grim determination, Kurt wished her luck in the new job and left the penthouse early for a meeting with his chief of security. There should be closed circuit camera coverage of the spot where Hernandez's vehicle had been found. The deep intimacy she and Kurt shared at La Luna was gone, replaced by tension and urgency.

Emilia's nerves were stretched thin as she drove, once again constantly checking her rearview mirror.

The address Claudia provided turned out to be a modern glass and steel affair on Avenida Almendros, a wide but short street studded with office buildings in Acapulco's posh commercial district. That hardly seemed right for a police unit and Emilia continued past.

The Torre Metropolitano skyscraper loomed ahead. The structure was complete now, but Emilia could not suppress a shiver. She'd been shot on top of the half-constructed building and only the hand of the Virgin had kept her from falling to her death.

The GPS told Emilia to turn around. Once around the block and the metallic voice said once again that she'd arrived. Emilia showed her police badge to the guard at the entrance to the lot but he asked to see her *cédula*. She waited while he consulted a clipboard and was mildly surprised when he handed her a laminated pass and pointed to the front row of parking spaces. As Emilia pulled in she saw a sign proclaiming that the space was reserved for the City of Acapulco.

The lot in front of the building could hold at least 30 cars and there was a sign for underground parking, too. Yet there were only three cars in the lot, including her white Suburban.

She checked her watch. It was 8:15 am. Claudia's text said to report at 9:00 am. Las Palomas apparently wasn't an early riser.

Time for a little reconnaissance. Emilia grabbed her shoulder bag, the jacket to her dependable gray pantsuit, and headed into the world of police fantasy.

She found herself in a soaring two story foyer, the spacious effect amplified by the creamy limestone floor's herringbone pattern. A steel and glass stairway rose to her immediate left while a gallery wall showcased half a dozen abstract oil paintings. The bright slashes of blue and magenta were taller than Emilia.

The dramatic space was devoid of receptionist or furniture save for a narrow leather and chrome bench and a man-sized saguaro cactus in a silvery pot.

The herringbone floor pointed to the far wall, which was a dramatic panel of tinted glass. As Emilia approached, she saw that the wall was in fact two sets of doors leading to a patio dotted with umbrella tables, dark wood chairs, and more plants in shiny pots.

Claudia had instructed Emilia to go to the second floor but she still had plenty of time to explore. Emilia wandered past the oil paintings, her footfalls amplified by the pale stone. The gallery wall ended in a long white corridor. To the right, Emilia found two darkened office suites and a set of restrooms.

Whatever business was conducted by Consolidated

Solutions and Vector Analytics, it wasn't done in the morning. Glass doors revealed reception areas in both office suites. They were both outfitted with a tall counter in the middle presiding over space for waiting clients complete with water cooler, plush chairs, and a coffee table with a flower arrangement. In each suite, the company name and logo hung on a sign mounted behind the counter.

The corridor ended in a stairway to the underground parking garage. Emilia retraced her steps, passed the foyer and found another office suite. The layout was the same; reception counter, client seating area, and a sign proclaiming Soledo Enterprises. The lights were off; no one was there.

Twenty meters past the Soledo Enterprises suite, Emilia came across a door labelled "Gymnasium." She pushed it open, flicked on a light switch, and was rewarded with the sight of a fully outfitted gym. Brand new weight machines, a rack of free weights next to a bench, two rows of treadmills, floor mats for stretching and wrestling, even a heavy bag suspended from the ceiling and a speed bag bolted to the wall.

The job wouldn't be a total loss.

Emilia heard the rattle of pans and someone talking; the first human sounds in the so-far deserted building. She quickened her steps, her heels tapping, and found a small restaurant. The building's address was etched on the glass door. The place was at once dramatic and comfortable, with oil paintings and the building's signature limestone floor tempered by rustic Mexican pine furniture.

"Can I help you?"

An older man in a maroon uniform shirt and pants smiled at Emilia from behind the tall steel-topped serving counter. He was quickly joined by two women in the same uniform.

"An omelet, perhaps, señora?" the man inquired. "A fresh omelet with *queso* and *jamón*? Or maybe a fruit plate? We have mango, papaya, *piña*." He turned to one of the women. "Delores, show the señora how fresh the mango is."

Emilia held up her hand. All three were a little too excited to have a customer. "Thank you," she said. "Just a coffee, please."

"Cappuccino, latte, café Americano?"

"A latte, please."

Her order galvanized all three into action. After much ceremony, Emilia left the café with a piping hot latte and new friends in the form of Esteban, the owner, and his wife and daughter.

She went back to the foyer and climbed the airy staircase. It led to a mezzanine. Emilia walked the length of it and found two doors, both with a discreet label that read "City of Acapulco." Both were locked.

Emilia continued up to the third floor. It was a mirror image of the second, with doors labelled "Building Services." Those doors were locked as well.

Back in the soaring foyer, Emilia sat on the bench and sipped her latte. She didn't have long to wait. Promptly at

9:00 am, half a dozen women walked in, Claudia Sanchez at the center of the gaggle. She wore a suit similar to the one she'd had on the day Emilia met her; a navy affair with brass buttons like a sea captain's blazer cut down to size. The salon-perfect hair was curled as artfully as before and her nails gleamed with lavender polish.

"Detective Cruz!" Claudia caroled, the corner of her mouth lifted in a knowing smile. "Right on time."

Emilia stood, feeling dull in her gray pants and jacket, her hair scraped back and secured with a rubber band. It was the same outfit she'd worn to the mayor's breakfast. It coordinated nicely with the fading black eye.

She'd lost the first round already.

"Good to see you again, Claudia," she said.

Introductions were made. The four women were administrative assistants for one thing or another. Emilia quickly got the impression that at Las Palomas, titles were more important than names.

"We have a busy day ahead and I want you to get settled in quickly," Claudia said. She led the way up the staircase, her minions trailing behind. Her stiletto heels clacked against the steel stairs. "It's a shame you weren't available last week."

"I was investigating a murder last week," Emilia said.

"Of course," Claudia said, without changing her buoyant tone. "We have a deadline set by the mayor and the chief of police. Things simply have to get done."

Claudia swiped a card against a key reader, a low tone

sounded, and the glass door released. The administrative assistant for liaison activities pulled it open and they all filed into a reception area.

The space looked so new that it hurt Emilia's eyes. Every surface reflected, whether it was glass, steel, or glossy paint. White walls gleamed like crystal.

"Our administrative assistant for customer service sits here," Claudia said, waving a hand to indicate a large lacquer desk and pale gray upholstered chairs clustered around a marble coffee table "Of course we still need artwork."

"Of course," Emilia said, looking around. This wasn't a police department office; it was a picture from one of the hospitality trade magazines Kurt left lying around.

"Emilia." Claudia cocked her head to one side. Despite her breezy demeanor, her lower lip trembled with nerves. "Paola will be your administrative assistant for operations. She can get you situated in your office. Your first meeting is in the conference room at noon."

"Fine," Emilia said.

A girl, presumably Paola, detached herself from the gaggle around Claudia. She was stamped out of the same mold, in a severe business suit and platform heels. Emilia was sure they'd get along great.

Paola led her down a gleaming white hallway, the brightness accentuated by modern chrome sconces. Claudia's office was right next door, Paola explained, and the administrative assistants were across the hall. She stopped by a simple black nameplate reading "Emilia Cruz

Encinos, Chief of Operations."

The office was the size of the entire detectives squadroom.

A picture window overlooked the patio with its bright umbrellas and dark wooden chairs. The desk was even bigger than Kurt's desk in his office downstairs in the Palacio Réal's administrative offices and that was as big as a cruise ship. Emilia ran her hand along the shiny gray lacquer, which matched the desk in the reception area. Two gray upholstered chairs fronted the desk while another two flanked a console that resembled a silver torpedo. Built-in shelves ran the length of the wall behind the desk.

"You'll be wanting some artwork," Paola said.

The rest of the Las Palomas office suite was just as impressive. There were easily a dozen private offices and a large staff area with 20 cubicles. The place also boasted a coffee bar, two bathrooms, a conference room, and a work room with printers and a copier. Everything looked brand new, from the color copier to the espresso machine.

The rest of the morning passed swiftly. Emilia received a keycard on a lanyard so she could open the doors. Next came a briefing by the administrative assistant for information technology, after which Emilia was shown how to access the new Las Palomas network.

She logged on easily but couldn't navigate to any familiar database. "How do we access the police intranet?" Emilia asked.

"What police intranet?" the girl asked.

"This is an Acapulco police unit," Emilia said. "We have to be tied into the network."

The girl shrugged. "Don't worry. We're on a commercial server so it's blazing fast."

"I'm not talking about speed," Emilia said. Apparently, all the Las Palomas network allowed her to do was access the open internet. Even the unit's information was stored in folders hosted by a commercial service. "We have to be tied into the main police network in order to do background searches and find arrest records. Be connected to Dispatch and the radio network."

The girl gaped as if Emilia had suddenly started speaking a different language. "No one's told me anything like that."

Emilia opened her notebook and began a list.

At noon, Paola took her to the conference room. It was as magnificent as the rest of the office space, with a giant lacquered table topped with a rose-colored bowl the size of a small car. The chairs were upholstered in mauve leather. More chrome wall sconces and views of a grassy courtyard completed the modern and impersonal effect.

The room was packed with people Emilia remembered from the meeting in Carlota's office. Public relations types. A few men from Chief Salazar's office.

Victor Obregon Sosa.

The corner of his mouth lifted when he saw Emilia. "How nice to see you again," he said. "Detective." He lingered over the last word, letting her know that it was now merely an honorific.

Emilia didn't speak as Claudia sat at the head of the table, her every word and manner copied straight out of Carlota's playbook. The first item on the agenda was the Las Palomas logo and the public relations people had several for them to choose from. The debate ranged on for an hour, while Emilia thought about finding Hernandez dead in his car, if Loyola could be the El Trio killer, and what Silvio was doing right now. Talking to Rio to find out more about the circle man? Or prowling a house that stank of blood and feasting flies?

The meeting droned on. Emilia was grateful she'd brought her notebook and a pen. She flipped open to the timeline of the El Trio murders she'd made on the weekend and added last night's events. If nothing else, Hernandez's murder meant she could cross out the half-baked theory that the El Trio killer was a woman killing old lovers.

"Emilia, do you have a preference?"

She jerked up her head to see Claudia looking at her expectantly. "For what?" Emilia asked.

Claudia pursed her lips together in a line of disapproval. Obregon's mouth twitched.

Madre de Dios, but they were still nattering on about a logo. "The one with the greatest contrast will look the best on the badge," Emilia said shortly.

"Number four?" asked one of the consultants. He had several designs on an easel. Number four was a simple white dove against a circle of stylized blue waves.

"Sure," Emilia said. "Clean and simple, with good contrast."

All of the consultants looked at Claudia. She bit her lip.

"I agree with Detective Cruz," Obregon spoke up. "Number four makes the statement the city and the union want to make."

"Our signature color isn't on it," Claudia pouted.

"We could add a thin outline," the consultant said. He leapt to the easel and outlined the logo with a pink marker.

Claudia brightened. "Perfect, that's settled."

The next agenda item was uniforms. There was no debate over design choices this time; apparently Carlota had designed the uniforms herself.

Emilia was amazed to see a model walk into the room dressed in a brown polyester two piece pantsuit. The pants were straight and simple, but the top was a short-sleeved button-down affair with a rounded collar and a peplum that nipped in the waist and flared over the hips like a big ruffle. All of the edges were piped in hot pink. The matching hat was a caricature of a military officer's lid, with a black brim far too small and shiny to be useful anyone patrolling in the hot sun all day.

The model walked the perimeter of the room to polite applause. Claudia stood by like a fashion designer on the runway. "Such a beautiful design," she gushed when the clapping died down.

It was an utterly ridiculous uniform for a cop. "We have

to make some adjustments," Emilia said bluntly and motioned to the model to stop promenading about. "Everybody knows that brown is the color of traffic cops." She tugged on the peplum; it stayed in place and wasn't the detachable item she'd hoped for. "This has to go, too. It'll get in the way of the gun belt."

Claudia flinched as if Emilia had lobbed a sack of onions at her. "What belt?"

"The gun belt," Emilia said impatiently. "Home to gun, nightstick, handcuffs, pepper spray. All the shit that cops carry."

"Las Palomas are the doves of peace." Obregon's voice had a humorous sting to it. "An unarmed police force."

Emilia raised her eyebrows at him. "There is no such thing as an unarmed police force in Acapulco."

"There is now, Detective." Obregon's tongue stretched out the last word.

"The collar is reinforced for the radio," Claudia chimed in, as if that would keep cops safe.

"Excellent," Emilia managed. There was no way she would patrol the streets of Acapulco without a gun. But the room was full of people and this wasn't the place to argue. She went back to her seat. First no access to the police intranet and now this.

The meeting ended with a discussion of hiring. Las Palomas could hire 40 officers. An advertisement had already gone out and prospective candidates were supposed to apply in person at the central police building at the end of the week. Paola passed Emilia the ad, which was already in all the Acapulco newspapers. Self-congratulations ensued for getting the ad so widely distributed on such short notice.

Emilia knew she passed right over the ad that morning, too engrossed in the coverage of Hernandez's murder to notice anything else. Now she read it with mounting concern. The only requirements were to love the city and be female.

"There are going to be thousands of applicants," she said, aghast.

Claudia beamed. "We'll be able to hire the very best."

"No, you don't understand," Emilia said. "Thousands of women are going to show up at the building's gates and they are all going to want this job."

"But it's a police job." Claudia frowned and her lower lip wobbled again. "Women who qualify for a police job will apply."

"What qualifications?" Emilia exclaimed. "Minimum age? Level of fitness? Ability to read and write reports? Basic English skills so they can talk to tourists? The ad doesn't say any of that."

Claudia shrank away from the table.

"There's nothing in this ad that is going to discourage any woman who can walk and read from showing up." Emilia couldn't believe Claudia didn't understand what she had offered in the ad and how many women in Acapulco were desperate for a better life. "I'm not kidding when I say thousands will apply."

"Do you have a suggestion, Detective?" Obregon queried.

"Notify Internal Security, for a start," Emilia said.

Claudia straightened up. "I don't think that's necessary," she said. "We have this well in hand."

They were fucked before they even started. Emilia leaned forward. "Internal Security controls everything that goes on at the central police building. If they don't know what's happening, come Thursday when they see a horde of women descending on them, they might start shooting."

"Is that true?" Claudia turned to Obregon."

"Detective Cruz knows her department," Obregon said.

"We have to notify Internal Security," Emilia said. "Request the big gymnasium for a processing arena. Get some uniforms to act as crowd control." She thought about events Kurt had hosted at the hotel which brought in scores of people and how the Palacio Réal staff handled everything so smoothly. "We'll divide the gym into zones. First zones will be English and writing tests. That should narrow the field pretty quickly."

"Of course," Claudia said, as if it was her idea. "If they pass the tests, they'll get an immediate and personal interview with the chief of operations."

Emilia stared across the table at Claudia. "You want

me to interview a couple hundred women in one day?”

"You have to train them, Detective Cruz," Obregon said, with no attempt to hide his smile. "You should have the privilege of choosing them."

"Well, thanks," Emilia said.

The rest of the day passed in a blur of more introductions, lengthy phone calls to Internal Security, and fruitless discussions about the uniform and computer access. But at 5:00 pm, as if a whistle had blown, everything shut down. Emilia was happy to head out as well. The move from street detective to executive planner had been too swift. There had been no time to corral her emotions and prepare for the change. Emilia didn't even have the right clothing for the job.

As she passed through the lobby, Obregon fell into step beside her. Emilia wondered if he'd been waiting.

"You made quite an impact on your first day," Obregon said.

"Thank you," Emilia replied. "Although I feel like more of a babysitter than a cop."

"Las Palomas will come together," Obregon said. "You have plenty of time."

"Thirty days." Emilia tried not to sound bitter. "It could take that long just to clean up the applications mess."

"Come now, Detective Cruz." Obregon's voice was silky.

"You can't tell me this isn't nicer than being in the detective squadroom. It always smelled like stale coffee and sweat. Your computer was from before the Fox administration."

"But we had a new copier," Emilia parried. He'd been the one to supply it when she was acting lieutenant for a brief period.

Obregon laughed out loud, the sound bouncing off the walls of the expansive foyer. "You'll do well here."

"Why me?" Emilia asked. "Why was I picked for this job?"

"Bigger and better things," Obregon said lightly. "Chief Salazar knew you were ready for something bigger and better."

"I didn't ask for bigger and better."

"It was time. Besides we had to get you away from Silvio. His career has been in a death spiral for years."

"Silvio is a hell of a good detective," Emilia said.

"Was," Obregon said. "I heard he resigned."

"Can you blame him?"

"You have admirable loyalty, Detective."

She knew things about Obregon, knew that he served only himself. He knew that she understood him, but it never seemed to matter. Obregon always had the upper hand.

Emilia stepped away and pretended to admire one of the big oil paintings. "Is Las Palomas really going to be an unarmed unit?" she asked. "You of all people should know that's a prescription for disaster."

"An unarmed unit is a signal that the city is rebounding," Obregon said.

Emilia looked at him over her shoulder. "How many Las Palomas are going be dead before we've officially rebounded?"

"You get to redefine the rules of engagement." Obregon came up behind her, so close that he brushed her back. "How many women get to do that?"

Emilia felt the rise and fall of his chest as he breathed. He probably slept with anything that wasn't red hot or running away. She felt trapped by the testosterone surging against her and was suddenly reminded of Castro and Gomez. Without thinking, she spun and shoved Obregon with both hands.

He nearly overbalanced and his brow darkened.

"Don't you have somewhere to go?" Emilia snapped. "A busy man like yourself."

"Victor!" From the stairs above them, Claudia's girlish voice echoed against glass and steel. "I'm so glad you're still here."

Both Emilia and Obregon looked up. Claudia started down the stairs, high heels announcing her descent.

"Did we forget something, Claudia?" Obregon asked.

"I was hoping to catch you," Claudia reached the lobby, wearing a strained smile as she looked from Obregon to Emilia. "Did you two have some unfinished business?"

"Detective Cruz and I have known each other for a while," Obregon said. "But we don't often get a chance to catch up."

Claudia's unspoken thoughts were so plainly written on her face that Emilia didn't know whether to laugh.

Or cry.

"I've got to be going," Emilia said. She ignored Obregon and smiled at Claudia. "He's all yours."

As Emilia drove back to the Palacio Réal, she couldn't remember the last time she'd left work so early. She could work out in the hotel gym or go swimming before it got dark. Even cook dinner, another simple pleasure she'd sacrificed for life in the hotel, instead of eating restaurant food.

Or she could call Macias and Sandor, see what the squadroom had on the Hernandez murder. Calling Ibarra was out of the question; he wouldn't share anything with her.

As she passed the spot on the road leading to the hotel where they'd found Hernandez's body, Emilia found herself wondering why she'd been plucked out of the squadroom and reassigned to Las Palomas.

Obregon said that Chief Salazar had selected her. But Chief Salazar had insisted that Carlota wanted her for the job.

Emilia had never been so popular and she wondered why now. The timing couldn't have been worse.

CHAPTER 13

The week passed with lightning speed as the Las Palomas office got ready for the big hiring event. Emilia's evenings were busy as well, accompanying Kurt to Copa America events sponsored by the Acapulco Hotel Association. She didn't have the right clothes for those events, either.

There was no time to think about Isabel's death, Hernandez, or anything else related to the El Trio murders. No one from the squadroom called. Neither did Silvio. Loyola didn't come looking for his missing file.

It was just as well. Emilia found herself involved in almost every decision about Las Palomas. She'd never imagined all the issues involved in setting up a new police unit: training plans, testing, record keeping, patrol routes, radio signs and frequencies, union-mandated lunch breaks. Everything was complicated by the lack of access to police systems. Emilia found herself at the central police building every day, trying to wrest lesson plans from the police academy or establish the unit's radio protocols. No one had heard of Las Palomas and it was difficult to get traction.

By Thursday, Emilia was sure she'd worked for Las Palomas for four years rather than just four days. At the noon meeting every day, she alone talked about the actual work of finding, training, and deploying the Las Palomas officers. Claudia and the others listened to her politely, agreed that she follow up on her own suggestions, and went back to their debates over public relations.

Obregon was in and out but ignored Emilia. More staff appeared yet Emilia remained the only actual cop.

Las Palomas came to life at 9:00 and closed promptly at 5:00 pm. As far as Emilia could tell, the office suites on the first floor stayed dark all day. She wondered how Esteban in the little restaurant made enough to stay afloat.

As she came back to her office after the noon meeting, her cell phone rang. The display read *Silvio*.

"*Bueno*," she answered neutrally.

"It's Franco," he said.

Emilia swallowed hard. In all the time they'd been partners, he'd never, ever, implied permission to use his first name.

"Hi," Emilia said. "How are you doing?"

"I'm getting by." Silvio cleared his throat. "How's the new job?"

"It's okay." Emilia looked around the office. "Cleaner than the squadroom."

"Yeah?"

"My office is as big as a cruise ship," Emilia babbled. "I've got a secretary, too. Excuse me, administrative assistant for operations."

"Yeah," Silvio said. "Maybe I can come check it out one of these days."

"Sure," Emilia said. "Anytime."

Silvio cleared his throat again. "Isabel's funeral is Sunday." He gave her the time and directions to the church. "You can bring Hollywood if you want."

Emilia couldn't help but smile at the familiar taunt. "I'll ask him."

"Good." Silvio paused. "Listen. I looked for that kid. The one who punched you. Rio."

"Did you talk to him? Did he say anything about the circle man?"

"He's dead. Heroin overdose."

Emilia caught her breath. "He was a glue boy. He didn't have money for heroin."

"He was somebody's lookout and probably got a payment in horse."

"Come on. This is not a coincidence." She was suddenly back in the squadroom, sparring with her partner and digging for answers at the same time.

"Look, I just thought you'd want to know," Silvio snapped.

"Okay." Emilia let it go. Silvio probably didn't even believe the whole key story. "Look, have you heard anything from Macias and Sandor? About Isabel?"

"If there is anything they want me to know," Silvio said brusquely. "They know how to get in touch."

The connection cut off.

Emilia put down her cell phone and closed her eyes. Was Rio's death really just a coincidence? She wondered if she should call Silvio back and tell him about the original ballistics report that Hernandez had signed. Was it fair not to tell him? What would he do if he knew? Silvio's temper was legendary and after what had happened with Loyola in the squadroom, anything could happen. More importantly, would Silvio end up like Hernandez?

Someone coughed and Emilia's eyes flew open. Paola was in the doorway. "Detective Cruz, would you like a cup of coffee before your next meeting with Claudia? I've just made some fresh."

Emilia stood. Paola could hardly know where Emilia's mind had been but she was an alien intruder, whisking Emilia away to a foreign place and time. "Thank you, Paola. I'll get it myself."

As she went into the gleaming little kitchen, following the aroma of espresso, Emilia missed the detective squadroom with a longing that was almost physical. She missed the crappy coffee made in the scummy Señor Café machine, made drinkable by an invariable bag of pastries, a tradition she'd started. Missed Silvio cursing at his computer screen. Missed Macias and Sandor holding their private conversations. Ibarra's smokestack cologne and Loyola's indecision. Everything except the nerve-sharpening exchanges with Castro and Gomez which always came with the knowledge that her fist had connected with both of their faces and a rematch was inevitable.

She poured herself some coffee. Being a detective was the high point of her career and nobody could take that away from her. She'd fought hard for that job because it was a job worth having. A job where she could make a difference. Or at least believe a difference was possible.

The coffee was piping hot and there was real *crema* in the refrigerator. Two of the assistants giggled over a cell phone. They looked up when Emilia coughed. One of them swiped at the screen and they left the kitchen, leaving dirty cups in the sink for the cleaning service to deal with.

This wasn't that job.

"Thank you for coming," Claudia said primly. She rose from her desk and closed the door behind Emilia.

"Is this about the uniforms?" Emilia asked. Chief Salazar's office had quietly vetoed the brown and pink polyester pantsuits. Las Palomas officers would wear blue polo shirts and cargo pants. Emilia knew that Claudia blamed her for the change.

"I'm always open to suggestions," Claudia said. It was a signature line that Emilia recognized meant *shut up*. "Today we have to discuss something more urgent."

"Urgent?"

"Team building," Claudia announced, as if broadcasting the national *lotéria* winner.

"Team building," Emilia repeated warily. She perched on the edge of a plush upholstered chair, part of a suite that gave Claudia's office all the warmth of a furniture store. "What did you have in mind?"

Claudia clasped her hands together. "I want to help my

team achieve success. Don't you agree success is important?"

"Sure."

"Don't you think that being able to rely on each other is important, too?"

"Sure," Emilia said again.

Claudia nodded encouragingly, as if Emilia had said something significant. "We should know each other's strengths and weaknesses."

"All of the Las Palomas candidates, you mean?" Emilia questioned. "Is this about the training program? It's not complete yet—."

"No, no." Claudia blinked in surprise. "That's not what I meant. I'm sure you have the training program well in hand."

She smoothed her hair, today pulled into a glossy side ponytail draped over one shoulder. A crystal and emerald brooch decorated the opposite lapel of her sage green skirt suit. Emilia knew that her own outfit of skinny black skirt, white tee, and cotton jacket with flat sandals was far too casual for this place.

"When I said team," Claudia went on. "I meant those I supervise."

As far as Emilia could tell, that was about three people. The rest of the staff didn't belong to Las Palomas but were either on loan from the mayor's office or public relations consultants from a marketing company.

"What did you have in mind?" Emilia asked. She

thought about team building events she could contrive to miss. "Group lunch? Drinks somewhere after work?"

Claudia beamed at her. "Not exactly." She handed Emilia a magazine sized booklet. "It's a strengths finder questionnaire. You fill it out and all your personal strengths and weaknesses are revealed in a way that tells us how to build an action plan to maximize your good habits and address the bad ones."

"You want to talk about my bad habits?" Emilia demanded incredulously.

"I mean identify areas for improvement. We all have them." Claudia looked away from Emilia's unblinking stare and gave a self-deprecating little laugh. "Fill it out right away so we can get started on an action plan to help you make positive changes."

"Positive changes?" Emilia echoed. "This sounds like a witch hunt."

Claudia gave a nervous trill. "Of course not. I told you. It's a strengths finder instrument. All the big companies use them. It's our team's prescription for success." She smiled, no doubt pleased to have remembered the right slogan.

"You said this was team building," Emilia said. "Will you be doing one of these questionnaires, too?"

"I did one long ago," Claudia said. "With my mentor."

"Who's that?"

Claudia gave another trill of laughter. "No one you know."

"No, I guess I don't." Emilia rolled the questionnaire

booklet into a stick.

"Let's review your answers on Monday." Claudia's voice followed Emilia out the door.

Kurt roared with laughter when Emilia recounted the conversation. And again when she told him that she'd trashed the strengths finder booklet in the dumpster behind the building.

CHAPTER 14

Standing in the shade of the little church's side entrance, Emilia could see that Silvio had lost weight and his gray crew cut had grown out. He wasn't wearing his trademark white tee, jeans, and leather jacket, nor a police uniform. Emilia had never known him to wear anything else and was inexplicably shaken by the sight of him in white button-down shirt and gray trousers.

"Rucker." Silvio shook Kurt's hand. "Thanks for coming." He turned to Emilia and extended his hand. "You, too, Cruz."

Emilia wanted to hug him, or at least greet him with the traditional kisses between friends. But Silvio's bearing invited no familiarity.

The only family standing with Silvio was his cousin Antonio and his wife, both of whom Emilia had met the day she fetched the house key. Isabel must not have had any family; if she had they would be with Silvio, accepting condolences.

Emilia introduced Kurt to Antonio and his wife and saw the shadow of surprise cross their faces. Once again, Kurt stuck out, tall and blonde and wholly noticeable in his expensive suit and tie. Emilia wore the simple and elegant black shift she'd bought when she and Kurt first started dating. Her black eye had faded away and her makeup was minimal.

Their reflections in the penthouse bedroom mirror had said *sober and tasteful*. But both she and Kurt were overdressed for El Roble. Emilia felt out of touch.

The queue waiting to go into the church wound around the block. All of El Roble was there, or so it seemed. The mourners at Isabel de Silvio's funeral were working class people who lived close to death and violence and had little to show for it besides a tenuous grip on survival. Most of the women wept openly and the men looked grim.

No one wore a hat with a circle logo.

There was no time to talk to Silvio in the receiving line and Emilia reluctantly walked into the church. Perhaps she'd get a chance to reason with him later. His badge was in her shoulder bag. Kurt had seen her put it there and raised his eyebrows. But she was still determined to try.

Inside the church, the coffin on the altar was closed and draped with a blanket of red roses. A framed picture of a very young Isabel faced the congregation. A guitarist sat on a folding chair and played softly.

Emilia guided Kurt to the line of people shuffling to pray in front of the coffin, wanting to say farewell to Isabel yet dreading it at the same time. When their turn came, Kurt knelt next to Emilia and took her hand. Emilia tried to say a silent Hail Mary but the words were pushed aside by indecision. If she was able to talk to Silvio, should she tell him about the ballistics report which had cost Hernandez his life? Would it convince him to rejoin the force or send Silvio headlong into danger?

They left the casket and found a pew as the church gradually filled with mourners. Emilia saw Macias and Sandor kneel briefly in front of the coffin. Numerous uniformed cops came in and she recognized several of the Ball Busters who'd gone door to door in the days after the shooting.

Finally, the church was full to bursting. Family, neighborhood friends, cops and the street kids who'd relied on Isabel for a few decent meals each week filled the pews and the aisles. Silvio and his cousin took their places in the front pew, the guitarist stopped playing, and the priest boomed out a prayer from the back of the church. All stood.

Emilia saw more familiar faces in the pews at the back of the church. Felipe Garcia was there, accompanied by a young woman, as well as an older couple. They were probably his parents.

The priest and his acolytes came down the aisle, chanting and swinging the censer and leaving a wispy trail of smoke. The acrid scent of incense filled Emilia's nostrils. When the small procession reached the altar, the priest motioned for the congregation to sit. Emilia sank into her seat, not before recognizing someone who moved more slowly than the others, as if like Kurt he didn't know Catholic rituals.

It was Victor Obregon Sosa, wearing yet another black suit with matching shirt.

"Fuck," Emilia said under her breath and got a startled look from Kurt.

The thought of Obregon coming to the funeral gnawed at her throughout the sad ceremony. Obregon and Silvio were bitter enemies. Obregon had once tried to set up Silvio for a murder rap and had implied Silvio was to blame for Isabel's death, too. As head of the police union for the state of Guerrero, it was a kind gesture to come in an official capacity, but Obregon didn't strike Emilia as someone who did anything out of kindness.

As the funeral went on, the air grew hot and sticky. The congregation waved paper fans handed out by the undertaker and emblazoned with his name and address. People wept continuously. Children cried in the pews and the street kids crouching in the aisles shuffled restlessly.

Emilia kept her own tears at bay with a clean tissue from her bag. She could see Silvio in front, looking carved from stone. He'd lost the woman with whom he'd spent half his life, the dream of being a father, his job, and probably his home. His wife's killer was still on the loose. But he displayed no emotion, no grief. Even during the priest's touching homily, the set of his shoulders never changed.

Finally the Mass was over, the censor swung a final time, and the pallbearers proceeded down the aisle with the casket. Silvio and his cousin followed. As if it had been choreographed, all the neighborhood children spilled into the center aisle and swarmed around the casket. Rio should have been among them, but of course he wasn't.

There was no music, just continued weeping as the congregation left the church.

Outside, Emilia and Kurt were swept up in the stream of mourners walking behind the casket to the cemetery. Someone handed out candles in little cups and they joined the procession as their candles twinkled against the hazy twilight. Emilia's eyes kept watering and she would have stumbled more than once along the route if she hadn't had her arm linked with Kurt's.

By the time they got to the cemetery, dusk had fallen. Everyone surrounded the hole in the ground, creating a wreath of candlelight. The street kids ranged uncertainly on the fringes of the crowd. Emilia saw a few glue bottles.

The priest said a blessing and the casket, still covered in red roses, was lowered into its resting place. The priest shook holy water over the flowers and began a decade of the rosary. He was joined by the congregation. The words of the Hail Mary filled the cemetery with emotion.

Silvio stood stony-faced, with his arms crossed, as the familiar prayer was repeated over and over. Again, his cousin Antonio stood next to him, an arm around his wife. The couple's children pressed against their parents.

Someone cried loudly.

Finally the priest intoned the painful words. "Ashes to ashes. Dust to dust."

Everyone waited for Silvio to throw a traditional handful of earth, a rose, or other memento on top of the coffin.

He stripped off his wedding ring and dropped it into the

grave.

An audible gasp rippled through the crowd.

Someone began to sing *Ave Maria*. Others joined in.

Finally, it was over.

Like a cloud passing, the tension lifted. The aftermath became a social event, with people chatting in small groups and slowly making their way toward the gates of the cemetery.

Macias and Sandor joined Emilia and Kurt. Both wore slacks and jackets but no tie. Sandor had on sunglasses.

Emilia introduced them to Kurt, stumbling a little over first names; they never used them in the squadroom and it took her a moment to remember.

"You're the guy who got the mayor out of the fire at the El Tigre restaurant," Macias said.

"Hope I never do anything like it again," Kurt said and shook hands with both detectives.

"How's Loyola?" Emilia asked. "Last time I saw him he looked pretty rough."

"Still in the hospital," Macias said. "Broken jaw and nose."

"Some argument," Kurt marveled.

"Loyola is still trying to run the squadroom from the hospital," Macias said.

"Even the investigation into Isabel's murder?" Emilia asked.

"You'd think that with all the people here today," Sandor said. "Somebody would have seen something. But we've got nothing."

"What about the hot line?" Emilia pressed. "Or the circle man tip?"

"Nothing." Sandor shook his head. "We actually printed out a bunch of circular sports logos and walked the neighborhood, asking about your circle man. Waste of time."

"Silvio told me he tried to find the kid who gave me the tip," Emilia said. "He found out that the boy died of a heroin overdose."

"*Rayos*," Macias swore. He pulled out a small notebook and scribbled in it. "We've heard that Silvio's been all over El Roble, asking questions. Talking to everybody who'd ever placed a bet with him."

"This is going to turn out to be all about his bookie business," Sandor said. "That's what Loyola thinks, anyway."

"I think it's relevant that the kid is dead," Emilia said. "Strange timing, don't you think?"

"You talked to an addict, Cruz," Macias said. "Addicts die all the time."

Emilia looked across the cemetery where Silvio was still with the priest. "What about the ballistics report?" she asked. *Tell me you know the same gun was used to kill both Isabel and Vega.*

"Dead end there, too." Macias flipped his notebook closed.

"No El Trio connection," Emilia said leadingly.

Sandor shook his head. "Everyone is chasing their tails

over the Hernandez murder, if you want to talk about El Trio. Shook up Ibarra, that's for sure."

Silvio was still by the graveside with his cousin, speaking to the priest. Mourners slowly passed through the gates of the cemetery, retracing the procession's path back to the church. The street kids drifted along, begging for money.

"Did you see Obregon?" Emilia asked Macias and Sandor. "He was in the church but he didn't come to the cemetery."

"No kidding?" Macias raised his eyebrows in surprise. "He hates Silvio's guts. But I guess that's what we have the union for. Suck dues out of our pockets and show up when family is gunned down."

The two detectives said goodbye and left the cemetery, falling in with other mourners still clutching lit candles.

"Detective Cruz?" It was Felipe Garcia. "It's good to see you again."

The long hair was just as distinctive as the day they'd met but today Felipe was dressed in a dark shirt and pants, a somber contrast to his cheerful store uniform. Emilia introduced Kurt. In return, Felipe introduced his wife and parents. They all murmured sympathetic things about Silvio. The elder Garcias looked tired and upset.

"Thank you for the socks," Emilia said when Felipe said they had to be going. "They're great."

"Anytime you need more, let me know." Felipe gave her a sad smile and moved on.

The crowds thinned. The priest gathered his acolytes and headed for the gate. Silvio and his cousin's family left the graveside.

"Wait for me at the car, okay?" Emilia said to Kurt.

"You sure this is the right time to talk to him?" he asked.

"I'm sure."

Kurt kissed Emilia's forehead and passed through the cemetery gate.

Emilia fell into step with Silvio. "Franco, can we talk for a moment?"

Silvio nodded to his cousin Antonio to go ahead without him. A moment later, Emilia and Silvio were alone in the cemetery except for the gravediggers piling dirt on top of Isabel's coffin. Their lantern threw a wide pool of light around the grave.

"A last goodbye, Cruz?" Silvio's expression betrayed neither sadness nor friendship. Nor anything else.

"What are you going to do now?" Emilia asked.

"I'm out of business as a bookie," he said. "Without the ledgers, settling up on the last match went all to shit. My reputation is gone. I'm going to get rid of the house. Maybe pick up some work as a trainer."

"A trainer?" Emilia repeated. "You mean, a boxing trainer?"

"Yes," he said. "My name still means something in certain circles."

Emilia pulled his badge out of her purse. "This still means something to a lot of people, Franco," she said. "Did you see all the cops here today? The department needs you."

Silvio stared at her, his expression flinty. "Did you forget what happened? I'm done with being a cop."

Emilia grabbed his arm. "You're throwing away your career and your pension. You could walk in the squadroom tomorrow and do exactly what you wanted. Loyola owes you and he knows it. Go collect."

"Peddle your advice somewhere else," Silvio said and threw off her hand.

The rattle of dirt falling on the coffin made Emilia flinch. She shoved the shield at him but Silvio made no move to take it. "This badge is your key to finding out who killed Isabel," she said. "Unless you're on the inside, no one is going to tell you anything."

"Spare me the lecture," Silvio retorted. "I'll find the bastard who did this myself."

"Don't be stupid," Emilia exclaimed. "This isn't as simple as finding some *pendejo* and taking him apart. The answers aren't all here in El Roble. Things are going on, Franco. You need to be inside. You need access."

"Fuck off," Silvio snapped "Who are you to tell me what to do?"

"Your partner," Emilia said. "And partners—."

"I never wanted to work with you," Silvio interrupted nastily. "You were a shit partner. At least one good thing came out of this. I'll never have to work with you again."

His words were a savage blow out of the blue. Emilia gaped at him. "*Rayos,* Franco," she swore. "I don't deserve—."

Silvio grabbed Emilia by both upper arms and shook her hard. The badge flew out of her hand. Her eyes watered and her teeth chattered.

"Did you hear me, Cruz?" he thundered into her face. "You're a shit detective and you made a shit partner. Do your pretty job for Carlota in your fucking big office. Better yet, stay home with Hollywood and pump out a couple of babies. It's the only way you're going to hold on to somebody like him."

Silvio thrust her aside and walked away.

Nauseous and dizzy, Emilia nearly fell over. She heard footsteps crunch on the gravel path as Silvio left the cemetery. The gravediggers continued to shovel dirt into the grave, oblivious to the exchange by the gate, as they argued over the Copa America standings.

Honduras and Bolivia were still hanging on. Argentina couldn't dominate forever. Mexico had won its bracket but how much farther could the team go?

New moonlight glinted on Silvio's badge cradled in the grass a few feet away. It took a few minutes before Emilia felt steady enough to pick it up.

CHAPTER 15

"Your name is Natividad Leyva Roma." Emilia scanned the application. The woman standing across from her was a 21-year-old high school graduate with a certificate from an accounting school. Her English was excellent.

Emilia looked up. "Why do you think you're qualified to become a police officer?"

"I'm used to working long hours," Natividad said. She had on jeans and a clean white cotton shirt with short sleeves that revealed heavily muscled arms. Like Emilia, she wore dark hair pulled back into a ponytail. "I can think fast. I'm honest. I'll work hard. Do what I'm told."

Out of the 1900 women who showed up that morning in response to the advertisements, fewer than a quarter completed the writing sample and English test. A dozen uniforms kept order as those who passed waited to be interviewed. Ten at a time formed a line to talk to Emilia as she sat behind a table with Paola to keep the paperwork organized.

Emilia's first victory, which Claudia had yet to recognize, was approval to use the gymnasium at the central police building, the same gymnasium where Emilia had won the hand-to-hand competition over the other patrol officers competing for a single detective slot three years ago. Emilia had also gotten permission for two dozen uniforms to keep order, which allowed her to divide the huge space into processing zones, just as she'd imagined.

In the first zone, candidates completed an application and a copy was made of their *cédula* identity card and school records. The second zone was for the English and writing tests administered by a team from the police academy.

Emilia commanded the third zone. She was the final decision point, selecting 60 women representing the initial cut.

The fourth zone was a circle of folding chairs where the lucky ones waited as their *cédula* was checked for a criminal record. Those who made it through that hurdle received a packet of instructions for training. Some would drop out, others would flunk the physical fitness and psychological tests. Eventually, Emilia would have the final 30 Las Palomas patrol officers Carlota wanted on the streets within a month.

Natividad looked like a good candidate but the woman's essay was terrible. Her handwriting was loopy and girlish, her spelling that of a student who hadn't paid attention in class. She'd need to be taught how to write the basics, much less a police report. It was too bad they didn't have time for that.

Emilia looked up and shook her head. "I'm sorry, but you don't have the qualifications we're looking for." She pointed past the line of waiting women to the exit. "Thank you for coming. There is a small *dispensa* you can pick up on your way out."

That was Claudia's idea. Every woman who didn't make the cut got a small box of household staples to compensate for the time they'd spent applying. It was a nice gesture that would go far in promoting Las Palomas even before it was up and running, and Emilia had to give her credit.

"I can't go," Natividad said. She spoke well, as if her education had been better than her writing sample suggested.

"Excuse me?" Emilia lifted her pen to mark the woman's paperwork as Disqualified.

"I need this job." Her voice shook with nerves.

Emilia put down the application packet. "You're not fully qualified. They should have told you after you took the writing test. I'm sorry."

"I'll do anything for this job," Natividad said. She repeated the sentence in English.

Emilia hesitated. There was an intensity and resolve about the woman that she liked. The other candidates who passed every test were giggly girls in spandex and halters, unsure of what they were signing up to do and more interested in their cell phones than in following directions.

She leafed through the girl's paperwork again. "You work on one of the boats at Playa Olvidada?"

"For now," Natividad said.

"That's a tough environment," Emilia observed. She looked at the woman's hands. They were well groomed instead of chapped and red from pulling in fishing nets and gutting fish.

"I do accounts for the fishermen so they know how much the broker should pay for each catch," Natividad said, as if she'd known what Emilia was thinking. "They don't mess with me."

"Okay." Emilia slid a numbered card across the table and indicated the chairs in zone four. "Take this and wait over there."

Natividad pressed the ticket to her heart as if it was gold. "Thank you, thank you," she breathed. "You won't be sorry."

Paola took Natividad's file. The next woman in line put her papers on the table.

Emilia started to read. Two hundred hopefuls to go.

Two hours and three cups of coffee later, Emilia found herself looking at a girl who couldn't be more than 16 years old. She was a tiny thing with pencil-thin wrists and eyes the size of saucers. She wore a pink tee shirt and skinny jeans and had a mass of black curly hair corralled by a banana clip.

"Can I see your *cédula*?" Emilia asked.

The girl's mouth hardened but she opened her purse and dug out a wallet. She held it for Emilia to look at the identity card through a cloudy plastic sleeve.

"Take it out," Emilia prompted.

"You can see it," the girl said.

Emilia plucked the wallet out of the girl's hand and extracted the *cédula*. It proclaimed that Tina Maria Velasco was 22 and lived in the upscale Las Brisas neighborhood. Emilia held the card to the light and saw where it had been carefully cut and another picture substituted. The forgery wasn't bad, but it wasn't the best she'd ever seen, either.

"Paola," Emilia said, turning away from the candidate. "Could you get some more file folders?"

"Now?" Paola asked, pen poised over her notes.

"Yes," Emilia said. "I'd also like a latte. Do you remember where the kitchen is? Get one for yourself as well."

Paola didn't have to be told twice. She trotted off, her dark suit incongruous amid the noisy sea of women in casual clothing.

The young candidate was still at the table. "How much did it cost you?" Emilia asked.

"Three hundred pesos."

"You got a bargain." Emilia handed back both the wallet and the false identification card. "How old are you?"

"Twenty-one," Tina Maria replied.

"Sixteen," Emilia countered.

"Seventeen," Tina Maria admitted, her voice barely a whisper.

Emilia returned the girl's paperwork. "The exit is over

there. You can—.”

“Do this job,” Tina Maria finished the sentence. “Doesn’t matter how hard it is. I’ve already done harder.”

There was an unexpected steel behind the angel face and cloud of hair. Emilia stared across the table. Tina Maria stared back, her jaw set.

“What else is fake here?” Emilia asked, indicating the application papers.

“Nothing.”

Emilia read the girl’s application. She’d gotten high marks for her English. Her essay was very good and her handwriting small and neat. Still, she was a child with fake identification. “I’m sorry,” Emilia sighed. “You can pick up a *dispensa*—.”

“No,” Tina Maria said. “I will be the best you have. I’ll work harder than anyone else here. You’ll see.”

Emilia shook her head. “You’re too young and too small.”

The young girl looked around the huge gymnasium and at the seating area where selectees in tight jeans and spandex tops checked their cell phones. She put both hands flat on the table. “There was no size or age requirement in the newspaper. Unless you lied.”

Emilia saw ugly burn marks on the back of the girl’s right hand. She had a larger scar on the inside of her left arm, possibly from the edge of a hot iron.

“You’re a *muchacha planta,* aren’t you?” Emilia asked.

“Yes.”

“What about your family?” Emilia asked. “Do they know

you want to be a cop?"

Tina Maria shook her head. "My family doesn't live in Acapulco."

Emilia considered. Tina Maria was a live-in maid, probably from a small village in the state of Guerrero. She might be the family's only source of income. No doubt Las Palomas would more than double her salary. "But if you join Las Palomas," Emilia said. "You'll have to find a place to live."

Tina Maria lifted her chin to indicate the women who already had tickets. "One of them will need a place, too," she said. "We can share.

"Being a cop is much harder," Emilia cautioned. "And dangerous."

"I love Acapulco," the girl said impulsively. "I can do something to make it better. Talk to people. Tell them where to go and all the things there are to see."

Emilia was suddenly swept back in time, to a shabby interrogation room at the police station, and a conversation with a thickset man. She'd said something similar to a detective named Rico Portillo and he'd given her a chance to become the first female police detective in Acapulco.

Rico was dead now and she'd never really thanked him for the chance he'd given her.

"Okay," Emilia said. Against her better judgement, she slid a ticket across the table. "You've made the first cut."

The girl would probably wash out in the physical fitness test, but there was something about her that Emilia liked very much.

The very last candidate was named Rosalita Riva Diaz. She was a striking woman about Emilia's age. She was the only candidate to wear a dress and the clingy fabric accentuated her considerable curves. Expensive sandals showed off manicured toes. The woman wore her shoulder-length hair in loose curls and her wary smile was brightened with red lipstick.

Emilia had seen that smile before, on too many downtown street corners.

Mumbling something to Paola about stretching her legs, Emilia took the application and slipped out from behind the table. She steered Rosalita a few steps away.

"You're a working girl," Emilia said.

The woman's smile faded into a thin line. "What makes you say that?"

"I've been around, too."

"Does that disqualify me?" Rosalita asked.

"Hooker to cop is pretty unusual," Emilia said.

Rosalita hitched the wary smile back in place. "You need somebody with street smarts."

"Who put you up to this?" Emilia pressed. "Who wants you to be their eyes inside?"

"I want a better life," the other woman said flatly. There was no guile or pretense in her eyes.

"Being a cop is hard," Emilia said.

"I said better life," Rosalita said. "Not an easy one."

Emilia looked down at the application. Rosalita knew English. The essay was fine, her handwriting was tidy. Her high school graduation information could be genuine.

"You got an arrest record?" Emilia asked.

"No."

"You know I'll find out."

"Go ahead. I don't have a record."

"You're an inside girl," Emilia ventured. Inside girls went to hotels to service tourists and were less vulnerable than common street walkers. Rosalita's pimp would be a fixer inside the hotel who set up the appointments.

"Yes."

"What about your pimp?"

"That's my problem, not yours." Rosalita didn't flinch or look away.

"Are you clean?"

The woman extended a bare arm. There were no needle tracks. Her fingernails were short and polished; no long nails for scooping cocaine up her nose.

"I drank," Rosalita said. "But that's all."

"And now?"

"It won't be a problem, I promise you."

"You have to pass the psychological and medical exams," Emilia warned. "Plus the physical fitness test."

"I'll pass."

Emilia pretended to study the application again, but her thoughts weren't on the printed page.

On one hand, Rosalita had the potential to be a decent patrol officer. Her test scores were high and she'd have the survival skills many of the other candidates didn't.

On the other hand, Emilia didn't believe Rosalita's reason why she wanted to be a cop. The distance between the two occupations was too great. She had a motive for joining Las Palomas and Emilia wanted to know what it was.

But the bottom line was that if Claudia knew Emilia had hired a hooker, she'd probably have a stroke.

Emilia handed Rosalita a ticket.

CHAPTER 16

The first week of training for the Las Palomas selectees was hectic. Claudia insisted on making a cheerleading speech every morning to the patrol officer candidates but other than that left everything to Emilia. Thankfully, instructors from the police academy were there with lesson plans and tests. Mornings were devoted to classroom instruction and the afternoons were for physical fitness training and instruction in the use of nightsticks, handcuffs, and pepper spray.

Emilia joined the afternoon sessions whenever she could but her administrative responsibilities were endless. No one else in the Las Palomas front office had a clue about police procedures or even the hierarchy of the police department. One minion or another was continually at Emilia's door with questions and problems for her to solve, keeping Emilia in the office long after everyone else had gone for the day. She barely saw Kurt at all.

But by Friday, a routine had been established, giving Emilia a chance to get her head above water. She grabbed the opportunity to get out of the office, which is how she found herself in the state's attorney general's office with a business card in her hand and a weak smile on her face. She was taking a huge risk requesting an update on their investigation into the Salinas murder; hopefully word would not get out that she was asking questions related to El Trio.

"Thank you for coming, Detective Cruz," the attorney said, opening the door to the conference room.

Emilia took the seat he indicated at the conference table. The man's name was Sergio Noriega Menendez and he was the senior investigating attorney. He'd been the late Javier Salinas Arroliza's boss.

Another man and woman, both well dressed in business suits, came into the conference room. Noriega introduced them as Javier Riviera Cortez and Josefina Vargas Guzmán. They were followed by another woman wearing a dark cotton dress and white apron and pushing a trolley laden with a coffee service.

Once they'd all been served, Noriega looked at Emilia expectantly. "We're very interested in what you have to tell us about the police investigation into Javier's murder."

Emilia lowered her cup into its saucer, too surprised to even take a sip of coffee. "I was under the impression we'd be discussing your investigation," she said.

"Our investigation?" Noriega frowned. "What are you talking about."

Emilia went cold. She distinctly remembered Chief Salazar telling her that there would be no unified El Trio investigation and that the state's attorney general's office would conduct their own investigation into Salinas's death while the *federales* did the same for Espinosa. Vega's death was being investigated by the Acapulco police and Chief

Salazar's office was in charge of that.

"Well, your inquiry," she ventured.

Noriega jabbed a finger into the air. "Your colleagues specifically asked us not to investigate. Said the Acapulco police department was all over it. Are you now telling me nothing has been done?"

Emilia took out her notebook and a pen and made a show of flipping through the pages of the notebook. "And you spoke to . . ." She let the question hang in the air.

Noriega looked at his colleagues with an expression like thunder. He was probably in his early fifties, with wavy hair distracting from a receding hairline. His colleagues were at least 20 years younger, with the weary looks of good people who had too much work and too little life. "Neither gave me a business card," he said. "I think I was so upset that day I forgot to ask for one."

"Lopez, or Loya," Josefina said. She was pretty, with long straight hair worn parted on the side. She wore a pale gray dress with a multi-strand silver necklace worth two months of Emilia's salary. "Something like that."

"He wore glasses," Riviera said. "The other was shorter. Stocky. Smelled like cigarettes."

Loyola and Ibarra. Emilia swallowed her surprise and nodded as if their names were written in her notebook. Inside, she was seething.

The three attorneys looked at her expectantly.

"We've had a miscommunication," Emilia managed.

"I hold your department responsible," Noriega barked.

Madre de Dios, but this was not what she had expected. "I have a few questions," Emilia said. "When I get back to the office, we can get things straightened out."

"This is deplorable." Noriega banged a fist on the table. "I don't know what you police spend your days doing, but it isn't catching murderers."

Emilia deliberately looked at the younger attorneys to give Noriega a chance to simmer down. "Can you each tell me the last time you saw Salinas?"

They had all seen Salinas the day he was killed. The attorney had left the office a little after 9:00 pm. That wasn't particularly late for him; the man often stayed in the office until 10:00 or 11:00 pm. He didn't have much of a social life. After work, Salinas either ate at a restaurant with a book or had a meal at home prepared by his housekeeper.

"Married?" Emilia asked.

"No," Josefina replied quickly. "Javier worked almost all the time. If Javier handled a case, you could depend that it would be perfect. Every detail considered, every thread followed. He never forgot a promise or let you down."

Noriega did most of the talking after that. Salinas had no commitments besides work during the week that anyone knew about. Salinas was an excellent attorney who knew the risks associated with his position. He kept a low profile and didn't attract the wrong sort of attention. Although he often handled important cases, he didn't seek out publicity.

"But he was a regular at several restaurants," Emilia said. "Do you know which?"

Noriega shook his head.

"The Octagon," Josefina interjected. "Tahoma. Leonardo's. El Jazz, but not as much as the others."

Noriega glared at Josefina. The look carried an undercurrent of hostility that was more than annoyance at an underling speaking out of turn.

"I have some pictures I'd like you to look at," Emilia said. She got out the graduation picture from Loyola's file, Espinosa's portrait from the newspaper, and the photo of Silvio and Isabel taken from their bedroom.

Emilia spread them in a row so the three attorneys could see them all at once. "Do you recognize anyone in these pictures?"

"Of course," Josefina said immediately. She put her finger on the graduation photo, indicating a man in a suit. "That's Javier."

Her finger was on the man standing third from the left. "Are you sure?" Emilia asked.

"Of course," Josefina said. "He had the same photo in his office. It was his graduation from a course he took in *El Norte* two or three years ago. There was some sort of exchange. Law enforcement from all over Mexico went."

"Do you recognize anyone else in the picture?" Emilia asked. Salinas and Vega knew each other. Trained together. Probably were friends. A little shiver of excitement went down Emilia's spine.

"No," Josefina said.

Emilia tapped Silvio's picture. "What about the man

in this photo?" she asked. "Did Salinas know him? Did you ever see the two of them together?"

"No." Josefina shook her head. Both of her colleagues did the same.

Emilia put all the pictures back in her bag. "I'd like to look through Salinas's office."

Noriega looked angry again. "It's been well over a month, Detective. His personal effects were boxed up and sent to his family."

"What about his cases?" Emilia asked. "There could be a connection."

"We thought of that while the police were chasing their tails," Noriega huffed.

"Of course," Emilia said. She guessed he was a difficult man at the best of times. "I'd like to get briefed on his cases. There may be leads that the police should follow up."

"You're not authorized," Noriega said testily. "These are extremely sensitive investigations and we're not in the business of distributing the information. If we had found anything that appeared to tie to Javier's murder, we would have let the police know already."

"But—."

"We've found nothing for the police," Noriega said with finality.

Emilia took a deep breath. She had no jurisdiction and no ability to force him to share anything. "I understand. Perhaps you could give me his family's contact information."

Noriega shook his head. "His next of kin has asked not to

be contacted further. Discretion for reasons of safety. I'm sure you understand."

Again, his voice had a cutting edge of finality to it.

Emilia realized that Josefina was looking down at her lap, as if she was no longer part of the conversation.

Noriega stood up. "If you'll excuse us, Detective, we have to get back to work. Javier's passing has left us with quite a bit of unfinished business. And every day brings that much more."

Emilia rose, as did the others. "Thank you for seeing me," Emilia said. "I'll be in touch if there are any developments in the case."

"I'm sure you will," Noriega said, his voice riddled with sarcasm. He didn't offer to shake her hand.

Two minutes later, as Emilia nodded to the uniformed security guard in the underground parking lot, she heard the clatter of high heels running on cement.

"Detective Cruz?" It was Josefina, slightly out of breath.

"Hello." Emilia smiled. "Did I forget something?"

"I wanted to give you my card." The attorney held out a small square.

"Thank you."

Josefina looked around the parking garage. It wasn't a very busy place. The uniformed security guards watched an old man wash a car two rows over.

"Noriega has his car washed every other day," Josefina said. "He likes things to be tidy."

"So it would seem," Emilia replied.

Josefina folded her arms, hands clutching opposite elbows. "I'm sorry my colleagues weren't more forthcoming," she said.

"It's a hard situation," Emilia said carefully.

"Javier didn't have much family." Josefina looked around again.

"My car is over here." Emilia gestured vaguely away from the security outpost.

Josefina followed Emilia around the side of the Suburban. "I only have a minute," she said. "But I thought you should know the whole story about Javier's family."

"I'd appreciate anything that could help," Emilia said.

"Javier was gay."

Emilia raised her eyebrows. "Do you think that had something to do with his murder?"

Josefina shivered and hugged herself tighter. "I don't know. It wasn't common knowledge. Noriega suspected. But he doesn't approve of alternate lifestyles and Javier knew he'd never have much of a career if he was open about it."

"But you knew," Emilia said leadingly.

"We were friends." Josefina teared up and pressed a finger to the inside of her eye. "He even introduced me and my husband to his partner. We were pretty surprised to meet Dario Delgado."

"Dario Delgado," Emilia repeated in disbelief. "The actor?"

"Yes," Josefina said. "They were extremely discreet. But Javier went to Mexico City at least once a month and I know Dario came here. He's got a place up the coast. In Ixtapa."

"Are you sure?" Emilia asked. "I mean, *Dario Delgado*."

Dario Delgado wasn't just an actor, he was a *telenovela* mega-star who'd gone on to blaze a new path in both English and Spanish-language movies. He was every inch a hell-raising, hit-making, *macho* Latino hunk who oozed testosterone and had saved the world on screen twice in the past year. The entertainment news always reported on his latest break-ups with super models and night club antics both in Hollywood and Mexico City.

"I know," Josefina said, with a noise between a laugh and a sniff. "He's nice."

"He's really gay?" It was hard to believe Dario Delgado was the gay lover of a workaholic attorney.

"Javier invited me and my husband up to Ixtapa once," Josefina said. "Not what you'd expect. Nothing like what's in the tabloids. Apparently, that's all drummed up by Dario's publicists."

"I don't suppose you could get me in touch with him," Emilia said.

"I can try," Josefina said. "It might help Dario to know someone is trying to find whoever killed Javier."

She took Emilia's card, the one with her first name and cell phone number on it.

"Thank you," Emilia said.

Josefina nodded and made to move away, but stopped. "The other people in the pictures you showed us," she said. "More murder victims?"

"Yes," Emilia said.

"Were they gay, too?"

"No," Emilia said.

"So lifestyle probably isn't a factor?" Josefina asked hopefully.

"I don't think it mattered who any of them loved," Emilia said.

CHAPTER 17

Emilia found herself worrying about Loyola's possible role in the El Trio murders all weekend like a dog with a bone. Both Loyola and Ibarra had weighed in on the squadroom's impromptu discussions about the El Trio killings without ever giving any indication they had gone to the state's attorney general's office after Salinas was killed. Why start an investigation into Salinas's murder without telling anyone else? How far had they taken the case? What were they hiding about the Salinas case? Was it connected to the ballistics report Loyola hid and which cost Hernandez his life?

Loyola had no motive to kill any of the El Trio victims and had been in the hospital when Hernandez was killed. Would Ibarra have killed Hernandez for Loyola? Emilia didn't think so. She'd been with the stocky detective when he identified the body. He wasn't that good an actor.

She didn't have any answers, of course, just more questions.

When Kurt went for a marathon bike ride Saturday afternoon, Emilia settled into the office in the penthouse and searched online for more scraps of information. The afternoon flashed by. When the front door opened and Kurt called hello, Emilia was surprised to see how late it was.

"Hey." Kurt came into the office, the pegs on the bottom of his cycling shoes clacking against the floor. "Did you forget? It's Mexico versus Honduras tonight and we have the big event in the bar."

"*Madre de Dios*," Emilia groaned. "I forgot all about it."

Emilia had skipped over the sports news but everyone in the country had high hopes that Mexico's team would score a slot in the Copa America semi-finals. The hotel had transformed the beach with huge screens for tonight's decisive match, with a buffet in the Pasodoble Bar.

Kurt tossed his bike helmet on the desk and bent to unfasten the Velcro straps on his shoes. "Did you see the report from Olivas?"

"Ronaldo Olivas?" Emilia asked. Ronaldo Olivas Camacho was a former cop from Monterrey and head of security for the Palacio Réal.

"Yes." Kurt got both shoes off and padded to the desk. "I meant to leave it for you."

He looked through the papers on the desk and pulled out a file folder. "Here," he said.

Emilia's jaw dropped as she read the security chief's report, which included several low resolution black and white pictures. The Palacio Réal's security cameras maintained coverage of the entire length of the private road linking the hotel complex with the highway. The vehicle in which Hernandez had been found was caught emerging from a villa midway along the road before it parked in the underbrush where Emilia and Kurt found it. The villa in question was empty and for sale. The sellers had not given permission for it to be used by anyone. Guards working the *privada* gate had been questioned; all said that no one matching the photos came through the gate on foot between the time marked on the video feed and the time Hernandez's body was discovered.

The bathroom shower turned on as Emilia studied the photos. The best image showed a man walking away from the vehicle in the direction of the *privada*. He wore a hooded sweatshirt that obscured his face.

Was this the El Trio killer? Between the camera angle and the grainy picture quality, there wasn't much Emilia could glean. The man was slender and of medium height. He worked alone and knew how to drive. He didn't have a hat with a circular logo.

Definitely not Loyola, Ibarra, or anyone else she knew.

"Aren't you going to change?" Kurt asked from the doorway, dressed in jeans and a white linen *guayabera* shirt.

Emilia put on a jersey tank dress and sandals. They went down to the Pasodoble Bar, where trouble greeted them. The projection equipment had a glitch, an order of liquor was missing, the hotel's reservation software crashed, and the extra waiters needed for tonight's event were late.

But none of this was apparent to the hotel guests enjoying the pre-match steel drum band and cruising the buffet line to scoop up *ceviche* in puff pastry shells, stuffed *nopales* with pomegranate salsa, truffle risotto, and a dozen other delicacies from Jacques's kitchen. The chef presided over a huge grill sizzling with mouth-watering lamb chops, bacon-wrapped slices of beef *lomo*, and shrimp the size of Emilia's hand. She went through the buffet line with two plates and grinned as Jacques heaped them high.

Emilia found a table on the bottom level of the Pasodoble and a waiter brought her a pitcher of mojitos. She ate slowly, wondering what Kurt was doing and if he could take a break to eat.

Right on schedule, the huge screens lit up, first with music videos, and then with the Copa America match. To the delight of the guests, sparklers soared into the night sky as the match began.

Forty-five minutes later, Kurt sat down next to Emilia and thanked her for the waiting plate of food. "That's it," he declared as he tackled a lamb chop. "I'm going to Las Vegas and hiring an assistant manager."

"Why Las Vegas?" Emilia asked.

"I've still got contacts there," Kurt said.

Before Emilia could say anything, a young employee from the reception desk skidded to a stop next to Kurt's chair. "Señor, I'm sorry to disturb you," he said breathlessly. "But the system is down again and there are no reservations anywhere."

Kurt dropped his knife and fork and followed the youth.

Sparklers shot skyward again, dazzling against the dark sky. The crowd cheered and applauded Mexico's first goal.

Jacques dropped into the chair Kurt vacated. "My dear Emilia, you look deserted."

"Kurt is having an awful night," Emilia said. "He said he needs to hire an assistant manager."

"I have been telling him this for months," Jacques said with a theatrical sigh, one hand over his heart. "He works too hard."

"He said he could find someone in Las Vegas."

Jacques gave a Gallic shrug. "After Paris, Las Vegas has the highest concentration of hospitality professionals in the world. That is where Kurt and I met. And I, of course, am a tremendous asset to the Kurt Rucker hotel brand."

Emilia shook her head, unable to suppress a smile. Jacques was so unlike anyone else she knew.

"They call it Sin City, you know," Jacques said. "For good reason."

"I'm sure you did your best." Emilia laughed.

"I am French," Jacques offered, as if that explained everything.

Emilia picked up her mojito, determined to sound casual. "Does Suzanne Kellogg still live in Las Vegas?"

But she had lost Jacques's attention, which was now riveted on the work of a sloppy waiter. "Excuse me, Emilia," the chef said and shot out of his chair.

Emilia finished her mojito but didn't refill her glass. Mexico lost and its Copa America hopes ended. The defeat matched Emilia's mood. At midnight when she went to bed, Kurt was still troubleshooting problems downstairs.

Emilia dropped her shoulder bag in her office and went into the conference room for the daily meeting. Everyone else was already there.

"Well, let's begin," Claudia said as soon as Emilia took her seat at the table.

Everyone always sat in the same places around the table and reported on their responsibilities in the same order. Publicity always went first, as if it was the most important thing. Emilia always went last.

It hadn't taken long to realize that no one cared about the training curriculum, if the candidates passed a final exam, knew how to subdue an unruly suspect, or operated according to Mexican law. What really mattered was how good the candidates looked in uniform and that they all spouted the same public relations garble.

"The Las Palomas badges won't be ready for the graduation ceremony," Emilia announced when it was her turn. "I've been at the requisition office. They said the order needed to be in months ago."

The table erupted in protest.

"There wasn't a Las Palomas months ago!" someone exclaimed.

Claudia raised her hands for quiet and turned to Emilia.

"Did you tell them the date of the graduation ceremony has already been set?" she asked.

"Yes." Emilia didn't go on to say that the requisitions chief had actually laughed at her, found the form submitted a week ago, and tossed it in her face. "They weren't motivated."

The table buzzed with suggestions ranging from giving the new officers cardboard badges to simply awarding certificates.

"You can't put cops on the street without real badges," Emilia said. "Their actions and arrests won't be legal."

"I think Detective Cruz and I will take this offline," Claudia said over the wails of dissent. Her voice was shaky yet determined. "The meeting is adjourned."

She led the way back to her office, perched on the edge of her desk and dialed a number from memory as Emilia settled into an upholstered chair.

"Gustavo?" Claudia sang out to whomever had answered her call. "It's Claudia. Yes, I'm doing wonderfully well. Las Palomas is the most exciting assignment. You can't imagine."

The unseen Gustavo said something that made Claudia titter. Emilia stared out Claudia's window at the empty patio one floor below. For as many times as she'd come and gone from the building in the past three weeks, and bought food at the café, she'd never seen anyone else besides the Las Palomas staff or officer candidates. The offices on the first floor remained empty and dark.

Claudia's voice interrupted her reverie. "I'm calling because I need to know what number Carlota wants on her badge. She's our patron, of course, and we want to make her an honorary Las Palomas officer." She paused, listening, then broke into a wide smile. "Of course, 001. Here's the ceremony information. Be a darling and make sure it goes on her schedule."

She had the unseen Gustavo send her a confirmation email verifying Carlota's attendance and badge number. A second conversation ensued with someone in Chief Salazar's office. Carlota would be included on the official roster of Las Palomas officers receiving badges. Claudia forwarded him the verification from the mayor's office and extracted a promise that the official badge request would be sent to the requisitions office within the hour.

Two minutes later, Claudia called Gustavo in the mayor's office again and asked him to call the requisition office to verify that they had the list with Carlota's name on it.

As soon as Emilia went back to her office, her phone rang. The requisitions office asked her to submit a request for badges and send along the design.

Claudia appeared in her doorway. "Is the crisis over?"

"Yes," Emilia said grudgingly. "That was pretty slick."

Claudia smiled, looking for all intents like a puppy who'd been praised. "How are you doing with the strengths finder questionnaire?" she asked.

"Coming along great," Emilia lied.

Emilia blew off steam with a hard workout in the gym alongside the officer candidates. Six had dropped out already, and she could tell a few more would leave by the end of the week.

The three women who had given her pause during the interview process were still there. Natividad was smart, capable, and a natural leader. She soaked up information like a sponge, stayed calm in all the simulations, had good observation skills, and didn't need to be told anything twice. Emilia chose her for a sparring partner. When the match was over, they both pulled off their sweaty head protection and bumped fists. Natividad held her own and gave as good as she got.

Tina Maria consistently scored high in the classroom but struggled when it came to physical training. She was roughly the same size as a nightstick and obviously leery about ever having to use one. She dropped handcuffs twice during a simulated arrest. Emilia felt a little guilty and wondered what would happen to the girl when she washed out of Las Palomas.

Rosalita was doing better than Emilia had expected. The hooker approached every task seriously, earned high grades in the classroom, and was in shape. The problem was her reserve. There was a noticeable gulf between her and the other candidates, all of whom were much younger.

Once again, Emilia wondered why Rosalita was there. It certainly wasn't for the camaraderie.

255

CHAPTER 18

The badge ceremony in the central police building auditorium was a big success.

Chief Salazar was there, of course, along with Obregon and a host of senior police and union officials. Carlota showed up as both the patron of Las Palomas and an honorary patrol officer.

Emilia managed to keep a straight face during the speeches. Chief Salazar, bald head glowing under the stage lights, spoke about progressive police tactics and how Las Palomas will create bridges to the community. Obregon congratulated Las Palomas for bringing a fresh attitude to the union as well as expanding the concept of police in Mexico. Las Palomas was a model for others to emulate.

Carlota made one of her trademark speeches, alternating between flowery phrases and dramatic flair. She praised her protégée, Claudia, for making Las Palomas the face of peace for the people of Acapulco and lauded the officer candidates.

Natividad, Tina Maria, and Rosalita had all made the final cut. Natividad's final essay showed great improvement and Emilia heard that Rosalita had tutored her. By the same token, Emilia was sure that Natividad had put in overtime to help Tina Maria make it through the final physical fitness tests. The youngest officer candidate had passed by the skin of her teeth.

One by one, each of the new patrol officers shook hands with the chief of police and received their badge. Pictures were taken with the mayor.

Kurt left for Las Vegas two days later.

Emilia hated being alone in the hotel without him. Rattling around in the big penthouse. Cut off from real life in Acapulco's neighborhoods where people talked in the market, debated which vendor sold the freshest *jitomates*, planned church celebrations, and walked their children to school.

Meals were the hardest. Emilia felt self-conscious about walking through the lobby with a bag of groceries, ordering room service for one, or eating by herself in the restaurant.

The solution was to work late every night. Spend more time in the gym in the building on Avenida Almendros.

And keep inching along the El Trio trail. She had to find the killer before he found out she was asking questions.

"I'm sorry, señora," said the stilted female voice on the other end of the phone connection. "This is Public Affairs of the Policía Federal Preventiva. Do you wish to schedule a briefing for your school or workplace?"

"No," Emilia said. "I'm Detective Emilia Cruz from the Acapulco municipal police department. I wish to speak to the commander of the late Captain Juan Carlos Espinosa from the Guerrero state office."

"I don't have access to state-level information," the voice said.

"I understand," Emilia said patiently. "Would you be able to direct me to the correct department, please?"

The woman exhaled loudly. "I'll transfer you to the operator."

The phone chimed in Emilia's ear. The line went dead.

Emilia gritted her teeth, stabbed at the phone until she heard a dial tone, then redialed the number for the local *federale* headquarters again. This was the third call to the same number; each time she'd been routed to different offices, either local or national, in an impressive display of either incompetence or deliberate deception.

Either way, it was having the same effect.

There was a *federale* liaison officer assigned to Chief Salazar's office but she certainly couldn't contact him and expect that her queries stayed under the radar. She dialed again.

It took 90 minutes and six more calls before a Captain Torres informed her that yes, he'd been Espinosa's superior but that no, he was not in a position to discuss the murder investigation. Out of respect for the family, as well as being a privileged and proprietary matter for the Policía Federal Preventiva.

"Of course," Emilia said, trying to inject as much sympathy into the words as possible. "But as I said, I'm a detective with the Acapulco municipal police. Some relevant information has emerged from other investigations that would be of use to you in the context of Captain Espinosa's murder investigation."

He didn't reply. Emilia heard scratching on the other end, as if Torres was writing.

"I'm proposing a collaboration, Captain," she pressed.

"To verify," Torres said. "You claim to have information regarding the death of Captain Espinosa."

"Related information," Emilia corrected him.

"What do you want in return?" The man's voice had changed from wary to openly hostile.

"We're both law enforcement officers," Emilia said. "We want the truth to come out."

"What did you say your name was again?" Torres asked, tension clipping his words.

Something had gone very wrong. Paranoia blotted out logic. Emilia hung up.

She left her office, shaken by the exchange. Had she given Torres the wrong impression? Or did he know something about Espinosa's murder that made collaboration with the Acapulco police department impossible? Did he know Loyola? *Madre de Dios*, maybe Torres was the El Trio killer.

Emilia walked on, her thoughts churning. Down the wide staircase to the lobby and past the empty offices. The signs were all there, waiting for people to come and open for business. Soledo Enterprises. Consolidated Solutions. Vector Analytics. All looked exactly the same as the day she'd walked into the swank building on Avenida Almendros. Nicely appointed and inexplicably empty.

The café was open. As always, Esteban was there and delighted to have a customer. Emilia bought herself an ice cream sandwich, the kind with the word *Mordisko* baked into the square chocolate cookie. She took it to a table, unwrapped it, and looked at the empty patio with all the tables and umbrellas shining in the afternoon sunshine. For some reason the clear sky made her think of being outside with Kurt and the way bright light always turned his blonde hair to silver. When he swam in the ocean on a day like this, his hair looked like molten metal in a jeweler's shop.

The cold ice cream helped her focus. Going through official channels to find out what the *federales* had on Espinosa's murder had been a mistake. She needed a personal connection.

Like Doctor Prade, the medical examiner.

When she met Espinosa, he had introduced her to the *federale* medical examiners working with him. Both of those men knew Prade; the medical examiner occupation was apparently a small circle. Acapulco's medical examiner always looked exhausted and his outlook often verged on morose, but he was addicted to his job as much as she was. If she asked him to connect her to one of his *federale* colleagues, he'd do it.

She licked a melted drop of vanilla ice cream off her thumb and was surprised to see Paola run into the café, her cheeks red with exertion. "Claudia needs to see you in her office," the secretary panted. "Right now."

"What's the matter?" Emilia stood up.

"She has a visitor," Paola said. "I was told to find you right away."

A heavyset man in a gray suit and red tie filled one of Claudia's upholstered chairs to overflowing. When Emilia tapped on the open door of Claudia's office, his eyes raked her up and down, taking in her pink blouse and gray pants, and came to rest on her chest.

Claudia half rose from her chair behind the desk. "Emilia, please come in and shut the door. This is Señor Leyva. He's the father of Natividad Leyva Roma." She smiled nervously. "Señor Leyva, this is Detective Cruz. She's our chief of operations and very familiar with all our staff."

Leyva nodded at Emilia but made no move to shake her hand.

"Emilia," Claudia went on. Her voice betrayed her discomfort with the visitor. "Señor Leyva has some concerns about Natividad being part of Las Palomas."

"Your daughter is an outstanding officer," Emilia said.

"I don't care," Leyva growled. "It's an embarrassment. A man of my standing and my daughter is a cop mixing it up with cheap *chicas* and living who knows where."

"If I may ask, señor, what is it that you do?" Emilia asked.

"Señor Leyva owns Pesca Estrella," Claudia murmured.

Pesca Estrella was a huge seafood company that distributed Pacific-caught fish all over Mexico and Central

America. The company supplied restaurants and hotels, including the Palacio Réal.

"I have a reputation in this community," Leyva growled. "No daughter of mine is going to embarrass me."

"Natividad is a fine officer, señor," Emilia said. "One of our best and representing Acapulco in a very admirable way. You should be proud of what she's accomplished."

"Huh," Leyva harrumphed.

"Keep in mind," Claudia said. "Your daughter received her badge from the mayor, no less. Carlota was very impressed with Natividad. Very impressed."

Emilia stared at Claudia. The mayor had barely acknowledged any of the Las Palomas officers at the ceremony.

"Would you like us to send you a photo of Natividad with Carlota?" Claudia continued rapidly. "I'm sure the mayor would be glad to sign it. We can set up a photo opportunity for you with Carlota so she can present you with it."

"Well." Leyva blinked, obviously torn between his original agenda and the allure of being associated with Acapulco's famous mayor.

"Thank you so much for coming." Claudia knuckles went white as she clasped her hands together nervously. "We'll contact your office with the details."

"All right." Leyva shoved his bulk upright. The gray suit shimmered like a whale caught in a spotlight.

Claudia buzzed her assistant to show him out. When he was gone, she flapped at Emilia to close the door and sank into her desk chair as if drained. "I can't say I was very impressed with the way you handled that, Emilia," she admonished.

"Me?" Emilia remained standing near the door. "I barely said two words."

"Yes, I had to jump in and smooth things over." Claudia straightened up and shook her finger at Emilia. "Señor Leyva is a very important businessman, the sort of person we need to cultivate, not alienate.

"He came to see you, not me," Emilia pointed out. "If I was supposed to handle things, you might have let me know."

"That's Paola's fault." Claudia clicked her tongue. "She should have told you."

"Leave Paola out of this." Emilia couldn't believe Claudia's readiness to blame a subordinate for her own mistake.

Claudia bristled. "If you'd completed your strengths finder questionnaire when you were supposed to, you would already be practicing your problem-solving techniques. You wouldn't have blundered so badly with Señor Leyva. I wouldn't have had to fix this for you."

Emilia felt her blood pressure go through the roof. "I barely said anything before you jumped in," she exclaimed. "Riding Carlota's coattails again. Have you ever solved a problem without invoking her name?"

Claudia gasped.

The intercom buzzed. "Señor Obregon to see you."

Claudia took a deep breath before pressing the button and telling her secretary to have him wait a minute.

"Don't let me keep you," Emilia said acidly.

"That will be all, Emilia," Claudia said, sounding like she was trying hard not to cry. "I'll expect to see your completed strengths finder on my desk the first thing tomorrow morning."

Obregon was in the hall. He flashed Emilia one of his predatory smiles as she went back to her own office.

Her cell phone rang as Emilia flung herself into the chair.

"Detective Cruz?"

"Speaking," Emilia snapped.

"Detective, we have a mutual friend named Josefina." The voice on the other end of the connection was male and well-spoken.

Emilia sat up. "Yes."

"She got in touch with my office, which does both security and public relations for popular personalities," the man went on. "To request a meeting between you and one of my clients. I assume you know who."

He meant actor Dario Delgado. "Yes," Emilia said again, her anger at Claudia forgotten.

"His schedule is extremely constrained but we can arrange something for tomorrow," he said. "The entire day."

"Tomorrow?" Emilia pulled up the online calendar that Paola kept up to date. The next day was full of meetings, as well as more scenario training with the Las Palomas officers. "That's fine."

"A car will pick you up in front of the downtown Sanborn's. Please carry a copy of today's *Jornada*, with the masthead clearly visible."

"All right." Emilia grinned to herself. This was like something out of Dario Delgado's latest spy movie.

"You will be required to sign a confidentiality agreement."

"That's not a problem."

"Also, we trust that you will not be identifiable as someone in an official capacity."

"No uniform," Emilia replied.

"Thank you for understanding."

He repeated the time and place and rang off.

Emilia put down the phone and checked that her shoulder bag still held the pictures she'd shown to Salinas's co-workers. The graduation photo was the most surprising and she couldn't resist another look. Salinas wasn't at all the way she'd imagined him when they'd spoken on the phone about the El Pharaoh money laundering case all those months ago. Then she'd imagined him as overweight, balding, and coping with a nervous tic. But Salinas had been a slim man in his early thirties, with wavy hair, a wide jaw and a thin-lipped, sensitive mouth. Even in this standard group photo, a positive energy surrounded him.

In contrast, Vega's long face and haughty expression exuded an attitude of privilege and entitlement.

She wondered what Dario Delgado could tell her. The connecting threads were still fragmentary. Emilia began doodling. Vega and Isabel were connected by having been killed by the same gun. Vega and Salinas were connected by a police exchange course they'd taken together in *El Norte* two years ago. Silvio and Salinas were connected by the failed money laundering case against the El Pharaoh casino. So far, nothing connected to Espinosa.

She was snapped out of her reverie by a knock on her office door.

"Come in," she called, sweeping pictures and notebook back into her bag.

It was Natividad. "Am I early?" she asked.

Emilia glanced at her watch. She'd timed the meeting for when most of the Las Palomas office staff had gone for the day. "No, you're right on time. Come on in and have a seat."

Wearing the final uniform of dark blue cargo pants and pale blue polo with the Las Palomas symbol embroidered on the sleeve, the younger woman could be a recruiting poster. Her hair was in a ponytail and her makeup was as subtle as the mayor's.

"Is there a problem?" she asked.

"Maybe," Emilia said. "I'm afraid you were hired under false pretenses."

Natividad winced. "I said I worked with the fishermen."

"Your father owns Pesca Estrella," Emilia said dryly. "Not quite the situation you led me to believe."

"Would you have hired me if you knew my family was rich?"

"We were looking for women who'd make good cops," Emilia said. "Not their families."

"How did you find out?"

"Your father came to the office," Emilia said. "Wanted Claudia to fire you. Said he didn't want a cop in the family."

Natividad turned scarlet. "Am I fired?"

"No. Claudia is sending him an autographed picture of you and the mayor from the badge ceremony. Hopefully that will be enough to convince him that being a cop isn't a blot on the family name."

"*Madre de Dios.*" Natividad spun off the chair, obviously too angry to stay seated. "Something else for the Look-How-Important-I-Am wall in his office. I'm so sorry, but it's the sort of thing he'd do to get me back under his thumb again."

"About that," Emilia said. "He also said he doesn't know where you live."

"That's right," Natividad said. She paced the length of the silver console. "I have my own place now. I don't want anything to do with him."

"What about your mother?" Emilia asked.

"She's dead." Natividad threw it out, almost as a challenge.

"Okay," Emilia said wearily. She wasn't in the business

of solving interpersonal issues; she could barely cope with her own. "You're an adult. A cop. Your family issues are no business of mine unless they get in the way of you doing your job." She paused and pointed to the chair across from her desk. "Now that we've cleared the air, I want to talk about something else."

Natividad sat back down.

"I'd like you to become the assistant chief of operations," Emilia said. "Eventually you can take over the day-to-day assignments, radio checks, that sort of thing. You can start tomorrow by organizing the scenario training with the academy instructors."

"Me?" Natividad gripped the arms of the chair in excitement. "Are you sure?"

"I'm sure." Emilia grinned, relieved the woman would accept. The new distribution of tasks would give Emilia more time to focus on El Trio. "I'll see if the increased responsibility can come with a pay increase as well."

It was a good conversation after that. Natividad was ready for more responsibility and Emilia was delighted to finally have someone else to talk to about real issues. When they got down to discussing patrol officer partnerships, Natividad had a very surprising suggestion.

"Tina Maria and Rosalita."

The oldest and the youngest. Emilia sat back in her desk chair. "Why?" she asked.

"They've become very close," Natividad said. "I don't think Rosalita would do well with anyone else as a partner.”

A loud thump against the wall interrupted their conversation.

“Construction?” Natividad asked.

A second thump was followed by a third.

“Let me check,” Emilia said. Normally, everyone else in the front office had gone home by now.

The thumping segued into a steady rhythm of taps coming from the common wall between Emilia’s office and that of Claudia.

Natividad followed her into the hall. Claudia’s office door was closed.

Emilia knocked once. “Claudia? Are you all right?”

There was no answer. Emilia pressed her ear to the door. The tapping was definitely coming from inside Claudia’s office.

“Claudia?” Emilia rapped again. She waited, then turned the knob and opened the door.

And wished she hadn’t.

Claudia was lying on top of her desk with her skirt hiked around her waist and bare legs in the air. Her shoes and panties were on the floor. Obregon stood against the desk thrusting in and out of her, his breath coming in labored grunts. His pants were around his knees but he was still wearing his black suit jacket.

Claudia’s eyes were closed and her hands clasped behind Obregon’s neck as if she was holding on for dear life. A corner of the desk banged against the wall in rhythm with his movements.

Emilia stepped back and closed the door, faintly revolted. Neither Claudia nor Obregon had seen her.

"Was that . . ." Natividad let the rest of the sentence go unspoken.

"You didn't see anything," Emilia said.

CHAPTER 19

Emilia sat alone in the back of a big town car as it wove through Acapulco's western suburbs. Houses and shops, darkened by the tinted windows, fell away rapidly, to be replaced by the beaches at Playa Piede la Cuesta as the car sped down the highway. Emilia couldn't hear the shriek of kids playing in the shallows or smell the salted coconut oil-scented breeze. The big vehicle was a hermetically sealed capsule. From the slight distortion of the landscape beyond the window and the weight of the door as the chauffeur had opened it for her, she knew the car was armored.

"There is a selection of beverages in the console." Like the chauffeur, the bodyguard in the front passenger seat looked like a movie character in a dark suit and narrow black tie. He spoke to her reflection in his visor mirror.

"Thank you." Emilia looked in the console between the back seats to find chilled bottles of sparkling water, an assortment of juices, and real glass tumblers.

"The ride will take about an hour," the bodyguard said. "Make yourself comfortable."

Emilia looked out the back window as the vehicle's speed increased. Another two armed bodyguards were in a car behind them.

An hour later, both vehicles passed through a *privada* gate overlooking the beach town of Ixtapa. As they continued on, Emilia saw more gates, each with its own guardhouse and uniformed security staff.

They turned and the road narrowed. A uniformed guard saluted and opened another gate. The vehicle continued uphill, revealing a panorama of rugged mountain and foaming ocean. The road curved and a rambling white house came into view.

The bodyguard murmured into his radio as the car came to a halt. The locks clicked and Emilia's door swung open. An older man in a white *guayabera* shirt and matching linen trousers held it as she climbed out of the car. "Welcome," he said with a formal bow "I am Fernando. Señor Delgado is expecting you."

He led her down a wide passageway roofed by a trellis and climbing jasmine. Nestled amid dark green foliage, the small white flowers gave off a heady and cloying scent.

They passed through open double doors and into a dramatic foyer. Blue and white floor tiles gave way to soaring stucco walls spliced by long narrow windows. An antique Spanish sideboard dominated one wall. A faded rug twice as tall as Emilia hung above it like artwork.

Emilia followed Fernando through an archway and into a more intimate room. The ceiling was as high as in the foyer, but the room was grounded by three large brown leather sofas arranged in a U configuration and centered by an enormous stone coffee table. The open end of the seating faced floor-to-ceiling glass doors. Beyond the glass, a terra cotta terrace beckoned and an infinity pool spilled into the ocean.

"I'll let Señor Delgado know you are here," Fernando said. He gestured to the sofas. "Please sit and rest after your trip."

"Thank you." Emilia put down her shoulder bag as he left the room. She was too edgy and the view too enticing for her to sit.

The scene was breathtaking.

Unlike the vista from the penthouse balcony at the Palacio Réal, which overlooked the placid bay at Puerta Marques, the ocean below the pool was aggressive, like the thunder of a storm continually bubbling up from the center of the earth. Ixtapa's heavy rollers attracted surfers from all over the world.

"Do you surf?"

Emilia turned to see Dario Delgado, followed closely by Fernando. The butler set a tray on the coffee table and withdrew.

Delgado came to the window. "The best surfing in the world is about a quarter mile north."

"Yes," Emilia said.

Up close Delgado was dangerously, fatally handsome, and Emilia had to repress a nervous schoolgirl giggle. He was big for a Mexican and nearly as tall as Kurt. Dressed in a white singlet that clung to a muscular chest and loose linen pants that emphasized narrow hips, he looked like the pictures in *HOLA!* magazine with captions attesting to his sculpted arms, sharp jaw, and perfectly tousled hair glinting with the merest suggestion of gel. A turquoise horn charm, suspended from a thick silver rope, rested in the hollow of his throat. He was barefoot.

"I beg your pardon for forgetting my manners," he said. "I'm Dario Delgado."

"A pleasure to meet you. I'm Detective Emilia Cruz." With great effort, Emilia kept her knees from buckling. She was shaking hands with Dario Delgado and would never be able to tell a soul. *Dario Delgado!*

"I was told that you are investigating Javier's death," he said. "You understand that I will never admit speaking to you."

Emilia gave herself a mental shake and reminded herself why she was there. "I signed the confidentiality agreement," she reassured him.

Delgado stared at the churning ocean. "I owe him at least this much," he said. "To try and help find his killer."

"I'm sorry for your loss."

"Do you know how many people have said that to me?" Delgado asked. "None."

Loneliness emanated from the man, raw and harsh like the waves outside. Emilia felt it beat against her.

"I would like to know who took Javier away from me," Delgado said.

"I would like to know as well," Emilia said.

Delgado led her to the nearest sofa and motioned to the tray on the table. "May I offer you something?" he asked.

"Water, thank you."

Delgado poured her some sparkling water and selected a juice for himself. He was rumored to be in his late thirties but could pass for ten years younger. Emilia watched in fascination as he put a straw into his glass and pursed his lips around it. She felt sure he never drank from a straw in public.

She found her notebook and pen. "When was the last time you saw Javier?" she began.

"A week before he was killed," Delgado replied without hesitation.

"Did he mention any problems?" Emilia asked. "Anything out of the ordinary?"

"He was nervous," Delgado said. "Jumpy."

Emilia tamped down a rush of excitement. "Was something wrong at work?"

"Javier and I didn't talk about work," Delgado said. "Not his. Or mine. We swam, watched movies. Made messes in the kitchen. Javier said he was fine, but like I said, he was jumpy."

Emilia felt the rush ebb as she led Delgado through as many questions as she could think of. He was forthcoming, but it was quickly apparent that while lovers, the two men mostly lived separate lives. They'd met through a professional matchmaking service that Delgado wouldn't name. Their relationship had been a tightly-held secret for the last seven years. Delgado knew few details of the legal cases in which Salinas had been involved. The only professional colleagues of Salinas's that he knew were Josefina and her husband. He never met Salinas's parents.

The attorney was estranged from both mother and father, neither of whom had ever come to terms with their son's sexual preferences.

As for Delgado, Salinas knew the actor's personal staff but never met his family nor any associates in the film industry.

Every question about Salinas's murder or involvement with law enforcement led to a dead end. Delgado wasn't hiding anything; he simply didn't know.

When Emilia ran out of questions, she spread the photographs on the coffee table: the graduation photo, Espinosa, Silvio and Isabel. "Do you recognize any of these people?" she asked, without much hope.

"Of course." Delgado straightened the graduation photo and put his finger on Salinas. "That's Javier."

"What about him?" Emilia edged the picture with Silvio closer to the actor.

But Delgado picked up the graduation photograph. "I can't be sure," he said. "But I think I know this person."

He pointed to Vega.

"A friend of Javier's?" Emilia asked.

"Oh no," Delgado said hastily. "Acquaintances, perhaps. But definitely not friends."

Something told Emilia to tread carefully. "Why do you say that?" she asked.

"He came to Javier's house," Delgado said. "It was the last time Javier and I were together." He gave her the date. "I didn't often stay in Acapulco with Javier. Usually he came here or to my house in Mexico City. But I was on my way to Los Angeles and there wasn't enough time to come all the way out here." He pursed his lips around the straw again.

"So you were at Javier's." Emilia let her voice trail off.

"My staff left." Delgado took up the thread. "Javier and I were alone. He was very busy, developing evidence for a case that was supposed to go before a judge very soon. I thought that was why he was so jumpy."

Emilia nodded sympathetically.

Delgado went on. "We'd finished eating when security for his building called up. Someone was there to see him. Helio. I remember the name was Helio." He shrugged, the sleek muscles in his shoulders rippling. "Just Helio."

Emilia nodded. "That helps."

"Does it?" Delgado smiled for the first time, flashing perfect white teeth against bronzed skin. "Javier said he was sorry, he'd have to talk to this Helio. I went into the bedroom but left the door open. Javier and this Helio went into the study and I saw their faces in the bedroom mirror as they went by. I shut the door after that but heard them argue."

"What about?"

Delgado leaned forward and put his hand on Emilia's knee. "Money. I assumed that this Helio wanted to borrow money. But when I asked him, Javier said no, Helio wasn't there for money. I think Javier was disgusted with him."

"Disgusted?" Emilia moved his hand.

"Maybe a little scared, too." Delgado acted as if the hand

thing never happened.

"How so?"

"Javier seemed nervous afterwards. He didn't want to talk about it."

"Do you think Helio threatened him?"

"No." Delgado took a sip from the straw. "I think Javier was concerned this Helio was going to do something stupid."

Emilia stared at her notebook. Salinas and Vega, arguing before they were both killed. "Go back to when this Helio arrived and you saw him in the mirror," she said. "Had Helio ever been to Javier's before? Did he seem to know the layout of the apartment?"

"No, not at all."

Emilia asked a few other questions but Delgado didn't know anything else. He'd apparently seen the interaction through the lens of a lover. Once he was sure that this Helio wasn't a rival, his attention evaporated.

"You worked with Javier, didn't you?" Delgado asked.

Emilia looked up from her notebook. "On one case," she said.

"An important case?"

"Money laundering," Emilia said. "He wasn't able to prosecute the way we'd planned but he still salvaged something."

"What did he do?"

"He charged a dirty cop with illegal amounts of foreign currency." It sounded feeble, compared to the money laundering charges they'd expected to come out of the raid on the El Pharaoh casino, but at the time it was a victory.

"And you helped him do that?" Delgado wasn't so much asking a question as confirming a fact.

"Yes."

"Javier was very good at his job, wasn't he?"

"I didn't know him well, but the people who worked with him said yes, he was very good."

Delgado leaned forward. "You're very good at your job, too."

He said it as a fact. Emilia interpreted his tone as seeking reassurance, but there was no point in offering him false hope. "May I ask you a final question?" she asked.

Delgado nodded.

"Why wasn't an autopsy performed on Javier?"

Delgado's eyes clouded and he sat back again. "His mother was the legal next of kin. She refused. I heard she said it would show that he was gay."

"And all of his personal effects?"

"Went to her." Delgado clasped his hands together between his knees. The wave of loneliness buffeted her again. "Would it?"

"I'm sorry?"

"Would an autopsy have shown that Javier was gay?"

He was serious. Emilia shook her head. "An autopsy determines the cause and manner of death," she said. "That's all. And in Javier's case, it probably wouldn't have given us much more information."

Delgado sniffed. "Thank you."

Emilia closed her notebook and gathered up the photos. "I appreciate your help. I know this wasn't easy."

"Do you have time for a swim?" Delgado asked and gestured to the pool beyond the glass doors.

They'd spent hours talking about his dead lover, yet there was a stilted flirtatiousness about Delgado's manner, as if he'd been schooled on how to behave with women. "No," Emilia said. "I really must be getting back to Acapulco."

Delgado stood when she did. "Is there someone important in your life, Detective Cruz?" he asked.

"Yes," she said.

"Have you been together long?"

"A year or so," Emilia said.

"I hope you are as happy as Javier and I were," Delgado said.

He held out his hand. When Emilia took it, he pulled her in and kissed her on the mouth. "I like you, Detective Cruz," he said.

"Thank you," Emilia replied. There was no glitter about having been kissed by the legendary Dario Delgado, just faint embarrassment at his clumsiness.

He released her with an awkward smile. Emilia was relieved when the bodyguard appeared and said the car was ready.

Alone in the back seat, she closed her eyes. She'd met

the famous Dario Delgado and all she felt was sadness. His sultry Latin looks made him the prettiest man she'd ever seen up close, but he wasn't the man the tabloid press knew. Maybe it was his lover's death, or the double life he'd led—and protected—for so long.

She dug out her notebook, flipped to the timeline of all the murders, and noted the date Delgado had given her. Vega and Salinas discussed money. The conversation had not been a positive one. It was a data point she didn't have before.

Had the cop and the attorney worked a case together? No one at the state's attorney general's office had mentioned it. Perhaps it was an unofficial investigation, which was why Vega went to Salinas's home rather than the office. Was Espinosa involved as well?

She made a list of what to do next. At the top was a conversation with Dr. Prade about his *federale* medical examiner colleagues and what they knew about Espinosa's death.

Emilia turned around to look out of the rear window. The follow car with Delgado's bodyguards was still there. It was a reassuring sight.

CHAPTER 20

The penthouse was dark and empty when Emilia got back from Ixtapa.

The refrigerator yielded a bottle of white wine and containers of fancy stuff stocked by the restaurant. Kurt must have arranged it before he left. Emilia rifled through the choices until she found a rice dish she'd had before. The risotto with capers and artichokes was a grudging substitute for *arroz rojo*.

She took the cold rice and the bottle of wine out to the balcony and ate standing at the wall. Happy sounds filtered up from the Pasodoble Bar but Delgado's loneliness was contagious. She was alone at what passed for home. The only person foolish enough to investigate the El Trio murders.

I hope you are as happy as Javier and I were. How happy had the two men been? Salinas was a workaholic estranged from his family. Delgado pranced around the world with supermodels to burnish his acting career. Seven years of hiding, seven years of living a lie. Seven years of being unable to make a real commitment. The proof was in his house. Totally impersonal. Nothing to suggest his commitment to someone else. No smiling picture of the two of them in a silver frame.

Emilia knew she wasn't winning awards in the commitment department, either. A Mexican cop and a wealthy *gringo*. It was laughable. Kurt wasn't helping by rushing up to the land of old girlfriends to hire staff.

Her mood darkened as the level in the bottle went down. Emilia knew she was tipsy when she brought the empty rice container back into the kitchen.

The floor felt slightly uneven as she walked into the living room and looked around. Masculine leather sofas, scrubbed pine tables, someone else's choice of artwork. No pictures of her and Kurt. The room was just a path she walked on her way to real life on Acapulco's mean streets.

"What did you lose, *gringo* man?" she said out loud. "What am I not supposed to find?"

She carried the bottle of wine into the hall and went through the closet, searching behind Kurt's surfboard and sports equipment. Boxes of clothes were upended and pockets turned inside out. Emilia didn't know what she was looking for, but it would be unfamiliar and upsetting.

From the closet she moved on to their bedroom, fortifying herself with gulps of wine before tackling his dresser. It was midnight before Emilia went into the office and slumped into the desk chair. "I used to be a detective," she mumbled to herself. "But I can't find shit."

The desk held no surprises, nor did the bookcase.

One by one, sitting on the floor, she combed through the file boxes Kurt kept stored on top of the closet. The papers were all in English and she actually laughed to think that the language refresher she was getting with Las Palomas was coming in handy.

She easily identified Kurt's visa paperwork from Mexican immigration and documents with the name of his college on top. Another folder held various professional certifications.

A file marked LEGAL was the thickest, with long papers folded to fit. Some of the documents looked like Kurt had bought and sold a property in Las Vegas. She studied the date of the sale; it was right before he moved to Acapulco.

Another long paper had a fancy seal at the top and the embossed words *San Miguel County, Fourth Judicial District Court*.

The document was in English. It started *In the matter of Kellogg v. Rucker*.

The formal prose and complicated verbs defeated her adequate but still basic English skills. Emilia picked out nouns: *paternity, child welfare, material support*. She didn't need a dictionary to know what they meant.

The paper swam in front of her. Kurt had a child.

Suzanne Kellogg had borne Kurt a child and sued him for child support. No wonder Kurt had been so oblique when Emilia had asked him about Suzanne.

The dopey effect of the wine was gone. Emilia felt cold and sober. Kurt had a child, whom he'd left in Las Vegas. Paid child support because of a court order, or whatever this document was called. Probably moved to Mexico to get away from the whole nasty legal issue. His trip back to Las Vegas wasn't to hire an assistant manager, it was to resolve some problem related to the child.

He'd seemed so honorable, so principled. Those qualities had drawn her to him, made her abandon the Catholic Church's teachings and live in sin with him.

But Kurt was a man willing to abandon his own child. How had she misjudged him so badly?

There were a few other documents in the file with the same seal and embossing but Emilia had seen enough. She stuffed everything back in the box and replaced it in the closet. Kurt would never be able to tell she'd discovered his secret.

CHAPTER 21

In the morning, Emilia had too much nervous energy churning through her bloodstream to stay in the office. She told Paola she'd be out and suited up with the first shift of La Palomas girls.

"I'm with you?" Natividad walked up to her as Emilia clipped on her radio.

"Is that a problem?"

"No, not at all."

Emilia watched as Natividad made the five pairs of officers perform radio checks and assigned their beats. Las Palomas patrolled the heavily touristed western side of the bay. No doubt Carlota would soon be touting the great success Las Palomas was having on reducing crime, without ever saying that the unit was assigned to areas of the city that already had the lowest crime rates.

Patrol routes overlapped so that each team met up with two others during a four hour shift. It was a lesson Emilia had learned as a beat cop years ago. The timed meetings cut down on efficiency but reduced the number of opportunities to take bribes or shake down tourists.

An unmarked van bought with the mayor's money dropped off the teams. It made six stops between the Fuerte San Diego fort and the intersection a block west of the Costera, where Teniente Jose Azueta intersected three other streets all lined with restaurants. Rosalita and Tina

Maria were the first to get out at the fort. Her nightstick clanked against the door as Tina Maria stepped out of the van. Rosalita quickly grabbed the end of the nightstick to make sure Tina Maria didn't trip. As she watched the pair walk down the street, Emilia was reminded of Macias and Sandor. Close together and a little apart from everyone else.

Emilia and Natividad got out next on Avenida Morelos. They got a few stares and smiled in return. Natividad was observant but at ease. Emilia felt like a target and had her gun strapped to her right ankle. Of course she'd never turned it in. She still had her detective badge, too. No one had asked for either badge or gun and she had no intention of voluntarily giving them up to be lost in the police department's arcane bureaucracy.

It had been three years since Emilia walked a beat but the city looked the same. Pastel high rises touched the bright blue sky. Neon signs and shop windows enticed tourists, which in turn attracted panhandlers. Royal palm trees lined the sidewalks, fronds dancing in the breeze. Bleating car horns, whiny motorcycle engines, and the whistle of *transito* cops were a continual traffic concerto.

Emilia and Natividad helped a few lost tourists and took pictures for people who wanted a group photo of their vacation. Bought lunch from a food vendor advertising *tacos a la canasta*. Connected with the other patrols as scheduled. Emilia relaxed a little after the first hour. It wasn't the El Trio killer's style to target victims on the street in broad daylight.

Natividad's radio crackled.

"Paloma 1, Paloma 1." The voice was clearly Tina Mara's. They could hear shouting in the background. "This is Paloma 5. We have a situation in front of the Casa de la Máscara and request backup. Now."

Casa de la Máscara was about two long blocks away. Natividad flipped up the end of her collar to radio their reply. "Paloma 5, this is Paloma 1. On our way. Three minutes out."

"Hurry," Tina Maria said breathlessly. "Paloma 5 out."

Emilia broke into a fast jog. Natividad kept up easily and the two dodged palm trees and pedestrians as they made their way down Jose Maria Morelos to the white stucco building which housed the state of Guerrero's impressive collection of indigenous masks.

Emilia saw the situation as soon as the building came into sight. Two *gringos* surrounded Rosalita, propositioning her in English. Rosalita was calm, but her voice was raised as she told the boys to move on. They looked like typical spring break college types; drunk at 10:00 am and likely to stay that way for the next four or five days. An equally wobbly friend blocked Tina Maria from helping her partner. He towered over the girl.

A small knot of people stood on the porch of the museum, watching nervously.

As Emilia and Natividad ran toward the scene, Tina Maria evidently had enough. With a move that the police academy instructors would be proud of, she swept her nightstick into the boy's right knee. He yelped and buckled. Tina Maria stood on tiptoe to deliver another blow to the side of his head.

The drunk sank peacefully to the ground. His friends reeled toward Tina Maria and were intercepted by Natividad and Rosalita.

Emilia caught up to Tina Maria and grabbed the nightstick before there was any more damage to Acapulco's reputation. "Easy now," she said. "Let's not go killing tourists, okay?"

"I did it just like in class," Tina Maria whispered.

"Dude," one of the drunks slurred to Natividad. "Did you see that?"

"Yes," Natividad said in English. "Identification, dude."

Tina Maria's lower lip trembled as she looked at Rosalita. "Are you okay?"

Rosalita nodded. "I'm fine."

Emilia knelt to check that the kid on the ground wasn't dead. Before she could find a pulse, however, he sat up and grinned.

"Dude, did you see that?" he called to his friends. "She was like Buffy or something."

Emilia helped him to his feet. His head was so soaked with liquor Tina Maria had hit sponge rather than skull.

As suspected, they were all college students, down from Texas for a few days. "Where are you staying?" Emilia asked.

Their hotel was two blocks away and conveniently past three liquor stores. The small pension catered to the less well-heeled tourist crowd. Emilia told Natividad to call in that the two teams were going off their standard patrol routes for 30 minutes to assist tourists in distress and would report back when they resumed normal patrol.

The four women in uniforms and the three wobbly *gringos* made a ridiculous parade but they got the boys back into their hotel with orders to sober up or they'd be arrested for drunk and disorderly conduct. As the Las Palomas officers left the hotel and started back to the Fuerte San Diego, Tina Maria abruptly burst into tears.

"It's okay," Rosalita said. She stepped between Emilia and the youngest officer, as if to shield the girl from a reprimand. Tina Maria raised a tear-stained face and Rosalita hugged her. It was an intimate scene and Emilia was momentarily nonplussed. She walked a few steps away

A yellow building was ahead. Something flashed gold on one side.

Emilia trotted across the street to get a better vantage point. She took in the grassy area in front of the yellow building, the red flowers, the gold edge of the sign.

"I sent Rosalita and Tina Maria to their scheduled meet with Paloma 2," Natividad said as she came up to Emilia. "I expect you'll want to talk to Tina Maria later."

"Yes," Emilia said distractedly. She walked a few steps to the left.

Natividad followed. "What's going on?"

Emilia shook her head. "Nothing, just getting my bearings."

At the end of the shift, Emilia participated in the debrief, showered, changed and went upstairs to her office. Most of the staff was gone for the day and the spaces were quiet.

She took out the *Las Perdidas* binder and flipped through the reports of missing women until she came to Lila's entry. She lifted out the copy she'd made of the torn photo Lila Jimenez Lata had sent her grandmother. A moment of careful study and Emilia was convinced.

Lila had been standing by the employee entrance to the El Pharaoh casino.

It was the one night in the week Mercedes didn't teach and the dancer accepted Emilia's spur-of-the-minute invitation. In a strappy dress that floated to her ankles and hair knotted loosely at the nape of her neck, Mercedes seemed quite at ease in the Palacio Réal restaurant. Emilia was grateful; she couldn't bear another miserable night in the penthouse alone. Besides, Lila had taken lessons from Mercedes and Emilia was eager to tell the dancer what she'd discovered.

"Are we celebrating something?" Mercedes asked."

The waiter came by, greeted Emilia by name, and poured them sparkling water from a bottle that alone cost more than

Emilia's coral jersey wrap dress. He left them menus and melted away.

"In a way," Emilia said. "I have some good news about Lila."

"*Por Dios*," Mercedes exclaimed. "You found her."

"No, but I found where she might be working," Emilia said.

"Where?"

"At the El Pharaoh casino."

"So why aren't we there?"

"I gave the information to Missing Persons," Emilia said. "They'll run it down."

"Well." Mercedes raised her water glass for a toast. "To Emilia and dogged determination."

Emilia touched her glass to that of her friend. "Thank you."

The waiter reappeared and told them about Chef Jacques's dinner specials. The sommelier was next. Emilia asked him for a suggestion, the way Kurt always did, and accepted what he proposed.

"I love it here." Mercedes leaned back in her chair and took in the restaurant's sea-faring décor, lavish linen tablecloths, gleaming silver, and spectacular views of the ocean. "You live in a fairy tale, Emilia."

The food was delicious and the wine the perfect accompaniment. Mercedes kept up a commentary about goings-on in Emilia's old neighborhood. Emilia listened but couldn't help her thoughts from wandering.

Halfway through the meal Mercedes put down her knife and fork. "You're pretty subdued for someone who is supposed to be celebrating," she said quietly.

Emilia dropped her head in acknowledgment. "You're right, I'm sorry."

"What's the matter?"

"Well," Emilia considered. Her head was full of things too dangerous to discuss. Time for humor and deflection. "I hate my new boss. Not all of the time, but most of the time."

"What's he like?"

"She," Emilia corrected. "She. Claudia Sanchez, head of Las Palomas. A know-it-all bureaucrat who thinks her shit doesn't stink."

"She must have some redeeming qualities," Mercedes said. "Otherwise, how did she get her job?"

"She's sleeping with the mayor's boyfriend."

Mercedes laughed. "Is that all?" she asked. "How is Kurt?"

"He has a child," Emilia blurted. She hadn't planned on saying anything about last night's unpleasant discovery but the words bubbled up. "In Las Vegas. He's there now."

"Oh, Emilia." Distress turned down the corners of the dancer's mouth. "Are you sure?"

"I searched the apartment." Emilia felt the heaviness weigh on her heart. "He had to be ordered to support the child. I found documents. Official orders or something. With a judge's stamp on them. His old girlfriend, that Suzanne woman, is the mother."

"Maybe there's an explanation," Mercedes said.

Emilia looked beyond her friend's shoulder to see Jacques, resplendent in his chef's jacket and checkered pants, making his way to their table. "I think Jacques knows the whole story."

The chef exchanged kisses with them and asked about their dinner.

"Do you remember," Emilia said to the chef after both women had complimented his food. "You told me about Kurt's friend Suzanne."

"Kurt's sordid past," Jacques said.

Emilia glanced at Mercedes. "And her child."

"Such a sad situation." Jacques clicked his tongue.

"A real surprise for Kurt," Emilia suggested.

"Of course," Jacques said. "But what do you care about that mess, Emilia? Suzanne and her unlucky child have nothing to do with you."

Emilia couldn't believe Jacques would have such a cavalier attitude. "Well, if it concerns Kurt," she said. "It concerns me."

"You'd certainly never play such a dirty trick on him, *non*?" Jacques glanced at his watch and bolted up from his chair. "*Mon dieu*! I must get back to my kitchen." He exchanged kisses with both but his glance lingered on Mercedes. "Will we have the pleasure of seeing you again, mademoiselle?"

"Perhaps," Mercedes said.

"I shall live in hope," Jacques said dramatically. He

threaded his way through the restaurant, stopping to chat with patrons, and finally disappeared through the swinging door to the kitchen.

Emilia didn't trust herself to say anything.

"He's different," Mercedes said into the silence.

"He's French," Emilia managed. She took a deep breath. "Always good to have your worst suspicions validated."

"What are you going to do?" Mercedes asked quietly.

"I guess . . . I guess I'll have to talk to Kurt," Emilia said.

Mercedes leaned forward and tapped Emilia on the hand. "I have an idea. Let's go over to Sinfonia del Mar and watch the sunset. You can stay over at my place tonight."

"I'd like that," Emilia said gratefully. The Palacio Réal held no appeal for her right now.

The Sinfonia del Mar was on the opposite side of the bay but traffic was light and they got there in time for the show. The outdoor amphitheater pointed due west and was the perfect vantage point from which to view Acapulco's legendary sunsets. Set on a promontory not far from the cliff divers at La Quebrada, the fan-shaped theater emulated ancient Greek amphitheaters but with a special Mexican twist; the bottom tier flared out into a striking red mosaic of the sun.

From time to time the mosaic served as a stage for outdoor concerts but for the most part the Sinfonia was simply a place for locals to watch the sunset. The atmosphere was always casual. Teens got drunk in a parking lot rite of passage, picnicking families left their trash, and lovers made out on the curved stone benches because they had nowhere else to go. Emilia felt safely hidden in the crowd.

The two friends found a bench close to the mosaic as the sun spread extravagant ribbons of pink and gold across the ocean. The amphitheater glowed with the last remnants of daylight while a string quartet played a classical accompaniment to the spectacle on the horizon. The voices of the crowd quieted, replaced by the clicking of cameras. Every other person had a selfie stick.

"I kissed my husband for the first time," Mercedes said. She pointed to the other side of the amphitheater. "Right over there."

"It must have felt very romantic," Emilia offered.

"It was." Mercedes smiled at the memory. "I knew right then that I was going to marry him."

Emilia looked over her shoulder towards the parking lot. "I got drunk once over there. Tagged along with my cousins. I was determined to show that I could do whatever they did."

"Were they impressed?"

"Absolutely." Emilia laughed. "I threw up more than either of them."

As the sky slowly deepened to crimson and rust, the spectators were almost enveloped in the sunset. Below the amphitheater, the restless ocean reflected the colors of the horizon.

"This makes up for a lot," Mercedes sighed.

The string quartet ended the concert to a smattering of applause. Darkness closed in, replacing the brilliant colors of the sunset with a purple veil pierced with stars. Spectators left the tiered benches and filed into the aisles leading up to the parking lot. Emilia and Mercedes made their way to the closest aisle, anticipating a slow walk behind those from the upper tiers.

Mercedes suddenly clutched Emilia's arm. "Lila had a knapsack like that. Do you see it? It's pink."

Several steps above them, Emilia saw a female figure with a bob haircut, denim jacket, and pink cartoon knapsack. The girl's back was to them as she climbed the steps surrounded by others making their way out of the amphitheater.

"*Madre de Dios*," Emilia gasped. "It's her. It's Lila."

She bolted up the steps, focused on the distinctive haircut and the pink knapsack. People protested as she shoved them aside, forcing herself through the throng until she could reach the knapsack. Emilia got a hand on the slippery fabric and pulled, forcing the owner to spin backwards. A scream stabbed the tranquil night air, followed by shouting.

Emilia found herself looking at a woman considerably older than herself. She had a narrow face framed by obviously dyed hair. "Leave me alone, leave me alone," the woman shrieked and threw up a hand as if to ward off danger. A little girl grabbed the woman by the leg and cried for help.

Before Emilia could apologize, a burly man slammed a hand into her chest. The force of the blow sent Emilia sprawling backwards into the crowd coming up the aisle. Shouts of panic echoed against stone as people fell. Emilia ended up in a thrashing tangle of arms and legs.

"Run, run," the burly man yelled. "Run!" He scooped up the child and pulled the woman with the knapsack up the steps, knocking over more people.

"Run!" The word careened around the amphitheater.

"I'm sorry," Emilia gasped, trying to pick herself up. "I thought she was someone else."

Her words were blotted out by a rush of sheer terror. What had been a peaceful evening at an iconic spot turned into a panicked stampede to escape a funnel and the unknown violence it contained. Emilia crossed her arms over her head to protect herself as frightened people clambered over her to gain the aisle. She crashed against the base of a stone bench and her right arm blazed with pain from the old gunshot wound.

Suddenly it was over, leaving a handful of dazed people. Shouts and footfalls of those thundering to the parking lot slowly died away. A few seagulls flapped to a stop near the top row of the amphitheater and pecked at the trash scattered behind. Someone laughed nervously.

Emilia levered herself onto a bench and sucked in air, trying to still her heart. Mercedes stood two rows below, scanning the upper tiers. Emilia waved to get her attention.

The dancer rushed up the aisle. "I saw you go down and I didn't know what happened," Mercedes exclaimed. "Are you all right?"

"I think so," Emilia said. Her right arm was killing her. Her dress was torn and dirty. The buckle on her sandal was broken. "It wasn't Lila."

"I saw," Mercedes said. She sat next to Emilia.

"I'll never find her," Emilia said miserably. "Or any of the others."

"Don't say that," Mercedes protested.

"My entire life has unraveled," Emilia gulped. "My job is taking photos for tourists and getting drunks back to their hotels. I'll never be a detective again and who knows what Silvio is going to do with his life. He hates me and thinks I was a terrible partner. He actually said that. All I wanted to do was help him find out who killed Isabel. Now he hates me."

"Don't say that," Mercedes repeated.

Emilia couldn't stop the tears if she wanted to. "Here I was so worried that I was a disaster as a girlfriend and that Kurt would break up with me. But he's a *pendejo* in disguise. Did you hear what Jacques said? I'd never play a trick on Kurt like that. Like a child is a trick."

It all came crashing down. Emilia sobbed because Kurt wasn't the man she knew after all. For the loss of her detective status, the hurt of Silvio's words, and the feeling that she was wasting her time in the Las Palomas office. For each of the more than 40 women in the *Las Perdidas* binder.

She cried out of fear, too. The El Trio killer was out there, watching her. He'd killed five people and warned that her turn was coming. She had collected a few scraps of information but in her heart, Emilia knew she wasn't good enough to catch him first.

After all, she was a shit detective, just like Silvio said.

Mercedes grabbed her hand. Emilia hung on as if she'd never let go. The pressure of her friend's fingers was the only thing preventing Emilia from flinging herself off the stone ledge at the bottom of the amphitheater. Plunging into the ocean and letting the water take her to the bottom. Her bones could sink into the silt, erasing the existence of a woman stupid enough to think she mattered.

The two women were alone in the dark amphitheater but for a few couples taking advantage of the relative privacy created by the sky's endless arch of royal purple. The ocean surged over and over.

Mercedes's grip was a lifeline. It carried a message for Emilia, telling her that tomorrow she'd be able to pick up the pieces and go on.

Telling her that she wasn't alone.

CHAPTER 22

Emilia and Mercedes were having coffee in the dance studio the next morning when Prade called with good news. The medical examiner's *federale* counterpart had agreed to meet with them at the Universidad Autónoma de Guerrero, where the man taught forensic science. UAGro, as the university was called, had several facilities across the state. Doctor Enrique Furtado's office was on the main campus in Chilpancingo northeast of Acapulco.

Emilia left a message for Paola in the Las Palomas office, picked up Prade at the morgue, and drove to Chilpancingo along the wide Carretera Federal 95 highway. They made small talk as the Suburban ate up the miles and Prade was pleased to hear that Emilia was still hunting for Lila. Prade had performed the autopsy on Lila's mother, discovering a lethal dose in the body that helped Emilia break a drug trafficking operation.

The large university campus was easy to find and their identification got them through the huge gates set beside the school's shield emblazoned on a blue background. The guard gave Emilia directions where to park and how to find Furtado's office. As they walked into the main building, the rounded steps and gleaming white architecture promised things Emilia didn't have: money, higher education, and professional respect. Last night's mood was still with her.

Furtado was expecting them. He met them at the door to

his office, where Prade introduced Emilia.

The office was a small, windowless, and claustrophobic room lined on three sides with wooden shelves, all bowing under the weight of thick hardbound books, stacks of glass trays, jars of fluids and jumbled piles of papers and laboratory notebooks. Emilia pulled in her elbows to avoid knocking into any of the precarious cargo, as she edged past to the wooden chair Furtado offered. Once seated, she found herself inches away from a jar of eyeballs floating in a cloudy solution. Coffee-flavored bile seared the back of her throat and she fought it down.

"Enrique," Prade began. "As I said on the phone, this is a private conversation. Detective Cruz worked with Captain Espinosa and needs some closure regarding his death."

Furtado nodded. He was younger and slimmer than Prade but wore the same professional exhaustion. When Emilia met him during the investigation with Espinosa into a killing field on the Costa Chica coast south of Acapulco, the doctor was a pair of eyes above a surgical mask and gown, orchestrating the recovery of body parts. Now he was the examiner who'd done the autopsy of Captain Espinosa.

"You'll safeguard any information I give you, Detective Cruz?" Furtado said.

"Yes, of course," Emilia said.

"This is extremely important." Furtado placed his

hands flat on the desk and leaned in. "I can't overemphasize the need for discretion."

How many times had Emilia heard that lately? "I fully understand," she said.

Furtado's narrow shoulders drooped. "Captain Espinosa's death was not murder," he said. "The poor man shot himself."

"But everybody knows he was the third El Trio victim," Emilia protested. "Same pattern. Shot in his parked car."

Furtado shook his head sadly. "It was suicide. He left a handwritten note for his ex-wife in the glove compartment."

"Why let everyone think he was murdered?" Emilia exclaimed.

"It served a purpose," Furtado said. He had large eyes ringed with circles and deepened by his grim expression. "Captain Espinosa was in a unique position to manipulate evidence for a case the *federales* were prosecuting and was, shall we say, encouraged to do so. When he refused, one of his sons was kidnapped."

The eyeballs in the jar stared at Emilia accusingly, as if she should have known. They seemed closer than before.

"*Madre de Dios*," Prade murmured.

Furtado went on. "The boy's body was discovered the day before Captain Espinosa killed himself. The note to his ex-wife said it was to protect the other children."

It was stuffy in the office, the air thick with dust and death. Emilia could barely breathe. It took a moment to find her voice. "Why hide the fact that it was suicide?" she asked.

"The investigation into his murder is ongoing," Furtado said carefully.

"Did he deliberately stage his death to look like a murder?" Prade asked.

Furtado didn't reply.

Emilia looked from one medical examiner to the other as the eyeballs silently taunted her. The suspicious reaction of Espinosa's boss, Captain Torres, now made sense.

"His note named names," she guessed. "With enough creative thinking, the *federales* will be able to charge someone for his murder. And the murder of his son."

"I can't overemphasize the need for discretion," Furtado said.

Both Emilia and Prade were silent as the Suburban rumbled along the highway.

"You're very quiet," Prade said finally.

"What happened to Captain Espinosa was awful," Emilia said.

"But does it help to know?"

"Yes. I guess so." Emilia felt sick at what Espinosa— and his family—had suffered. The cruelty of Mexico's drug war violence, and the choices it drove, was crushing the life out of the country. She almost wished that he had been murdered by the El Trio killer; it would be easier to accept.

Espinosa's suicide subtracted one victim from the El Trio scorecard. That left the killer responsible for the deaths of Salinas, Vega, Isabel, and Hernandez.

Out of the four victims, Emilia only knew why Hernandez had been killed. The reason for Isabel's death remained especially murky. Even if the killer had intended to kill Silvio and not Isabel, what was the motive?

As they passed the exit for Tierra Colorada, Emilia thought back to Dario Delgado's account of the quarrel between Salinas and Vega, possibly over money, the week before Salinas was murdered. Maybe money was the key, as it was in so many other cases she'd encountered as a detective. Her efforts so far had been scattered, what with everything else she was juggling, but maybe now she should focus on financial transactions. Of course, without the authority of a formal police investigation, her chances of finding out anything were slim to none.

"You were wrong, you know," Emilia said. Tucked into the corner of the big front seat, Prade wore half moon reading glasses, a trademark plaid shirt, and a rumpled sports coat that had been in fashion during the Mexican Revolution. He was a medical examiner and a friend but certainly not a fashion icon.

"A common occurrence," Prade replied.

"You thought it was possible that Silvio killed his wife."

"Ah, you are correct," Prade said. "I was unduly influenced by his political enemies."

"He's still got the personality of a gorilla," Emilia said.

Her cell phone was on the console between the two seats. It rang and Emilia glanced at the display. It was her contact at Missing Persons.

"Could you get that?" Emilia asked Prade and told him who it was.

Prade answered the phone. The conversation was brief. He thanked the caller and replaced the phone on the console. "No one named Lila Jimenez Lata is employed at the El Pharaoh casino, Emilia," he said. "Missing Persons has no time for further inquiries."

Emilia bit her lip to keep from crying. It was all too much. Hunting for Lila, suspecting Kurt, the echo of Silvio's words, the constant fear of the unseen El Trio killer, Claudia nattering in the background.

She'd fallen apart last night at the Sinfonia. Today was no better.

Kurt called that night as Emilia sat on the sofa in the penthouse living room, staring at some *norteamericano* police drama on television. In one hour, the tall thin lady detective and the rich handsome writer always solved the most perplexing crime. Later they danced around the issue of whether or not to have sex. They were never hopeless or overwhelmed.

"I miss you," Kurt said. He sounded happy and sexy

and wholly normal, as if he'd never keep secrets from her.

"You're not missing much," Emilia replied. "I'm not good company right now."

"Work?" Kurt asked.

"A lot of things." Emilia wasn't going to gossip over the phone about desperate suicides or El Trio murders or missing girls.

Or abandoned children. They had to talk face-to-face so she could see the lie in his eyes if he tried to deny it.

"Have you seen Silvio lately?" Kurt asked.

"No," Emilia said.

"Claudia making you crazy?"

"No."

Silence stretched across the miles between Las Vegas and Acapulco.

"Did I call at a bad time?" Kurt asked.

"Kind of," Emilia said.

He told her when he'd be home and the call ended. Emilia eventually fell asleep on the sofa in front of the television, her face wet with tears.

CHAPTER 23

Emilia came into her office the next morning to see Rosalita sitting behind the desk. The former hooker was in uniform with the *Las Perdidas* binder open in front of her.

"What are you doing?" Emilia demanded.

Rosalita looked up. "What happened to all these women?"

"I'm looking for them," Emilia said. "Why are you in here?"

"I . . . I." Rosalita sniffed hard. "I'm sorry. I came in to ask if Tina Maria was in trouble for what happened yesterday. Or if I was."

"And thought you'd sit down at my desk and look through my things?"

Rosalita closed the binder and covered her face with her hands. "My daughter is in your book," she choked out.

"Oh." All the air went out of Emilia.

She dumped her shoulder bag on the console, closed the office door, and waited.

Rosalita swiped at her eyes and gave a shaky cough. "She was 13. One night she vanished."

"Show me," Emilia said.

Rosalita reopened the binder. "I filed a report but no one cared that some hooker's kid was gone," she said bitterly. "Probably thought she was a hooker, too."

Leaning over the desk, Emilia scanned the entry for Rosalita's daughter. The first and last piece of information was a standard Missing Persons report over two years old.

"I'm sorry," Emilia said. "I don't have any leads on her. But I'm always looking in police reports and the news. Plus, I have friends on the street. In the morgue. They tell me if they hear anything."

"And this is where you keep it all."

"Yes. If I get anything else, I'll tell you."

Rosalita sniffed. "At least she's not forgotten. You're a detective and you're still looking for her. That's more hope than I had an hour ago."

"That's why you wanted this job, isn't it?" Emilia asked. It explained everything, including the close relationship with Tina Maria. So clearly in need of a mother herself, the youngest patrol officer was nearly the same age as the lost daughter.

"I thought maybe the police had information they weren't sharing," Rosalita admitted.

"No," Emilia said. "I hope that doesn't mean you'll quit Las Palomas."

"I won't," Rosalita said. "If you'll let me help. Is there someone you're searching for right now? What can I do?"

Emilia straightened up. Sometimes gifts came when least expected. "Did you ever work the El Pharaoh casino?" she asked.

"Once or twice," Rosalita said warily. "Why?"

Two women are hookers waiting for business, Rosalita had said, whereas four women are out to have fun. Emilia had to admit the logic of what she'd said and so Natividad and Tina Maria were with them.

All four were dressed for an evening out. Rosalita had on a slinky red dress that was going to attract more attention than they needed, while Natividad and Tina Maria both wore skinny jeans, heels, and strapless tops. Emilia fit in, too, in dress and high heels.

She gave each woman Lila Jimenez Lata's background story and a picture, piled them into the Suburban, and prayed that Tina Maria's false *cédula* would fool the doorman at the El Pharaoh.

It did and now they were at a table for four near the bar. Tina Maria's eyes were as big as saucers. Every man in the place noticed Rosalita.

The El Pharaoh casino was big, noisy, and crowded. Waiters and waitresses were dressed as ancient Egyptians. Costumes leaned heavily on metallic leather, imitation gold, gladiator sandals, and jeweled collars extending beyond their shoulders. Emilia's senses were assaulted by blaring pop music, incessant electronic bleeping and ring tones from hundreds of slot machines, and a circus of visual inputs including blinking lights and wide screen televisions broadcasting Copa America highlights.

Emilia ordered a mojito and looked around. The first and last time she had been in the El Pharaoh casino was with a detective badge around her neck and a warrant in her hand. She remembered telling Kurt that Silvio had walked into the place as if he owned it and shuttered the doors ten minutes later. Of course, it had all been for nothing, thanks to those idiots Castro and Gomez.

A costumed waitress with an elaborate headdress served their drinks. All of the croupiers, security staff, and money counters were male, as were the bartenders. If Lila worked there, she was either a server, kitchen staff, or part of the cleaning crew. Or a hooker trolling for business.

Slot machines lined the perimeter of the bar. Bells went off and lights flashed as a couple cheered their win. Noisy onlookers joined in.

Tina Maria was agog. Rosalita looked at home. Natividad grinned at Emilia. "Shall we circulate or stay here?"

"Let's take turns circulating," Emilia said. "In pairs. Leave your glass on the table so the sharks know the seat is taken."

"I see some familiar faces," Rosalita said. "Tina Maria, let's go over there." She indicated a horseshoe-shaped lounge area for smokers."

Tina Maria obediently got up. "Can I take my drink?"

"I'll take mine, too," Rosalita said. They'd both ordered non-alcoholic cocktails.

Rosalita and Tina Maria left, serious about their reconnaissance mission.

Excited bar chatter competed with English-language pop music. Three large screen televisions mounted above the bar formed a panorama of sports events, each with their own soundtrack.

"*Madre de Dios*," Emilia said. "This place is so loud I can barely hear myself think."

"You work a lot," Natividad said.

"What?"

Natividad scooted closer. "What else do you do besides work?"

"Besides work?" Emilia repeated.

"Yes."

Emilia shook her head. "I'm very one dimensional," she said and they both laughed.

They talked as they watched the flow of people through the bar, Lila's photo on the table between them.

"You know," Natividad said at one point. "We could give all the patrol officers pictures of this Lila. You'd have more luck with all of Las Palomas looking for her."

Rosalita and Tina Maria returned after a few minutes. Rosalita shook her head. "No one knew her," she said.

"I was just saying," Natividad said, as Tina Maria and Rosalita sat down. "We should give copies of this picture to all the Las Palomas officers."

"That's a wonderful idea," Tina Maria said.

"What about the others?" Rosalita was quick to ask.

"Others?" Natividad queried, looking from Emilia to Rosalita.

Emilia nodded. "Lila is one of more than 40 women currently missing in Acapulco."

"She has a binder of all the missing women," Rosalita said.

"What if we made playing cards with their pictures and details?" Natividad asked. "Officers would use them as reference and even hand them out if we made enough."

It was a promising idea, but Emilia knew Claudia would never go for it. "First things first," she said lightly.

She and Natividad strolled out of the bar, ignoring several lingering glances.

Below lurid murals of a Mexican version of ancient Egypt, endless rows of slot machines advertised *Double Diamond Sweepstakes* and *Hot Tamale Hot Cash*. Flashing lights and rolling symbols called attention to directions in both English and Spanish. *Bet twice and triple your winnings!*

Players sat on tall stools in front of the machines and punched blinking buttons or pulled a lever. The machines emitted a collective orchestra of electronic tones and clunking cogs. An occasional *dingdingding* and flashing red lights, along with excited squeals, indicated a winner. No coins tumbled out, however; everything was recorded on the casino's version of a debit card.

The area devoted to slot machines was a maze, no doubt designed to trap gamblers in front of all the excitement and promises of easy money. Emilia wasn't immune. She paused in front of a Double Diamond machine. Images of jeweled rings tumbled behind the glass display; rubies, sapphires, and the occasional lucky diamond horseshoe.

"You didn't say anything about my idea," Natividad said.

Emilia turned away from the hypnotic machine and its empty promises. "About making playing cards to find missing women?"

"Yes."

"I thought it was brilliant," Emilia admitted as they strolled on. "But Claudia will never go for it."

"Why not?"

Emilia didn't want to trash their boss to a subordinate. "She's focused on image," she said carefully. "The role of Las Palomas is to project a very positive image of Acapulco."

"What if it was her idea?"

"How would you do that?"

Natividad shrugged. "I'll think of something. After all, I'm the assistant chief of operations."

Emilia laughed.

They passed a couple squabbling over how many bets to place at once. "New gamblers," Natividad observed. "Probably still believe the odds are in their favor."

"Lila isn't here," Emilia said after their second circuit of the slot machine labyrinth.

"Why not just ask the management?"

"I was hoping to avoid that," Emilia said. "The casino doesn't have a great relationship with official Acapulco."

"Look, roulette," Natividad said. "Let's watch."

They drifted over to the table and watched the wheel spin. Half a dozen gamblers leaned over the side, hands drumming nervously on the felt or stacking colored squares of plastic embossed with the El Pharaoh logo. Emilia didn't know the denominations of the colored chips and was startled when one man pushed four chips into play and announced, "Twenty thousand pesos on black."

The El Pharaoh was too rich for her blood.

"Over there," Natividad whispered. "Isn't that the man from the union?"

It was Obregon, in one of his trademark black suits complete with black shirt and tie, coming out of a doorway marked "Employees Only." Through the open door, Emilia saw a long hallway with thick carpeting.

Obregon was accompanied by a jowly man with oiled curls swept back from a high forehead. Obregon's usual security detail wasn't around as the two men approached the opposite side of the roulette table.

The other man wore a navy blazer with the El Pharaoh logo embroidered on the breast pocket. His white shirt was open at the throat, the better to show off a thick gold chain. A white silk square bloomed out of his breast pocket, drawing attention to the logo. He was older and stockier than Obregon, and everything about him screamed ostentatious wealth.

The conversation between the two men paused as the El Pharaoh blazer consulted a heavy gold watch. Obregon looked around and saw Emilia. It was as if radar had directed his gaze straight at her.

"Shit," Emilia hissed under her breath.

The two men approached, coming through the scrum of gamblers at the roulette table like Moses parting the Red Sea. "Well, Detective Cruz," Obregon drawled. "Where is the heroic Señor Rucker this evening?"

Emilia managed a half smile as Natividad stared. "This evening is for Las Palomas," she said. "Celebrating our new badges."

Obregon gave her one of his predatory smiles before turning it on Natividad. "We haven't been introduced."

The four exchanged names. The jowly man was Pedro Duarte Ochoa, the owner of the El Pharaoh. Their host.

Emilia managed a smile as Duarte Ochoa fawned over her hand. Many of the high rollers must be regulars and knew him, which explained the reaction at the roulette table as he passed.

"Are you here to play table games, Detective Cruz?" Duarte Ochoa asked. "You don't have any chips."

"No," Emilia said. "Just the slots."

Obregon licked his lips. "Detective Cruz is always a table games player," he said. "Whether she admits it or not."

Duarte Ochoa laughed and snapped his fingers. Out of nowhere, a young man in a King Tut costume appeared. He opened a small wooden box and offered it to the casino owner. Duarte Ochoa took out a blue chip embossed with the golden logo of the casino. Five thousand pesos. Nearly a month's salary for Emilia. Double that for Natividad.

Emilia's gaze travelled from the chip to the young man dressed as King Tut. Despite the costume, which included a jeweled headdress covering his forehead, she recognized Felipe Garcia. The long hair flowed over his bare shoulders and the high cheekbones were on full display.

The sporting goods store wasn't doing so well after all. It was too bad that Felipe had to moonlight at the El Pharaoh.

She flashed him a smile of recognition but he didn't acknowledge her. Emilia wasn't offended; Felipe probably had to stay in character. Duarte Ochoa dismissed him with a wave and King Tut went back to his pyramid.

The casino owner held the chip between his second and third fingers as if toying with it. "Red or black, Detective Cruz?"

She certainly wasn't picking Obregon's favorite color. "Red," she said.

Duarte Ochoa put the chip on the felted table. The croupier announced that bets were closed and spun the wheel. The clatter of the ball bouncing inside the wheel was louder than the grinding pop music.

"Red wins," the croupier announced.

Duarte Ochoa smiled broadly as the croupier raked a combination of colored chips to his designated spot on the table. "Do we let it ride, Detective?" he asked Emilia.

Obregon lounged against the table, watching her with that

hawkish expression on his face that always made her so nervous. If he suddenly sprouted wings and talons, Emilia would not be surprised.

"It's your money," she said.

Duarte Ochoa let it ride.

"Red wins," the croupier announced again.

Another bet was placed, the wheel spun, and Duarte Ochoa won a third time. The pile in front of him grew. Emilia counted at least a dozen blue chips and an equal amount of red and yellow. A year's salary.

"If we win on red again, we'll share it four ways," Duarte Ochoa said. "With champagne."

Natividad dug her fingers into Emilia's arm.

The wheel spun again, the ball bouncing and clattering until finally settling into a numbered slot.

"Black wins," the croupier announced.

"*Que lastima*," Duarte Ochoa said as the croupier raked away all his chips. "When you are a gambler you know that tomorrow the odds will be better. I hope you ladies are not disappointed."

Obregon let his gaze linger on Emilia. "Don't worry about Detective Cruz, Duarte. She knows that sometimes you win." He licked his lips. "And sometimes you lose."

It had been a strange encounter and Emilia had had enough. "We'll say good night, gentlemen," she said hastily. "We have a celebration to rejoin."

She didn't wait for either protests or pleasantries but steered Natividad towards the bar.

"Why didn't you ask them if Lila Jimenez Lata worked here?" Natividad asked.

Because I'd forgotten all about her. "It didn't seem like the right time," Emilia said lamely. Maybe she could ask Felipe Garcia about Lila.

"That union guy," Natividad said. "I don't like him."

"I've run into him before," Emilia said. "He's always testing. Trying to find your weak spots, figuring out how to exploit you."

"I've met his kind before," Natividad said. "He likes to butt fuck because he knows it hurts you."

Emilia looked at the younger woman, surprised at her vulgar language. "What would you know about things like that?" she asked.

Natividad met her eyes. "You've met my father, haven't you?"

CHAPTER 24

"Oh Emilia!" The Palacio Réal's concierge waved from behind her tall counter. "Do you have a moment?"

Emilia transferred the gym bag containing her street clothes to her left hand, shoved her sunglasses up on her head, and stalked across the lobby. She was still in workout gear—sports bra, capri leggings, cross trainers—and couldn't resist a smile as Christine blinked at the puckered scar on Emilia's right bicep.

Emilia deliberately put that elbow on the counter. Christine pasted a hotel greeter smile on her pale *gringa* face.

"There is a gentleman waiting for you in Kurt's office," the concierge said. She inclined her head to indicate the corridor behind the reception desk where the executive offices were located.

"You mean Kurt is back?" Emilia asked. He wasn't supposed to return until tomorrow.

"Yes and imagine his surprise to find this gentleman waiting for you."

Emilia frowned. "If this person was asking for me, you didn't need to call Kurt."

Christine's mouth twitched. "He always wants to know if anything irregular happens," she said sweetly.

Puta. Emilia managed a smile. "You're always so on top of things, Christine."

The door to Kurt's office was closed but opened swiftly at her knock.

"Em." Kurt gave her a quick kiss on the cheek and tossed her sports bag in the corner. "You have a visitor."

Emilia looked beyond Kurt to see Dario Delgado's bodyguard. He rose from a chair at the conference table. "It's good to see you again, Detective Cruz."

"And you." Emilia realized she didn't know his name. "Is everything all right with your employer?"

"Thank you for asking. He's fine and sends his regards." The bodyguard indicated an oblong box wrapped in brown paper on the table. "He would like you to have this."

Kurt folded his arms, his face expressionless. There was a tray with a bottle of sparkling water and two glasses on the table next to the package. Both glasses still had water in them. Emilia wondered how long the two men had sat in the office looking at the view and saying very little to each other.

The bodyguard held out the package to Emilia. "My employer asks that you open it in private."

It was heavy. Emilia imagined what was inside. A piece of expensive artwork. One of Delgado's film awards. Something told her that whatever it was, the item was totally inappropriate. She tried to hand it back. "It's very kind, but I cannot accept his generous gift."

The bodyguard kept his arms at his sides. "It is not a gift, Detective Cruz."

He turned to Kurt. "Thank you for your hospitality, señor."

"I'll have your car brought around to the front," Kurt said.

The bodyguard inclined his head and walked out, closing the office door behind him.

At his desk, Kurt punched a button on his phone and murmured some directions into the receiver.

Emilia put the package on the table and sat down.

Kurt hung up the phone.

"Hi," Emilia said. "How was your trip?"

"Fine."

"You're back a day early."

"I missed you."

Kurt pulled Emilia out of the chair and kissed her hard. The embrace wiped Emilia's mind and her body responded the way it always did to him. When reason returned she pulled away, nearly breathless. Despite everything she knew, he still sent her pulse soaring. If he asked, she'd make love to him right here on the floor of his office.

She scrambled back to the relative safety of the chair. "Did you hire an assistant manager?" she asked.

"Yes. He'll be here in a couple of weeks when his visa gets squared away." Kurt sat down beside her.

"Great," Emilia said.

Kurt tapped the package on the table. "You want to tell me what this is all about? I walk into the hotel and find the international man of mystery asking for you."

Emilia took a deep breath. "You remember Javier

Salinas. The second El Trio victim."

"Yes."

"He and Dario Delgado were lovers."

"Dario Delgado, the actor?"

"Yes, that Dario Delgado."

Kurt gave a laugh. "Somebody is having you on, Em."

"The man who brought the package works for him."

"Okay," Kurt said. He rifled a hand through his hair. "So now you know Dario Delgado."

"One of Salinas's friends arranged for me to meet him." In a few sentences, her hand resting on the package, Emilia told Kurt about going to the state's attorney general's office to discuss the Salinas murder investigation, her discussion with Josefina Vargas Guzmán in the parking garage, and the subsequent trip to Ixtapa to speak with Delgado.

"Well, let's get this over with," Kurt said skeptically. He produced a pair of scissors from a desk drawer. Emilia cut away the heavy paper to reveal a cardboard box. She lifted the lid, pushed aside sheets of tissue paper, and saw two green linen-covered accounting ledgers.

"Silvio's books," Emilia gasped.

Kurt peered over her shoulder. "Why would some actor have Silvio's books?"

"I don't know." Emilia dug out the ledgers. Both were foxed on the edges from long use.

She found a blue note card underneath.

"'J gave these to me but I was not to tell anyone I had them,'" Emilia read aloud. Punctuated with blots from a fountain pen, the slashing handwriting was difficult to decipher. "'He said he was going to give them to you because you were the only honest cop he knew. You would fix what he'd done. Yours eternally, D2.'"

"'Yours eternally?'" Kurt echoed.

Emilia glanced at him. "The man is gay."

"He's not gay," Kurt said. "He's Dario Delgado."

"We can argue about him later." Emilia opened the first ledger. It was filled with columns of figures. "It's full of math," she said blankly.

"Let me see." Kurt pulled the ledger towards himself and slowly paged through it as Emilia watched. After a few minutes Kurt looked up. "My best guess is that this is a record of foreign exchange transactions. Euros, pounds, yen, you name it. Exchanged into dollars or pesos. I have no idea if the exchange rates are fair or not."

Emilia slid the other to him. Whatever they were, the ledgers were not Silvio's.

Nearly half an hour ticked by as Kurt studied it.

"This is a real estate business," he said at length. "A dozen commercial properties and a circle of investors who own shares. Each of the properties generates income from tenants who pay rent. The investors get paid a percentage of the rental income. Sounds like the investment club Tony Wilcox wants me to join."

"Show me," Emilia said.

"Okay." Kurt flipped pages. There was an address printed in block letters at the top of every few pages. He smoothed the center binding so that the ledger stayed open and swiveled it around so he and Emilia could read the page at the same time.

"Here's a good example," he said. "It's a building on Avenida Almendros. Three business tenants. Soledo Enterprises, Consolidated Solutions, Vector Analytics. Rent is received monthly. Investors are paid quarterly. My guess is that these initials are the investors." He showed her a column of initials with a percentage next to each.

"I work in that building," Emilia said with a catch in her voice. "All those businesses are on the first floor. Las Palomas offices are on the second floor."

"So this investment club is either the owner or the rental agent."

"No. You don't understand." Emilia took a deep breath. "There's nothing going on in those offices. Soledo and the others. There are signs, but no one ever goes in or out."

"They're fake?" Kurt asked. "Storefronts?"

"I never really thought about it," Emilia said. "I figured the building was so new the tenants hadn't moved in yet."

"If the tenants are fake this could be a money laundering scheme. I've seen it in the hotel business where chains try to say rooms or condos are rented when they're empty. Real estate is a great way to move dirty money around."

"As the so-called rental income."

"Exactly. The unwitting investors provide iron-clad legitimacy." Kurt flipped open the first ledger. "My guess is that all this foreign currency is cash from drug sales. It's basically washed through the real estate scheme, masked as rent in dollars and pesos."

"What about the investors?" Emilia asked.

Kurt leaned back. "If this is Tony Wilcox's investment club, they don't have a clue."

"How could that be?"

He shrugged. "The investors' money is recycled and paid out bit by bit. They think they're getting paid a dividend or whatever and that eventually they'll earn more than they paid in."

"But they won't?"

"They'll keep getting dividends as long as new members and fresh money keeps coming in." Kurt shook his head. "It's a classic scam. But in this case the scam is also a front for the money laundering."

"Would Tony know who's in charge?" Emilia groped for what to do next. "We could find out who's making the payouts, right?"

"Give me a minute to think, Em." Kurt passed a hand over his face. "This has been a hell of a day. I had to wait two hours in Mexico City while the drug dogs walked all over my suitcase which meant I missed my connection to Acapulco. When I finally get home, some spook is waiting to give you a present from superstar Dario Delgado."

"Are you jealous?" Emilia asked.

"No, I'm not jealous," Kurt said uncomfortably.

"Good, because I think this has to do with the El Trio

murders."

Kurt stood up in agitation. "Great, just great. The El Trio murders in my hotel again."

"You told me to tell you things." Emilia slammed the ledger shut and jumped up to face him. Who the hell was this *pendejo*, this father who abandoned his child, to get mad at her? "When I do, you don't want to hear."

Kurt raised a hand. "Stop. Stop." He inhaled and let it out slowly. "Look, I'm hot and tired, had a shitty flight, and this seems like bad news. Let's not take it out on each other."

Emilia took a deep breath, too. "Okay. I'm sorry, too. It's been an awful week."

"I'll call Tony Wilcox," Kurt said. He went to his desk and pulled out an address book. "Make like I want to join the club. There's no need to tell him anything else."

"Wait." Emilia interrupted. She leaned against the edge of his desk and pressed her fingertips against her temples. "Obregon's in it, too."

"Carlota's police union goon?" Kurt asked. "The one who always wears black?"

"Yes. Him."

"What's he got to do with all of this?"

"The building on Avenida Almendros belongs to the police union," Emilia said. The connections and implications came at her like an alarm ringing in a storm. "What time is it?"

Kurt checked his watch. "A little after 7:00 pm," he said. "Do you want some dinner?"

"I have to go," Emilia said.

"I just got home, Em."

But Emilia barely heard him. She scooped up the ledgers, grabbed her sports bag, and sprinted out of the office.

CHAPTER 25

"You called just in time," Josefina said. She closed the door to her office in the state's attorney general's building and motioned for Emilia to have a seat on a small beige sofa by a dark wood coffee table.

"Thank you," Emilia said. "You'd said that you stayed late and I was really hoping to catch you."

The attorney sat next to Emilia rather than behind the desk piled high with legal sized folders. She wore a chic charcoal linen suit with a ruffled white blouse. If she wondered at Emilia's capris, cross trainers, and wrinkled sweatshirt, she didn't say anything.

"I have a few more questions about Javier Salinas," Emilia said.

"Have you made an arrest?" Josefina asked hopefully.

"Not yet." Emilia took the ledgers out of her shoulder bag and placed them on the small coffee table in front of the sofa. "Have you ever seen these before?"

Josefina picked up one of the ledgers and fanned through the pages. The color drained out of her face. "Yes," she said in a small voice.

Emilia waited.

"I couldn't say anything before," Josefina faltered. "No one else knew. And Javier made me promise . . ."

Emilia waited some more. The silence grew awkward.

"I guess there's hardly any point in trying to protect his

reputation now," Josefina said. She closed the ledger and ran her palms down her thighs, smoothing the linen of her skirt. "Javier had a case a few months ago. Foreign exchange trading fraud, something like that. I don't remember exactly. I was in his office when a man came in. He didn't have an appointment and I remember Javier was upset with security that they'd let him in. Later, the security guard said that the man was a police officer. He had these ledgers with him. Basically he offered to trade them to Javier in return for getting the foreign exchange case thrown out."

"And Salinas took the bribe," Emilia said.

Josefina gave a lopsided smile. "Not really. Javier kept the ledgers and said he'd see what he could do. Then he followed procedure and the criminal went to jail."

"The man who brought the ledgers," Emilia said. "Was he thin, kind of lanky? Dressed in jeans and a tee shirt? Ponytail?"

"Yes." Josefina clasped her hands together. "Do you know him?"

Castro, of course it was Castro. Trying to get his brother out of a jam.

"I know who he is," Emilia said. "Did you ever see him again?"

"No."

"Did you know where the ledgers came from?"

"They're from the El Pharaoh casino." Josefina's mouth tightened with tension. "Javier was assigned to that case. Money laundering charges but there wasn't enough to prosecute. Noriega ordered him to drop it. There's only time for the most solid cases."

"But Javier had the ledgers," Emilia said. "Didn't they prove the case?"

Josefina shrugged. "He never did anything with them that I know of."

"So Javier kept the ledgers but didn't use them to prosecute the money laundering case," Emilia said. "He didn't drop the fraud case, either."

"That's right." There was little decoration in the office except for a silver frame on the coffee table. Josefina moved it an inch to the left.

"Wasn't Javier afraid of retaliation?" Emilia asked. Castro had connections, although she didn't think he had the gall to murder a member of the state's attorney general's office. "After all, Javier didn't keep up his end of the bargain."

"We talked about it." Josefina fiddled with the photo again. The picture inside was of her and a handsome man. The photo was posed but their smiles were genuine. "Javier said he knew a cop who dealt with financial crimes. Someone very senior. Well placed within the department. Javier thought this officer would protect him. When I asked him who it was, he said he wanted me to forget I'd seen the ledgers. He was adamant and I promised."

Vega. Emilia remembered the partial biography that Loyola had filed away. Vega had led a financial crimes task force for Chief Salazar. "That's all he said?" Emilia pressed. "That this police officer was protecting him from retaliation?"

"There's something else," Josefina said slowly. "A few days before Javier was murdered, he said that things weren't going his way. He'd been left with a choice between two evils. I thought that meant that he and Dario were having problems. You know, whether to come out or not."

"Two evils?"

"Yes, that's what he said."

Emilia replaced the ledgers in her shoulder bag. "But nothing else about the senior police official? You're sure?"

"Is that how you got them?" Josefina asked. "From this other police officer?"

"No," Emilia said. "Javier gave the ledgers to Dario for safekeeping."

"Did someone kill Javier because he kept the ledgers? Because he tricked them?"

"I don't know," Emilia said honestly. "But do us both a favor and forget you saw the ledgers tonight. I was here . . ." She hesitated and looked at herself. "Because you asked about my health club."

"Are you afraid sometimes, Detective Cruz?" Josefina asked.

"Yes," Emilia said simply.

Josefina picked up the picture in the silver frame.

Emilia was reminded of the photo of Isabel and Silvio she'd taken from their house. It, too, had been in a silver frame.

That's what people in love did, she thought. Capture happiness in little silver frames and think it will last forever.

Emilia drove slowly around the parking lot of the police station. Given the late hour, there weren't many cars. Castro's SUV was gone. But a certain dented piece of crap was still in the lot, which was even better. She parked in an unlit corner where the big Suburban was less noticeable, got out, and waited.

An hour later, her quarry emerged from the rear exit of the building, wearing his Australian canvas duster. He paused and lit a cigarette.

"Hey, Ibarra." Emilia sidled around the back fender of the dented sedan as the stocky detective jammed the lighter in his pocket. She was gratified to see him jump and dart a glance at the guard shack on the other side of the parking lot. "Haven't seen you in awhile," she went on. "How're you doing?"

"*Rayos*, Cruz." Ibarra pulled the cigarette out of his mouth and spit out a chip of tobacco. It snagged on the sleeve of his coat. "What the fuck are you doing here?"

"Thought we could have a chat," Emilia said. She leaned against the driver's door.

"That business with Castro and Gomez is over," he said,

trailing smoke out of both nostrils. "No sense travelling over an old road, you know what I mean?"

"I'm not here about that," Emilia said.

"You better go home," Ibarra cautioned. "It's late." He pulled out his keys and jingled them impatiently.

"Not so late."

"There's nothing for you here, Cruz."

"I want the ballistics report from the Javier Salinas murder investigation."

Ibarra shrugged and drew hard on his cigarette. "Good for you."

"You and Loyola opened the case into Salinas's murder," Emilia said. "You two showed up at the state's attorney general's office. Talked to at least three of his colleagues there. Made them believe the Acapulco police department was taking point on the case."

"Never happened," Ibarra said coolly. He walked directly at Emilia with his keys ready to unlock his car door. "Nice talking to you, Cruz."

"They described both of you," Emilia said, folding her arms and standing her ground. "You and Loyola without a doubt. They wondered why it was taking so long to get back to them. What should I tell them?"

Ibarra snaked an arm around her to get his key in the door lock.

"I never took you for a coward," Emilia said. "Or a thief. Must be something in between."

Ibarra stepped back, leaving the key in the lock, and

blew smoke into Emilia's face. White tendrils drifted by the mercury light mounted on the massive wall surrounding the parking lot.

Emilia snorted out ash and waited.

"You have no idea what you're talking about," he said finally.

"Enlighten me," Emilia replied.

Ibarra met her eye and drew hard on the cigarette. The end was hidden by his cupped hand.

"I've got all the time in the world," Emilia said.

Eventually Ibarra threw down the butt. He ground it under his heel, the buckle on his boot jingling softly.

"Okay," he said. "Loyola told me he was directed to do a preliminary inquiry into Salinas's murder the day after the body was discovered. Orders were to be discreet, talk to the family and the office. Keep them quiet."

"Who gave the orders?"

Ibarra shook his head and took out the pack of cigarettes again. "We looked at the car, asked a few questions at the office, talked to the family. Got the body shipped off to his mother."

"And then?"

"Then nothing. Loyola was told that was enough. Acapulco jurisdiction didn't allow us to do anything else. Our part was over."

"So you and Loyola walked away without a word to anyone?" Hearing it from the pompous ass in the state's attorney general's office was one thing, hearing Ibarra admit it was another. Emilia was stunned. "As many conversations as we all had about the El Trio murders and you never said a word. Never logged it in, made any record, asked any more questions?"

"Loyola had his orders. It was an inquiry, not a murder investigation."

"So what happened to the crime scene reports?" Emilia demanded. "The ballistics report?"

"Never happened," Ibarra said.

"What do you mean, never happened?" Emilia forced herself to stay calm. "The techs had to be there."

"Doesn't mean there's a report." The stocky detective lit another cigarette with his cheap plastic lighter.

"There would be a ballistics report," Emilia insisted. "It was a high profile murder."

"Leave it, Cruz."

"What about the final ballistics report for Isabel?" Emilia persisted. Loyola might have shared the original report with his former partner before hiding it in his safe. "No match for anything. Wasn't that a surprise?"

"For fuck sakes," Ibarra said, his casual attitude gone. He waved the lit cigarette. "Have you forgotten Hernandez?"

"No, I haven't forgotten about Hernandez."

"Want to stay alive?" Ibarra was too close now. A cloying mix of tobacco and sweat thickened the air. "No questions."

"You're willing to let this killer go?"

"I don't know about you, but I like breathing." Ibarra stuck the cigarette in his mouth, grabbed Emilia by the shoulders and muscled her aside. He snagged his keys and wrenched open the car door.

Emilia caught the sleeve of his duster before he could get in. "Who told Loyola to stop investigating Salinas's murder?"

"Go home and keep your mouth shut, Cruz." Ibarra angled himself into the car, nearly dragging Emilia along with him.

She hung on, stooping in the door opening, and suddenly they were face-to-face, inches apart. The interior of the old car smelled like an ash heap. "Vega or Obregon?" she asked softly.

Ibarra stared at her, the cigarette dangling from the corner of his mouth. "Leave it alone, Cruz," he said.

Emilia stood. She didn't need his answer; it had been inside Loyola's file all the time.

Ibarra slammed the door closed and the engine groaned into life. She stepped aside and let him go.

CHAPTER 26

Emilia didn't get back to the Palacio Réal until after midnight. Kurt was asleep. She crawled into the bed next to him and stared at the ceiling, her thoughts a stew of conspiracy theories and crippling paranoia. She slept fitfully. Nightmares shook her awake more than once.

Daylight helped. Emilia and Kurt discussed next steps as they stood on the balcony, cups of strong coffee in hand, and watched the sun climb into the brilliant blue sky.

Just another day in paradise.

Kurt called Tony Wilcox, who agreed to an 11:00 am appointment. Emilia wondered if she'd make it through the entire morning without screaming to relieve her nerves.

As Kurt showered, Emilia sat on the bed with the ledgers, drawn to the entries for the building on Avenida Almendros. Those empty office suites on the first floor supposedly brought in thousands of pesos in rent every month. How could she have been so blind?

"I'll run downstairs for an hour while you're scanning the ledgers," Kurt announced as he came into the bedroom dressed in a towel.

Emilia's heart twisted. Sometimes he was so beautiful that it hurt.

Kurt picked out his clothes; navy pants,

monogrammed shirt, loafers buffed to a high sheen. "I need to catch up on a few things," he said as he dressed swiftly. "When you're done scanning, send me the file and I'll copy it onto a dozen flash drives. Then I'll get a driver to take us over to the Santa Rosa to talk to Tony."

"Thanks for all of this," Emilia said. "You didn't want El Trio to touch the hotel. Now you're in the middle of it."

Kurt came over to the bed and cupped his hands around Emilia's face. "When this is over," he said. "We have to talk. About some serious stuff."

"Agreed," Emilia said, keeping her voice neutral.

Kurt kissed her and left. Emilia took a long shower and found a tank top, pencil skirt, and sandals. He was probably going to tell her he was moving back to Las Vegas to be with Suzanne and their child.

Emilia went into the office. As she started the tedious process of scanning each page of the ledgers, she wondered how long it would take to pack and move in with her mother and Ernesto again.

When this is over.

The driver stopped the car in front of the Santa Rosa and they got out. The hotel was a gracious shrimp-colored stucco affair in the traditional Spanish style. Pots of vibrant hibiscus lined the steps to the massive carved front door.

Tony and Jane Wilcox lived there during the cold months

in Canada, Kurt had told her, and owned another hotel property in Toronto where they spent the rest of the year. Emilia had only a vague idea where that was.

The lobby was an exaggerated version of the reception hall in Dario Delgado's house, cluttered with antique Spanish furniture and makeshift racks of postcards and brochures. Piles of Acapulco's weekly tourist magazine sat on a priceless table next to a pottery lamp with a large crack and a grimy shade.

Staff were overdressed for the Acapulco heat in tuxedo pants, white long sleeved shirts, satin vests, and cotton gloves. Although ceiling fans turned overhead, the receptionist who led them to Tony Wilcox's office door looked ready to melt.

"Kurt. Emilia." Wilcox rose from his chair behind a yacht-sized mahogany desk. He shook hands with Kurt and landed a blubbery buss on Emilia's cheek. "Let's go into the bar. You're in time for the midday cocktail."

The bar at the Santa Rosa was a small intimate affair, the way the inside of a coffin was a small intimate affair. The place was dim and mahogany paneling absorbed what little light there was. Banana plants in dark pots drooped as if they'd lost the will to live.

Wilcox steered them to a tall table by a window. On the other side of the leaded glass, coconut palms shaded an Olympic-sized turquoise pool. Dozens of teak loungers ringed the water. An outdoor bar sported a *palapa* roof, a bored bartender, and a sign offering free margaritas.

Everything that an Acapulco hotel should have, except guests.

The bar where they sat was also empty.

Wilcox saw Emilia looking around. "Wrong season, don't you know," he blustered.

"Of course," Emilia said.

At this time of the day, the Palacio Réal ran like a well oiled machine. Bartenders at the Pasodoble made fruity drinks. Each of the three pools at the Palacio Réal was busy, as staff stocked clean towels, ferried drinks, and led water aerobic classes. Guests relaxed in the spa or enjoyed wine tasting and gourmet cooking lessons in the restaurant. Tour groups assembled in the lobby. The marina hummed with private boat trips, fishing excursions, and water skiing lessons.

"Boy." Wilcox snapped his fingers at the Mexican bartender. "Make us some cocktails. Vodka tonics, with Grey Goose. None of the cheap stuff." He grinned at Kurt. "Sergei Porchenko gave me a case of Kalashnikov vodka. Tastes like piss but the wetbacks lap it up."

The conversation was in English. Emilia struggled with Wilcox's twangy accent.

Jane Wilcox came into the bar wearing a strapless dress. Her chest and arms were tanned, accentuating her skin's crepe-like texture. Emilia thought she looked like an over-fried *churro* wrapped in a form-fitting napkin.

"Emilia!" Jane nearly fell into Emilia's lap as they

exchanged air kisses. Her breath smelled like vinegar and mint. "And the handsome Kurt Rucker."

"Jane. Nice to see you." Kurt grabbed the woman's upper arms before she stuck her hand in his crotch. He eased her into a chair next to her husband.

Tony Wilcox mimed another drink to the bartender.

"Are you staying for lunch?" Jane asked. "I'll have them make Mexican. *Pollo con* something. Emilia, you'll like that."

Under the table, Kurt put a restraining hand on Emilia's thigh. "Thanks, Jane," he said. "We have to take a rain check on lunch."

The bartender delivered three vodka tonics and a glass of wine for Jane.

"Cheers, all." Wilcox slugged down half his drink.

Emilia stirred the ice cubes in her glass with a finger. She never drank vodka and guessed now was not the time to start.

Wilcox put down his glass and grinned at Kurt. "So, you two are doing some financial planning?"

"Emilia and I are thinking of a run at that real estate investment club you told me about a few weeks ago," Kurt said.

"I thought you said you and Kurt don't talk about money," Jane said archly to Emilia.

"Emilia and I are expanding our conversation," Kurt said before Emilia could reply.

"That sounds serious." Wilcox guffawed and reached

across the table to clap Kurt on the shoulder. "But hells bells, Kurt. As I always say, why buy the cow if you can get the milk free?"

"Oh, Tony," Jane warbled. "Don't be so crude. You'll make Emilia nervous."

Emilia managed half a smile, unsure if she'd understood. The renewed pressure of Kurt's hand on her leg said she had.

"So is this real estate club for real or what, Tony?" Kurt got Wilcox back on track. "Are you making any money or is this a tax dodge?"

"It's legit," Wilcox said with an expansive gesture that nearly toppled his wife's wineglass. "Nothing complicated. We buy top commercial buildings, rent out office space and collect rent. You get a share of the rent in proportion to your original investment."

"Great." Kurt nodded. "What's the minimum?"

"Here's the deal." Wilcox leaned forward conspiratorially. "It's a nice fat 20 percent return if you come in with at least half a million US. Cash money. No pesos, for crissakes. If you bring in a full million you get a guaranteed rate of 25 percent." He leaned back. "Can't get that kind of guarantee on the stock market. I tell you, doing business in Mexico is like finding gold in the street."

"That's a lot of cash," Kurt said. "I mean, you're a business owner. You've got collateral. Who else is bringing that kind of cash to the table?"

"Well, I don't know," Wilcox said. "It's not the kind of club where you sit around and drink together. You should liquidate whatever else you're holding and grab a piece of it."

"If you haven't met anyone else, how do you know it's legit?"

"I didn't say I haven't met anyone," Wilcox huffed. "Most of the other Acapulco Hotel Association board members are in. The ones who are owners, at least. Real estate types are always looking for a good investment."

Emilia found it hard to stay still. Kurt's hand on her knee kept her focused.

"So who runs the show?" Kurt asked. "I don't want to lay down a wad of cash and find out I'm dealing with a crook."

"Would I steer you wrong?" Wilcox inhaled the rest of his drink and snapped his fingers for a refill. "That's the beauty of this. Everything's local. No shadowy corporate assholes you never heard of. The man at the top is Pedro Duarte Ochoa. Fat guy. Dresses like a fop. But he's got a mind like a steel trap. Runs the El Pharaoh casino, don't you know. Takes a fucking bushel out of there every night."

CHAPTER 27

It was a surreal experience to arrive at the Avenida Almendros building as if it was an ordinary day. Emilia felt as if she had a bull's eye on her forehead and a sign that said *I know this place is a scam* on her back. Maybe she didn't need the gun strapped to her ankle beneath black pants but she wouldn't have had the courage to walk in without it.

She made a circuit of the silent and empty storefronts. *Consolidated Solutions. Vector Analytics. Soledo Enterprises.* Exactly the same as the first day she'd walked into the building.

The Las Palomas office was the same, too. Busy with press releases and nonsense for Carlota. Emilia checked in with Paola, went into her office, and closed the door.

She called Silvio's cell phone. It rang a dozen times without going to voicemail.

Too agitated to stay behind a desk, Emilia went down to the Las Palomas ready room and reviewed the patrol schedule. Natividad had everything in order. There was little for Emilia to do.

She went back upstairs and called Silvio. No answer.

The day crawled. The main issue at the daily meeting was what color lipstick the Las Palomas patrol officers should wear. One of the PR hacks proposed a cross-marketing campaign with an upscale department store like Palacio de Hierro.

Emilia thought nothing more could surprise her but this left her simply aghast. "Las Palomas are cops," she exclaimed. "We don't sell cosmetics."

Everyone around the table looked embarrassed. Someone giggled.

The discussion resumed as if Emilia had never spoken. Claudia asked questions but was more subdued than usual. No doubt she'd eventually approve the idea.

Emilia excused herself and stalked out of the conference room. She went into her office, slammed the door, and jabbed at the redial button on her cell phone.

Silvio picked up on the third ring. "Cruz," he said, his voice neutral.

"Where have you been?" Emilia snapped. "I've been calling you all day."

"Run out of other ways to waste your time?"

"Don't give me any of your shit, Franco," Emilia shot back. She pressed the heel of her free hand to her forehead, trying to control the stress swimming through her bloodstream. She took a deep breath. "I need to talk to you about El Trio. And Isabel."

"The circle man?"

"I think I know who hired him."

Silvio was silent, but she heard the shift in his attitude. "I'm listening," he said at length.

"I have to show you," Emilia said. "Can we meet?"

"Where?"

"The place with the good *tostadas* and ceviche. You

remember?”

“Sure.”

“Stay in your car,” Emilia said. “Pick me up on the sidewalk in an hour.”

She churned through her emails, cleared off her desk, grabbed her shoulder bag, and set off for the restroom. The space gleamed with white porcelain tiles, volcanic stone basin sinks, and enamel partitions that stopped a few inches shy of the terrazzo floor. As Emilia pushed open the door, she heard the unmistakable sound of someone vomiting.

One stall door was closed. Emilia peered underneath and saw a pair of beige pumps with red soles.

The vomiting stopped and was replaced by soft coughing. An unseen hand flushed the toilet.

Claudia came out of the stall and flinched when she saw Emilia. “Oh, hello.”

“Are you all right?” Emilia asked.

Claudia stepped to a sink and turned on the water. “Yes, I’m fine, thank you,” she said primly. “A touch of food poisoning, that’s all.” She splashed water on her face and swished out her mouth.

“Okay.” Emilia used a different stall.

When she came out, Claudia was still standing at the sink with the water running. Tears and mascara streamed down her face.

Emilia went to the other sink and tried to pretend she hadn’t seen. She got a paper towel, swiftly dried her hands, and reached for the door handle.

"Emilia?" Claudia's voice was small and broken.

Two minutes. She'd give the woman two minutes. Emilia turned around. "What's going on, Claudia?" she asked. "Palacio de Hierro tell you to take your lipstick idea and shove it?"

"No." The younger woman gulped several times. "I'm pregnant."

"*Madre de Dios.*" Emilia reluctantly came back to the sink and turned off the faucet. "Are you sure?"

"Yes." Claudia brushed at her tears, leaving a messy smudge under both eyes.

Emilia knew the answer but had to ask. "Is Victor Obregon the father?"

Claudia nodded. "Yes, it's Victor."

"Have you told him?" Emilia handed Claudia a paper towel.

"No." Claudia took the paper towel and clutched it in both hands, like a frightened little girl. "I can't."

"You have to," Emilia said.

"He'll be furious," Claudia whimpered.

"He has to know," Emilia insisted. The parallel between this news and Kurt's situation with the mythical Suzanne hit her hard. "The child is his responsibility, not just yours."

Claudia dabbed at her face with the paper towel even as she teared up again. "I never meant for this to happen," she sniffed. "Victor was so helpful. One day he was in my office. He put his hand on my knee, and said if he didn't have me, he'd lose his mind. Before I knew, we were doing it."

"Didn't he use a condom?" Emilia asked.

Claudia shook her head. "You don't ask an important man like Victor things like that."

"Then how could you have thought that nothing would happen?" Emilia wanted to shake the teary woman. Like a bird of prey, Obregon had swooped in, seen Claudia the rabbit, and eaten her alive. This was what happened when children were given grown-up jobs.

"He's so exciting." Claudia's eyes filled again. "And he wanted me. Not Carlota. Me."

"Sleeping with him could be a real career builder, too," Emilia observed.

Claudia hiccupped and turned scarlet. "That's not a very nice thing to say."

"Well, nobody likes the whole truth." Emilia picked up her shoulder bag from where she'd left it by the sink. "You have to tell him. It's his child and he's responsible. You'd better tell Carlota, too."

"I'll lose my job if Carlota finds out," Claudia gulped.

"Ask her to be the godmother. Maybe she won't fire you."

Claudia brightened. "That's a good idea, Emilia."

Suddenly, Emilia couldn't stand being in the confined space, where every word bounced off the hard tile, echoed in her brain, reminded her of the situation with Kurt, and made her late to meet Silvio. She jerked open the bathroom door and fled down the hall.

CHAPTER 28

The timing worked as if they'd practiced. Silvio's truck pulled up to the sidewalk as Emilia passed a table of workmen shoveling down *tostadas* and tunes blasted from the food stand's boom box. She threw her shoulder bag, weighted with the ledgers, onto the seat and climbed in after it. Silvio swung away from the curb as she slammed the door.

Silvio looked even thinner than when she'd seen him at the funeral. No, not thinner. More like ripped, as if he'd spent every waking hour since in the gym. The skin over his jaw was stretched tight. The veins and sinews of his neck stood out like knotted rope. He wore a black tee over black jeans, an outfit which accentuated his overall look of taut muscle and constrained menace.

"Where are we going?" he asked without preamble. No greeting, no apology for the harsh words he'd thrown at her after the funeral.

Emilia told him how to get to the church. Last night, it had seemed the best neutral ground with the privacy needed to show him the ledgers and test out her theories. Now, with the dynamite in her bag, she wasn't so sure she should create a trail that led to Padre Ricardo. But she didn't know where else to go that would be private.

The old priest greeted them without asking questions and opened the door to the sacristy. "No one will disturb you."

"Thank you, Padre," Emilia murmured. "If anyone asks, this was couples counseling, right?"

Padre Ricardo turned to Silvio. "May I offer you some tea?"

"No," Emilia said before Silvio could respond. Padre Ricardo reused tea bags until the recipe was hot water and hope. "No, thank you."

Padre Ricardo left. Emilia sat at the big table which served the priest as desk, ironing board for his vestments, and conference center when he met with Confirmation candidates, planned funerals, or conducted marriage counseling.

Silvio stayed by the window, his arms folded. "So what's with all the drama, Cruz?"

Emilia pulled out the ledgers and let each drop on the table with a heavy thud.

Silvio crossed the room in two steps. "You found my books."

"They're not your books," Emilia said. "They're from the stash we hauled out of the El Pharaoh casino a couple of months ago. The money laundering case that tanked because of Castro and Gomez."

"Where did you find them?" Silvio snatched up one of the ledgers and paged through it.

"Remember Salinas? The first El Trio victim."

Silvio closed the ledger and tossed it on the table. "Okay, you've got my attention," he said.

"I think you'd better sit down," Emilia said.

It wasn't the most coherent account of what she'd found out over the past few weeks, but Silvio listened intently and didn't interrupt. Emilia showed him the documents from Loyola's file and flipped open her notebook to make sure she remembered every detail of the conversations with Dario Delgado, Josefina Vargas Guzmán, Tony Wilcox, and Ibarra. She told him the *federale* medical examiner's grim story about Espinosa, too.

"It's all there," Emilia finished. "A giant money laundering scheme that washes drug money through real estate holdings, using a legit investment club as cover. The owner of the El Pharaoh runs the whole thing. We should have found this out months ago, after the raid."

It grew dark as Silvio silently processed what Emilia had thrown at him.

"If Vega stopped the investigation into Salinas's murder," he said finally. Silvio found the handwritten questions posed to Emilia before her suspension. "Who's pulling Loyola's strings now? This isn't his handwriting."

"I don't know, but—."

"What did you think about Vega?" Silvio interrupted her. "When you met him in the office?"

Emilia blinked at the abrupt change in direction. "He was pompous. Power-hungry and not very nice."

"Not very nice," Silvio mimicked. "*Rayos*, Cruz. Vega was a mother-fucking *pendejo*. Chief Salazar's very own mother-fucking lapdog *pendejo*.”

“Well, yes.”

“Here’s what I think happened.” Silvio spun out of the chair and began to prowl the sacristy, from the closet where Padre Ricardo kept vestments, to the cabinet for candlesticks and altar linens. “Salinas comes to Vega for help. Vega sees it as a money-making opportunity. Get some cash out of this Duarte Ochoa.”

“Blackmail?” It was a twist Emilia hadn’t considered.

“Exactly.” Silvio punched the air for emphasis. “Salinas told his colleague, this Josefina, that he had to choose between two evils.”

“She thought he meant coming out as gay or not.”

Silvio snorted. “His choices were to cooperate with Vega, whose price for protection from Castro was help blackmailing Duarte Ochoa, or face Castro alone with Vega breathing down his neck for the ledgers.”

“You’re right.” Emilia felt sick. Salinas had made two fatal mistakes. The first mistake was accepting the books from Castro and the second was asking Vega for help.

“Salinas tells Vega he won’t go along.” Silvio was on a roll. He backed against the cabinet, his body tense. “He’ll take his chances with Castro. But Vega can’t leave Salinas out there knowing about the blackmail plan. So Vega shoots him and makes sure there’s no investigation.”

“But if Vega killed Salinas, that means there’s not just one El Trio killer.”

Silvio grimaced. “The evidence didn’t make up the

legend of El Trio. The press did."

Emilia held up her hand, palm out. "Hold on. Why would Vega have killed Salinas unless he got the ledgers first? He needed them to blackmail Duarte."

"Salinas made some mistakes but he was at least smart enough not to show off the ledgers," Silvio said. "If I was him, I'd have waved a couple of pages at Vega and inferred I knew where to get the rest."

Emilia nodded. "Vega leaped to the conclusion that you kept the ledgers after the El Pharaoh raid. It's what he would have done."

Silvio nodded. "That's why whoever killed Vega also killed Isabel."

"Somebody working for Duarte," Emilia supplied.

"But how did they know we wouldn't be home that particular night?" Silvio launched himself away from the cabinet and slammed his hands down on the table by the ledgers. "*Rayos*, Cruz. Where's the picture from Hollywood's security camera?"

Emilia rifled through the documents she'd brought along with the ledgers. She found the grainy photo taken from the closed circuit video feed featuring a slender and hooded figure by Hernandez's car. "Here," she said.

"Fuck," Silvio breathed, his eyes fixed on the photo. "I know who the circle man is."

CHAPTER 29

Emilia's heart was in her throat as she and Silvio plunged into the casino. She'd shown her badge to get them past the metal detector at the entrance and they probably had less than two minutes before casino security intercepted them.

The noise inside the casino was deafening and the crowd was thick. It wasn't just the ring and tumble of the slot machines. Tonight, televisions blared out the final Copa America match from at least a dozen huge screens. Patrons with key cards on lanyards around their necks and drinks in their hands filled every square meter of floor space as they screamed support for underdog Honduras against the seemingly invincible Argentina.

"There he is," Emilia shouted and pointed to the pyramid montage by the roulette tables.

In front of the giant mock-up of an ancient pyramid, King Tut was resplendent in his jeweled headdress, spangled leather collar, and shoulder-length hair. He had a large wooden box and exchanged gambler's plain poker chips for special chips with the El Pharaoh symbol stamped in gold, the kind Duarte Ochoa had used. A steady stream of casino patrons posed for a picture against the pyramid with the casino's theatrical version of ancient Egypt's child king.

Emilia stayed close to Silvio as he muscled aside a tourist to face King Tut. "Hello, David," Silvio said. "Felipe told me you had a new job."

"Franco?" The color drained from the man's face.

So fast that Emilia only saw a blur of hands, Silvio grabbed the collar of David's costume with one hand and knocked off the headgear with the other.

Emilia gasped. David Garcia Diaz looked enough like his older brother Felipe to be his twin, except for a whorl of dark hair that interrupted the hairline. The pronounced cowlick created a circular wave that he combed straight back.

David stared from Silvio to Emilia, his mouth open in fear. Then he thrust the wooden box full of chips against Silvio, breaking the other man's hold. Silvio stumbled back as golden chips clattered all over the floor, prompting a raucous melee as tourists and gamblers dove after them. As pandemonium reigned, David disappeared through a doorway concealed in the pyramid's side.

Emilia was nearly dragged down by the frenzy of grasping hands and slippery plastic scattered across the floor. Silvio's firm grasp kept her on her feet. He led her through the hidden doorway, following David.

In three steps the corridor turned. The door sighed shut behind them, muting the clamor of the casino. Emilia recognized the hallway ahead; she'd seen it beyond the Employees Only door when she was with Natividad. White walls, tile floors, bleached pine doorframes, and sudden quiet.

"David," Silvio bellowed.

Faster than Emilia would have thought possible, Silvio

was on the costumed man, hands locked around his throat. "You killed, Isabel, David. For what? What did they promise you?"

"I didn't mean to hurt her, Franco," David gurgled, eyes bulging in terror below the distinctive cowlick. He clawed at Silvio's arms. "Felipe said he was going to a party with you. She wasn't supposed to be home."

"You killed her, David." Silvio shook him like a dog with a bone. "Why? Tell me why!"

"The books." David writhed in Silvio's grasp. "That's all. Just the books. I never meant—."

"Who sent you to my house?" Silvio shouted. He slapped David across the face. Once, twice, three times.

"Franco, let's take him and go." Emilia's eyes were glued to the cowlick. Rio's description was perfect.

"I didn't mean to kill her," David gasped. Blood streamed out of his nose and mouth.

"Who sent you to my house?" Silvio said again and slammed the younger man against the wall.

Emilia expected to see security at any moment. They were close to an open doorway. "Franco," she said urgently. "Let's get out of here."

David punched Silvio in the ribs and face. It made no difference. Silvio moved down the lushly carpeted hallway, blind to where he was going. He hauled the costumed man along by the neck and threw David against the wall with every step.

"Who." *slam* "Sent." *slam* "You." *slam*

"Franco! Let's go!" Emilia pleaded.

Silvio ignored her as he halted across from the doorway, his back to it. "Who sent you, David?" he repeated.

"My boss," David mumbled. "Get the books. That's all I was supposed to do."

Silvio propped up David's head. "And the others? How many cops did you kill?"

"I was getting rid of the bad guys," David said, his hands wrapped around Silvio's wrists. Blood and tears streamed down the young man's face. "They told me I was just like you and Manuel."

"Isabel didn't do anything bad."

"I'm sorry, Franco. I didn't mean to kill her."

Silvio and David were still locked together when Emilia heard the shot. She saw Silvio whip his head around and for an agonizing second, she was sure he was shot. But it was David's expression that slackened and his eyes that rolled up to the ceiling. Silvio let go.

David's shoulders sagged and his knees buckled. A split-second later, his body jerked as he was shot a second time. David crumpled to the floor.

Before Emilia could process what had happened, Silvio pulled a handgun from his belt under the black tee and plunged through the open doorway. Emilia followed recklessly on his heels, her own gun in her hand. She had no conscious memory of drawing the weapon from her ankle holster.

They were in a spacious office with shiny wallpaper, crystal chandeliers, shuttered windows, and pale wood furniture. Both Duarte Ochoa and Obregon stood in front of an enormous desk. Both men were armed.

"You used him," Silvio said to Obregon. "You fucking used him and then threw him away."

Emilia heard the click of a safety being released. Silvio's weapon dug into the soft flesh under Obregon's jaw.

Obregon dropped his gun and raised his hands.

"Who the fuck are you?" Duarte Ochoa shouted and trained a polished gold pistol at Silvio's heart.

Emilia jammed her gun into Duarte Ochoa's back and felt him stiffen. "My safety is off, too," she said.

No doubt Duarte Ochoa had closed circuit cameras all over the casino. His security was going to flood the hallway and shoot them all.

The tension in the air was like boiling fog and it took Emilia a moment to realize they'd formed an armed lineup. Obregon kept his hands in the air. A half a smile flitted across his face as he realized the same thing.

"Pedro." Obregon's voice was as silky as ever. He flicked a finger at Silvio. "This is the famous detective Franco Silvio. Until a few weeks ago, he was my brother-in-law.

Emilia gasped.

"Yes, Detective, Cruz," Obregon said. His eyes flickered between Emilia and Silvio's gun. "Isabel de Silvio was my sister."

"You don't even deserve to say it," Silvio snarled. He

pulled one of Obregon's hands behind his back and wrenched it upwards into a wrestling hold. "You spent 20 years treating her like dirt and trying to knock me down so low that she'd leave. When she didn't, you had her killed."

"You always think it's personal, Franco," Obregon mocked breathlessly. Silvio's grasp bowed him backwards even as the gun threatened his throat. A trickle of sweat ran down the union chief's forehead. "You have no idea. Isabel simply got in the way."

"You killed Isabel, as sure as you pulled the trigger yourself." Silvio ratcheted up the pressure. "This time she's not here to keep me from killing you."

"I'll take your head off," Duarte Ochoa spat at Silvio.

Emilia gave Duarte Ochoa a hard shove with the snout of her gun. "Don't be stupid," she hissed. The only reason casino security wasn't there had to be the noise and excitement of the Copa America final.

"I'm unarmed, Franco," Obregon said and cut his eyes to the gun on the floor. "Two witnesses would see you kill an unarmed man."

"You piece of shit," Silvio snarled. "You used David. Knew that he was Manuel's brother and you could manipulate him. How many people died for your fucking real estate scam? What would one more mean?"

Emilia heard barely-controlled rage in Silvio's voice and knew he would murder Obregon in cold blood, right here, right now. Twenty years of conflict and hurt had boiled down to this moment of fury and revenge. She saw David's inert body through the doorway. The Egyptian costume looked oddly out of place in the hall, as if men were supposed to die in dark pants and bloody tee shirts.

"Franco, listen to me," Emilia said. Her right arm ached already. She couldn't hold this pose for long.

Obregon cut her off. "Your hands are dirty, too, Franco," the union boss said. "Vega said you kept the ledgers after the raid. Shared them with Salinas. You probably still have them."

"Vega didn't know shit." Silvio gave a grating laugh. "He had you going."

"Look, we can cut you in," Duarte Ochoa said urgently.

"Shut up, fat man," Silvio said. "No deals. Just justice for the dead."

"That other cop," Duarte Ochoa said, eager to deflect guilt. "Vega. He got a little too greedy. Lied about everything. This was all his fault."

"You see?" Obregon's voice was rough; the bird of prey was caught in a trap. "This isn't what you think, Franco."

"Vega made it like you had the ledgers." Duarte Ochoa took up the argument. His small gold pistol wobbled in his hand. "He said you must have them, because you led the raid. That's the reason David went to your house. Killing your wife was his mistake."

"Shut up, Pedro," Obregon said savagely.

Even as the pain in Emilia's upper arm quivered up her shoulder and licked at her neck, everything made sense.

Silvio was right. There never was only one El Trio killer.

Vega murdered Salinas in their dispute over the ledgers, and with sketchy information, tried to blackmail Duarte Ochoa and Obregon. David was dispatched to kill Vega and recover the ledgers from Silvio's house. Isabel was collateral damage.

Loyola wasn't involved, although Vega's orders made him suspicious enough to collect some information.

"Was Hernandez a mistake, too?" Silvio went on. Every muscle in his body bulged with tension. His arm was an iron bar trapping Obregon and the muzzle of his gun was still jammed into the other man's throat. "I know the same gun killed Isabel and Vega. So did he."

"Look, Franco," Obregon said. Sweat beaded his upper lip and his eyes squinted against the pain. "For Isabel's sake, we can both walk away from this."

Silvio's face twisted with cruelty. "She's dead. She'll never know I killed you."

"You're better than this," Obregon rasped.

"Pretty weak last words, Victor," Silvio said.

"Franco," Emilia said. Her right arm was ablaze with the effort to hold the heavy handgun against Duarte Ochoa and she knew Silvio would do what he said. "Don't do this."

"Shut up, Cruz." Silvio didn't waver.

"Isabel didn't marry a killer," Emilia said. "She wouldn't love that sort of man."

"This doesn't concern you," Silvio replied.

"He's going to be a father," Emilia burst out.

Silvio darted a glance over his shoulder at Emilia. "What are you talking about?"

"Claudia Sanchez is carrying his baby," Emilia shouted. Adrenaline coursed through her body. Life had boiled down to the pressure of Silvio's finger on the trigger. "Franco, please. He's going to be a father. If you kill him, you're letting him abandon that child."

Disbelief flashed across Silvio's face.

"I can sweeten this for you," Duarte Ochoa said. "I'll give you 100,000 pesos for the ledgers and cut you in for a share of the real estate club profits."

The shot was deafening in the room without anything to soften the flash or the bang. Duarte Ochoa cannoned into the desk and knocked Emilia off balance. For a moment she was disoriented. Had she shot him? Her right arm was alive with pain with the effort of holding her gun steady, but she could swear she hadn't fired.

Duarte Ochoa sank to the pale carpet and his head knocked against the edge of the desk as he went down. The small gold pistol was still in his hand as he stared sightlessly at the ceiling. He had been shot once in the chest.

Emilia slowly turned away from the dead man, her heart thundering.

Chief Salazar stepped into the office, his handgun trained on Silvio. He was wearing a suit with a starched white shirt open at the collar and his bald head reflected the chandelier's dangling prisms. With his free hand, he closed the door, blocking the view of David's body in its elaborate costume.

"Well, Detective Silvio," the police chief said. "Detective Cruz. Every time there's a problem, the two of you show up."

Emilia found herself panting like a racehorse; there wasn't enough oxygen in the room. She'd lowered her gun when Duarte Ochoa fell; now she knew without a doubt that if she tried to draw on Salazar he'd kill Silvio without hesitation.

"You're hardly going to shoot the head of the police union, Detective Silvio," Salazar went on. "He's unarmed."

Silvio kept his gun pointed at Obregon. "He killed my wife."

"David Garcia Diaz killed your wife," Salazar said. "Señor Pedro Duarte Ochoa killed him and was about to shoot you in a killing spree I just averted. So it would seem that justice has been served today. Mexican-style, I admit, but justice nonetheless."

"What about justice for Salinas and Vega?" Silvio asked bitterly. "And Hernandez?"

"What happened to Salinas was entirely between him and Vega," Chief Salazar said. "On the other hand, Vega got what he had coming. He wanted money he didn't earn."

Obregon's eyes darted nervously between Chief Salazar and Silvio. Sweat streamed down his face and disappeared into the collar of his black shirt. Emilia had never seen him like this; broken and at someone else's mercy.

The sight was a tonic. She moved away from Duarte Ochoa's body, gun at her side, and faced the police chief. "You must have been thrilled when Captain Espinosa was found dead," she said.

"The *federale*?" Chief Salazar raised his eyebrows.

"The *federale*," Emilia confirmed. "Another dead body, with a crime scene that looked just like the first two. Espinosa's death was a gift that created an entire cover story for you. Suddenly the El Trio killer was on the loose."

"You're a smart girl, Detective Cruz," Chief Salazar said.

"Vega was your big problem, wasn't he?" Emilia challenged. "He killed Salinas, ordered Loyola not to investigate, and left a stinky trail you knew somebody was going to follow. The viper in your nest, the right hand man in your own office. The big question I have is who did Vega trust so much that he shared his theory about the ledgers from the El Pharaoh? His boss?"

Chief Salazar bared his teeth in an angry smile. "The department is going to miss you."

"She's got your fucking ledgers," Silvio said with a harsh laugh. "And Hernandez's ballistics reports."

Chief Salazar slowly lowered his gun. "So it would seem negotiations are in order," he said.

"I've got the ledgers and the reports," Emilia confirmed. "Digitized, with a copy going to every member of the

Acapulco Hotel Association board, including Carlota and the press secretary, with an explanation of what it all means, if anything happens to me or Silvio."

"I presume you want something to keep from having to share those digital copies." Chief Salazar's voice was ice cold with fury.

"Silvio and I walk out of here," Emilia said. "He takes his badge back."

"And, I assume, gets promoted to lieutenant? Or captain?"

"No," Silvio cut in. "But Loyola's out. He's been your stooge long enough."

"His jaw is broken," Chief Salazar said. "Isn't that enough?"

Silvio pushed his gun under Obregon's jaw so hard the union chief was forced to raise up on his toes. "We'll bring in an outsider," Silvio said. "Through the union's law enforcement exchange program."

"Someone you approve?"

"Yes."

"Is that all?"

"Cruz is done with her special assignment," Silvio said. "Back in the squadroom on Monday."

"Done."

"And this *pendejo*." Silvio prodded Obregon's throat with the gun, making the union chief cough. "He takes care of his child."

"What's he talking about?" Chief Salazar asked

Obregon.

"I hear Claudia Sanchez is pregnant. Supposedly I'm the father."

"Of course you're the father," Emilia said furiously. "You banged her on her desktop. Probably everywhere else, too."

Chief Salazar laughed.

"While you're thinking of baby names," Emilia went on. "The real estate investment club is over. Everybody gets their original investment back and it's done. Considering that the president of the club is dead, that shouldn't be too much of a problem. Any delay and everybody gets a very interesting email."

"Well, then," Chief Salazar said. He replaced his gun in the holster hidden under his jacket. "If Detective Silvio would like to drop his gun, we have a deal."

CHAPTER 30

Emilia woke to the sensation that her head was a block of stone. Her eyelids felt like cement. She managed a squint.

The bedroom in the penthouse slowly came into focus. The long draperies were closed over the sliding glass doors to the balcony. With an effort that sent an electric shock through her skull, she rolled onto her side and found her phone plugged into the charger on the bedside table. The time was 6:00 pm.

Next to the phone, some angel had left two aspirins and a bottle of expensive electrolyte-infused water. Emilia inched her way to a sitting position, breathing in little grunts.

The aspirins and water didn't come back up, which was a good sign. After a minute or two, she took inventory.

She had on panties and one of Kurt's white tee shirts.

She had a monumental hangover.

She had no recollection of anything after she and Silvio left the El Pharaoh.

No, that wasn't true. Silvio had driven them to a tiki bar on some nameless beach. The place had cheap El Patrón shooters and a canvas roof stretched over bamboo joists. Plastic chairs plugged into the sand. No TV, no Copa America crowd.

The rest of the night was a blank.

She struggled out of the bed, trying not to tilt her too-heavy head, and found the flannel shirt she used as a robe. Cool water on her face helped a bit, enough to send her down the hallway in search of answers, the bottle of water in her hand.

Kurt was in the living room, wearing an old Marine Corps tee and board shorts. His bare feet were propped on an ottoman as he watched the television. It was a replay of Argentina's Copa America victory.

The glass doors to the balcony were open. Pulled to the side, the white draperies rippled in the salty breeze. Far below, the ocean kept up a rhythmic sigh.

The apartment had never felt so safe, so much like home.

"Hi," Emilia croaked.

Kurt muted the television. "How are you feeling?"

"Awful." Emilia lowered herself to the sofa, one hand cradling the side of her head.

"Did you find the aspirin I left for you?"

"Yes, you're a saint."

Kurt chuckled. "I figured you'd need it."

Emilia winced. She never realized that his laugh sounded like a meat grinder. "What happened last night?" she asked.

"You and Silvio rolled up in a taxi about 4:00 am," Kurt said. "The valet on duty called me. You were both impressively drunk and didn't have enough money to pay the driver."

"*Madre de Dios*." Once again she'd made a scene at the

hotel. The staff was probably buzzing about her again. "I'm sorry. I'll pay you back."

"You were still coherent, however." Kurt grinned. "You came in and announced you were going to bed. Threw up twice and passed out on the bathroom floor."

Emilia covered her face with her hands. "I am really, really sorry."

"Silvio told me what happened at the El Pharaoh," Kurt said, serious now. "Finding out that his late partner's brother killed his wife."

Emilia dropped her hands. "Did he tell you Chief Salazar showed up?"

"Yes. I'm amazed the two of you walked out of there." Kurt paused. "Silvio said you kept him from shooting Victor Obregon. He owes you."

"Where is he now?"

"He spent a couple of hours on the sofa in the office. I had one of the drivers take him back to his car."

"Did he seem okay when he left?"

"As well as could be expected." Kurt pulled his feet off the coffee table and leaned forward with elbows on thighs. "Is it over?"

Emilia drank some water. "I guess so."

"Good," Kurt said. He clicked the remote to turn off the television. "I'd like to talk. About us."

"I know." Emilia didn't really feel strong enough to do this, but after what she'd been through last night, she could handle whatever happened with Kurt. "It's about time you told me the truth."

"Well, okay." Kurt looked startled. "The truth is, the night we had the Copa America party, the night Silvio's wife was killed, I didn't like our interaction."

Emilia gingerly repositioned herself on the sofa, drawing in her legs and crossing her arms. If he wanted to get to the Suzanne story in a roundabout way, she would play along. "Our interaction?"

"Not you and me," Kurt clarified. "I didn't like the way our relationship got talked about. Like I was fooling around with some Mexican *chica*. Playing *casita*." Anger traced through his words. "You heard Tony Wilcox say garbage again when we were at the Santa Rosa."

"I don't know what that has to do with anything," Emilia said.

"It's exactly what we need to talk about," Kurt admonished her. "Our relationship. Do we have a real commitment here or not?"

Emilia held up a hand. "We can't talk about commitment until you come clean about your child."

"My child?" Kurt's eyes widened in surprise. "You're pregnant?"

"No, I'm not pregnant," Emilia flashed back. "I'm talking about the child you abandoned."

"What?"

"Don't pretend you don't know!"

"What else besides tequila did you and Silvio drink last night?"

Emilia pulled herself off the sofa and ran down the hall. In the office, she hauled boxes out of the closet. Kurt folded his arms and leaned against the doorway as Emilia scrabbled through papers until she found the court document.

"There," Emilia said in triumph and flung it down on the desk. The seal of the County of San Miguel mocked her. "Your child with Suzanne Kellogg. The child you abandoned and the judge ordered you to support."

Kurt sauntered over to the desk. "You haven't been practicing your English, Em."

"My English is fine."

"Not as fine as you think," Kurt said. "This is a summons to appear in court for a paternity hearing. If you look through the rest of the box, you'll find a DNA test proving I wasn't the father, plus the final decree throwing out the case."

Emilia blinked.

"You were right that this is about Suzanne, but that's all," Kurt said. "Suzanne and I were pretty serious but it ended when I found out she was sleeping around. A year later, as I got ready to move down here, she showed up with a baby and tried to get child support out of me."

Emilia found her voice. "You mean you weren't the father?"

"No."

"Who was?"

"I don't know." Kurt walked to the sliding glass doors

and stared out. The sun was low in the sky and pink streamers decorated the horizon. "Suzanne simply wanted money. I knew that, yet the whole thing turned my life upside down. It was a long time before I was ready for another relationship."

"I thought, I mean," Emilia stammered. Everything Jacques said now held a different meaning. "But you were looking for something in the apartment. At night. Something you hid from me. When you went to Las Vegas, where you'd been with Suzanne, I thought, I thought. Umm, well, you know. And then I found the papers . . ."

Kurt walked out of the room.

Emilia covered her face with her hands. Her head pounded. She had misjudged him very badly. It had never occurred to her that the commitment Kurt gave so freely came at a personal price. The way he was—open, direct, caring—was always easy for him and hard for her. How wrong she'd been; so immersed in her own insecurities, so ready to assign to him the same callow attitudes she saw in men like Obregon.

The only thing left to do was apologize, pack, and go to her mother's house.

She found him in the kitchen, uncorking a bottle of red wine.

He looked up as she hesitated by the doorway. "Want some or are you sticking with water?" he asked.

"I'll have what you're having," Emilia said uncertainly and sat down.

Kurt set out two glasses and poured. He sat across from her.

"Look, I'm sorry," Emilia started. She stopped when he tossed a small green envelope across the table.

"This is the key to my safe deposit box in Las Vegas," Kurt said. "I thought I lost it, and yes, I searched the apartment like a mad man. I finally found it in my duffel the day of the half marathon in Zihuatanejo."

"Why didn't you tell me?" Emilia asked. "I would have helped you look."

"You would have wondered why I wanted it now." Kurt plucked a small object off the counter and handed it to her.

It was a square box no bigger than a plum. It was covered in brown leather worn thin and scratched with age.

"I didn't want to lie just so I could surprise you later," Kurt said and jerked his chin at the box. "I guess we're past that now. Go ahead and open it."

Emilia pried open the lid to reveal an oval ruby ring nestled against pale blue satin. The deep red stone sparkled inside a gold rim. "Oh, Kurt," she breathed.

"It was my grandmother's engagement ring," Kurt said. "I knew when I met the woman I was meant to be with, I'd ask her to wear it."

Emilia touched the ring. It was simple and perfect.

"Are you asking?" she said, not meeting his eye.

"Should I?"

Emilia shook her head. "I'm not ready."

"I know," Kurt said. "But when you are, it'll be waiting for you."

"What if I get pregnant?"

"The child's name is Rucker, whether or not we're married," Kurt said matter-of-factly. "We'll get a house with a yard. My children aren't growing up in a hotel. They'll go to a bilingual school. Your mother can visit any time, but she's not reliable enough to take care of our children."

"Oh." He'd been thinking of their future while she groped toward the here and now. She hardly deserved what he was offering.

Te amo. I love you.

Such little words. Such a big commitment.

"I'd like to take a picture together," she heard herself say.

"Now?" Kurt said. He looked down at his tee and shorts.

Emilia smiled and reached for his hand. "Sometime when we're all dressed up, let's have a nice picture taken. And put it in a silver frame."

CHAPTER 31

The reunion in the squadroom was less than overwhelming. Loyola was gone, retired on disability. Ibarra was acting lieutenant but had already filed his papers for a transfer to Vice. Macias and Sandor weren't there but at a conference on criminal network analysis. Castro and Gomez were subdued, unsure of what all the changes meant for them.

Emilia went to her old desk. The *Las Perdidas* binder went back into the big file drawer. She'd already gone over to the building on Avenida Almendros, collected her things, and said goodbye to everyone.

Natividad would step into her shoes, ready to make Las Palomas part of the hunt for missing women. The younger woman would be a better advocate for the unit; she was already more politically adroit than Emilia. They would stay in touch.

Ibarra avoided her eye as he handed out a robbery report from Dispatch. Silvio looked in Loyola's office and found the keys to his official vehicle. Clad in leather jacket, white tee, and jeans, Silvio led the way to the parking lot as if he'd never been gone. Like him, Emilia pretended it was simply another day.

She settled into the passenger seat. Silvio put the key into the ignition and started the car.

Emilia tapped the address from Dispatch into the GPS

app on her phone. "Got it," she announced. "Should take us about 15 minutes."

Silvio turned on the air conditioning, found the control for the side view mirrors, and played with the settings. Emilia looked out the window and waited. The lot was full of standard Acapulco police cars, emblazoned with lights and lettering, as well as unmarked official vehicles. The morning sun glinted off chrome and paint. Three rows over, a couple of uniforms milled around the guard shack, trading weekend war stories and waiting to check the identification of incoming drivers.

"You ready?" Emilia finally asked.

"Yeah." Silvio fiddled with his seat, adjusting it back and forth.

"What are we going to do about Castro?" Emilia asked. "He stole evidence to use as a bribe."

"I'll think of something."

"Regretting not having taken the promotion?" Emilia asked. "Chief Salazar would have made you lieutenant. Even a captain, you know."

"Stuck in an office with a mountain of paperwork." Silvio gave her a sideways look. "No, thanks. I'm better off on the street."

"Yeah," Emilia said. "That's what I figured."

Silvio played with the side mirrors again. The electronic whine of the adjustment mechanism got on Emilia's nerves. She checked her phone for text messages.

"I shouldn't have said that you were a shit partner," Silvio mumbled.

Emilia lowered her phone, surprised that Silvio would offer anything even remotely resembling an apology.

"I didn't want you involved," he went on. "I knew this thing was fucked up and if you poked around, something bad would happen."

"You were right," Emilia said softly. "I was a shit partner. You called when you needed me. I didn't answer."

Silvio looked away.

"I thought you were drunk," Emilia continued. "Calling to tell me I'd lost my bet. A better partner would have known you were in trouble. I should have known."

A hoarse gasp cut the air. Silvio's shoulders heaved and he began to weep, making no effort to hide his tears. The car filled with the raw and rusty sound of the big man's breakdown.

His pain, hidden for so long, was gut wrenching. Emilia reached across the console and pried his right hand off the steering wheel. Silvio hung on to her as if he'd never let go.

Emilia didn't say anything. She kept her hand in his as Silvio wept, letting the pressure of her fingers be a message, telling him that tomorrow he'd be able to pick up the pieces and go on.

Telling him that he wasn't alone.

El Fin

Discover Emilia's next case in PACIFIC REAPER

You're invited to stay up to date with Emilia and the team in the Mystery Ahead newsletter. Get behind-the-scenes details and must-read recommendations every other Sunday.

Subscribe and receive the Detective Emilia Cruz Starter Library with 2 novellas and the Who's Who guide to the series.

Go to carmenamato.net/starter-library.

There are extra goodies ahead, too.
A **favorite recipe** from a meal featured in the book,
A **Glossary** of Spanish words, and
An **excerpt** from the next Detective Emilia Cruz novel.

The Pasodoble Mojito

1 ½ oz white rum
1 ½ cups club soda
12 mint leaves
juice from ½ lime
1 tbsp simple syrup
1 blood orange, quartered (optional)

To make simple syrup, dissolve 1/4 cup superfine sugar in 1/4 cup hot water. Stir until sugar is dissolved. Let cool.

Place mint leaves, lime juice, and tbsp. simple syrup in bottom of a tall glass. "Muddle" the mixture together with a wooden spatula, bruising but not tearing the mint leaves.

Add ice, rum, and top with club soda. Stir well and garnish with a lime wedge and sprig of mint. For added zest, squeeze a quarter of a blood orange over the top.

Glossary of Spanish Terms

Commonly used words in the Detective Emilia Cruz series

Abarrotes: snacks

Agua de jamaica: cold tea made with dried hibiscus

Alcaldia: town hall and/or mayor's offices

Amigo: friend, buddy

Barrio: neighborhood

Bayos blancos: white beans

Cabrón: slang meaning dumbass

Campesino: subsistence farmers, country dwellers

Casita: little house

Cédula: identity card

Cerrado: closed

Chatarra: junk

Chica: girl

Comida: the main meal of the day, usually eaten in early afternoon

Conchas: sweet rolls topped with sugar and shaped like a conch shell

Coyote: guides who take people over the US-Mexican border illegally for a price

Dios mio: my god, an exclamation

El Norte: the United States

Falta: lack of

Federales: slang for the Policía Federal Preventiva, federal law enforcement agency

Guayabera: men's button-down shirt with a straight hem and multiple pockets

Halcone: word meaning falcon, used to mean a person acting as a lookout

Hojalateria: brake shop for cars

Hombres: men

Jefe: chief, person in charge

Jitomate: tomato

Las Brisas: upscale neighborhood on the eastern side of Acapulco bay

Libraría: bookstore

Libro: book

Llantas: tires

Loco: crazy

Lotéria: lottery

Madre de Dios: Mother of God, used as exclamation

Maldita: damn, damned

Mercado: market

Mujeres: women

Muertos: papier maché skeleton figures used to decorate Day of the Dead altars

Narcomanta: banner bearing a message from a gang or cartel

Norteamericano: North American

Ofrenda: altar

Palapa: traditional Mexican shelter roofed with palm leaves or branches

Papel picado: streamers of tissue paper cut into silhouette designs

Parrilla: grill for food, usually assumed to be for meat

Pastelería: pastry shop

Patrón: boss

Pendejo: asshole, jerk

Permiso: excuse me

Peso: Mexican monetary unit, roughly equivalent to $0.10.

Placas: license plates

Por dedazo: expression meaning "by the finger" to indicate patronage

Prima/primo: female or male cousin

Privada: enclosed subdivision and/or the gate to the property

Prohibido el paso: "Keep out" warning

Queso fresco: soft cheese common in Mexican recipes

Rayos: exclamation, similar to "oh hell"

Reina: queen

Salsa verde: tart green salsa usually made with tomatillos

Sicario: cartel henchman or assassin

Talavera: hand painted pottery from Puebla

Taqueria: taco restaurant

Telenovela: television soap opera

Tiendita: little store

Tío/Tía: uncle/aunt

Tumbadore: person who steals drug shipments

Zocalo: town square

An excerpt from PACIFIC REAPER. the next Detective Emilia Cruz mystery

"Young guy," Detective Emilia Cruz said. "His throat is slit." She'd seen enough dead bodies to know that the man in the tent had only been dead a few hours.

"Even I can see that." Senior detective Franco Silvio held open the tent flap to let in the light and encourage the stink to float out as he squatted by the entrance. The early October morning sun seemed to thicken the smell of death in the fabric-bound space.

"He didn't put up a fight." Emilia held up her latex-gloved hands as she knelt by the body to indicate that she'd found nothing in the pockets. "No identification except the El Machete tattoo. No signs of a struggle. Like he just laid there and let someone cut his throat."

"He was asleep," Silvio said. "Or passed out."

"Probably," Emilia agreed.

The body lay on top of an old sleeping bag, clad in faded jeans and a black tee shirt with some sort of logo on it. The feet were bare but looked to be the same size as a pair of nearby cross trainers. The head was nearly severed from the body and blood had pooled and then congealed under the body.

"Needle tracks?" Silvio asked.

"I can't tell." Emilia backed herself toward the tent flap

and Silvio moved to the side. The tent was small, just big enough for two people and their camping gear. Or one dead body and a strange collection of souvenirs.

"Let's get him out." Silvio took her place inside the tent, grabbed the bottom edge of the sleeping bag and eased it out of the tent, the body sliding along as if on a stretcher.

Seagulls screamed overhead and the waves lapped at the shore only a few sandy yards away as Silvio straightened up. Emilia stripped off her latex gloves, her palms sweating despite the fact that it wasn't that warm yet.

The victim looked even worse in the bright sunlight, although neither detective saw any indication he'd been a junkie. The break between the lolling head and the supine body was a clean, deliberate slash. The distinctive design on the inside of the right arm marking the man as a member of the El Machete gang was a good quality tattoo with thick greenish lines. He would have been a powerful man; even in death his arms were weighted with muscle and his hands looked powerful.

"Doesn't really look like a camper," Emilia observed.

Silvio's cell phone rang and he punched a button and put the phone to his ear. The senior detective was a big man with a face that betrayed his years as a boxer. His hair was a gray crew cut and he wore his invariable uniform of white tee shirt, jeans, and shoulder holster hidden by a khaki bomber jacket.

Emilia took pictures of the face and body with her cell phone as Silvio gave the crime scene techs directions from the run-down hotel near the road. When she'd snapped enough of the body, she walked towards the water's edge, then turned and snapped a few more pictures of the tent and a grove of scrubby pines and rusty seagrass that separated the beach from the road. The sand was rippled but there was nothing useful; an overnight storm had scoured away the killer's footsteps.

There were a few makeshift tents further along the beach, a stretch of desolate sand ringed with rocks on the inland side that made it less attractive to Acapulco's mainstream tourists. The surfers who'd called to report the body had been a young *gringo* couple with bad Spanish made worse by what Emilia was fairly sure was their own drug use. They'd probably found the body in the tent while looking to score drugs from the motley assortment of surfers, junkies, vagrants and penniless adventurers who often camped out on this lonely strip of beach near Coyuca Lagoon, a few miles northwest of Acapulco. There weren't many actual residents, just a vagrant population that would be hard to locate and question. They got all the information they were likely to get out of the couple, warned them to stay in the area and to call if they remembered anything else. They wouldn't. Emilia had encountered that sort of tourist before.

She knew Silvio didn't want the case and he had a point. Coyuca Lagoon was outside what was normally the Acapulco police department's jurisdiction. But the new lieutenant now running the detectives squadroom had decided that they'd respond to any and all calls that came in. This was despite the fact that they still hadn't replaced the two detectives lost a few months ago in a drug smuggling bust. Emilia and Silvio had a dozen open cases already and hiking out to Coyuca Lagoon wasn't going to help them close any of them.

Silvio pocketed his cell phone and clumped across the sand to Emilia. "Found the hotel but couldn't find the beach behind it," he growled. "Like nobody's ever been out of the fucking city before."

Emilia glanced at her watch. They'd only been there about 40 minutes, which was a relatively short time. The crime scene technicians often took an hour or more. Or didn't come at all, tying up detectives' time waiting for a body to be collected and the crime scene to be dusted for fingerprints. All the detectives had learned to carry latex gloves and plastic zip-lock bags in their pockets so they could handle any evidence they came across.

The crime scene technicians weren't lazy or incompetent. They were simply overloaded with work.

They had a shit job, Emilia reflected as she finally saw the van. Crime scene techs earned little more than an ordinary beat cop—less than half what a detective earned—and had to handle dead bodies all day, much of the time in the hot sun. Yet they faced the same dangers as the rest of the cops in Mexico; all of them lived as perpetual targets of drug cartels determined to break down civil authority. Emilia often wondered which side was winning.

"Cleaner than most," the lead tech said by way of greeting as he dumped his case down beside the body lying on its blood-soaked sleeping bag.

"Looks like a dead junkie," Silvio said. "Killed by some surfer for his stash. But it isn't."

"Why not?" the tech asked.

Emilia held open the flap. "You'll see."

She crawled into the tent ahead of the tech, trying to keep from getting any more sand in her loafers or embedded in the knees of her jeans. The tech came in after her. He got all the way in before suddenly stopping and rearing back on his heels.

"*Madre de Dios*," he exclaimed, his face working with fear.

"Tell me about it," Emilia said.

An altar to the dead, similar to an *ofrenda* commemorating the Day of the Dead, had been created against the tent wall opposite the spot where the body had been. A plank as long as Emilia's arm held the offerings. A shriveled bouquet of marigolds, the traditional Day of the Dead flower, was a brown and brittle mess next to a bottle of cheap tequila. A trio of thick white candles were wrapped in black gauze, the most deadly color in Santa Muerte's arsenal of ritual. A few peso coins were scattered across the plank as well and Emilia saw a half-smoked cigar, long cold.

But it was the frayed poster-sized banner decorated with

the image of Santa Muerte that caused a shiver to run down Emilia's spine, the same as when she'd first spotted the image. Pinned to the tent canvas, it depicted the Death Saint as a skeleton in a long black hooded robe. One bony hand held a scythe like a religious Grim Reaper. The other held out a globe to indicate Santa Muerte's mastery over the earth.

"Look at this." Emilia nearly had to snap her fingers to get the tech's attention as he gazed slack-jawed at the banner. "What do you make of all these broken pieces?"

Several *muerto* skeleton figurines, common items on Day of the Dead altars, were nearly hidden under the wilted marigolds. On a traditional *ofrenda*, the figurines might represent something related to the deceased, like their occupation, hobby, or pet.

But these *muertos* were simple male figures. Each was broken cleanly and deliberately in several places, with clean slashes through the thick papier maché. The heads were all severed, with a red substance like lipstick outlining the gash.

The scene, with Santa Muerte leering down from the gently billowing canvas tent wall, was a strange parody of a traditional *ofrenda*. But a Day of the Dead altar was meant to attract and celebrate the spirits of the deceased. This strange altar devoted to Santa Muerte was made to punish them.

"I'm not touching this shit," the tech said. Still on his hands and knees, he scrambled backwards, tangling himself in the canvas flap in his haste.

"Hey," Emilia said, surprised at his reaction. She grabbed the sleeve of his papery jumpsuit. "We got work to do here."

"Not me." The tech pulled away from her, his eyes bulging in terror. "They can fire my ass. Anybody who touches this shit, they're dead."

Find PACIFIC REAPER on Amazon or your favorite bookseller.

ABOUT THE AUTHOR

Carmen Amato turns lessons from a 30-year career with the Central Intelligence Agency into crime fiction loaded with danger and deception.

Starting with *Cliff Diver*, her award-winning Detective Emilia Cruz mystery series pits the first female police detective in Acapulco against Mexico's drug cartels, government corruption, and social inequality.

The series was awarded the Poison Cup for Outstanding Series from CrimeMasters of America in both 2019 and 2020 and has been optioned for television.

Her Galliano Club historical thriller series was inspired by her grandfather who was a deputy sheriff during Prohibition.

Originally from upstate New York, Carmen was educated there as well as in Virginia and Paris, France, while experiences in Mexico and Central America ignited her writing career.

Every other Sunday, Carmen shares her top secret(s) in the Mystery Ahead newsletter.

Subscribe at carmenamato.net.

www.ingramcontent.com/pod-product-compliance
Lightning Source LLC
Chambersburg PA
CBHW030104310726

48970CB00004B/1138